Prais
Y

MW01008519

"*You Between the Lines* is almost indescribably good: fresh and smart and tender, with not just some of the most gorgeously crisp prose, but poetry I'd pin to every one of my Pinterest boards. Leigh is my soulmate, and Will is the gold standard for book boyfriends. Katie Naymon has a forever fan."

—Jessica Joyce, *USA Today* bestselling author of *The Ex Vows* and *You, with a View*

"It's no surprise that a novel about poets would feature some of the best romance writing I've encountered in years. I melted into this book. It's rare that a debut author becomes an instant auto-buy, but whatever Katie Naymon writes next, please inject it into my veins."

—Kate Goldbeck, bestselling author of *You, Again*

"A fresh, intoxicating voice, Naymon delivers a brilliant, poignant love story perfect for fans of Emily Henry. With vibrant characters, *You Between the Lines* is a master class in the art of the romance novel. I will read anything she writes forever."

—Peyton Corinne, author of *Unsteady*

"Like the loveliest and most profound poems, *You Between the Lines* is instantly captivating and rich with depth. Naymon's debut is an ode to writers and a literary love story both sweet and nuanced that will have you underlining every romantic detail."

—Emily Wibberley & Austin Siegemund-Broka, authors of *The Roughest Draft*

"*You Between the Lines* marks the debut of a stunning new voice in romance. I was captivated by Katie Naymon's tender, lyrical prose, and my heart ached—in the best way possible—through every page of Will and Leigh's journey to embrace the messy vulnerability of both love and art."

—Ava Wilder, author of *Will They or Won't They*

"*You Between the Lines* is the kind of book that gives you butterflies. Beautifully written with just the right amount of steaminess—I swooned through the entire thing."

—Kate Spencer, author of *In a New York Minute*

"Like the best poems, *You Between the Lines* is poignant, lyrical, and true. I thoroughly enjoyed Leigh and William—their rivalry, their pining, and their crackling chemistry. The immersive, academic setting shines. An absolutely beautiful debut. I can't wait to read what Katie Naymon writes next!"

—Naina Kumar, *USA Today* bestselling author of *Say You'll Be Mine*

"Everything I hoped for in a romance about two poets—captivating sexual tension and emotional push-pull. This novel that centers a Taylor Swift–loving main character is itself a Swift banger in book form. So intimately human that it feels as if your own diary has been mined for material."

—Melanie Sweeney, *USA Today* bestselling author of *Take Me Home*

"Lyrical and lovely, *You Between the Lines* is the perfect romance for anyone who has ever worried that they are not enough. Deliciously sexy and so deeply real. Prepare to fall in love!"

—Laura Hankin, author of *One-Star Romance*

You
Between
the
Lines

KATIE NAYMON

FOREVER
New York   Boston

Copyright © 2025 by Katie Naymon

Cover design and illustration by Caitlin Sacks. Cover copyright © 2025 by Hachette Book Group, Inc.

Forever
Hachette Book Group
1290 Avenue of the Americas, New York, NY 10104
read-forever.com
@readforeverpub

First Edition: February 2025

Forever is an imprint of Grand Central Publishing. The Forever name and logo are registered trademarks of Hachette Book Group, Inc.

The publisher is not responsible for websites (or their content) that are not owned by the publisher.

The Hachette Speakers Bureau provides a wide range of authors for speaking events. To find out more, go to hachettespeakersbureau.com or email HachetteSpeakers@hbgusa.com.

Forever books may be purchased in bulk for business, educational, or promotional use. For information, please contact your local bookseller or the Hachette Book Group Special Markets Department at special.markets@hbgusa.com.

Print book interior design by Taylor Navis

Library of Congress Cataloging-in-Publication Data

Names: Naymon, Katie, author.
Title: You between the lines / Katie Naymon.
Description: New York : Forever, 2025.
Identifiers: LCCN 2024036433 | ISBN 9781538768556 (trade paperback) | ISBN 9781538768563 (ebook)
Subjects: LCGFT: Romance fiction. | Novels.
Classification: LCC PS3614.A965 Y68 2025 | DDC 813/.6—dc23/eng/20240826
LC record available at https://lccn.loc.gov/2024036433

ISBNs: 9781538768556 (trade paperback), 9781538768563 (ebook)

Printed in the United States of America

LSC-C

Printing 1, 2024

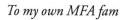

To my own MFA fam

Prologue

When Will Langford drags his pen over each line of my poem, slowly, as if to not miss a single word, I feel the movement scraped over my legs.

He's the kind of student Mrs. Lincoln's creative writing elective was made for. The class is a big deal to get into. You had to apply with a short story or three poems, and there's only room for ten students, to create an intimate feel. As one of the only two juniors selected, I feel a need to prove why I'm here.

But Will doesn't. He's a senior, the president of the Rowan School Literary Club, the editor in chief of *Expressions*, our student literary journal, and next semester, he's graduating and going to Middlebury to study English. Will wants to be a writer when he grows up, and if you know him, you know *that*.

I want to be a writer, too. In middle school, I won all sorts of local writing competitions. I scribbled short stories under a timer in drafty auditoriums and felt like a pop star when my name was called hours later, accepting gold plastic and certificates like they were Grammys. I liked the way they glinted along my bookshelf's edges, obfuscating the actual books behind them. I wasn't the most popular or the prettiest, but I *did* write Cuyahoga County's third-best short story for a seventh grader.

Writing's my escape. As an only child, I never grew up playing house or doctor or any of the other games siblings play together. Instead, I made things up, just for me. And now, while other kids are first-kissing and kicking soccer balls over summer break, I go to creative writing camps, exchanging poems with braces-clad boys who look at me like I'm the kind of girl who knows how beer tastes.

In a poem, I can be whoever I want to be, even if it's just for six stanzas.

So yes, I want to be a writer. But not the annoying kind. It feels like most writers are very, very annoying—particularly the population of straight, white literary men. The kind that everyone hates but craves approval from anyway. You know the type. The guys with three names—David Foster Wallace, Jonathan Safran Foer. I haven't read anything by them and I won't. Maybe because I'm in high school and, quite frankly, have better things to do than read *Infinite Jest*.

But it's not just the contemporary guys. I SparkNoted my way through Ernest Hemingway in ninth-grade English. I skimmed *The Sound and the Fury* and suffered through *Madame Bovary* (in French, no less). I love reading, I swear. But I've never been able to sink my teeth into these lauded literary classics—the ones written by men, the ones set in wartime, with stream of consciousness as their stylistic mode of choice, the poverty and depression of men as their focus. Give me Brontë, Austen, Lorde. John Steinbeck, though? Ralph Waldo Emerson? I'm good.

But Will is different, I'm sure of it. On the first day of this workshop, when Mrs. Lincoln asked who our favorite writer was as an icebreaker, Will said the poet Mary Oliver. Everyone else said Sophocles, Ayn Rand, Charles Dickens. I was going to say Erica Go, a young poet who plays with pop culture, but I got intimidated and lied, saying F. Scott Fitzgerald instead. (I *did* dress up as Daisy for Halloween, but that's only because I look amazing in a flapper dress.)

That's the problem with me. I constantly read the room and cater my movements, words, thoughts, which-comma-goes-where to other people.

Because he's a year older, I've never been in class with Will before. I've only watched from afar—Will, making a call for submissions to *Expressions* during morning assembly, Will, reversing out of the school parking lot, his hand on the back of the passenger-seat headrest. The curlicue of caramel hair he can never seem to get off his forehead, a stark contrast with the perfectly symmetrical bunny ears of his boat shoes, the knot of his tie. While the other popular senior boys are going to party schools for football or planning senior pranks, Will Langford writes poetry in faultless cursive in his Moleskine notebook in a Middlebury crew neck and khakis.

Absolute catnip for girls like me.

Outside of class, we've spoken exactly once. It was at this year's homecoming dance, when my best friend Gen (who snagged the second junior spot in this class) tried to orchestrate a meet-cute by steering me in his direction. I bumped into him mid "Mr. Brightside" and spilled Sprite on us both. He apologized even though it was definitely my—well, Gen's—fault. He couldn't even look me in the eye as my hot-pink dress clung to my body, soda-wet and sticky.

"Oh my god, I'm so sorry," I'd said.

He shook his head. "No, it's my fault." He ran his eyes across my body. "Here, maybe paper towels in the bathroom…" He set off in the direction of the accessible bathroom right outside the gym, and Gen violently shoved me once more, to get me to follow.

"I'm really sorry." I watched soda drip down the chest pocket of his light-green button-down. He handed me a paper towel and we dabbed ourselves, not making anything better.

"I actually…" He looked through the bathroom's open door toward the mass of students. "I don't mind the interruption. I'm not sure I can really dance."

In the yellow-tinged light of the bathroom, his eyes were a choppy mosaic, twinkling with shards of copper, sage, and seafoam.

"I'm Leigh, by the way."

He nodded. "I know. I'm, uh, Will."

A wildfire erupted in my stomach. "I know."

We stared at each other like we didn't know what to do next. I hugged my arms around me, suddenly cold in my wet dress. How awkward it is to have a body.

"Okay, well. Sorry again." I smiled, my face heating up.

"Should we, should we, uh—"

A gaggle of freshman girls catapulted into the bathroom for a lip gloss refresh. Will and I walked silently back to the gym, where the music had moved on to Usher's "Yeah!"

"Should we what?"

But he had already slipped into the crowd. The interaction ended there, to Gen's dismay.

So last night, when I emailed everyone my poem ahead of

class, all I could think about was what Will would write on the poem I'm about to present.

Most of the class is hesitant to critique, even when Mrs. Lincoln reminds us that this is a safe space and constructive advice is always appreciated by the author. But from day one, Will's comments have been direct and helpful. They're so good, I feel like he's reading different works than the rest of us. While I get the shallow stuff, the fluffy layer of foam on top, Will's able to envision what the writer intended to do and provide notes to help them get there. After each workshop, we pass our comments around the table to the author, and every time I pass Will's, I see long blocks of cursive in the margins, squiggles throughout stanzas and paragraphs, underlines and exclamation points.

"Go ahead." Mrs. Lincoln nods at me to begin reading my poem. I glance across the table at Will. He is already underlining, and my stomach swoops in anticipation.

" 'Introduction to Feminist Blogging,' " I begin, and take a deep breath. " 'Step One: Write a think piece / *37 Reasons Why We Need Feminism.*' "

Pause. I look up. Everyone is staring at the paper except Will, who is looking straight at me, his hazel eyes dark and unreadable, his hands clasped neatly on his desk, pen down. A current of electricity flashes over my skin with every second of his focus. I cross my legs and then uncross them.

My pause grows, and Gen gives me an encouraging smile. I start reading again.

First comment: Shelton from Arkansas:
Women should keep their legs together, sparking
Guest: *Don't get your panties in a bunch!*

Pam1992 informs the group that feminism
just means equality
(that didn't go over well)

I continue with the rest of the poem, taking idiotic comments from a recent article and pairing them with my imagined "steps" of the woman journalist. Step one, write a think piece. Step two, get doxxed. Step three, get a death threat. I thought it was provocative, and there was so much good material in the comment section, the poem basically wrote itself. I was especially proud of the last line, "Simone de Beauvoir is spinning in her grave," when I wrote it last week.

"Great, Leigh," Mrs. Lincoln says. "Now, class, let's open it up to discussion. What is working well in 'Introduction to Feminist Blogging'?"

Gen raises her hand first, almost too on cue, but I appreciate it nonetheless. "I think this is such a clever idea, combining the words of female writers with the nasty male commenters. It's a really cool juxtaposition." I grin in her direction.

A senior, Michaela, raises her hand next. "I agree. The title pulls you in, and I like how Leigh structured the lines into step one, step two, step three. Like a how-to guide to being a woman on the internet."

I breathe easier now, but the conversation starts to stall, and Will is still silent. Mrs. Lincoln asks the class what they think my poem could expand upon or revise for more clarity. I'm *okay* with taking constructive criticism—as long as I agree with it—but my stomach tenses anyway, as if in anticipation of a punch.

To this question, Will raises his hand. While I know he's chosen to include his comments in the criticism section of the workshop, I somehow think this is maybe all a misunderstanding, that he just *has* to find something minuscule to criticize out of his otherwise glowing feedback lest anyone think he's not the literary wunderkind teachers say he is. He's going to recommend separating my block stanza into couplets for more flow, maybe. Or a title change. Some small cosmetic fix.

"I'm just not really sure what the speaker is saying in this poem," Will begins, and like his slow pen dragging over my lines, I feel these words raze over me, too, harsh and spiky across my chest. "It's found poetry put together in a fun way, I guess, but what is it trying to say? It feels very surface-level."

I'm not sure what my face is doing but Gen's jaw drops, and she jumps in first. "The message is that men on the internet are dangerous and that female journalists have a lot to put up with."

Will shrugs. "That's nothing new. Where's the turn? The complication? There's no vulnerability from the speaker here, and while I acknowledge that there's good momentum and speed in the poem as the male commenters keep interjecting, I don't understand the speaker's opinion of all the back-and-forth. What's going on between the lines here?"

I can't look at him anymore, or at anyone else in this classroom, so I stare at my page until the words blur into a black-and-white pattern, like hieroglyphs with no obvious meaning.

"Okay," Mrs. Lincoln says, "but we need to be more constructive here. The point of this class is to revise these workshopped poems, and I think we should delve into the specifics of why you're confused so that Leigh can identify which parts of the poem to revise."

"I'm not confused by any of the lines. They all make sense." Will's voice is slow and measured. Not angry, just flinty and pointy and frustrated. "My feedback is more overarching. When I get to the end of the poem, I don't feel anything. It's all style, no substance."

And that's the kicker. That's the thing that coaxes the tears in my eyes to start bunching up, threatening my Maybelline Great Lash.

All style, no substance.

I want to stand up, shove my chair back, and leave the classroom, but I don't have it in me. Because how would that look? What would the seniors or Will or Mrs. Lincoln think? *Sensitive. Dramatic. Takes things too personally.*

Instead, I sit there, keeping my eyes down until I can blink back the tears. The class has moved on to other points of feedback, but I hear none of it, just a lull of white noise.

Eventually I receive everyone's comments, passed to me from both sides of the circle. Will's are on top, and while his perfect blue cursive with absolutely no slant is lovely and legible, I can't seem to read any of it, and I don't want to. I put his comments at the back of the stack and shove them into my backpack while we move into the week's reading material.

I don't plan on reading them. I don't want his feedback. Any semblance of a crush I had feels irreconcilably snapped. Evaporated. No evidence it was ever there at all.

All style, no substance, I hear once again in his low, sure voice.

And that's the thing about straight, white literary men. They're all the same at the end of the day. Even the boys who've barely yet learned what power they have.

Chapter One

___❤___

WHEN I RECEIVED THE ACCEPTANCE letter to the Perrin MFA program four months ago, my first thought was *I am an unbelievable scam artist. I am the Anna Delvey of poetry. The Tinder Swindler of graduate programs. I am that guy from the NXIVM documentary. Equally good hair, significantly less dangerous.*

But the letter is still here—shiny and shocking and addressed to me, Leigh Simon, no typos. It's not a mistake. I'm sitting in my new apartment in Perrin, a suburb near Asheville, filled with IKEA furniture and some remnants of undergrad, driven down by my dad all the way from Ohio. And in an hour, I'm going to the Welcome Barbecue.

Mom couldn't come to Perrin. She was scheduled for some urgent surgeries she couldn't get covered. I'm not sure how pleasant it would've been in the car with her and Dad, anyway, or if they would've even taken the same car.

I applied to Perrin on a whim. When my parents' fighting escalated last year, I picked up the proverbial pen for the first time since college, processed my emotions through words, and submitted a poem to *Goldfinch Review*, which (shockingly) published it a few months later. That bit of external validation led me to consolidate my old college poetry and submit applications to a handful of MFA programs. Maybe someone took pity on me or the competition was particularly low this year, but the Perrin English department took a chance.

But even after getting the acceptance letter, I didn't think I'd actually *enroll*. Up until two days ago, I was living in Boston, (over)working as a copywriter for the ad agency Coleman + Derry, writing manifestos for a diaper company while clients questioned whether I was an intern instead of a twenty-seven-year-old mid-level copywriter. It took one bathroom breakdown and an impromptu panic attack for my manager to recommend, nay, *insist* on therapy. And I'm the kind of girl who aims to please.

Bridget, my therapist, has an Anna Wintour bob and a collection of chic sweater-vests. During our session, she suggested that my parents' separation a month ago might have played a role in my burnout, but that's clearly not the case. I told her it had to do with taking something I loved—writing—and turning it into something I hate—also writing.

"I hate the clients and half my co-workers," I said. "I thought going into advertising meant I'd get to be super creative, but there are always parameters. Restraints. Budgets."

"That's got to be really frustrating as a creative person." Bridget's chin teetered on her knuckles, absorbing every word like I was the most important person in her life. I desperately wanted her to invite me to brunch.

"It makes me hate writing. There's so much pressure around it now. I can hardly look at words without self-editing them through a client's eyes. It's a creativity-killer. But what choice do I have? I'm not good at anything else."

Bridget looked at me, bemused. "How do you know when you're good at something?"

"When someone else tells me I'm good at it. Is that bad?"

She scribbled in her notes and offered a feline smile. "I don't know. Is it?"

Damn you, Bridget.

She then asked what I'd do if I wasn't copywriting. The only thing I could think of was still writing. But not for clients. Just for myself. I studied creative writing in college because I liked making words breathe—and because I couldn't imagine studying anything else. But then I pivoted my attention to copywriting instead of attempting the scarier kind of writing, the kind where you spit yourself out on a page and lay yourself bare for strangers to dissect.

"Copywriting's an art, for sure. But I've never been attached to it in the same way," I told Bridget.

For a billboard or a digital ad, you have to sculpt a sentence until it's crisp. Strong. Weight bearing. Until it's sailor-knot-tight, black-and-white, with no underbelly of feelings that could be misinterpreted.

"Maybe you're ready for the underbelly now," Bridget said.

I told her I'd gotten into an MFA program but wasn't sure I should go. She politely informed me she couldn't tell me what to do (I, obviously, had asked) but that I could *pretend* to make a decision and then do a body scan to determine what choice felt better "in my body."

Obediently, I sat in front of her, eyes closed, envisioning one life stuck at Coleman + Derry, constrained by pencil skirts and too-high expectations, and another at the MFA program—an easy excuse to quit my job without looking weak; a chance to fall in love with writing again. Bridget hypothesized that maybe I was going through life making decisions using my head over my gut; that maybe my gut should have a bit more say.

As I stand in front of my mirror in Perrin, North Carolina, applying makeup to look as hot as possible in front of my new classmates, you know which option won out.

But Bridget offered some departing advice before billing me an ungodly fee and scheduling another session:

"Leigh, I think you need to be careful not to fall into the old patterns you've created for yourself over the last twenty-seven years. The chasing validation, the people pleasing. If you decide to go, hunker down and enjoy it. It can't be a competition. It can't be for other people. Just for you."

It's her words now that strum over my body, jostling my fingers as I apply mascara in the mirror. I've taken the leap to pursue the writing career I've always wanted, and I'm pushing everything that happened in high school and college behind. This is my blank slate.

And there's something important at stake: What to wear on the first day of grad school?

I've thought a lot about this. Made the Pinterest boards, devoured the university Instagram for clues on how students dress. Mapped out three distinct options—three different moods to evoke as I begin a new chapter of life where no one knows me.

I considered going full poet. All-black, eyeliner, definitely no bra, thrift store top, some sort of satchel. Or I could dress incredibly casually, as if this MFA First-Year Welcome Barbecue is *nothing* to me. A blip on a full social calendar, a common occurrence out of a schedule of readings, informal workshops, art gallery openings, et cetera. That would call for wide-leg jeans, a black tank top, Birkenstocks, maybe lipstick. Model off duty, French girl, New York girl—something like that.

But I go with option three, which hinges on a never-before-explored concept in my twenty-seven years of life: being, with no agenda, myself. A Taylor Swift–enthusiast sorority-girl Ohioan entering a Master of Fine Arts program. In poetry.

In other words—a seersucker dress and sandals. I'd texted my best friend Gen a photo of the outfit an hour earlier and received enough flame emojis to fill up the screen.

Armpit-sweat-stained in mid-August, I stand outside the one-story brick house calculating the appropriate amount of cleavage to wear to a party of overeager, neurotic writers who are about to name-drop all over me. After pushing up the off-the-shoulder neckline of my dress, I ring the doorbell. Within seconds, it opens.

"Why, hello!" booms a red-cheeked bald man with translucent acetate glasses and a polo shirt, looking more like a rich golfer than the longtime director of the Perrin MFA program.

I haven't seen Professor Daniel Kitchener in months. Not since the video call where he went over my funding options after I accepted the offer of admission. But he remembers me, no doubt, because—

"Leigh? *The* Leigh Simon? Poet of Cleveland?" His voice carries all the gravitas of a sixty-four-year-old novelist and National Book Award winner—deep, rich, buttery. The croissant of voices.

"That's me," I confirm, ignoring a deep-seated urge to curtsy.

"We're just delighted to have you." Daniel steps aside to leave room for his wife—Sharon, a professor of art history at Perrin—who materializes next to him holding a glass of something bubbly.

"I'm delighted to be here!" I chirp. I walk into the house after the Kitcheners and check myself out in the mirror above a tasteful side table. I am positively dripping. Maybe I *should* have worn black.

"We're still waiting on some more, but we've got a handful of each genre so far. A few poets, a few prosers." Daniel leads me down a hallway and into the living room, which has one focal wall of shelves, filled to the brim with the tattered spines of books I've probably never heard of, family photos, antique clocks. And in front of it are five first-years, mingling.

This is the moment of truth. I majored in English but never found much in common with the other students. On-campus readings and student literary clubs seemed to attract a certain type—the tattooed, the pot smoking, the ones who brought books to parties, the ones with ill-cut bangs and nose rings and an aversion to neon. They didn't seem much impressed with me, either. So I didn't try to make friends with my Intro to Fiction & Poetry classmates. Instead, I rushed a sorority and tasted beer for the first time, liking how something so bitter could be so easy to swallow. With the Greek system, I got a built-in family—the perfect antidote to my only-child existence. Back then, an arbitrarily assigned "big sis" was more appealing than a book.

"Everyone, everyone, allow me to introduce you to another fine poet." Daniel extends his arms as if he's a celebrity talk-show host. "Leigh Simon of Cleveland, Ohio!"

I'm reminded of the time at sophomore-year summer writing camp when we sat in a circle in the grass, introducing ourselves with epithets that started with the same letter as our first names. I said, "Legendary Leigh," like the first word I thought of hadn't been *lonely*.

The group smiles politely and I shake hands with everyone as Sharon Kitchener presses a flute of sparkling wine into my left hand.

There's Wiebke—a thirty-year-old German fiction writer who's spent the last ten years in New York: loose handshake, light accent, smells amazing. Then Hazel, a twenty-seven-year-old poet from Portland, dressed in all-black with chunky loafers and an eyebrow piercing. I meet Morris, a scruffy-cheeked and blazer-clad fiction writer from Brooklyn with a pack of cigarettes in his pocket. I'm pulled into a hug by Southern-drawling Athena, another fiction writer, fresh out of college judging by her UNIVERSITY OF FLORIDA T-shirt. Lastly there's Kacey, a Texan poet in ripped jeans with a warm, toothy smile. This year's cohort is five poets and five fiction writers—and we're waiting on more to arrive.

Hazel speaks first, and I see she's gone the full-poet-outfit route, no bra included.

"So, Ohio—cool! I've never been," she says, as if Ohio is Luxembourg—someplace random and far away that you know exists but will never have a reason to visit. But less rich.

"You're hardly missing out," I quip, my standard boilerplate response, which reliably gets a chortle from our New Yorker, Morris.

"You're the second Ohioan in the cohort, actually," Hazel says. "Daniel said there's one more. Maybe you'll know each other."

I stave off a snort. It's a big state. "Maybe!"

The small talk continues, and more students appear. Houston, a handsome six-foot-four fiction writer from Chicago—you can already tell he'll be trouble. Christine, a North Carolinian fiction writer in a periwinkle maxi dress with a bulging satchel. Jerry, a twenty-four-year-old poet who appears to be suffering immensely at the intense back-and-forth of names, ages, locations.

But it's nice. Despite the mental work it's taking to smile, to nod emphatically at other people's introductions, to find the exact time to look away and grab a potato chip, it's nice to be with a group of writers. People who actively want to be here and aren't just fulfilling a college requirement.

Ideally, though, it would be an environment free from pretension. Maybe that was too much to ask for.

"I actually didn't even apply to Iowa," Hazel says, gulping wine, to the small group around us. The fiction writers self-segmented and are standing by the unlit fireplace, leaving me alone with the poets. "I just feel like it's overhyped."

Kacey shrugs. "I have a close friend there in fiction now, and she absolutely loves it."

"Oh, sure. But it's still in *Iowa*," Hazel says.

"Yeah, location's important, but I was drawn to Perrin for the opportunities outside of class," Kacey continues, while I have absolutely nothing to add to this conversation. "I really want to teach Intro to Fiction and Poetry to freshmen next year. Not sure if I want to be an editor of the lit journal."

Our MFA is fully funded, thank god, due to every student getting an assistantship or editorship, which they complete alongside their studies. In the second year of the MFA, we can apply to be an editor for the university's literary journal or teach undergraduates. In addition to that, two writers are offered a prestigious fellowship with a famous visiting professor, which could be very interesting depending on who the visiting professor is.

"Oh, Perrin's got a great lit journal," Hazel says. "Personally, I've been published in *Ploughshares*—"

"So is this everyone?" I interject. The poets slowly reintegrate with the larger group.

"We're missing the final poet," Athena says, twirling her black hair around her finger.

"The Ohioan." Hazel nudges my shoulder. "Maybe this is him?"

I see him in the hallway first, shaking hands with Daniel and Sharon, handing them a bottle of wine. I can't make out his face from where I'm standing, but his silhouette is striking. And there's something familiar about him. He's tall and broad-shouldered and is wearing a loose button-down shirt with rolled-up chinos, loafers with no socks. His hair is wavy and light brown, a lock hanging in front of his forehead. He looks put together enough to be a professor. Did Daniel invite professors, too?

Within seconds, he's in the living room with the rest of us, and something in my stomach drops low, then lower.

"Finally, we are complete!" Daniel announces as the walls close in on me. "Friends, I am pleased to introduce our final poet—William Langford of Cleveland!"

Will starts making the rounds, introducing himself and shaking hands. The air's been sucked out of the room, the scene playing out in slow motion, my ears clogged like I'm underwater. As if from far away, I hear his voice—deep, like honey, trickling over my skin.

He's in front of me now, and because for the last minute I have been stick-figure-still, I can sense the entire room watching us, trying to decipher what's going on behind my eyes. He extends a hand, then suddenly, as if someone poured ice water over his head, jerks it back to his side and stares at me in disbelief.

"Oh! Hi!" he says, and I cannot begin to imagine the flush my face is betraying me with.

"Will?" I hear my voice, pitched higher with the cadence of a question. But it's not a question. Not really.

Chapter Two

THE LAST TIME I SAW Will Langford was an accident.

He was always *supposed* to stay in the high school section of my brain, where I keep disappointing math grades and embarrassing prom photos. But I saw him by chance four years later, when I went to Middlebury to do a summer program and he was moving out after graduation.

Then *that* was supposed to be the last time I saw him. If it were up to him, at least.

But he's here now, at Perrin, in front of me, taller than I remember. Not that my memory is trustworthy. In the last six years, I've replayed the last time I saw him so many times that the memory is both crisp and blurred. My mind never knows what to do with it.

He looks tired. Crow's-feet, faint under-eye bags. He smells like how I remember—some uniquely him medley of spice and salt and musk.

"Do you guys know each other?" Hazel blurts out, watching our strange, strained interaction.

Will's jaw muscle tightens just a hair, then releases. "Yes—"

"We went to the same high school," I say quickly, though I

wonder how he would've put it had I let him finish. Social decorum may dictate that now would be a good time to give him a loose hug in lieu of a handshake, but I can't make my body do it, and he clearly isn't going to initiate contact, either.

Will nods and looks me dead in the eye, his own wide and puncturing. "It's been, what? Six years?"

Six years, two months. I say "Yes" instead.

The group moves on, chatting among themselves once again. Will stays in front of me and I feel the urge to touch him, just to prove he's neither ghost nor myth.

"I didn't know you would be here," he says.

Obviously. I haven't kept up with Will, and frankly, I haven't wanted to. I was never his friend on Facebook, didn't follow him on Instagram. Standing before me now, he has the same expression he did six years ago, when he abandoned me on a sun-drenched sidewalk in Vermont: cold and unwavering.

I laugh. "I guess we haven't really spoken since Middlebury."

He grimaces, which satisfies me. "I saw your poem in the *Goldfinch Review* last year." His eyes leave mine to drift to my feet, my hips, my mouth. I feel the movement like the crash of a wave.

"Yeah, well . . . that was just sort of a random piece I sent out."

He nods and looks at me searchingly, as if waiting for me to say something else. I don't.

"But you've been well?" He angles his body away, glancing around the room as if begging for someone to save him.

"Yeah, great." I twist the stem of the wineglass between my fingers. "And you?"

He opens his mouth, then hesitates, and I see something brewing behind his cold gaze, some sort of energy in his body that makes him flex his hand, purse his lips. But then he stands up straighter and becomes more looming than ever.

"I've been good." And that's that.

I desperately need an excuse to leave this conversation. Luckily, Sharon Kitchener opens the door to the deck and ushers us outside, where Daniel grills peppers and chicken breasts, the smells of paprika and fresh-cut grass intermingling in the day's heat.

Will leaves my side to grab a beer. Within seconds, Kacey is next to me, whispering, "He's very attractive," turning to make sure he's not there. She says it conspiratorially, as if we've known each other for years and she wants to gossip. My stomach tightens, but I also very much want to make a friend, and Kacey's willingness to confide in me so early is a good start.

"He's okay," I whisper back, and she snorts as if I've said something inconceivable.

Outside, on the patio, Daniel's backyard is glow-glazed with early evening. I want to see if Will is looking at me, but that would require looking at him, and I won't give him the satisfaction. I try to concentrate on the group of writers in front of me—Wiebke, Athena, Christine—but I'm too distracted. A strange tension in my chest threatens to bubble over.

Daniel sets down his spatula and claps. Everyone quiets. "Well, friends, I am just so impressed with this cohort of fiction writers and poets. So, so many talented writers apply to our program every year, and you should feel very proud to be here. We've selected you based on your work and the fierce intellectual curiosity you demonstrated in your personal statements, and we've tried to create a diverse cohort with diverse styles."

I eye the group, but Will, several feet away from me, stares straight at Daniel.

"I hope the next two years are those of great development and growth, both as writers and as humans. The people standing around you today are the ones who will push you, elevate you, learn with you. By the end of this program, I hope you emerge with work you are proud of, as well as relationships that will define your artistic and personal lives."

We all offer one another shy smiles.

"So with that, please enjoy tonight—we have plenty of wine, plenty of beer, and in about an hour, the second-year cohort will join you for even more merriment." Daniel claps again and raises his own glass. "To a year of growth and lots and lots of writing!"

We all raise our glasses and cheers. And that's when I notice Will is looking at me.

*   *   *

It's 8:00 p.m. and I'm buzzed on wine. Everyone else is, too, and our conversations have finally pivoted from the other MFA programs we were deciding among (Hazel wants everyone to know she almost went to Michigan; I share with no one that this was my only option) to the writers we admire, which is only nominally better. I imagine it will take another round before everyone relaxes and stops talking about writing.

Kacey is the best friendship bet so far. She reminds me a bit of Gen, a bit of my sorority clique at Tufts. She doesn't seem to have the natural pretension the others have. In her ripped jeans and tank top, she looks more like a camp counselor than a poetry student.

But I'm not sure about the others. They all want to talk about poetry and writing. I want to talk about the food we're eating, maybe the logistics of our schedules, the cities we're from, how nervous I am about the MFA. How I hope they're nervous, too.

"So what kind of poetry do you like?" Hazel asks. It feels like a trick question, and I'm not sure how to answer. Beyond what I was assigned to read in college, I didn't really *read* poetry in my spare time. The rare times I went looking for it, I enjoyed online lit mags with more experimental, pop-culture-focused poems. The only poet whose body of work I really know is Erica Go. But I'm certainly not about to announce that on day one.

"Oh, I read a bit of everything." I volley it back to her. "What about you?"

She rattles off five or six names. I've only heard of one of them (Ocean Vuong).

Christine, the fiction writer from North Carolina, joins the conversation and tells us she writes in a surrealist style, like a recent short story about a woman giving birth to a fish that won a prize at a small literary journal.

"It's less about the fish and more about the mother's capacity to love her child," she adds.

"Wow, that's really interesting," I say, like an idiot.

Across the backyard, I see Will talking to Wiebke and Morris. I imagine they're discussing all the fancy journals they've been published in, the fellowships they're going to get after the MFA, the famous writers who wrote their recommendations.

But the low din of voices and indie music is soon cut by a ruckus in the house. And out comes a group—the second-years.

"Hey y'all!" drawls a girl with thick purple-rimmed glasses and an arm covered in geometric tattoos. "We're here to pick up the first-years and take you to my apartment for a cozy little after-party!"

There's about five of them there, and they all look to be around the same age range as us—mid-twenties to early thirties. One man is very handsome with cornflower-blue eyes and long blond hair he's tied in a bun on top of his head. He makes brief eye contact with me, and my stomach fizzes.

We say goodbye and thank you to the Kitcheners and are then led three blocks away to the girl with tattoos' apartment. Her name is Penelope and she's a twenty-five-year-old poet from Boston. Her apartment is significantly less nice than the Kitcheners' house, but it is indeed cozy and has a cooler full of Pabst Blue Ribbon. A record player spins something I don't recognize, and North Carolina's humidity has our faces dewy.

Will talks to the guy with the blond bun and a tall, lanky girl with a mullet and an angular, modelesque face. I sit next to Hazel, Penelope, and Kacey in the living room. And for the first time all night, I'm able to take my time looking at Will.

He stands with all his weight on one leg, shoulders leaning against the door of the kitchen as if he can't balance on his own, his chest oriented toward the living room. I watch his lips tug upward. I watch him chuckle. A sliver of dark chest hair peeks out from where he's unbuttoned his linen shirt.

Across the room, his eyes meet mine and his entire expression calcifies like stone. My immediate urge is to look away, but as if to test him, or maybe myself, I stare back. He breaks away first, and I feel immense satisfaction.

"Leigh?"

I jump back into consciousness. Penelope stares with a kind smile. "Sorry." I force a laugh. "I'm definitely feeling the wine. I'm going to get a cup of water, actually."

She points to the kitchen. "Cupboard above the sink has cups."

"Great, thanks." I walk toward the kitchen, passing Will and the two second-years, careful not to look at any of them.

In front of the sink, I steady myself and drink two cups of water in a row.

"Whoa, slow down there."

I turn, and it's the guy with the bun, grinning. "Too much wine," I say, extending my hand. "Don't think I've introduced myself yet. I'm Leigh."

He shakes it, and his blue eyes are pretty enough that I feel self-conscious looking for too long. He must know they're pretty, from the way he smiles.

"August. Let me guess. You're a . . . poet?"

"What gives it away?"

"Poets always get drunk first at MFA parties." A pearl of sweat forms above his lips.

"So you're a poet, too?" I smirk back.

"Yes, but I must say, after a year of this, I've gotten better at holding my liquor." He takes a sip of PBR and leans forward, smelling like tobacco. "I think it's time for shots," he whispers. Turning his head from me, he cups his hand around his mouth to yell, "Shots!"

I hear woos in the background. The light is dim, the mood is light, and within minutes I'm shooting Fireball with everyone else.

Kacey appears next to me, and she's just as tipsy. "Hi, Leigh!" she says with great enthusiasm and a subtle Texan twang. Despite our drinking, her dark-brown eyes look alert.

"August is going to guess if you're fiction or poetry," I announce as August sips on water.

"Oh! Okay, do it." She stares at him pointedly.

August looks her entire body up and down. He's shameless in the way his eyes linger at her neckline, her breasts spilling over in her low-cut tank top.

"Poet," he declares after a moment of thought.

"Oh my god, that is amazing," Kacey exclaims, slapping her palm to her chest in disbelief. "How can you tell?"

August goes to stand behind her and dips his head low to hover in the crook of her neck. He points to the couch at the center of the living room, where Hazel, Jerry, and a few second-years are sitting. "Half the fiction writers went home already. It's the wild ones who are left."

This makes me snort. I'm drunk, but I'm hardly wild. I'm wearing seersucker.

Kacey seems slightly more impressed.

"In what ways are you wild?" she coos, turning to face him.

I'm no longer interested in this conversation and how it will inevitably play out, so I take another glass of water to counteract the Fireball and turn back into the living room. But instead of making it to the couch, I stumble into something firm and musky, and watch water slush out of my cup in horrifying slow motion.

"Oh my god." I jump backward, but a steady hand grabs my bicep to still me.

"Maybe shouldn't have taken that shot," a cool, low voice says. Of course it's Will, whose linen shirt is now dripping from the center of his chest down, like a bleeding heart.

"I'm not drunk," I declare, drunk. "Not drunk enough to do this, at least." I point to his chest, then my chest, then back again. I'm about to turn away when I realize he's still gripping my arm.

"Leigh." It's almost like a scold, but there's an undercurrent there that I can't identify in my haze. His eyes are so dark, and I feel their blackness against my throat.

"Will."

He releases me. "I, uh"—he coughs—"go by William now. I sort of transitioned to that in the last few years."

"Why?" I look him up and down as if that will reveal the answer.

"Just...grew out of 'Will.' Wanted to try something different, and it stuck."

"I'm not going to call you that."

He clearly has no idea what to say to that, so he ignores it altogether. I'm not sure if it's just the alcohol, but his face shades a deep strawberry.

"So how have the last six years been for you?" I lean my body against the doorframe for support.

He hesitates. "Good."

"Do anything fun? Get published in *The New Yorker* yet? Are you living the dream?"

"I did a master's in English at Bucknell. Then worked as an editor for a magazine in Pittsburgh for a bit. Now I'm here." He pauses, looking at me as if he's waiting for something. "And you?"

"Graduated. Was working as a copywriter for an ad agency in Boston up until last month."

He nods. "Sounds productive." Then adds, in a low voice, "You look good, Leigh."

He looks better, but I don't tell him that. Instead, I do something even more self-indulgent, something I absolutely know I'd never do if I were sober.

"So, you bring your girlfriend to move here with you?"

There's a glint in his eye, and his lip curls, and I hate that in that moment, he knows he's won something.

"I'm not seeing anyone right now."

"Ah," I say dumbly. "Well, that's great, it's always more convenient to—"

"Are you?" He cuts me off.

"No."

"Cool."

"Is it? Cool?"

"Yep."

"Great. Sorry about the water." His now-damp shirt is molding into the planes of his stomach like a taunt. "Okay, bye." I shoot across the room onto the couch next to Hazel, who is still regaling her audience with hot takes about Iowa.

"We were thinking of going to karaoke at the dive bar down the street," Penelope says. "You in, Leigh?"

In the kitchen, Will blots his shirt and says something to August and Kacey, who look like they're about to devour each other.

"Yeah…think I need to sleep, actually. But next time." Penelope nods. The rest stand up and start grabbing bags and wallets.

I take one more glance at Will, the sharp edge in his voice pond-skipping across my brain. And in that moment, I already know how this is going to end.

Chapter Three

THERE'S A KNIFE IN MY head, surely. I wake up on Saturday hungover, lying in the same twin bed I had in high school that my dad drove from Ohio to North Carolina. Something about that feels poetic—how I'm clearly no smarter than I was at seventeen.

The harsh morning sun peeks through the blinds of my rented apartment, a 610-square-foot one-bedroom in Perrin, a seven-minute walk from campus. Because I'm still in the throes of unpacking, the place is messy, cardboard boxes scattered along the perimeter, my closet bursting with unorganized color. The hangover lets me ignore the mess. My throat is dry and my head is spinning, so I chug the bottle of water I had the foresight to put next to my bed.

"Fuck," I say aloud, to myself, to this room.

Small pulses of last night come back to me. The most harrowing image is Will's chest, broad and firm, and I close my eyes and try to re-imagine that moment. The jolt of force where we collided and I soaked his shirt. The low gravel of his voice spiraling into the dip of my spine.

This brings up another image of Will's chest pressing me firmly into his apartment wall, the afternoon six years ago at

Middlebury, one hand snaked around my waist, the other twirled in my hair.

But I push that image down, down, down.

My phone buzzes with a notification from Instagram. Kacey and Hazel have requested to follow me. I accept and follow them back. I scroll through photos of Hazel—her backpacking in Turkey, her fishing on a lake in Oregon, her posing with lit journals with captions like My poem has found a home!, as if her poem is a sentient being with housing needs. Her bio reads MFA candidate @PerrinUniversity. Closer to my own aesthetic, Kacey's grid is filled with pictures of her rescue dog Bruno and well-lit selfies with friends.

While I'm on Instagram, I go to Will's account. It's public, but I never followed him. Instagram didn't get big until after he and I last saw each other, and it always felt like out of sight, out of mind was the safer route when it came to us. But now that he'll be in sight for the next two years, I can't help but take a look.

There's not a single photo of him. His feed is all landscapes, still lifes, billboards, nature. Some in black-and-white, some in low-saturation color. There's a photo of a stack of books, a giant Maine coon cat, a lone evergreen tree at what he's tagged as the Cuyahoga Valley National Park, a field trip staple of my own childhood.

It's all completely insufferable, like he always has been. I toss my phone across my bed.

What I need to do with my only weekend before school officially begins again is grocery shop, unpack, and decide on a first-day-of-school outfit. I've already taken my schedule and added it to my Google Calendar, and the color-coded classes feel deliciously structured after working full-time. On Monday, I'm in a nonfiction seminar in the morning, then poetry workshop in the afternoon. In between is my first shift at the University Writing Center, where I'll be helping undergrads tweak essays for abysmal pay.

I gulp down the rest of my water bottle and finally manage the strength to go into the bathroom cupboard and pop two ibuprofen. Then I go through my closet to plan my first workshop outfit, mixing and matching skirts and tops until I find something that feels put together. I decide on a pink slip skirt and a ruffled blouse, which I quickly swap for a white tank top. Less girly, more serious.

I pull up Will's Instagram again. Its somber aesthetic is coated in a thick layer of ennui and Cleveland kid angst. He would hate my pink skirt.

Tapping on the photo of the stack of books, I pinch my fingers to zoom in—a tattered copy of the *Goldfinch Review*, a W. H. Auden collection, a *Poetry* magazine.

Pretentious, pretentious, pretentious.

I set a goal for myself for the next semester: Do not engage. Be civil. Create the kind of art *I* want to create, and not what people like Will or Hazel probably think is cool.

And absolutely do not bring up Middlebury.

*   *   *

The first thing I learn in grad school has nothing to do with writing at all.

It's Monday morning, Gilman Hall, Creative Nonfiction, first class ever, and Kacey takes the seat next to me. All ten of us first-years are piled around a large oak table. Kacey's to my right;

quiet poet Jerry is to my left. Will is several seats away, making it hard for me to accidentally make eye contact with him, which is a plus.

"So," Kacey begins in a whisper, setting her *New Yorker* tote bag next to her seat because even she, apparently, can't help it. "Friday night. August. Things happened." She can barely hide her grin.

"Oh? Things we are happy about?"

She smirks. "You could say that, yes."

"So did I miss everything after I left?"

"Hardly. Once you left, William left, and the rest of the first-year poets went to karaoke." She pauses, scanning the room as if August could possibly walk into a first-year class. "But I went back to August's place."

Once you left, William left, is the only part of her story that sticks with me, the five words repeating in my brain like an incantation until the sudden quiet of the class brings me back. Professor Jen Stewart-Weiss, acclaimed journalist and essayist, has entered the classroom.

She's a petite woman with frizzy blond hair, red lipstick, and truly excellent fashion sense. Her chunky black-heeled booties click-clack across the floor as she settles in her seat and looks at us, arms folded and ready to go, like we're already off schedule even though class doesn't start for another minute.

"In your other classes, you can feel free to hide behind whatever personas you create for yourself. In this class, it's just you. Or whatever you decide to be when you write." She makes direct eye contact with every person in the room. It feels too intimate, like you should look away but can't.

"Over this semester, you're going to write two works of creative nonfiction and spend the time in between workshopping one another's work and reading and discussing excellent examples of essay, memoir, literary journalism, et cetera. But it's not about what you write or who you are—it's purely about the craft. How you hook us, how you keep us, how you release us back into the world after your piece."

Her evergreen eyes pierce into me with such closeness, and I feel like I would tell her every secret I have, if only she would ask. She writes the first assignment across the whiteboard in sloppy, all-caps handwriting that feels like a scream.

BIRTH STORY. 10 PAGES.

"The first assignment," she says, "is to explain your birth. The circumstances around it. The actual birth. The immediate aftermath. Whatever you want and feel is necessary."

"Our conception, too?" asks Houston, the handsome fiction guy, smirking in his Chicago Bulls sweatshirt. A few of the other first-years groan and laugh in disgust.

"Could be, if you deem it important to the story." Jen's eyes glitter. "I'm interested in the factors that created you and what shaped that actual first moment before you were taught the tricks to disguise and change yourself. As we all learn to do."

The factors that created you. I think of my parents and my stomach dips low.

Will—*William*, I suppose—writes down the details of the reading assignment Jen wrote on the whiteboard, even though she promised to email us with the details. Out of the corner of my eye, I study him. Strong nose, thick eyebrows. The lightest dust of stubble coating his jaw.

"Your birth story is due in two weeks to my email in a Word doc. One of our English department assistants will consolidate the work and put the printouts in your mailboxes in the department office. We'll spend the first month reading and dissecting these alongside our regular reading material, looking at two or three pieces per week. I'll send out whose work will be read which week in an email after class."

One hour into grad school, and I'm already intimidated. Lovely.

After class, Kacey walks with me to the café in the building's atrium, filled with silver laptops and students. The combination of high ceilings and a checkered-black-and-white marble floor create an echo effect when we walk in.

"Okay, tell me more about August." I nudge Kacey as she receives her flat white.

Kacey scans the atrium quickly. "So everyone else was going to karaoke, and he asked if I wanted to come over. I don't know, like I know hooking up with someone in the program is intellectually a bad idea, especially in the same genre. But he's a second-year and we'll only have that one workshop together..." Her voice dips low, and she looks me dead in the eyes with a grin. "It was good, let me tell you."

I barely know Kacey, but I love this intimacy, how she talks to me as if we've been high-school-friends-forever, as if I drew a big heart in her yearbook. We sit down at one of the marble tables dotting the atrium floor, and I feel like I want to confide in her, too.

"So Will left after I left on Friday?"

Kacey narrows her eyes. "Yeah. You left around eleven, right? I think he went home pretty soon after that, and then it was

just me, Hazel"—she closes her eyes, counting on her fingers—
"Houston, Athena, and Christine with some second-years."

"I know Will from high school, actually." I sip on my latte, the
picture of casual.

"Oh, right, classmate?"

"He was the grade above. I saw him once after high school, but
not after that."

"So, not close?"

"What?"

"Well, you didn't know he was coming to Perrin. So I assume
y'all haven't stayed in touch."

"Oh, yeah." I'm not sure how to describe this thing I can
hardly describe myself. "I wasn't his biggest fan in high school.
He said my writing was *surface-level at best* in a workshop once."
My stomach sours at the thought of that exchange, ten years ago.

Kacey's whole face scrunches up. "Excuse me? What the actual
fuck."

"I guess it was the beginning of this holier-than-thou pretension he's got going on now. He wasn't always like that. But he
seems to be really leaning into this *Poet* thing." *Poet* comes out in
a British accent for some reason.

"You got into the same program, so clearly you're just as good."
Kacey shakes her head. "William can get out of here. There is
nothing worse than a straight white male poet."

I'm glad that so many others agree with my philosophy. But
also:

I snort. "You hooked up with one three nights ago."

Kacey nods in acceptance. "Isn't that terrible? I hate them, and
yet here I am."

Both of our phones vibrate at the same time—it's an email from Jen with the schedule. My nonfiction essay is being workshopped in the first batch of writers—Leigh Simon, Wiebke Fischer, William Langford.

Kacey scans the email. "Oh, fuck me, my story is being workshopped with two fiction writers. I'm sure mine will be the worst in the bunch."

"You never know. I feel like poets are better with vulnerability than fiction writers. Yours could be the best."

Kacey grimaces, and the focus of her eyes shifts to something behind me. "Oh hey, your workshop partner is here," she whispers, and somehow I know it's not Wiebke. My body stiffens and I pretend to put my phone away in my tote as an excuse to turn to look.

Will's in line for the café, wearing navy chinos that he's cuffed with loafers and no socks, a striped, blue linen button-down, a Cleveland Museum of Art tote bag. He looks like he's about to go teach a history class and get hit on by freshmen.

"He's coming over," Kacey mumbles. I take a deep breath.

He stops in front of our table. "Hey."

"Hey!" Kacey says. "We were just talking about Jen's class. What did you think?"

Will puts a hand in the pocket of his chinos. "Think it'll be good. She sounds like she'll be a good workshop leader."

I nod silently as he and Kacey volley small talk back and forth, but I can't look him in the eyes. Instead, I stare at his chest, thinking about his smell, both familiar and somehow foreign; the corded veins of his wrist; the small hairs that lace his forearms.

"Well, I have to be off to my assistantship." Kacey swipes

through her phone, looking at her schedule. "I'm in the Digital Media Center in Murray Hall. Do you guys work today, too?"

"Yeah, I need to be in the Writing Center in ten minutes," I say, careful to keep several feet away from Will as I stand up and grab my bag.

Will sounds like he's choking on his cappuccino. "I'm also working in the Writing Center this year." It comes out almost like an apology.

I wish it were an apology. A preemptive one—to all the undergrads he's about to make cry with his snide comments.

*   *   *

If Will is uncomfortable that we've inconveniently been placed together for our assistantships, he doesn't show it. He's sitting across from me at a long rectangular table in the middle of the University Writing Center, the place where we'll now spend twelve hours together a week. The room is stately and cold, with marble floors and stained-glass windows like a church.

We're here with several other cohort members, as well as graduate students from other parts of the English department, including some linguistics master's students and a few English PhDs. Thalia Loren is at the head of the table. The longtime director of the UWC, she's taking us through a week of orientation before the center officially opens next week.

"You're going to get a variety of students coming to you." She tucks her gray hair behind her ears, scanning us carefully. "From freshmen who need help full-on revising their history essays to master's students with English as a second language who just need a copy edit. And you need to be ready to provide all of them with empathetic listening and gentle guidance."

I flash Will a dark look, but it's wasted. He's taking notes in his Moleskine.

Thalia explains what the next week will include—a crash course in Writing Center theory, aimed at helping us understand our own biases, being mindful of different learning styles and abilities, and the most common scenarios we'll encounter from the student body. We'll then be assigned twelve hours of work, spread across shifts during the week and weekend.

"So not what I signed up for," Houston huffs beside me under his breath, and I do feel his pain. But it's a necessary evil to get full funding and not have to pay out-of-pocket for a program that the internet warns will do almost nothing for our résumés.

Thalia passes out a five-page essay titled "Class Consciousness in Rap Music of the 2010s," and we're given five minutes to skim it and, as a group, come up with three concrete ways to improve the piece.

Fiction writer Christine from Chapel Hill, in a hand-knit tank top from what she called "the best Goodwill in the state," starts us off. "I think structure is the main issue here. The writer's body paragraphs don't logically flow from the thesis statement. I think we could help the writer take the thesis and then break it up into manageable sections."

"That's great, Christine," Thalia says. "Anyone else?"

Will drags his pen down the edge of the page while he reads paragraph-to-paragraph. My shoulders tense as he looks up and makes eye contact with me, raising his hand.

"Yes, William."

"The main issue for me is coherence." He runs his long

fingers over the text. "The introductory paragraph touches upon maybe eight different ideas, only some of which are tackled in the paper. There's no throughline—it's almost like the writer has no idea where she wants to go with the paper, and by the time she decides, the paper is over and no real conclusion has been offered."

I let out a small scoff. "Why are you assuming they're a she?"

"The top of the paper says *By Maria Thompson*." The corners of his mouth turn up like he's suppressing a smile.

I frown. "Okay, yeah, but maybe the writer is nonbinary. That's quite the assumption you're making." I'm emboldened by Christine next to me, nodding with her eyebrows raised.

"Of course, fair enough, but I think the main focus of this conversation is the paper's contents, not the gender of the writer. Or?" He places his hands flat on the table and looks to Thalia for validation.

Thalia closes her eyes in a slow blink. "Let's focus on the topic at hand. But don't worry, Leigh. We aim to make the UWC an inclusive place for all students, and we encourage everyone to wear name tags with their pronouns if they're comfortable with that. Carry on, William."

I'm not sure who won this particular argument, but it hardly feels like me.

Finally, Thalia releases us, and we bust out of Gilman Hall. We have to return for workshop in a few hours, so I take the opportunity to explore the campus—its red-brick buildings and archways, paved sidewalks lined with oak trees, the scurry of freshmen wearing lanyards. It feels nice to be back at school again, far away from sales directors and marketing managers and berating clients.

I pull out my phone and see two texts from my parents. My dad's is first:

> Hope first day is fun honey. FaceTime today? Can
> do tomorrow too, but would love to hear how it's
> going ASAP! Let me know

Then I read my mom's:

> Are you free now? Have time to chat between
> patients—otherwise can't until Sunday

Before the separation, I'd video-chat with my parents every week to give updates on my work and life in Boston. My mom would tell me horror stories about patients and my dad would complain about clients at the marketing agency where he worked in sales, both sitting shoulder-to-shoulder on the living room couch, holding the phone too close to their faces.

Once they separated and my mom moved out of my childhood home, those calls stopped. I've only texted or called them separately. And now I realize that if their separation becomes permanent, for every major life moment I have—moving to a new city, starting school, getting married, new jobs—I'll be telling them separately. There will no longer be an *us*.

I'm about to call my mom when I get another text from my dad: What about FaceTime in an hour actually? Or 6pm? You tell me what's convenient.

I sigh and make the call to Mom, who picks up on the last ring.

"Dr. Anna Simon," she answers, an authoritative edge to her voice.

There's a shot of serotonin from how she says our last name. I like knowing there's something connecting me, her, my dad. Even if they're fighting. Even if they're talking about divorce.

"Mom, it's me."

"Oh, sorry, baby. I'm so distracted I didn't even see the caller ID. How's school? Dad help you settle in?"

"Yeah, it's good." I almost stumble into some poor girl on the sidewalk. "Very different from Boston. Humidity is awful."

"Did he bring you the box with the vases? I bubble-wrapped them and brought them to the house, but I'm skeptical he remembered."

Oh. He clearly didn't remember, because I don't have them. "Hmm, yes, right. I haven't unpacked everything yet, but I think I know which box you're talking about. It was heavy."

"I knew you'd want them to make your apartment look pretty, but your father seemed to think there wasn't much room in the SUV. He wanted to mail them, but I don't trust USPS. They're fragile."

"Yeah, don't worry, Mom, he brought them to me." I stare into the pale sun until my eyes tighten.

"Wow, I must say I'm surprised. But good. How's everything else? Nice classmates?"

"Yeah, everyone seems nice. How's everything there?"

"Well, today was supposed to be the day I started at Mayo."

My tongue presses firmly to the roof of my mouth. "Oh. Right."

Last year, my mom got a call from the Mayo Clinic, offering

her the directorship of their Surgical Innovation Center. I was ecstatic for her—and relieved for myself, knowing I likely would have shouldered the burden of comforting her if she hadn't gotten it. It was the end of a long road; at last, she'd achieved the kind of leadership position she'd dreamed of since she was a med student.

Instead, it was the beginning of what might be the end of her marriage.

My mom said yes to the position, of course, and gave notice at work. The goodbye party was planned. Desperate to make her happy, Dad crafted a façade of excitement, of pride—until the boxes for the move were delivered and he revealed that *he'd* never given notice, never planned *his* goodbye party. Caught between wanting to please my mother and preserving his own life and comfort, he stood still and made no decision at all.

I just…can't leave, he'd said, dejected, in a video call to me in Boston.

Another person might have said, *To hell with it. I'm going to Minnesota, you stay.* But Mom comes from a place of duty; she thought it made more sense to stay with her husband. So she bottled up her disappointment, swallowed her pride, and brushed off the intrusive questions at work when she asked for her job back. For a few months, it was okay—a barbed remark here, a jab there. Then Mom's disappointment came to a boiling point. Six months later, she moved out of the house, renting a condo in what she and Dad call a temporary solution.

"I hope your father's happy staying put in Ohio. Why uproot your life for an amazing opportunity when you could waste away in Cleveland doing the same thing you've done for twenty years?"

"Mom, I mean, there's such a thing as compromise."

She snorts, loud and inelegant in my ear. "You sound exactly like your father."

My body stiffens, bringing me to a halt in the middle of the sidewalk. "Sorry, no. I mean Dad also should compromise."

And he never did. Not really. Before Mom even considered applying to positions in other states, she sought out leadership roles in Cleveland—to no avail. But even without the prestigious title I know she craves, no one could say she wasn't thriving as an attending surgeon at the Cleveland Clinic. My dad, in contrast, flitted between sales jobs, dealing silently with bad bosses and measly base salaries. Until his most recent company. He finally had a good thing going. He deserved it. And Mom was asking him to pack up and leave? Head to a new state where he wouldn't have any network of friends or family?

I wonder what would have happened if he'd had these discussions with my mom at the beginning instead of letting his need to people-please cloud his judgment. Maybe this would be a three-person call, instead of just two.

"Yes, he should compromise," she sighs. "But he didn't."

She goes on, asking about my classes. Then her voice dips.

"You sure you're liking it, sweetie? I mean, I love that you're pursuing something fun and creative, but as someone with years of experience, I'm telling you, money *does* matter. Titles matter, too. Your father's prioritized comfort over those things, and..." She trails off, then says, "Do you think you can get your job in Boston back when you graduate? If you want it, I mean. I'm just worried—"

"Mom, I'm heading into my first workshop soon, I have to go."

"Yes, yes, of course, baby. I'm getting pulled into a consult anyway, but keep me updated, okay?"

I nod into the phone before realizing she can't hear my body language. "Mhmm. Bye, Mom."

When I hang up, I see three more texts from my dad. Now he's worried about me and is proposing yet more inconvenient times for our video chat.

Writing this birth story is going to be a nightmare.

Chapter Four

PAUL RUTGER WELCOMES US INTO our first poetry workshop like we're being ushered into a church. He's quiet and unassuming—a total contradiction from his poetry persona, which is bold and loud, according to Cindy from Arkansas. I wouldn't know, so I made sure to skim the reviews of his work on Amazon before class.

The first-semester poetry workshop combines both the first- and second-year MFAs. Along with the five of us first-years, there are five second-year students, most of whom I recognize from the barbecue after-party. Including August. He makes no attempt to sit next to Kacey, although she tries to catch his attention. I take a seat next to her, with Will on the other side of the round table. It's hard not to look at him, but I don't want to give him the satisfaction.

"Welcome, first-years, to poetry workshop," Paul says from the head of the table. "The real fun begins on Thursday when we look at *your* work, but today is just a little primer where we'll go through some of my favorites to get the discussion going."

This has never been my strong suit. In college English courses, I tended to take a back seat, preferring to let other people talk while I learned from them. I'm okay talking about classmates' work, but when it comes to famous published people, a block goes up in my brain. I find the words difficult to play with, to interpret. It's the same issue I had in client meetings. Unless I'm 1,000 percent sure what I'm about to say is brilliant, I can't risk saying it at all.

We're each passed a thick packet of poems, and I flip through it quickly, looking for something I recognize. I see Dorianne Laux and Ada Limón and then a bunch of old white guys whose names I remember being taught, but I hardly know anything about them.

The first one we read is "Skunk Hour" by Robert Lowell, whom I recognize as a confessional poet from the late 1950s, but that's about as far as my knowledge extends. August reads it out loud, and although he's from Michigan, it comes out with a Florida twang for some reason.

Paul opens us up to discussion, and I have no idea what I'm supposed to say.

"I think it's really interesting that for the first several stanzas, we don't have a sense of where the poet is," Hazel begins, and quotes a few lines. "Then in the end, we get the first *I*, and I'm thinking of what it means to be an active participant versus a passive one."

What. I feel stupider by the minute. I look over at Kacey to see if she's going to say something, but she's too busy underlining words in red pen.

Paul nods at Hazel's comment. "That's a great observation. There's a real voyeurism to Lowell's persona in the last stanza, and it feels like we're unearthing an inner struggle."

Julian, a second-year poet with a nose ring, chimes in. "I think we should discuss the metaphor of the skunk."

"By all means!" Paul says. "Start us off."

While Julian is talking about how the skunk in the poem is an outsider or something, Will's face volleys back and forth between him and Paul. He raises his hand.

"Yes, William?"

"I'm intrigued by the tension between what it means to be exposed and what it means to hide," Will says. "And I wanted to note the structure of this, too—"

I zone out. In the hope of looking like maybe I'm just severely introverted like Jerry and not an idiot who is clearly not smart enough to be here, I start moving my pen across the lines to make it look like I'm highly invested in these skunks.

Then, a minute later, even Jerry raises his hand to make some useful comment on the matriarchy, which everyone nods at. So I do, too.

After another hour, class ends, and I know I have an even more daunting task ahead: writing a poem for next week that proves why I'm even here.

*   *   *

"Tell me *everything*."

Gen's ponytail swishes distractingly as she holds the phone up to her face, jogging to catch the T, her cheeks as red as her hair. She's late to work as usual. She's still in Boston, where we purposefully reunited after spending college apart—she being the safety blanket I didn't want to go without again. She works as the social media manager for a popular language learning app, spending all day in a glass-walled office, explaining memes to boomers who can barely copy-and-paste.

"I'm the dumbest person in the entire class." I lean back into the pillows of my bed and stare out my window.

Gen must have made her train, because now I see her smushed against a million other commuters, the peering eyes of an older man behind her, looking right into the screen. I don't miss *that* at all—spending rush hour feeling like you've been forced into a petri dish of stressed-out, too-close people who were never taught to cough into their elbows.

"So what? You're probably the hottest, and *that's* the real currency, baby."

"Gen," I moan.

She laughs. "There's no way you're the dumbest. I refuse to believe it."

I run through a mental list of the entire cohort. "Fine, I don't think I'm *dumb*, but I don't feel prepared. Or like this is going to come especially naturally."

"It's like day five. Give it more time. At least you're not doing this anymore." She looks to her left and right, and the man over her shoulder nods solemnly into the camera in agreement. Then she gets an evil glint in her eyes. "Anything new with Will?"

I'd told her everything, of course. Gave her the full play-by-play of the barbecue, the Writing Center orientation, how he stares at me in poetry as if I'm his moldy sourdough starter. "I'm ignoring him. He's ignoring me. Just two strangers who happened to go to the same high school."

At that, she gives me a look. "*Total* strangers, who six years ago were about to ki—"

"No, stop, not going there," I cut in. "I'm here to write, not to…"

"To what, sweet Leigh, to what?"

"To *date*," I grit out, like it tastes bad in my mouth.

Gen raises her eyebrows, a glittering smile undercutting the seriousness in her eyes. "Come on, every poet needs a muse. You haven't dated in ages. Maybe, fine, don't date anyone in your class, but you're on a college campus filled with eligible grad students. Get yourself a PhD candidate. Some hot guy in glasses and a blazer hanging out in the library? I'm dripping just thinking about it."

She's right. I *haven't* dated in ages. But in general, I don't do long-term relationships. Not since my college boyfriend Andrew. Not since Middlebury. There have been guys, of course. I'm a modern woman with a variety of apps at her fingertips. Over the last six years, beyond the one-and-done dates, I've had a handful of relationships, but nothing designed to last. Four months with a software engineer who had Regency-era facial hair. Two months with a McKinsey consultant who, while he could not stop bringing up the fact that he went to Penn, was completely mystified by my camisole's shelf bra the first time we slept together. Almost five months with a local high school AP Government teacher who was terrible at listening but very good at being listened to. None of them stuck, and it was never too difficult to say goodbye.

"Let me settle in first, and yeah, okay, I can look into the PhD crowd in a few months maybe. But writing comes first."

"Great, because I need some entertainment. Work is kil-il-ing me." She says *killing* like it's a three-syllable stab to the heart.

"What's going on?"

She casts a look around the cramped train. "Every day in this madhouse, I am seconds away from quitting. My boss is always up my ass, and fuckin' Cassandra is micromanaging the hell out of this product launch. I had this amazing idea for a video post and they shut it down faster than my last salary talk."

I grimace, knowing too well the feeling of your creativity being stamped out. Gen's had a similar trajectory to me—graduated our high school, Rowan, went on to study English at Ohio State, worked in marketing ever since, drowning in stupid corporate lingo and too-small raises.

"They're idiots," I offer, though I know it's no consolation.

"Okay, I'm at Arlington, gotta go get my soul sucked," she laughs. "Another day in paradise."

She blows a kiss and waves and suddenly she's gone. A good reminder for me to buck up and make this program work for me so I never have to go back to *that*.

* * *

Three days later, I join Kacey and Christine in the atrium of Gilman Hall, where we are simultaneously "writing" and also drinking lattes and eating expensive oat cookies from the café. I like Kacey but have no idea what to make of Christine and her ponchos. Still, I don't want the MFA to be a repeat of four years of English-major-ing where I couldn't quite make friends in class. I'm trying harder now.

"What did you think of workshop, by the way?" I ask Kacey.

"Good, I think. It'll be more interesting when we're looking at each others' poems, of course, but everyone seems engaged and smart, which is such a departure from what I experienced in undergrad. This is really a breath of fresh air."

"Totally agree!" I ignore the tightness in my throat.

Christine is telling us about her fiction workshop when all three of our phones ping at the same time with an email.

"'The 2023 Distinguished Writer Fellowship,'" Kacey says, reading the subject line out loud. She clicks into the email. "Oh *shit*, it's Erica Go for poetry."

I feel my entire body harden like an icicle. What are the odds? "Are you kidding?" I open the email myself and immediately start scanning.

Every year, the Perrin MFA offers two second-years, one poet and one fiction writer, special fellowships where they get to have one-on-one tutorials with distinguished visiting professors, sponsored by alumni. It's an excellent networking opportunity, but even more so, it's a year of full funding without work. No Writing Center, no assistantships, no teaching. Just a full year to write and rewrite. It's a great deal that any student would die for.

To apply, first-years submit a statement of interest as well as a small sample of work. The English department, with input from the visiting professor, decides in the spring.

But the fact that the visiting professor is *Erica freaking Go* makes this opportunity not a want but a need. She's the poet who made me feel like poetry was even something I was interested in. The first poet I read who wrote like a human, who wrote about womanhood and girlhood and pop culture. Slang, playfulness, sexuality. She's outstanding. And I've been reading her work for the last ten years. I feel almost entitled to this.

"Erica is really good," I say, tempering my response, trying not to give away how utterly thirsty I am. "I wonder how many poets will want the fellowship."

"Probably most." Kacey raises her eyebrows. "Though to be

honest, I maybe won't apply. I genuinely want to teach next year, get that on my CV."

"I'd fucking kill for the fiction one," Christine says with a huff. "Jeremiah Brandon got the Booker Prize two years ago."

"If you want it, though, Leigh," Kacey adds. "I'd say basically everyone else in the cohort is your competition."

I didn't even know it would be Erica until two minutes ago, but I want it. I want it for the middle school Leigh, who thought being a good writer could make her popular. I want it for the high school Leigh, who never thought she'd end up at an MFA program after that confidence-killing workshop. I want it for this version of me now: the one who doesn't know what else she will do—*can* do—if not for writing. I don't want to go back into marketing, but I know the odds. Poetry is hardly a stable career, and I don't want to be a hobby poet who thinks she'll write lines over lunch breaks until life inevitably gets in the way. This fellowship could be my best, most sure shot at being a full-time creative writer.

I re-read the email carefully. Statement of interest. Four to five poems. Due in January. Bridget warned me not to do anything too stressful, said I should be viewing this program as more of an artistic space than a competitive academic program, but surely this is fine. It's not like I have to do anything additional beyond the statement of interest essay. I'll submit the poems I'll write for workshop. Easy. It's hardly an application at all.

"Hey, Penelope!" Kacey yells across the atrium, and the second-year poet who hosted the after-party waves and trots over, backpack in hand.

"How are you all settling in? I'm guessing you got the email?"

"About the fellowships? Yes. I'm foaming at the mouth," Christine says.

Penelope laughs. "Definitely apply. You never know who'll get it."

I nod. "What do you think it takes?"

We all lean in as Penelope takes a seat at our table and begins spewing insights. In their year, Julian got the poetry fellowship and Vanessa got the fiction; the secret, Penelope says, is to submit work the visiting professors will know what to do with.

"What does that even mean?" Christine asks, eyes wide.

Penelope shrugs. "If you're good, you're good, but I'll say this: If the visiting professor is only writing magical realism and you just don't fuck with that, it's not gonna be a good fit. If you're committed to only writing poems with meter and they bring in someone who lives and dies by free verse, they're not going to pair you. At least not from what I've ever heard."

That's a good sign. I feel like Erica will respond well to the pop-culture poems I tend to write, since that's where she finds so much inspiration for her work as well.

"I'm sure it'll be a great fellowship with Erica and Jeremiah. They always are. Amazing experience, amazing connections. You could basically set up your writing career with this," Penelope says. She lists what the fellowship winners in the years above her have gone on to do—regular placements in *The New Yorker*, professorships at Iowa, making the *New York Times* bestseller list, the prestigious under-thirty Ruth Lilly fellowship. Not to mention that Julian and Vanessa apparently hit it off so well with this years' visiting professors that they're being invited to literary scene parties like they're already members of the community and not just two MFA students. At the thought, every tendon in my body tightens with want.

Penelope's off to work on our own university lit journal, the *Perrin Review*.

"What're you thinking, Leigh?" Kacey asks as my eyes glaze over in deep thought.

"I'm getting that fellowship," I say, and it's the most confident I've felt all week.

Chapter Five

THERE ARE THREE THINGS I need to accomplish in order to get this damn fellowship and thus become a real, actual writer.

The first is to impress in workshop. I know they're not explicitly evaluating this, but *of course* it matters. Paul and Daniel aren't reading our work anonymously. Everything they know about us will subconsciously seep into their assessment, and if I don't participate or if I say basic, dumb shit in class, they will notice.

The second is to, obviously, submit poems designed to win. Paul and Daniel will probably have a large say, but so does Erica, and that's where I have the advantage. But I still need to pick a handful that are really going to scream potential to her.

And finally, I'll need to put in a great performance at the First-Year Reading Series. It's our last chance to make an impression before the fellowships are announced, and I want to show the faculty (and my classmates) that I'm the full poet package. A writer with unique wordplay, an entertaining voice, and a compelling stage presence to boot.

But it's easy to forget that the MFA is not strictly poetry classes until you have a ten-page nonfiction assignment due in mere days. Poetry's an opportunity to transform into someone else, but with nonfiction, I'm forced to be myself.

And this "birth story" is not coming easily. I know when I was born (March 1, 5:06 a.m.), where I was born (Chagrin Falls, Ohio, a suburb of Cleveland), to whom I was born (Anna and Jeffrey Simon, a couple of thirty-two-year-olds with a plan), and what stars were aligned when I was born (Pisces sun, Capricorn rising, Libra moon). But I don't know what any of this should mean for Jen Stewart-Weiss.

As most of our idiosyncrasies emerge from our parents, I start by focusing on Anna and Jeffrey, composing a collection of vignettes in the third-person point of view about how they met, what they did on their honeymoon, how my mom knew she was going into labor, and the immediate aftermath—the pale-pink nursery room with the baby monitor on the changing table, ready to pick up the sounds of unrest in the night.

Then I extend the essay further. I interweave a series of anecdotes about early childhood and beyond with my parents. How despite how much they loved me—I asked for that confirmation over and over again, my dad says—they separated six months ago, the end result of years of fighting.

I know this isn't relevant to my *birth*. But it feels strange to talk about their marriage without mentioning that it might be ending, because right now, that feels like the most important thing.

My parents met their senior year of college at Ohio State, Jeff Simon, the work-hard-play-harder president of the OSU Delta Psi chapter and Anna Dunn, the precocious med school applicant. The pairing that shouldn't have worked but did. Until it didn't.

I inherited my dad's anxiety, my mom's stick-straight blond hair, my dad's sweet tooth, my mom's propensity to downplay pain.

Anna had planned it all to a T. Get married at thirty, have one kid at exactly the age of thirty-two ("You still have the energy, but now you have money"), send that kid to the same private school she'd gone to, and make sure they had enough money for college.

Life went according to plan.

In the early morning of March 1, Anna gave birth at home with a midwife. While she herself was a doctor, she didn't want to have her baby in a hospital. That was a place for work, not a place where she wanted to be screaming and crying, skin salty with sweat, vulnerable. But it didn't matter. She approached birth like the MCATs. She was terribly prepared, answered the questions efficiently, and kept a straight face despite the life force breaking her body open. As usual, she left the screaming to Jeff.

"We did it!" Jeff said at the end of the endless pushing.

"Well, I did the hard work," Anna said. Jeff planted an enormous kiss on her head.

And then there was me. Something in between.

What a bunch of melodrama. I delete all of it and start again, the cursor at the top of my document blinking with judgment.

In search of more inspiration, I pull up the poem I'd gotten published in *Goldfinch Review* last year, "Usually, Two Lefts Off Belvoir Blvd." When my parents originally separated, I'd written it in a rush, not knowing any other way to process what I'd felt. And then, I wanted to get rid of it—the fever-dream of words, the unwieldy feelings. Put that burden on someone else. So I submitted it to a handful of journals, sending it through the ether as cathartic release. I was confident no one would ever do anything with it. When *Goldfinch*—bafflingly—wanted it, all I could think was, *Who could possibly see me stripped bare—exposed, vulnerable, unedited—and find something beautiful?* Even I don't. Seeing the words now elicits a full-body cringe.

Usually, Two Lefts Off Belvoir Blvd

Nothing will change, you said, except
how I look in a mirror—lifeless
bangs (mine), eyes that whisper

tight-wound secrets (his), unwilling
chin—expectation-dimpled with age
(yours)—which is to say, everything

is now gaunt. *Aren't you too
old for this?* And it's true: I am
cotton candy at Cedar Point, backyard

treehouse Barbies, sunset scraped
knees, punch-drunk and asking too
many questions. *Are we there*

*yet? Is God a woman? If you build
a home and then break it, who is
to blame?* No one, you'd say, but

then why am I crying at Sephora,
raspberry-stained and ruddy, not answering
when the sales associate asks, *Where's*

home for you? Later that night, scrubbing
my face, I realize I didn't know what to say.

I exit the Word doc. I can hardly read it, much less use it to write this birth story. No one was supposed to like it—it's embarrassing, frankly, to think of it being printed on good paper, read by poets way more accomplished than me, who can weave their unruly emotions into something more sophisticated. And the fact that *Will* has read it? Kill me.

I know I can do better in the MFA. What can set my essay apart from everyone else's? How can I make it fresh and interesting? I decide to write the entire thing from the point of view of the midwife.

It's too exhausting to pour yourself out onto a page with no one to pour you back in. My best bet is to delight the reader with something unexpected.

*   *   *

A week before nonfiction workshop, we receive the printed packet of three birth stories to critique—mine, Wiebke's, and Will's.

I tackle Wiebke's first, pulling it up on my phone, reading it on the way to my Writing Center shift. It's about how she was born and had to immediately begin negotiating language (and therefore her personality)—the result of being the child of an

American father and a German mother, born in Berlin in the early 1990s. The language is precise, almost clinical, but with a careful joy simmering underneath. It's all very good, with a few sentences that make me so absolutely bitter I didn't come up with them first.

I move on to Will's. As I pull it up on my phone, crossing the threshold into the Writing Center, I smell his woodsy cologne.

He's getting in for his shift now, too. He looks the same as usual: polished. He's in dark, well-tailored jeans (probably something obnoxious, like Japanese selvedge) and a beige button-down, rolled up to his forearms. Nothing is askew, except for the wavy tuft of hair that sometimes gets in the way of his forehead.

He sets his tote bag on the table in the center of the room where we're supposed to wait until we're assigned students and takes a seat across from me.

"Hey," he says first.

"Hi." I shove my phone into my jean jacket pocket.

He opens his mouth to say something else, then doesn't.

We're interrupted, anyway, by Houston, the tall fiction writer from Chicago, who shares a shift with us and sits next to Will at the table. If you squint he almost could be a frat guy, but that's only until you catch the Sewanee Writers Conference T-shirt.

"You guys," he says. "Erica Go and Jeremiah Brandon. What do you think?"

"I'm not super familiar with Go's work," Will says, and I bite the inside of my cheek. Of course he's not. Erica once used a flame emoji in a poem. Will would find that sacrilegious.

"But Brandon is really good," he continues. "I read *Stars Made of Cinnamon* when it came out two years ago, and I couldn't put it down."

"Agreed." Houston nods. "I would actually die if I got the fiction fellowship."

"Erica is amazing, too," I say, pulling out my laptop to pretend to work.

"Isn't she, like, an Instagram poet?" Houston asks. He says it innocently enough, but there's the smallest edge of the condescension you'd expect from an MFA student.

"She has a presence on Instagram, but her books of poetry came first."

"Cool, cool. I should pick one up." It's an attempt at diplomacy, but I know Houston will do no such thing.

Before the conversation can continue, Houston and Will are whisked away by the shift manager for appointments. I'm on drop-in duty and have time to work or read while I wait for students to appear. I take out my phone again, unwilling to pull up Will's essay on the big screen of my laptop, and start to read.

I was born eight pounds, eight ounces, and eighteen inches long—which is to say, both too much and not enough.

I feel a light stab in the center of my chest. I look at Will across the room, sitting with a student. His posture is rigid, his back a wall.

My parents tried to make it a perfect pregnancy. Kristen read all the books; William accompanied her to pregnancy yoga.

He prepared her watermelon with flaky sea salt and shot glasses full of relish to eat with a small spoon. Every craving satisfied.

Kristen saw Dr. Newman at any sign of trouble. Not a stretch mark was created under her vigilance.

Right on time on September 3, the preparations made and the nursery ready, I, with matted brown hair and a glass-breaking cry, was born. But despite my excellent timing, Kristen and William were taught a lesson they perhaps never truly understood: When it comes to children, you can't control everything.

Kristen Hummel and William Langford met at Oberlin College, where William was a tenured professor in the English department and Kristen was a new hire to the admissions department. They met by chance at a prospective student luncheon Kristen had organized. She wanted to invite some of the college's most popular professors to woo potential students, but soon found that she was the one being wooed. William was charming and older by ten years, and they bonded over their love of words. Kristen was a reader, William was a writer, and once they got married, they hoped their child would be, too.

I read the rest of the essay. Will plays with anecdotes, but focuses on the nine months of pregnancy, as well as his parents' relationship prior to that. I learn that his parents made spreadsheets with different baby names, ultimately forgoing all of them to pass down his father's name instead. How they hoped the move would be prophetic—that their tiny new son would grow up to be as erudite and quick-witted as his dad.

I'm jolted out of the essay when Will comes back. I notice slight bags under his eyes, his thin forehead wrinkles a little more pronounced.

"Good session?" I ask, turning my phone off once again.

"I'm not sure how much I helped, but I think it went okay." He runs his hand through his hair, pulls out a journal from his tote, uncaps a pen, and starts writing. I try to parse out his handwriting, but it's loopy and a bit wilder than I remember his crisp cursive from high school being.

"Ahem."

I snap my eyes up to his face, heat flooding my cheeks as his gaze takes inventory of every divot, cranny, crease of me.

"I'm jotting down ideas for this week's poem. If you're so curious."

I cross my legs tightly. "I was just staring off into space. I'm not reading your journal."

"Have you started your poem yet?"

No. "Yes."

"Looking forward to reading it."

"You won't like it. It's more in the vein of Erica Go than anything you're probably reading."

He raises an eyebrow. "Good reminder. I need to start getting familiar with her work for the fellowship." He writes something down in his journal, then closes it, puts it in his tote, and focuses all his attention, unsettlingly, on me.

"You're applying?" *Of fucking course.*

He nods exactly once, resolute. "Don't sound so shocked. I imagine the entire cohort will apply."

"But why?" I stammer. "You've never read her work, ever."

"Any one-on-one opportunity with a professor, plus the ability not to do an assistantship, is huge. Of course I want it. I haven't read Erica Go, no, but I obviously will before I send in my statement of intent."

"You won't like it," I hear myself say. "She uses emojis. Slang. She's not like the old white men you're usually reading."

His gaze turns steely. "You have no idea what I like."

The way he says it, all low and direct, somersaults through my body.

"You'll think she's all style, no substance, I'm sure."

He folds his arms and leans back in the chair. "Leigh."

It's a scold. It's a *Why aren't you over that? Why can't you be fun?* That's how I hear it, at least.

I open my mouth, hoping to retort in some incisive way that will leave him reeling. But before I can come up with something, there's a tap on my shoulder.

"Leigh, we have a drop-in for you."

*   *   *

This man is staring at me. He needs help with an essay, which is about economics or something. It's hard to know.

His name is Lucas and he's well over six feet tall, skinny and lanky, with dark-brown hair and a patchy beard. He wears jeans and a fraternity sweatshirt with white athletic socks and Adidas slides. He's mildly attractive in a familiar kind of way, reminding me of all the frat guys I knew back in college.

While I read his paper out loud, I can see out of the corner of my eye that he's not looking down or following along. He's just staring.

"So what do you want to focus on today?" I ask when I finish reading, brushing the paper with the palm of my hand as if it's a cat.

"I just know the entire thing is wrong. The structure, the words, even the formatting."

"I don't think we'll have time to go through all of that in this session, so maybe let's focus on the structure?"

He grunts. He doesn't smile, really. I get the sense he's here because a professor told him he would get extra credit for coming—a common bribe among undergraduates, it seems.

I try to pick apart his essay, but he's resistant. While he said he wanted to change the whole thing, he also seems determined to keep everything the same, just with my validation. We spend the next twenty minutes setting up a plan for restructuring the essay, moving paragraphs around, and creating a new conclusion.

"Can you sign this sheet for me?" He shoves a pink slip into my hands. It's signed by the head of lacrosse at Perrin. "My coach needs to know I came."

"Um, sure." I sign and date it.

"Thanks." He keeps staring at me. It's not in a way that makes me feel *seen*, though. More like assessed. Like he's trying to ascertain if I'm attractive enough to keep talking to.

"Appreciate it." His eyes graze over my body one more time, and I immediately feel self-conscious about my V-neck shirt. "I'll be back."

"Great!" I say, and it comes out as a chirp. Relief that he's leaving, and maybe somehow also that I've passed his assessment.

*　　*　　*

My first-ever MFA workshop is here, and my stomach is in knots.

Wiebke and Will went way more personal with their essays. I took a creative risk by writing in the point of view of the midwife, one that I hope will impress the class and pay off.

I'm first up. Because the stories are too long to read aloud, Jen leads us right into discussion.

"Who wants to start us off with feedback on Leigh's piece?" she asks.

No one raises their hand, which feels *amazing*, so Jen calls on Houston, who makes the mistake of making eye contact with her.

"Felt like there was really good momentum at the beginning." He looks me in the eye and nods encouragingly. "But I thought it lost a little steam in the end, so that's just something to think about."

"Can you isolate the moment you felt like that?" Jen prompts.

"Around the fifth page, when Leigh is...born, I guess. Then the midwife no longer needs to be there, and I think she's used ineffectively at that point. I hate to say it, but I don't really see the point in hearing any of the midwife's day-to-day journey. It doesn't illuminate anything about Leigh's birth."

My thighs melt into the chair.

Hazel, not to be upstaged in her role as head critic, chimes in. "I also felt like it didn't fully fulfill the assignment. It's a *birth story*, but this essay seems to want to extend into something else, which could be good reading, but I think this could be tightened if it stuck to the scope. By the end of the birth story, I should feel like I know the circumstances surrounding Leigh's birth, and instead all I know is how babies are delivered via midwife."

It takes everything in me not to roll my eyes. Her words cue up flashbacks of the Coleman + Derry office, sitting in a large glass conference room with clients who never seemed to understand my vision. But underneath the irritation, there's a pang of embarrassment. I probably *should* have stuck more closely to the parameters of the exercise. I just couldn't figure out how to do it without looking at my own words and cringing.

The back-and-forth continues for another few minutes, and I jot down people's comments on my own copy of the essay. By the end, I feel wrung dry.

Then Jen chimes in with her final take.

"Leigh, this was a creative setup, but not quite the assignment. In nonfiction, it's essential to use the craft of fiction to create a real *story*. But I think this crosses the line into actual fiction, not nonfiction. You can't possibly know what the midwife who delivered you was feeling twenty-some years ago, and even if you did, we come out of your piece not knowing anything about you. There's some beautiful language in here, though, so that's all working great. This feedback is more on the concept."

It's polite, but it's still the most direct *Didn't hit the mark* I've ever gotten from a teacher. At least out loud like this in front of everyone. My skin feels itchy, my face burning hot. There's nothing I can do other than nod and force my lips up into a smile that says *Got it!*

Wiebke goes next. Hers is flawless, everyone loves it, Europeans are better, we get it.

Finally, Will goes.

"This was really lovely," Hazel says, her words only deepening my feeling that everyone in this class is better than me. "Just that first sentence—*both too much and not enough*—it struck me in the chest."

Athena chimes in. "I totally agree, Hazel. But I also want to call attention to structure here. I wonder what would happen if William were to switch some vignettes around..."

Will's piece *is* great, but I don't want to say it out loud, so I spend the remainder of class flipping through the pages, looking for a constructive comment, something intelligent I can say to show Jen and everyone else that I, too, have a critical eye.

By the time I come up with something, class is over.

As we get up, over the rustle of backpacks and zippers, Hazel goes up to Will.

"I don't know why I didn't put two and two together, but wow, William Langford is your dad! I've read all of his pieces in *The New Yorker*. Damn, that is the coolest thing ever."

My stomach braids into a knot. I've known Will's dad is an English professor for years now, but like all the other useless data on him I've accumulated since high school, I've stuffed it in the back of a drawer, never to be touched. But I didn't know he's a writer.

She tucks her hair behind her ear, and I press my tongue hard against the roof of my mouth.

"Yep," he replies.

"So does he still teach at Oberlin? I almost went to Oberlin for college. How crazy would it have been if I'd had him as a professor?"

I watch Will's body perform a sigh. He doesn't actually make a sound, but something in his shoulders tightens, then releases. "He, uh, passed last year."

I'm not sure how Hazel responds because I don't stick around to listen. My ears clog with water, my belly clenches. How neutral his face was when he said it. How his body told a different answer.

Chapter Six

In HIGH SCHOOL AND COLLEGE, I usually had a specific assignment for poetry workshop. Write a poem in the vein of some famous poet. Write a poem in iambic pentameter. Write a sonnet.

In the MFA program, you can do whatever the fuck you want, and it's a looseness that doesn't seem to agree with me. Sure, it's one of the main selling points of the program, as opposed to just writing in your free time. But I'm a person who likes structure and deadlines. It's why I like group exercise instead of improvising at the gym. I need someone to tell me what to do. Otherwise I barely know where to start.

Now, though, with the fellowship on the line, I need to use every workshop strategically, testing out the kind of work I think Erica will respond to. In writing this specific poem, I even tried to channel Erica. How would *she* approach her first MFA poetry workshop?

We receive the first packet of poems on Monday afternoon, meaning we have until Thursday to read through and annotate them with comments. I slip into the English department office to go to my mailbox and grab the stapled papers, containing ten poems—one from each of the five first-years and five second-years. Kacey's is on top, a two-pager peppered with couplets. I skim it as I walk down the hallway, trying to assess how embarrassed I should be by my own writing level and whether I belong in this class. Her poem is titled "This Is My Body Lying to You."

It's very good. It's better than mine. Fuck.

I continue flipping through the pages. Hazel's done some long free-form poem with lots of irregular stanzas. August has written a massive block of text that hardly looks like a poem at all. Jerry sent in what appears to be a sonnet: "Sunday River at 2:01 p.m."

My poem sits in the middle of the packet, both literally and quality-wise. It's not significantly better or worse than anyone else's. It's a deep relief, and I wonder if any of my other classmates feel the same way.

Will's poem is the last in the packet. It trickles down three-quarters of a page, written in couplets where the second line of each stanza has been indented, causing the entire thing to look like a reverse staircase. He's titled it "An Apology to the Oberlin College Department of Geology."

The poem is both gritty and lush. It sounds like it's about a time he snuck into a college office with a girl after dark while waiting for his dad. The whole thing flows with geological words like *agate* and *lava*, but each stanza has a disjointed quality, like he has no idea where it wants to go. I'm not sure if that's the point or not.

When I get home, I read it several more times, then write my comments, keeping them clinical. I don't want him to think I spent more time on his than anyone else's.

I wonder how much time he will spend on mine.

*   *   *

By the time Thursday rolls around, I'm buzzing on unused energy. Gen sends a well-timed text right before workshop begins: Don't let these try-hards knock you around bitch you're Leigh Simon the best writer I know

It's sweet. But she's biased. Nevertheless, after nonfiction, I go into *this* workshop feeling much more confident. Maybe my poem isn't the best in the class, but it's by no means embarrassing. This is the kind of stuff I know how to write.

Paul begins with Kacey's poem. In the Perrin MFA program, the rules are as follows: When a poem is up, someone other than the poet reads it out loud. Next, the poet reads it out loud in their own voice so the class can hear it with the intended inflection. Then the first reader goes back and walks the group through a brief synopsis of what is working well and not-so-well in the piece before opening it up to discussion for about five to eight minutes. Finally, Paul chimes in with his take. And repeat.

Harriet, a second-year from Alaska with curly brown hair and a perpetual frown, reads Kacey's first. "This Is My Body Lying to You" is a bona fide hit. The first-years, clearly a bit afraid to critique, ooh and ahh, but the second-years have good constructive criticism:

Consider the point of view, maybe it should be in third person.
Ending feels like it's missing a beat.
Maybe some of the imagistic language could be heightened.

It's all very reasonable and respectful. An acknowledgment that there's always room for improvement, but still, Kacey's first attempt was excellent. I make a note to study the poem in detail later for tips.

Jerry's poem, "Sunday River at 2:01 p.m.," is more mixed in its reception. Hazel's "Poem with Stale Cake, Golden Hour and

Grandpa" is met with enthusiasm, and August's "Soliloquy for Michigan Highway 75" is a mess and hardly anyone knows where to begin. Kacey is the only one who says something remotely positive, and even she is reaching when she comments on its "energy."

Then we move on to mine. Jeananne, a second-year with platinum-blond baby bangs, decides to present it.

"'Taylor Swift Sets the Record Straight,'" she begins, stating the title.

I'm drowning deep blue easy
    as Everest wonderland bodies

constrict and contract & I'm suffocating,
    choking on December, no, I'm not

fine. He's unbuttoning fast but yes there
    and *there*, red cranberry fall, no

scarves—bolder. Rocky, sure but when
    he says north I follow. I know

places, know headlights, lipstick smears
    on white T-shirts and never-evers, rosy

everything and granny smith green eyes
    in which I see my reflection—

I'll be cheekbones, good girl, oil painting,
    geometry proof you cannot solve,

all style, all stay, all wine-stained blank
   space you won't let me wear

anymore. Call me calculating, clean,
   mean, mine, innocent—and yours.

I read it next, then Jeananne starts off the discussion.

"So we have a poem with nine couplets in the voice of, I guess, Taylor Swift? I'm guessing some of these are snippets of lyrics, but I'm not a Taylor fan, so I don't know for sure. I assume in this poem we have Taylor 'setting the record straight,' which I imagine has to do with her reputation and the gossip around her? But it also feels like this is directed to one specific person. Maybe a past lover? I think the images in this poem are working well. It's quite visceral. I guess I don't know what's going on, though. It feels like the speaker is hiding behind a mask of images that the audience is familiar with, but we don't get to see the *real* Taylor. If she's setting the record straight, shouldn't we see the real her?"

Jeananne sets her pencil down as if she is dropping a mic.

If I wasn't embarrassed before, I am now.

"I agree, Jeananne," Kacey says with a kind smile. "I loved the flow of it on the page, but was also not fully sold on the content. Could that be the point of the poem, though? Like Taylor *thinks* she's being true to herself, but once again it's a performance. That's kind of interesting, actually. Maybe that's something that could be leaned into more."

I'm trying to take notes, but I can't focus. It's like a flashback from high school workshop only worse, since these are highly intelligent peers in a selective grad school program and not seventeen-year-olds with no life experience. All I want to know is what Will is thinking. I want him to chime in. Some sort of penance for high school. I want him to defend me.

But he never does. I hardly hear Paul's feedback, I'm so distracted. I flunked my first nonfiction workshop, and now I've flunked my first poetry one, too. Excellent, fabulous, great.

Everyone passes their poems to me, filled with comments and underlines. Somehow, Will's ends up on top.

Written there, in navy ink: *Taylor can be whomever she wants to be. So who will she choose?*

*   *   *

There's something intimate about reading each other's poetry every week. I learn that Jerry's dad is an alcoholic. Kacey seems to be hung up on body issues stemming from her childhood pursuit of ballet. Hazel is estranged from her grandparents.

And Will? His writing is like being welcomed into a supernova. Bright and suffocating and dazing.

To be sure, I don't always get it. His poems are sometimes obtuse, masked in foggy descriptions and contradicting emotions. I write about pop culture; he writes about death. I write about teen dramas; he writes about his late father. Every poem I get from him, it's clearer and clearer: We are not the same.

But even so, there's something familiar to how he writes. His poetry feels lived-in. Like the individual pieces are part of a bigger universe and he was kind enough to cut us a slice.

Reading his work makes me even more nervous about us both competing for the fellowship. I so badly want to prove that I can write poetry, but he's a natural talent. My only hope is that Erica sees more of herself in me than in him.

By the end of September, we've spent a month and a half as a cohort, and even though we haven't been together long, I feel like I've known everyone for longer. That's maybe why Christine already feels comfortable inviting us to her parents' mountain vacation home for the weekend.

"Drive down Friday morning, stay two nights, leave Sunday afternoon," she says after workshop. After Thursday workshop, all the first-years have congregated at Pete's, a bar a block from Gilman Hall, where townies mingle with grad students and compete to be "Patron of the Week," written on a chalkboard every two months. "I've been wanting to get away from campus to an environment more conducive to writing, and it'd be so fun for all of you to come with me! And we can just chill, too."

"Hell yeah," Houston proclaims. "I'll bring the beer."

"Do you have enough beds for all of us?" I ask. I'm not really a sleep-on-the-floor kind of person. My idea of roughing it was sharing a room with a stranger freshman year of college. I definitely have no tolerance for a camping situation.

"Oh yeah," Christine says. "We've got multiple bedrooms and then also bunk beds and several couches. No second-years, though. Let's just do our year."

I catch Will's eye over sips of beer. His eye contact is always so unselfconscious. If he catches me looking at him, I avert my eyes out of discomfort. But not Will. He just keeps staring.

"So will you go?" he asks when the group has changed topics. He sits in front of me and leans in over the table slightly.

"Of course. You?"

He nods. "Good for a change of scenery. To write."

Classic Will—turning what should be an opportunity to bond as a cohort into his own personal writing retreat.

"Oh, so this is purely a business trip for you?" I arch an eyebrow. "Don't you want to enjoy the company?"

"Eh. Not everyone. Maybe a few."

It's embarrassing how little things he says get me so worked up. It makes me want to hit myself for reading into everything. Bridget would probably tell me to stop. But it feels embedded in my nature. I can never just hear his words. I have to take them apart with my hands.

"Should be fun," I say.

"Let's see."

I insert myself into Morris's discussion of craft coffee, which is going on next to me. But even as I'm pulled in, I feel Will's eyes linger, and I try not to think about what it would take to get him to lean over the table again, his hushed, low words snagging in my brain.

Chapter Seven

THE CAR PULLS UP TO Christine's family's vacation house, a giant mishmash of cobblestones and gray wood. We're spending the weekend in the Blue Ridge Mountains, and you can feel the elevation gain in the air. It's cooler up here, clearer. Outside the garage, the gravel of the driveway is dappled with fallen leaves in almost neon red. I packed horribly for this.

Christine parks the car, and Kacey and I jump out. We are the first to arrive, but less than five minutes later, a second car carrying Morris, Will, Hazel, and Wiebke pulls up. A third car is expected within the hour—to no one's surprise, Houston and Athena got a late start. Everyone was able to make it except Jerry, who was probably too busy contending with his own demons.

"Thank you so much for bringing us up here," Kacey gushes to Christine as she surveys the house, which looks like it's on the verge of teetering off the cliff.

Christine unlocks the front door with a key on her keychain. "We come up here for the holidays and summer, but not so much in the fall. My parents are just happy I'm making use of it."

"Damn, this is nice," I exclaim as we file through the mudroom into a massive kitchen, all granite and hardwood cabinets.

It's the kind of place you can tell isn't in use most of the year. There's a slight musty smell, some cobwebs. A daddy longlegs spider in the ceiling corner. But Christine was right—it is huge and very lovely.

She takes us onto the deck, off the kitchen and living room, outfitted with five gray Adirondack chairs and a glass table. The house overlooks a woods painted in garnet, amber, coral leaves, surrounded by crystal sky.

We continue the house tour, and people start calling dibs on beds. I end up with Hazel in a room downstairs because there's no good way to object. Will and Morris get the room next door. Everyone else scatters to guest rooms and bunk beds.

We head back upstairs to admire the view and help unload groceries.

"I think it's time to start drinking," Christine says, and indeed, the clock is about to strike 4:00 p.m. "The others will come." She goes back into the kitchen for the heavy shopping bags of beer we stopped for on our way in. Based on the way she and Kacey start popping open bottles, I think the goal is to hit the weekend's peak tonight.

It's exactly the kind of reset I need. Back in Boston, I was constantly go-go-go, no time to be outside beyond a once-every-two-month run. Here, now, the goal is to just chill and take advantage of the new environment, which I hope will inspire me to work on new poems.

I walk out to the giant deck and look out into the trees, enjoying the calm.

"Sort of feels like the tenth-grade overnight trip to Tennessee."

Will is next to me, peering off into the abyss of foliage, steadying himself with his large hands on the railing.

"Oh? Was your year nice? I got stuck with some jocks in my group and was forced into a canoe." I grimace at the memory. "I was wearing a white T-shirt and they made it their mission to tip us over."

"Luckily, no jocks in mine. I just remember a really productive impromptu writing workshop I set up with some friends. We spent the free evenings having fruitful discussions of each other's work. As fruitful as it can be at sixteen, I suppose."

"Productive workshops? You? Hard to imagine."

A faint blush appears on his skin, and it's satisfying to know I put it there.

"Leigh." His voice drops to something lower, some decibel that's just for me. "We haven't really talked yet."

"Is there something you'd like to say?"

"We're going to be classmates for two years, and I think this is going to become a little uncomfortable unless we clear the air."

Something drops in my stomach. I hate how my first instinct is to want to make things more comfortable for him, to not be the root of someone else's issues. I hate how my second instinct is to want to pull his stupid corduroy shirt by the collar until he slams into my body.

"The air has never been clearer," I say into the subtle breeze that washes over us. "We're in the mountains, after all."

His jaw tightens almost imperceptibly, but I catch it. I go back into the house before he can respond.

The third and final car has arrived, bringing with it Athena, Houston, and their clinking grocery bags of glass bottles.

"We also brought pasta," Houston announces as they enter the kitchen.

"Put on some music." Christine shoves her laptop to me with

a music app open. Seeing my panicked expression, she adds, "Whatever you like. Just need the vibes."

What *I* like is whatever's currently on the radio—anthemic fluff, girl groups, glittery pop. I have no idea what my cohort wants played. I look around the room for inspiration, racking my mind for obscure indie groups.

Thankfully, Houston walks by, and I tap his shoulder. "Music recs?"

"Oh, word." He nods, pulls the laptop from me, and types. Rap music I don't recognize begins playing.

In the kitchen, Christine puts water on to boil, and the atmosphere swirls pleasantly around me. Two beers in, I can feel my façade fade—the one that's been telling me, all day, *You're not cool enough to be here.* I keep my distance from Will, who talks mostly to Morris and Hazel, and instead try to connect with the others, who seem more amenable. It's no sorority, but maybe it can be something good, too.

*   *   *

Hours later, the fireplace is on, and I'm utterly relaxed. Everyone is loose now, talking over one another, acting like we've known one another for years and not just a month and a half.

Kacey announces that we should play charades, but everyone boos. Houston and Wiebke go into the garage to play beer pong that Christine's set up, Athena helps Morris with his Tinder profile, and the rest of us mingle between the living room and the kitchen and the deck, spilling and sharing drinks.

As the hours pass and everyone gets both sleepier and even less inhibited, we move on to a group game of Fuck, Marry, Kill and start in the most obvious place: the second-years. We're draped over the various couches, chairs, and rugs of the large living room, the slow pulse of music sneaking in between conversations.

"Okay, okay, hear me out," Athena says. "Fuck Penelope. I just feel like she could really ruin me." This earns her nods of agreement. "Marry Willa, who is too pure for this world. And kill August. Obviously." There are snickers among the group.

"Oh my god, really? What's wrong with August?" Kacey slurs.

Athena shrugs. She definitely knows Kacey is hooking up with him. "Nothing, nothing. I'm just too gay for his toxic heterosexuality."

Kacey doesn't look pleased at all. "This is boring because I barely know the second-years. Let's do our year instead."

"Is that not inappropriate?" Wiebke questions. "We're all sitting right here."

"Okay, rule: Everyone be nice and mature about it after," Kacey exclaims, and that solves everything, I guess.

Christine goes first. "Fuck William, marry Kacey, kill Jerry. Sorry, Jerry." I have a feeling that even had Jerry been in the room, he would have simply nodded in bemused acceptance.

Will goes bright red. Hazel raises her glass. "I would also fuck William, kill Jerry, but maybe I'd marry Wiebke."

Wiebke crawls across the floor and plants a kiss on Hazel's cheek. "I accept."

Of course she likes Will. I force my face to stay neutral.

"Leigh, go, go," Christine urges.

Shit.

It's like solving a calculus equation drunk. When playing Fuck, Marry, Kill with people you know, you can't lie *so* much that people think you're intentionally obscuring your answers.

It's a cop-out if I say I want to fuck sweet, quiet, innocent Jerry. So what options do I have? Houston's gay, Morris is Morris. Will is very obviously the hottest straight guy in the cohort, and all the other girls chose him. If I *don't* choose him, it'll feel intentional. It'll feel like there's a reason why I won't say his name.

And there's not.

"Marry Christine." Christine blows me a kiss.

"Um. Kill Houston?"

Houston guffaws. "I would kill me, too, honestly." We all laugh.

"Fuck Will…iam." I add the *iam* late and it comes out more like *Will, yum.* Which definitely makes all of this worse.

I try not to look at him when I say it, but I find myself gauging his reaction anyway. He blinks slightly more than normal, but otherwise he looks like he always does. Jaw tight, cold hazel eyes, closed-off posture. No laugh, no blush. Nothing to suggest he's happy about the answer. In fact, he looks decidedly *unhappy* about it. Even in my tipsy stupor, I know then and there I should've played the whole thing as a joke and said I'd fuck Kacey or something.

"William, go next!" Christine yells. My entire body freezes, and I beg my drunk brain to sober up and listen.

Will shakes his head. "I'd kill all of you."

"Lame!" Kacey cries. "You have to answer."

Will shakes his head again, then puts his hand on his jaw. He's clearly buzzed at the very least, because the tension that normally lives in his shoulders is looser.

"Kill Wiebke."

Wiebke bellows with laughter. "He hated my musical taste in the car," she says. "William is not into Eurovision."

"Marry…Christine, because she has such a nice house, and I'd love to stay here more often."

Christine nods genuinely. "*Some* of you are welcome anytime." She shoots a mock look of disdain at Houston, who spilled beer on the coffee table earlier.

I realize I'm holding my breath as we await Will's last answer.

"Fuck…Morris. The suspenders really do it for me."

Morris wraps his arm around Will's shoulder and whispers something in his ear with a grin, causing Will to roll his eyes and smirk. "I could definitely handle you," he says darkly. God help me.

This is a nightmare of my own creation. Will played it off as a joke and I didn't and now he probably thinks I actually *do* want to fuck him. I make it my goal for the rest of the trip and potentially year to not make eye contact with this man whatsoever.

Eventually the night dies down as the alcoholic buzz of the last six hours starts to wane. Everyone disappears into their bedrooms and scurries around the various bathrooms, fighting for space to wash faces or brush teeth.

Because I'm sleeping in the kids' room, I'm sharing a large bathroom with the guest room next door—namely, Will and Morris. Hazel is already passed out, courtesy of the final tequila shots we all took, starfished in her twin bed by the window.

I play on my phone until I hear the boys' door close outside our own. After changing into some low-slung sleep shorts and a ratty Tufts orientation T-shirt (since I left the Delta Gamma swag at home), I grab my makeup bag and go upstairs to use the bathroom. I want to take off my makeup in peace and not worry about someone down here, especially the boys, needing to use the bathroom.

The house at this hour is spookily quiet and dark. There's a dim light on in the crack of the master bedroom where Kacey and Christine are, and I wonder what they're talking about, what gossip I'm missing out on. I tiptoe into the hallway, finding the small bathroom off the kitchen, and flick on the light.

I cringe at my reflection. My bangs are plastered to my slick forehead, and my mascara has started to slough onto my cheekbones. I dip my face into the sink and wet my bangs, then proceed with my skin-care routine. The steps are soothing; I like that there's a formula. Cleanser, serums, moisturizer, oils.

When I'm satisfied, I zip up my makeup bag and grab my small towel. I need water. While I've mostly sobered up, I want to ensure I'm at least semi-able to go on the group hike tomorrow.

In the dark kitchen, I flip open cupboards. It's a real hodgepodge of glasses and plastic cups, the markings of a vacation home rarely in use. It must be nice to have a family that still wants to vacation together.

"Leigh?"

I can feel a body next to me. The creak of a floorboard.

I scream for approximately two seconds. I can't go longer because a warm hand is pressed firm against my mouth and another hand grips my shoulder.

"It's me—it's William—it's Will."

I jump backward and the hand releases me. "Holy fuck," I scream-whisper. "I thought you were a kidnapper."

"You're twenty-seven. Wouldn't I just be an abductor?"

In the ghost of moonlight from the window, I see his outline. He's a few feet away from me now, and he grabs the water glass I was going for from the cupboard, fills it up at the sink, and hands it to me.

"Why are you up here?" I say, my pulse slowing by the second.

"I'm not a great sleeper." He flicks the switch next to the cupboard, and a harsh overhead light comes on. He's wearing sweatpants and a very baggy T-shirt with a tattered collar that makes his shoulders look absolutely enormous. I pry my eyes off his collarbone and back to his face.

"Pity. Have you considered medicating?"

"Oh, I'm medicated. Just not for this."

I finish my glass of water and set it down on the counter. There's a sensation that the conversation is over, but I find myself wanting to push it forward.

"Not insomnia, got it. So what *are* you picking up at Walgreens?" Jesus, what's wrong with me?

"Wow, personal. I don't usually tell my abductees my prescription list like this. Prefer to take them to the bunker first."

"You know, you actually do have serial killer eyes." I stare at him, past the circular glasses that balance so perfectly on the bridge of his nose, not a millimeter askew.

"You'd be surprised how often I get that."

"Not surprised at all. I've always thought your eyes were very intense."

You'd think I'd just said *Your eyes are very sexy and I want to sleep with you* by his stupid smirk. He grabs his own glass from the cupboard and fills it.

"Are you tired?"

I raise my eyebrows. "Well, I was until you scared the shit out of me."

He eyes me once over and I become acutely aware that I'm not wearing a bra, that my shorts are relatively short, and that my legs are prickly with a day's worth of stubble.

"Want to go out on the deck?"

I stare at the deck, only illuminated by a few porch lights installed near the gutters.

"Don't you think it's cold?"

"Wrap a blanket around yourself then."

He walks to the well-loved leather armchair in the reading nook of the kitchen and grabs the cable-knit throw blanket from it. He hands it to me. And then we go outside.

The crispness of the air hits me immediately. It has that signature fall smell, earthy damp leaf air with a subtle burnt note. I wrap the blanket around my shoulders and follow Will across the expansive deck. It's peaceful. I listen for the scamper of an animal over leaves, the gentle swell of wind through the trees.

We don't speak for a minute, each soaking it up, but I feel like I'm waiting for something. There's a thickness in the air between us, especially for me, now that he and everyone else in the cohort thinks I want to fuck him. Standing here, quiet and waiting, takes me back to that summer afternoon at Middlebury—*that* silence was even harder to bear.

Will stands about two feet away, his hands on the railing overlooking the blackness, his posture tense, as if he's waiting to see who will speak first.

"I don't want things to be super weird," I say. "Between us."

"Right."

There's something detached and clipped about his tone, like he's reciting lines from a script. His discomfort is obvious, but it's clear that this needs to be said, lest it float over us for the next year. And now that he knows I would sleep with him and I know he's got a prescription list, well. We might as well lay all our cards on the table.

"You know, six years ago I was really drunk at your apartment, and I hardly remember what I said or what you said," I continue.

"You don't." It's a statement, not a question.

"I came here to focus on writing. That's it. I want this to be my career and I want this fellowship. We don't need to get bogged down by the past. Not that anything really happened in the past... but you know what I mean."

He studies my face. Really takes his time with it, and as the subject of his full focus, I feel almost immobile. I watch him catalog my wet-dog bangs and my eyebrows and my eyes, my moisturizer-dewy cheeks, my lips. He looks at me like I've told him I have a terminal illness. Some soft gaze. Some mourning.

High school Leigh, or even college Leigh, would have spent weeks dissecting every crinkle of his expression. The new me chooses to put it aside because I know no good can come of it. Some call it avoidant. I call it *progress*.

"You're right." He looks away into the darkness. "I was drunk, too. Nothing happened."

"Great." I pull the blanket around me more tightly. There's silence again and I feel the cold wrap around my legs. "I guess we should go back in."

Will nods, walks to the door, and holds it open for me. I drape the blanket back over the armchair.

"Okay, well. Good night," I say.

"We both have to go downstairs to our rooms." His mouth tips up in amusement. My cheeks heat.

"Right." I laugh.

We march in silence through the kitchen, through the living room, and down the stairs until we're standing in front of the doors of our respective rooms, as if we're going home after a long night out. He puts his hand on the knob and, before opening it, turns to me.

"Zoloft, by the way."

I'm at a total loss for what he's talking about.

"What?"

"That's what I'm picking up at CVS, at least. Not a Walgreens family."

"Ah," I say, because what else is there to say. He looks down at his feet for a second and then back up at me.

"But it's fine. I'm fine."

My chest feels heavy suddenly—the incoming hangover, maybe. I lean against the back of my door; he leans against the back of his, as if we both need the support.

"It would be okay, though. If you weren't fine," I murmur.

There's a small night-light plugged into an outlet at the foot of the stairs, so I can only see the faint outline of his features, the ones I've memorized and then tried so hard to forget. But now, everything about him seems softer, more vulnerable.

He makes a low exhale, nods slowly, and tips his head toward my door. "Sleep well."

"You too." I turn to open the bedroom door, set one foot into the darkness before I look back over my shoulder out of reflex.

And when my stomach unexpectedly twists to find his eyes still on me, I realize I see him more fully than I have in years. And this time, he'd wanted me to.

Chapter Eight

Despite Hazel's best efforts to keep me up with her teeth grinding, I sleep better than I have in months. When I wake up, she's in bed reading Pablo Neruda and chugging her Nalgene full of water. I scroll through my phone a bit on my side and then turn over so she knows I'm awake.

"Morning," I say.

She looks up immediately. "Sleep well?" She puts her book to the side, obviously a morning person very interested in chatting.

I make an *mhmmm* sound as I stretch my legs and arms long. "Not sure I'm ready for the hike today."

Hazel rolls her shoulders back a few times and circles her neck around. "Oh, it'll be great. I hike a ton in Oregon. The best trails are in the Pacific Northwest, you know."

"Sounds like it."

This is what I've been fearing—a cohort full of Nature People who love to sit on the forest floor and wax poetic about death.

"What are you going to wear?" I sit up and pull my hair into a bun.

"Oh, I brought a merino wool tee and my hiking pants. Wool is much better than cotton, you know. Better to sweat in. And the pants are what I wear in Oregon. I see girls sometimes who hike in yoga leggings and they're just not at all right for this activity."

"Ah nice, I'll do something similar then."

I packed maybe three different outfits for this weekend but the best I can do is a pair of leggings (fuck me) and a college sweatshirt with white leather sneakers in lieu of hiking boots. Didn't need those in Boston and certainly didn't want to be the person to buy a new outfit for an MFA sleepover.

"Those Lululemon?" Hazel asks as I pull on my plain black pair.

"Yeah."

"I hope they don't snag on a branch and tear. I hear they're really fragile."

I change and put on a pair of jeans instead, the uncomfortable kind without stretch.

We go upstairs to the kitchen, where maybe half of everyone is awake and assembling breakfast. Christine's propped the door to the deck open, and the air has that early-fall briskness, the smell of maple syrup filling the kitchen as Houston flips pancakes.

"Morning, everyone," Hazel says as we join the group at the granite island. Despite our drinking last night, no one looks too hungover, save for maybe Morris, who blames it on his elderly age of thirty-four.

Will isn't upstairs yet, and I wonder if he's hungover, if he regrets anything he said last night. I mull the conversation with a coffee until he emerges from the stairs. He's wearing jeans, L.L.Bean boots, and a baggy, faded crew-neck sweatshirt that says ROWAN SCHOOL on it. It takes me immediately back to high school, peering at him out of the corner of my eye as he hunched over a notebook in the library. Wondering, but always doubting, if he could ever be writing about me.

"Go Gators," I mutter when he moves next to me, grabbing his own coffee mug.

"Sometimes I like to pretend I'm still there. Feels like I peaked then, unfortunately."

"I sure hope that wasn't your peak."

He does something unexpected: He laughs, and the sound of it, breathy and warm, fills me up even before we've eaten.

Houston serves us pancakes and we all chat and eat on the deck, scattered across the Adirondacks and kitchen chairs we've pulled outside, the sun slowly warming us up.

"This hike is chill, right?" I ask Christine. "I'll be fine without, like, serious hiking boots?"

"Oh yeah, I wouldn't say the trail is that strenuous or even that muddy. It's like a two-hour thing. You won't even need to pee outside."

"I love peeing outside," Houston chimes in.

I grimace next to him. "I don't think I could physically make myself even if I needed to."

"But let's just enjoy a casual walk and then, I don't know, we can do whatever. Read, write, talk. Go on Morris's Tinder," Christine says.

"A productive workshop, maybe!" I chirp, looking at Will, who pulls out a chair next to me with his pancakes.

"I couldn't even fathom a more perfect afternoon," he says, just to me, smooth and buttery in my ear.

*   *   *

There are nine of us walking on a zigzagging trail full of families and other walkers, and despite the chaos, the one thing that's certain is that Will always ends up next to me.

I've always been *aware* of his body, where he is, where he's looking. One time in high school, I remember he was behind me in morning assembly. He'd been sitting first in the row, and I could have filed in beside him, but I didn't want to sit next to him. I figured it was better to act like I didn't know he existed. Like his voice, his body, his entire demeanor didn't affect me at all. So I sat one row away, dragging Gen next to me. Will got up during the assembly to announce that the student literary journal was now open for submissions, and I remember vividly how he made a split second's worth of eye contact while making the announcement, how he leaned forward slightly before he sat down behind me. And then I remember thinking how stupid I was for thinking anything of it at all.

Walking next to him now on the leaf-strewn dirt trail, it's strange how even ten years later I can feel myself falling into the same pattern. Always watching him, always being conscious of where he is, where he's looking.

You can take the girl out of high school, but you can't take the fractured remnants of an obsessive crush out of the girl.

I think back to what I've discussed with Bridget in therapy. How I need to consciously stop caring so much what other people think—especially when it comes to Will, who is the exact type of person I can already feel myself wanting to tailor my behavior to.

So when he speeds up, I don't. When he slows down, I find myself going a bit faster, all in a conscious effort to do what *I* want to do, and not what I think *he* wants me to do, which was surely the point of Bridget's last monologue to me.

"Not a big outdoors person?" he asks as I tiptoe around a wet pit of leaves that threatens to stain my white shoes.

"Tried it once. Not for me."

He nods solemnly. "I don't know if I'm the biggest fan, either."

"Really? You seem like the type who knows exactly which mushrooms not to eat."

He laughs, and the sound ripples through my body.

"Avoid the red ones with white spots, that's all I know."

I take a swig of water from my bottle. "I like the sun and the fresh air. I'm just more accustomed to city sidewalks at this point."

We walk in silence for a moment, and as the group starts separating, I find myself wanting to hang back with Will instead of talking to the others.

"How was Boston?"

I shrug. "Fine. Expensive. Stressful, but that was my job's fault, not the city's."

"The ad agency, right?"

I nod. "It started out cool. It was kind of a fancy agency, and we had big-name clients and everyone was really smart and talented. I liked being in that group. But then it just became too much."

"In what way?"

It's still embarrassing how things ended at Coleman + Derry. I was grateful to have the "excuse" of the MFA to quit, but everyone who worked with me surely knew what was happening under the surface. Leigh Simon couldn't take the heat, so she got out of the kitchen. It's terrifying to think I might have to go back to that world after graduation.

"After writing things you don't believe in or care about and sucking up to clients who think *you* suck, you just sort of lose what you even liked in the first place. You know, when I started it was kind of fun. You'd get a brief from a client: *Okay we need to promote X product for Y audience segment, and you have to create some catchy tagline in eighty-seven characters or less for this digital ad.* It was like a puzzle, and I liked being given parameters and rules. I knew exactly what someone wanted from me, and I could mold my words to fit that."

I watch the ground as I talk, avoiding muddy patches. I notice how the feet next to me step completely in sync with my own—left, right, left, right. The old me would have made something of that.

When I look up from our feet, Will's full attention is on me. Even though I'm warm from the sun, I shiver.

"At some point, you drown in it, all the corporate bullshit language. The agency would encourage us to think big, be creative, whatever, and the client would just stamp it out immediately. I started to dread putting words on a page."

I skip the parts about my weekly bathroom crying sessions or my inability to fall asleep on Sunday nights out of anxiety.

"So that's why you're here," Will says, and I raise my eyebrow. "To rediscover what you like about writing."

"Maybe." We walk in silence for a few beats. "Why are you here? One master's degree wasn't enough?"

"Well, it's felt like my whole academic career has been leading up to this point. So why not?"

"The English-major-to-MFA pipeline can be quite the conveyer belt."

He runs his hand along the bark of a tree, as if he's looking for something stable to touch. "I'm not on a conveyer belt. I've always wanted an MFA."

"Of course."

The others are walking faster now, and I feel like I should rejoin the group. Getting stuck in these one-on-one conversations with Will seems dangerous. Like I'm teetering on the edge of a cliff and only the faintest gust of wind could topple me over. Back into the old habits that got me so preoccupied with what other people think to begin with.

We approach a bridge over a rushing creek, relatively high off the ground and flimsier than a city girl who's petrified of heights would want a wooden bridge to be. It's held together by nothing more than wood, rope, and faith, swinging slightly as people cross it. I watch Christine and Wiebke and Hazel walk over it like it's nothing to them. The last thing I want is to embarrass myself and seem like even more of a dumb sorority girl than half the class probably already thinks I am.

Almost everyone is across the bridge, which is at least eighty feet long, but Will and I straggle behind. I feel my body reject the bridge just looking at it. I pause a foot away, my legs unable to go farther.

"Let's go a different way," he says.

"What's wrong with this way?" My teeth start to chatter.

"You're clearly afraid of heights."

"No I'm not."

Will gives me a horrific, glorious smirk.

"It's too embarrassing. I'm an adult. I should be able to walk over a stupid bridge," I whisper.

Christine is now on the other side, looking back at us, waving, ushering us to come.

"Who cares? Why torture yourself?"

"Because everyone already thinks I'm some prissy...girl. It's just a bridge. It's nothing."

"Then why aren't we walking over it?"

Indeed, we're standing right in front of the first wooden slab. I can't make my foot move. Instead I see the rushing water below and imagine myself drowning.

"I...I..."

"We'll catch up with you!" Will's low voice bellows. "I dropped my wallet!"

Christine gives a thumbs-up on the other side, and the rest of the group continues on.

"What are you doing?" I hiss, suddenly aware that I am (A) alone with the very person I shouldn't be alone with, and (B) still no closer to the other side of the bridge.

"Let's just go another way. People will think you're helping me now."

"How do you even know there is another way? We're going to get lost and then we'll have to come back this way and cross the bridge anyway and then we'll be late to join the group and everyone will be pissed at me and think we held them up from going home."

"People don't think like that," Will says, as if it's a universal fact. "Come on. I think I saw another direction we could go if we backtrack a little. I'm sure it all ends up at the same spot."

I look back at the group, now just shards of color between the trees. And then I look at Will and his ridiculously broad shoulders, his caramel hair glowing in the late-morning sun.

"Fine," I sigh. "Let's backtrack."

* * *

It's obvious that neither Will nor I has any real insight into trails or hiking. I'm not sure why I thought he knew his mushrooms—he was seconds away from touching poison ivy until I intervened. He walks with a perpetual frown plastered to his face, but when we get to forks in the trail, he chooses which way to go confidently, despite having no idea where we are.

At this point, I'm pretty sure we're lost and going in circles. Perhaps Will's years in Vermont gave him access to the outdoorsy aesthetic via his Bean boots, but he's still ultimately a guy in a smartwatch and a prep school sweatshirt. Admittedly, it's a step up from my woefully unprepared ensemble of crisp white sneakers and extremely uncomfortable jeans.

I'm resentful that I should probably be nice to him now, given that he's created this lie on my behalf, god only knows why. Still, talking is easier than I expected. In high school, had I found more reasons to have a conversation with him, I would've been stilted and worried about not liking the right books, not saying the right things. But given everything—which is nothing, I remind myself daily—that has happened between us, maybe I'm less guarded than I'd be otherwise.

"I'm sorry about your dad." My voice is low even though the trail is hardly busy. "I heard you and Hazel talking after class...I didn't know."

"I wouldn't have expected you to have known."

Will's voice is tight. He looks straight ahead as if suddenly determined to find the rest of the group.

"What was he like? I guess I only met him…that one time." The words get stuck in my mouth.

Will raises his eyebrows, and I wonder how much he thinks about that moment—his parents walking in on us at Middlebury. Probably not that often.

"Our relationship was…" Will pauses. "Complicated."

"Complicated?"

He flinches. "Well, you read the birth story, I guess. But it wasn't just that he taught English. He was also a writer. A creative writing professor. He wrote short stories. Not like super big, but he'd been in *The New Yorker* a few times over the years. Had a few collections published."

"Oh wow, so family business."

Will chuckles. "Hardly. I don't know if my dad even thought I was a good writer. He wasn't very forthcoming with the compliments." There's an edge to his voice. "He was more interested in having me read his shit and explaining to me exactly how 'the mechanics' functioned. And then telling me how my own writing process was wrong, how I should outline instead of just proceeding with *feeling.*"

"Sounds like he was jealous of you."

Will lets out the heartiest laugh I've ever heard from him, and it sends a rush of blood to my chest. "No. I'm quite sure he wasn't."

"You knew him best. But I know overcompensation when I see it."

We reach another fork in the trail and, not knowing what to do, debate if it's best to turn around completely in order to go back to the cars. There may be another way there, a way over the bridge, but we can't figure it out. And my biggest concern is wasting everyone's time waiting for us.

"I don't want to lead you even more astray," Will says.

It occurs to me that I don't want to join the others just yet.

"Let's risk it. Let's try this one." I point to the left trail.

We walk into a large muddy section over which someone has resourcefully laid a wooden log so passersby can teeter across instead of sinking into the mud. Will traverses it, no problem. I'm worried about slipping off and embarrassing myself, though, so I approach hesitantly.

"I wouldn't really consider this a height, Leigh."

I send him a dirty look. "I'm not *afraid*. I just want to be careful so I don't ruin my shoes."

He smiles. "Come on before a group comes behind you. Then you'll be even more stressed."

He's right. He stands at the very end of the log, about ten feet from me, and I take one step at a time, holding my arms out for balance. Near the end of the log, I make the mistake of looking up at Will instead of watching my feet, and I lose my balance.

"Shit—"

In the split second before I fall into the deep mud, Will's arms are on either side of my waist, steadying me. I don't remember doing it, but my arms are on his shoulders. I'm still on top of the log and I'm a few inches taller than him from up here. He's looking up at me and his eyes are wide, as if I've caught him doing something he shouldn't.

He doesn't take his hands off me until I'm back on the ground, now looking up at him.

"Sorry," I mutter, and move my hands off his shoulders.

His brow furrows. "What do you have to be sorry about?"

I shrug but don't respond.

We continue down the path silently, meandering in and out of other hiking groups. When other walkers go by, I step behind him in a single-file line. And then I'm irritated once more that I'm the one who steps behind him, as if he's leading. Why doesn't he step behind *me*?

Bridget is right. I constantly accommodate, but then I secretly resent other people for not being as accommodating.

It turns out the left turn worked. In another fifteen minutes, we find ourselves on the other side of the original parking lot where we parked the cars. And our classmates only had to wait ten extra minutes for us to catch up.

Kacey pins me with a look when we return to the group standing in front of Christine's car. I feel her grin, but I avert my eyes.

We pile back into the cars—me with Christine, Kacey, Houston, and Wiebke. Will goes with Hazel, Athena, and Morris. In our car, everyone starts discussing dinner, Wiebke insisting she take charge in the kitchen because Americans don't even know where to begin when it comes to seasoning, which Houston takes as an affront to last night's pasta.

I'm hardly listening. Instead, I feel the ghost of Will's hands on me for the rest of the ride.

*   *   *

I was dead wrong about peaking on Friday and taking it easy on Saturday. Tonight is clearly the night we'll be peaking, which is to say, I anticipate a painful Sunday morning.

Houston tends to be the ringleader when it comes to drinking. He puts us on a tight shots schedule, but also insists we follow each one up with water, the mark of a true professional. Wiebke, maybe because she is European and has been drinking since she was twelve, can easily keep up with him but is miraculously never drunk. Morris had a brief stint as a bartender in New York, so we beg him to make us drinks, which he is happy to accommodate as long as we indulge his long-winded stories, like the time he fucked up a martini for Conan O'Brien, who, he offers with the smile of a conspirator, is perhaps a bit meaner than he looks.

Prior to the MFA program, I was only a casual drinker, but since everyone else is drinking, I obviously want to participate. So I do. I drink Houston's shots and Morris's old-fashioneds and whatever cheap beer Kacey pushes into my chest.

The alcohol probably doesn't help my state of mind when I see Hazel and Will by the fireplace, sitting on a luxurious faux-fur rug, her knees skimming his.

I pull Kacey aside in the kitchen after she hands me my second beer. "Do you think Hazel likes Will?"

"Why do you keep calling him *Will?*" she whispers with a grin.

"Because that's who he is. Do you think Hazel likes him?"

Kacey takes a step around the kitchen wall to look at them on the fur rug. "Probably. I could see that happening."

"I guess they're the most pretentious people in the cohort," I muse.

Hazel throws her head back in laughter at something Will said. They're probably talking about Poet Twitter drama or something else stupid and niche and insignificant to 99.9 percent of the population.

"I think he's definitely her type," Kacey says. "But you know William from before. Do you think she's *his* type?"

It's a great question. What is Will's type? He never brought anyone to high school dances until his senior prom, when he brought Maddie Katz. She was a National Merit Scholar and the co-editor of *Expressions* and had extremely long eyelashes. She ended up going to Yale. Then, he dated someone named Katherine in college. I don't know much about her, but there's something pretentious about a Katherine who doesn't go by Kate or Katie or Kat, isn't there?

I don't answer fast enough, so Kacey continues: "Or what about you? Is he *your* type?"

I choke on my beer. "Absolutely not. No, no, I mean, we—no. I don't like him like *that*. And please, you've seen him, there's no way. He would never—with someone like *me*—right?"

She gives me a sly look as if I'm lying. I shake my head again in aggressive confirmation.

Her eyes flit back to Hazel and Will. "I can tell Hazel judges me for hooking up with August. Can you imagine how hypocritical she would be if she went and hooked up with someone in the same genre *and year*?"

"So hypocritical," I slur. "Such a bad idea."

"Right. Gonna keep my eye on this. Let me know if you see any further developments."

I salute her with a "Yes, ma'am." She's right. There's no worse idea than starting something with someone in the same year and genre. We're all up in each other's emotional and artistic business every single day. Adding sex and, even worse, real feelings to that mix would be a disaster. What a grave mistake Hazel would be making if she got involved with Will. I continue nodding to myself self-righteously about this as I go back into the living room and join the people on the couch.

"Conan was a good tipper, I'll give him that, but I just don't *know*," Morris says over the din of chatter and indie music in the background. "I see an ego there, you know what I mean?"

"Let's play a game!" Christine shouts before Morris can continue his Conan Slander Tour.

"Spin the Bottle!" Houston chirps. There are groans.

"You're twenty-seven," Christine says. "Aren't we all way too old for that? Half of us have partners anyway."

"'Twas a joke, Chris, chill. Was just thinking that *some* may be into it." He flips his gaze to Will and Hazel, who are still on the rug; Hazel is showing Will something on her phone. I don't think they heard Houston. But is everyone catching on that Will and Hazel could become a thing?

Athena says, "My favorite party game is when you name a famous person you think you could reasonably attract. Like, not who *you* find hot, but who do you think you could go up to at a bar and like hit that? It's actually very revealing. Says a lot about you, what you're attracted to, what league you think you're in, et cetera. For example, I know it may be vain, but I think Megan Rapinoe would be utterly fascinated by me."

Christine starts us off. "This is niche, but I seriously think I could get the pop-music critic from the *New York Times*. I just have a weird feeling I'm what he's looking for."

"He's my cousin's best friend!" Morris chimes in. "I'm going to text him now to tell him!"

"Oh, I love this," Kacey says. "I think I could get the hot Texas Senate candidate. Does that count?"

She shakes Hazel's shoulder and explains the game to her and Will.

"What about you, Leigh?" Christine asks.

I mull it over. "Okay, not a celebrity, but my English teacher from tenth grade. I'd swear to anyone there was a vibe."

Will's gaze jolts over to me. "Mr. Carson?"

A laugh breaks out from my mouth. "Yes."

"Oh my god, juicy!" Kacey says. "Tell me about this Mr. Carson, you guys."

I look at Will first, and he holds his palm out to me as if to say, *Go ahead*.

"I don't know. Your standard tall, dark, and handsome. Bookish. Cheeky. He just found a lot of excuses to talk to me, more than other students. He was professional always, but I don't know, sometimes you can just tell. He was quite young, in my defense. He couldn't have been that many years out of college."

"Tell us, William, could Leigh pick him up in a bar?" Athena asks.

"I'm sure. Leigh could probably pick up anyone in a bar."

I guffaw so loudly I surprise myself. Will looks over to me, his eyes glassy from drinking. We make a moment of eye contact so uninhibited on both sides I feel a chill in the center of my body that extends to my fingertips.

The night winds down after that. Some people pass out on the couch; the more cognizant ones help tidy the kitchen. I lie on the faux-fur rug with my eyes closed, the room slowly spinning. Then I feel a gentle tap on my ankle and open my eyes to see Will standing above me.

"Time for bed."

I'm vaguely aware of lights flickering off around me and people going to their rooms.

"Mhmm."

He leans down to hoist up my shoulders and suddenly I'm standing, pressed into his neck. How easy it would be for him to turn his face to the right, if I nudged to the left, until there was nothing between our lips but hot breath.

"So was that true?" I slur as he places a hand on my lower back, guiding me down the stairs to the bedrooms. It feels like a branding iron the way my T-shirt rides up and one or two of his fingers touch the skin above the waistband of my jeans. Even drunk, I clock every sliver of skin-to-skin contact.

"What?" His voice rasps, as if the muscles in his body are strained, pulled taut.

"You think I could pick up anyone in a bar?" When he moves his hand off my back at the base of the stairs, I grab his hand before I can convince myself not to.

He's quiet for a second. His thumb trails a path across my knuckles, and a low hum buzzes under my skin. Then he steps away from me, dropping my hand, and opens the door to his and Morris's room.

"Good night, Leigh."

Chapter Nine

WHEN I GET MY NEXT poem back, Will's annotations are different. They're invites to conversation. He still writes his in-depth summary of feedback, still asks questions where my words don't make sense for him, but now he provides commentary on the rest of the workshop or unrelated musings. Sometimes his annotations spill over to the blank side of the paper.

August doesn't get metaphor, he scribbles in his small, precise cursive on the opposite side of the page, so as not to interfere with my poem. *Should we inform him that the apple in Kacey's poem is not* actually *an apple? In fact, is an apple* ever *just an apple?*

Another week, he writes: *Best verb of the day.* The verb I used was *tussle*.

And another: In a poem where I write in the persona of a pop-music star having sex to her own music, he underlines the couplet "how his palm unfurls / like spilled ink on my hip bone." I have no idea how to interpret the underline, but I spend way too long thinking about it.

I absolutely do not think about Will's large hands. How they could pull and spread and push and take.

I've started to do it back, only because I told Bridget and Gen that I'd try very hard to make chill, non-competitive friends in grad school. And even though Will and I are competing against each other for the fellowship, I can't let it get in the way of our friendship. Is it a friendship? Something like that at least. It's better than whatever weird relationship we had a month ago.

His poems have become a safe space for me to be more pointed in my feedback. The first few weeks of workshop, I'd been hesitant to comment on something unless I was positive it was worth mentioning. But last week, Paul pushed me to comment on Will's poem structure. Caught off guard with no time to formulate the perfect response, I had to improvise—"It's a bit choppy for me. I'd suggest longer lines in this case"—and ended up contradicting what everyone else in the class had said.

That day, Will commented on the bottom of the poem he handed back to me: *You were right about my poem. Longer lines will give it the meandering cadence I was looking for.*

It took everything in me not to look up at him when I got my poem back, but my neck flushed, like I'd seen something in him, hidden, that no one else had.

The comments go beyond just poetry workshop. He'll write on my nonfiction pieces, too. We'll have our own conversations that span weeks at a time, lazy and slow in their own way.

I hope I never meet Houston's sister, he writes on my piece, about a nonfiction essay Houston presented that day as well. *I bet she actually did blackmail that professor about the drugs.*

The next week, I respond: *Houston's sister also wishes to never meet you. And hey, maybe one day I'll tell you the story of how my college friend group convinced a couple frat guys to buy cocaine from us for an excellent price. It was powdered sugar but they were none the wiser. It funded our brunch habit for at least two months.*

He signs off his next comment with: *I definitely need the full story. The suspense is killing me. Not sure I can wait until next week's workshop for your response.*

And then he gives me his number. The 216 Cleveland area code is the same as mine, a revelation that is so obvious and yet reminds me he's not someone I just met. Even though it's much easier to think of us starting with a blank slate.

I create a new contact in my phone. Will Langford, I type, adding his number. I'm not sure if I should use it. But there is a sort of thrill in being given something that is his.

*   *   *

I don't use the number until a week later, and only when I have no choice.

It's a long weekend for the university. Kacey's gone home to Austin, Christine's in Chapel Hill, and I'm still here. My usual grocery store drivers are out of town, and I don't realize the problem until I'm one dirty bowl into making pumpkin bread and I have zero pumpkin to use. The campus shop definitely doesn't sell cans of pumpkin, and I'm not going to Uber all the way to the closest Harris Teeter for a single can that costs two bucks.

After living in Boston, I was unaware that I needed a car to live in North Carolina. I assumed when my dad dropped me off that it'd be walkable, but I was clearly mistaken.

Do you need to go grocery shopping today? I text.

I receive a response one minute later. Leigh?

Yes. Sorry should've said that.

I usually do my grocery shopping on
Sundays. Why?

> I'm out of pumpkin and don't have a car. Thought
> maybe if you were going to go today . . . but no
> problem! I'll pivot to zucchini bread. Hope you're
> having a good weekend! :)

I delete the smiley and press SEND.
He responds thirty seconds later.

What's your address? I can be there in 20.

Nineteen minutes later, he texts again: I'm outside.

Nineteen minutes is hardly enough time to look presentable, but I'm used to tight deadlines. I throw on a bra, jeans, a purple sweater, and sneakers and manage to do a face of no-makeup-makeup because I need to look good for the cute cashiers at Whole Foods, that's all.

I leave the apartment and sure enough Will is parked outside with his OHIO: BIRTHPLACE OF AVIATION license plate, which is immediately recognizable in a sea of needlessly competitive NORTH CAROLINA: FIRST IN FLIGHT plates.

"I'm so sorry, you really didn't have to do this. I could've waited until your usual Sunday grocery day," I say when I open the passenger-side door.

He shakes his head. "You say sorry way too much."

"Yeah, sorry, should work on that."

He raises his eyebrows. I give him a quick once-over. He's wearing black high-top Converses, muted green chinos, and a cream sweater. His Cleveland Museum of Art tote bag is by my feet. His car is a manual, which is something that should not be as hot as it is.

"So, um." Now I'm very aware that my arm is a foot away from Will's and the entire car smells like coffee and his cologne and I'm starting to heavily regret putting myself in this position. "How's your Saturday been so far?"

He shrugs and pulls out of the parking spot, putting his hand behind my seat back as he turns to look out. I avert my eyes and try to concentrate on the weave of my denim and not how close his hand is to my neck.

"It's only two. Can't say much has happened yet. But things are looking up."

I nod. "Nice. Cool. Yeah."

He rolls up the sleeves of his sweater, exposing the tops of his forearms with thick veins and a smattering of light brown hair, and I'm beginning to truly understand the meaning of *You played yourself.*

"What else do you need besides pumpkin?" He maneuvers us onto the main thoroughfare of the campus, in the direction of town.

"I'm running low on eggs and laundry detergent, too, but I guess only the pumpkin is urgent. There's a bowl of flour and baking powder and salt sitting in my apartment as we speak."

"What's your schedule like for the rest of the day?"

I can't even imagine why he's asking—or maybe the problem is that I can, and playing out what the rest of the day *could* be feels like maple syrup dripping down my spine.

"No plans." I hate myself, and I am so, so weak.

"Good." The word bursts into confetti somewhere deep in my chest.

*   *   *

If you can believe it, Will doesn't take me to Whole Foods, which is a real waste of this Effortless Cool Girl Grocery Outfit, but where we end up is arguably better: Willow Organic Farms, home to North Carolina's largest pumpkin patch and corn maze, a fact proudly proclaimed by the sign at the entrance.

"They have pumpkin and eggs, but I'm guessing not laundry detergent," he says, after we're out of the car and standing in front of the farm complex.

"Oh, but laundry detergent can wait." I glance around, not knowing where to look first. The buildings are littered with pumpkins of all shapes and sizes. "This reminds me of Ohio."

"I thought you might enjoy it."

The place is swarming with people—particularly children. I hear campy Halloween music and laughter and shouts like, "You *cannot* eat a decorative gourd, Billy, what did I tell you."

There's a country store where the farm sells things like milk, apples from their orchard, eggs, and cider donuts, and an outdoor part with massive rows of pumpkins, squash, and gourds, all ready to be cooked or painted or shucked for jack-o'-lanterns. A giant corn maze unfurls next to the parking lot, where cornstalks over six feet tall bleed into the orange landscape of trees and slightly overcast sky. The entire place smells like apple cider and cinnamon.

"Maybe this is lame, but would you want to do the corn maze?" I ask, my face reddening slightly.

He grins. "No self-respecting Midwesterner would turn down a corn maze."

And I agree. I don't make the rules.

We enter the maze, finding our own way among the parents, children, and two teenagers who look like they're on an awkward first date.

"Do you miss Ohio?" I run my fingers along the cornstalks, feeling like a kid on a field trip.

"Sometimes. But in many ways it hasn't felt like home in a long time. Even so close in Pittsburgh, I didn't visit much. Do you still go there often?"

"Couple times a year. Thanksgiving, a long weekend here and there."

I think back to going home to see my parents. How I might never do that again, not in the same way I always have, in my childhood home. Back in college, I'd look forward to flying home, to a weeklong reprieve from navigating the social dynamics of sorority girls and English majors. But now "home" is the place where I have to be *on*, constantly managing the emotions of two people who are no longer sure they like each other enough to hang out with me anymore.

I quickly change topics.

"How'd you end up at Perrin, anyway? You seem more like the New York MFA type. Like, I see you in the NYC literati crowd, drinking cocktails at *Paris Review* parties with agents and publishers and *Vanity Fair* interns."

Will laughs. "I applied to a handful. Iowa, Michener, Michigan, BU. Perrin's the only one I got into. Got waitlisted at Iowa. Straight rejections everywhere else."

"Really?" I raise my eyebrows. "You know, that humanizes

you, actually. I would've assumed you'd have your pick." *Why did I just say that?*

Will flinches, so fast I almost forget to feel guilty. "I'm shocked I even got into one."

"Perrin was the only one I got into, too," I add quickly.

We don't say anything for a bit, and when I move to turn down a corner in the maze, he grabs the sleeve of my sweater to pull me back, so we go straight instead. His fingers touch absolutely no skin, but the tug of fabric against my wrist is a chord thrumming deep in my belly.

I do *not* think about him undressing me, because that would be completely absurd.

We continue meandering through the maze at his slow, lazy pace—a noticeable difference from how I see him move on campus, where he's a fast walker by anyone's definition. We talk about the MFA and writing, what he thinks about our various professors, and then about his family, the pressure he felt from his father to go to his dad's alma mater, Columbia. It would be an easy segue into talking about his time at Middlebury, but I feel his resistance, so I switch topics. I don't want to talk about Middlebury, either, especially when the day has been so nice, so civil, so easy. The exact opposite of how I felt the last and only time I was on his college campus.

Eventually, it becomes apparent that five-year-olds are flying by us at an embarrassing rate. We've been in the maze for over an hour, and my stomach's begun its loud campaign for sugar.

"We're lost," I declare. "I need an apple cider so badly."

"It feels like we've already been over here." But he doesn't look particularly concerned. The signs said the corn maze would be difficult, but I think we expected that if gourd-eating children could do it, two Ohio-bred late-twenty-somethings in graduate school would breeze through.

"I think we need to cheat," he says finally.

"I don't think they put a map on their website, Will."

"No, I mean, I'll pick you up and you can see which direction the entrance is in."

"What?"

"Here." He gets down on one knee, and my stomach loops at the sight. "Get on my shoulders and then you'll be tall enough to see where to go."

"I'm afraid of heights, remember?" I take a step back.

"I will hold on so tightly," he says, maybe a little impatient. "Come on, I'll buy you as many pumpkins as you want. We don't want to be out here when it gets dark."

"Donut and cider, too, please."

"Come here. I won't let you fall. Just trust me."

Come here is a phrase I know my subconscious will hold on to for far too long; how he says it so cool and commanding. Willing my expression neutral, I step behind him and wrap one leg over his shoulder and pray to god that the jeans I put on today are clean now that my crotch is literally at his neck. I loop the other leg over and don't know what to do with my hands, so I hold on to his head, feeling the soft strands of his wavy hair.

Then he stands up, and his palms splay roughly over my thighs. A gasp leaves my mouth at the quick boost into the air.

"See, you're very secure." He tightens his grip around me as if to make a point.

From where we are now, I can see that the pumpkin patch is to our left and we're pretty close to the front of the maze.

"Okay, so what's our move?" he asks.

"Hmm, it's sort of hard to see, can you walk a bit straight ahead?"

He does, taking slow, steady steps. "Now?"

"No, sorry, can you keep walking? There's this one stalk that's really high and I can't see over it."

He keeps going. And then I feel myself lift up even higher; he must have raised his heels. "You don't see the entrance?"

"Not really. Maybe if you keep going straight and then once you get to that bit up there, I would take a left—"

"You just like the ride, don't you?" I hear the smug smirk in his voice.

"Me? I would never," I say in an exaggerated scoff. I half expect him to release me now that my cover is blown, but he doesn't. He walks straight, then turns left, right, left, then straight. In about forty seconds we're back at the start of the maze.

"I'm going to let you down now." He slowly lowers himself until my feet touch the grass and hunches over so I can wiggle off his shoulders. A couple of teenagers in skinny jeans walk by and check Will out. I become acutely aware that we were the oldest people in that corn maze without kids to chaperone.

"That was fun," I say.

"Apple cider time?" It's almost 4:00 p.m. and the sun has started to creep out from the clouds, bathing the farm in a copper glow.

"And donuts."

We walk to the corner inside the shop where donuts are being swirled in a vat of sparkling sugar. We order twelve donut holes and two cups of hot cider.

"Let me pay for yours." I butt him out of the way at the register. "Since you drove us here."

"No, it was nothing. I'll pay." But I swipe my credit card before he can.

"Fine." He puts his card back in his wallet, grumbling.

We probably should've split it. It's not like this is a date. It's a grocery store errand interpreted a little too creatively.

We go over to a bench outside and sit, watching kids slalom between the neat rows of pumpkins. And I etch a tableau in my head for later: the air's crispness as the sun dies out, giddy donut-mouthed laughter, Will's cologne laced into my clothes after he lifted me onto his shoulders. It feels like how it could have felt when I was sixteen, had I ever gotten the courage to maybe just ask him for a dance at homecoming.

"Being here reminds me of high school," I say.

"Did you hang out in a lot of pumpkin patches?"

"I don't remember the name—there's some big farm in Medina I've been to a few times. I got my first kiss there, actually."

"With whom?"

"Let me set the scene for you. October, sophomore year. The recession is on its way. The weather, crisp. The time, three p.m. on a Sunday."

Will laughs.

"Gen planned a little double date for me, her, Marcus Wolznak, and Evan Borowitz. Marcus was for me. She was hooking up with Evan."

"Marcus Wolznak." He runs his hand through his hair, closing his eyes as if he's scanning his memory. "The name rings a bell, but I can't place his face. Was he your year?"

I nod. "You wouldn't have run into him. He was on the baseball team, not super academic. Cute, though. Frankly, he was a huge get for me. I don't think he would've come had Evan not been there."

Will shakes his head with a laugh. "Okay, so what happened at the pumpkin patch?"

"Gen does the very transparent thing of *Oh my god I need to pee so badly, Evan can you please go inside with me to help me find the bathroom?* Which is a total joke, because if she really needed to pee, she would go with *me*, not Evan."

"Of course."

"So Marcus and I are walking around the pumpkins and eventually we sit down on a bench much like this one, waiting for Evan and Gen, and he says something like 'So...do you want to come to the fall dance with me?' and obviously I say yes, and then he says, 'You're actually pretty pretty,' which was too many qualifiers in retrospect, but what was I supposed to do? There was some silent moment and I kissed him."

"You initiated your first kiss? Wow, Simon. Bold moves."

"I saw my opening. Marcus probably wouldn't have been my top pick, but I wanted to get it out of the way, and he was attractive and popular. It made me feel cool...to be associated with him."

And it's true. I remember the moment vividly—how when his autumn-chapped lips touched mine, I thought that this, possibly, was some sort of peak. After we pulled apart, I had the strange thought that maybe it hadn't happened at all—that I had blacked out and the slight wetness on my lips was nothing more than wishful thinking. Because how *could* a guy like Marcus, with his Rowan baseball sweatshirt and boyish grin, like a girl like me? It wasn't until Gen greeted me with an extremely-not-subtle wink that I realized it had indeed happened.

"How was the kiss?"

"Fine. I mean, there was no tongue, my god. I think I was

afraid somehow my parents would *know* when I got home if a boy's tongue had been in my mouth."

Will chuckles, sipping his cider. "So who would have been your top pick?"

"Oh, I don't know." I look at him straight-on because I know averting my eyes could be interpreted in a particular way. "Ryan Fraiser from your year, maybe? Or Trent Walker from mine?"

He stares a second too long, but I plaster on a smile. "Ryan. Really," he murmurs.

"What's wrong with Ryan?"

He maintains eye contact while he takes another sip. There's some hard glint in his eye, as if he's daring me to press him on it. But I don't owe him that satisfaction, so I ignore it.

"Who was your first kiss?" I ask.

"Nicole King."

"Oh, really. I would've thought Maddie Katz."

He shakes his head. "I did, uh, kiss Maddie, but that wasn't until junior year. Nicole was freshman year."

"Okay, Nicole King. And where was this?" I knew of Nicole King, and she sounded exactly like the kind of girl he's always dated. I don't know what she was like back in high school, but I know she ended up at Dartmouth for law.

"It was just a stupid house party. No cute pumpkin patch."

"Did you guys, like, date?"

"I would hardly call it dating. But I guess technically we did throw around the words *boyfriend* and *girlfriend*. I could barely hold her hand, I was so terrified. I think at the time I worried I had some sort of skin condition because my hands were perpetually clammy. But she never seemed to mind. We'd spend every study hall period together in the library and she would give me reading lists like mixtapes, telling me which authors to read and who to skip."

The idea of tall, handsome Will Langford being afraid to hold someone's hand is so charming to me.

"She sounds like your type."

Will gives me a weird look. "Oh yeah?"

"Hot academic girls. Rory Gilmore types."

"I don't think I have a type."

"That's what everyone says."

"Well, what's your type, then?"

You, you, you. My brain's synapses fire to a steady drumbeat. It's one syllable, three letters, and 100 percent the worst thing to say if I want to keep this where it is—some sort of safe, loose friendship. It's the best-case scenario I could've hoped for after the weirdness that's simmered between us since Middlebury. And with the fellowship as my ticket out of the life I have and into the one I've always wanted, it's too risky to get distracted. Forearms and tugs-on-sweaters be damned.

"I don't have a type, either."

He doesn't believe it. I see my lie reflected back at me in the crinkles of his crow's-feet when he smiles. I switch my focus to the corn maze in the distance.

"Can I ask a personal question?"

He shifts on the bench. "Shoot."

"When did you start taking antidepressants? Was it after..." I trail off. I'm not sure if I'm supposed to say the words *your dad's death.* I have no idea what's appropriate in this situation.

"No." He plays with the hem of his sweater. "I've been on Zoloft since sophomore year of college. But I did consider increasing the dose. After."

"And it helps?"

"I like to think so. At least, mostly. I'm still prone to feeling low even on them."

"Do you think you'll be on them forever?"

He laughs. "Honestly? I hope so. I didn't like who I was off them." I must look sad because his face cracks into a wide smile, his eyes kind. "It's a low dose. And I mean, this is an MFA program. I'm pretty sure half the cohort is on *something*. Why do you ask?"

"No, I—I was just curious. My dad can be quite anxious, and I've wanted him to go on meds for ages, but he never does anything about it."

"Yeah." Will sighs. "You have to want to get better."

Dad's never done a good job of hiding it—his bitten nails, his insistence on working from home on subzero days when lake-effect snow coats the roads in ice. It's bad enough to affect him (and me, and definitely my mom), but not enough to catalyze any desire for change.

"You know, I've, uh, discussed meds with doctors, too." I twist a ring on my finger.

"Not into it?"

I shake my head vehemently. "No, it's more like, and maybe this is hard to explain, but being an anxious person, burdening someone with anxiety . . . I associate that with my dad. A doctor's never said to me, *You need to be on anti-anxiety meds*. It's more been like, *Okay, you show some signs of anxiety, but it's ultimately up to you to determine what you can live with*. I guess I haven't decided if I can live with it."

The way he's looking at me, unblinking, is almost too much. I redirect my eyes to a parent trying to corral her kid, who's zigzagging among pumpkins almost as large as he is.

"I know it's stupid. But admitting I need them feels like saying, 'This is my natural state. And my state is a problem.' For me, and for other people."

Will turns on the bench, orienting his shoulders toward me. They're so big they block out the landscape behind him, and it's oddly comforting. "With or without meds, your natural state is not a problem. Leigh, you're, you're—"

He trails off and I stop breathing in anticipation of what possible adjective he will attach to me. Behind my eyes a list emerges, scrawls of words: hilarious, clever, jaw-droppingly gorgeous, charming, deep—

"You're conscious," he says, meaningfully, as if the word could be anything but a nice way to say *nervous*. It takes everything in me not to deflate before his eyes.

"Oh. Well. Thank you."

He shakes his head, frustrated. "No, what I mean is you're so aware. You know, I watch you, and you're conscious of others, making space for people in workshop to talk. You're generous in the Writing Center, too; you make other people feel comfortable. It's a good thing."

His stare climbs across my skin like ivy. *He watches me.*

"My mom would say I'm a people-pleaser, but... Thanks."

"What I mean is, it's not about changing who you are or your personality. You're the same person on or off meds. I mean, I'm no scientist; I have no idea how they work. All I know is that *not* being on meds was untenable for me. You knew me in high school. I wasn't pleasant."

"Come on." I nudge him in the shoulder, static catching between us.

"Everything I did, every book I had to read for class, every essay I had to write—it all required so much effort. I felt like I was moving through sludge. A professor I liked finally noticed and recommended the student counseling center. It got better on the Zoloft."

"And so this is the real you." I say it like a statement, but it's a question, of course.

"Sure. But that was the real me, too. I don't buy into the idea that antidepressants show you the 'real you' or whatever. I accept that that was me."

"Even though you actively didn't like yourself?"

"I don't think many people did. Certainly not my dad. You'd think I'd shown him a warrant for my arrest when I handed him the acceptance letter from Middlebury. Dinners that entire semester were just, 'Hi, how was your day? Good? Great. See you tomorrow,' and then I'd spend the evening in my room reading. Everyone in Lit Society was probably wondering why everything we read that year had to be so moody."

The Will I knew in high school wasn't a disappointment. He was someone to look up to. The person I wanted more than anyone else to validate my work. Moody, yes, but also brilliant. It's why his comments about my poem in workshop hurt so much.

"Well, you already know what I thought about you in high school."

It comes out breathier than I wanted. He knows what I thought about him because I *told* him, at Middlebury six years ago, drunk on whiskey and nostalgia. I have no idea what he remembers of that afternoon, but his lips part and his throat bobs. His eyes move to my mouth and the crisp autumn air coasts the exposed skin of my neckline. Every word is a twist of the kaleidoscope of his eyes—sage twirling into ocher. As if I'm a marionette doll, governed by base instinct instead of my mind's hyper control, I lean forward an inch. Another.

Will says, his voice low and gravelly, "Your poem. In *Goldfinch* last year. I'm guessing you didn't get my—"

My shin is jolted by an ear of decorative corn. "Ow, fuck," I say, wincing.

"Sorry! Sorry!" a parent yells to me, chasing after a toddler who's laughing maniacally.

"It's fine!" I call back, running my hand down my leg while turning back to Will. "Sorry, what were you saying? About my poem?"

Will's face is flushed, and he stuffs his hands in his pockets. "Nothing. I was just going to say, uh, I guess you didn't work with Priya Gupta? I, uh, went to school with her, and I know she's a poetry editor there."

I frown. "Oh. Yeah, I did. I'm pretty sure she's the one who emailed me when they accepted the poem."

"Cool." His smile is detached.

A chill washes over me—the sun is setting. "Maybe we should start heading back." I have my bowl of flour waiting, after all, and we both have poems due tomorrow.

Will helps me load my two pumpkins and three spiky gourds into the car, along with a jar of apple butter, a bushel of Pink Ladies, and a carton of eggs. On the way home, he swerves into the local grocery store.

"No really, I don't need canned pumpkin," I protest. "These ones will be great."

He shakes his head. "Detergent."

He casts a quick glance in my direction before parking.

"Oh," I say. "Thanks."

Chapter Ten

I start my poem like I do all homework assignments: the night before it's due. I like the anxiety of it, the blood rush of adrenaline. The pressure of having no choice but to just write. In many ways, it seems counter to who I am—the careful girl who aims to avoid pain and confrontation at all costs. But with a deadline and a blank Word document, I somehow prefer the chaos.

This isn't high school, though, or even college creative writing. Now I'm in a real MFA program where someone in a fancy English department decided *Leigh Simon shows promise* and gave me a spot over god knows how many other people. People who don't write their poems the night before they're due.

So I need to get serious. I need to write at least four poems good enough to submit to the fellowship application in January, and so far, everything I've submitted to workshop has been met with a lukewarm reception. There've been a few that people liked, of course. But they never seem to reach the *whoa* of Will's, the *damn* of Kacey's, the *clever* of Hazel's. Maybe it's time to try something new. A little less pop culture, a little more me.

I glance at the time—8:21 p.m. What to even write about? I scroll through Instagram searching for an image to inspire me, a common practice I used in college when writer's block hit. But there's nothing.

I pace the apartment. The window outside reveals a sliver of setting sun in the distance. People on the street below speed past one another, holding take-out bags. Four girls, probably undergrads, walk by in short, highlighter-color dresses. They're all fresh-faced and pretty and struggling to balance in heels on the sidewalk.

My mind pulls up a memory from college. Stopping at the liquor store in Medford, a few blocks away from the Tufts campus, buying Natty Light on the way to a party with my sorority big sister Marnie. The hot-pink dress I'd brought from high school. My then-boyfriend Andrew's hand at the small of my back, introducing me to other deep-voiced college boys with fancy parents and fancy cars when we got to the off-campus party. The feeling that I had *made it*. That a lonely girl from an uncool town could be here. Could belong.

I walk back over to my laptop and start typing.

All leg, all mini dress so pink
you can chew me up, spit me out, don't
bother holding back

the gape of glossed lips, bunched neon fabric,
the frat house bathroom light bulbs
flickering like a paparazzi camera.

I pause to keep thinking. Stand. Walk around the room. Go to my bathroom, open the cabinet behind the mirror, and pull out my makeup bag. It's stuffed to the brim. I curl my eyelashes, slick on mascara. A smear of crimson lipstick, topped with sticky clear lip gloss. A fluffed brow, a silver-struck cheekbone.

When I no longer recognize myself, I stop. I always wear makeup—I love makeup—but I do the same six steps every day, maybe a wash of lipstick if I'm feeling particularly bold. Now, in the mirror, there's something freeing about transformation for no one but myself.

I slip on a black velvet dress from the back of my closet, stuff my toes into high heels. My fingers move across my phone to a music app, and I turn on something bubblegum, pulsating.

Then I stand in front of the full-length mirror I've stuck to the inside of my closet door with Command strips. Slinking down to the floor, I sit, arching my back, pursing my lips, hollowing my cheeks. I pretend I'm in a music video. I pretend I'm in control. I put on an entire performance and I win an award for it. I cry an acceptance speech; my eyes splinter to the camera flashes.

When the music fades, I kick off my heels and go back to typing, the Word doc filling before my eyes.

*   *   *

On Monday, I do my usual routine: Get a latte and a cookie on my way to pick up this week's poem packet from the English department office, then head to my Writing Center shift.

Two poems past mine is Will's, and this one stops me in my tracks. Each word on the page is an undone button, a fraying thread threatening to take the whole thing apart.

I stand still, reading. Then I read it a second time and a third. I'm on my fourth go when I'm interrupted by a voice and the unnerving smell of Axe body spray.

"Leigh, right?"

It's the frat guy I helped with his essay, all six foot four of him, wearing a hoodie and jeans with a baseball cap. He's holding a cup from the café downstairs, and I see crumbs of something in his facial hair.

"Oh hi," I say, slightly flustered. "Yes, Leigh."

"Are you okay?" His eyes flicker across my body. "You look a little disturbed."

I shake my head. "No, sorry, I was just caught up in reading something." I stuff the poetry packet into my tote bag.

"I wanted to thank you for your help on my essay. I felt really good about it when I submitted it, and I just got feedback from my professor, which was great."

"Oh, I'm so glad!" I wish I hadn't forgotten his name. "Well, please let me know if you need anything else."

I don't particularly want to help him—our session was frustrating and too long and he sat too close. But it's nice to get positive feedback and to feel useful.

"Really?" His eyes light up. "Do you have a shift now?"

I'm walking into a trap, but one where there's absolutely nothing I can do to keep myself from getting entangled in a net.

"Yeah, actually."

"Great, I'll follow you."

I study him again before nodding, fixing a small, polite smile on my face. He's sort of attractive, if you were to shave off his scraggly beard, update his wardrobe. He has a few things going for him. Like how tall he is; how even though he smells like a mall, he smells familiar. But most of all, how he clearly likes me. How easy he is to read.

We walk together to the Writing Center. Will's there, but he avoids my gaze. He must know that by now I've read his poem. My eyes roll to the back of my head at all of these mixed messages he's sent over the last six years.

"Okay, well, can we do a session now?"

Seeing Will made me forget about the frat guy in front of me. "Um, yes. You just have to sign in with Thalia at the front desk, and she can assign me to you."

He does just that. Will has started a session with some girl. He's fully focused, his broad shoulders hunched over a piece of paper, his pen tracing the words.

"Leigh, we signed in Lucas—he's all yours," Thalia says, pulling me out of my own head.

We sit at a small table together, and Lucas takes out a thick packet of paper from his backpack. This time it's an English paper.

"Oh fun." I skim the first page—it's an essay about Virginia Woolf.

"You think?" he asks, but instead of looking in my eyes, I find his gaze lower.

"Yeah, I like Virginia Woolf."

He nods. "That's helpful, then. You can tell me what to write about."

I laugh—is he being facetious? "Absolutely. One A-plus Virginia Woolf essay coming right up."

He seems to realize *I'm* making a joke, but he mansplains *A Room of One's Own* to me anyway—a book I haven't read since AP English my senior year of Rowan. His essay right now is a stream-of-consciousness mess with no cohesive thesis. My goal is to get him there.

But he can't concentrate. He didn't bring me a note for his coach this time, so I have to assume he's here because he genuinely thinks I'm helpful, as opposed to getting extra credit. And while that feels good, what doesn't is how his eyes linger more on my body than the words I'm pointing to with my pen.

Eventually, he gets what he came here for: a solid thesis statement written by me with an outline for his second draft.

"How was your session?" Christine touches my elbow in hello when I sit at the consultant table.

"I thought I was helpful. But no idea if he thought the same. He was too focused on my cleavage." I look down to the very slight vee of my top.

"You should tell Thalia."

"Really? I might be overreacting."

Will is listening. I can tell because he's stopped typing on his laptop, even though his eyes are glued to the screen. His hands flex, as if he's having an internal debate with himself over whether or not to join our conversation.

"That guy is clearly creepy, and he shouldn't be allowed to leer at you," Christine whispers.

"It's fine. If he does it again, I'll say something to Thalia."

Christine shrugs. "Your call. But I get a bad vibe from him."

Will starts typing again and for reasons I can't explain, it infuriates me. I almost want him to say something, even tell Thalia himself.

But then I remind myself—he's not my boyfriend. He's not here to protect me. He's a classmate. One who's decided to trounce all over whatever fragile friendship we'd struck in the pumpkin patch with a poem. A stupid poem that teases me with something he's never wanted to give. A dangled grape, a bait and switch.

Thursday workshop can't come soon enough.

Chapter Eleven

THE PROBLEM WITH WRITING WORKSHOPS is that there's always one student who talks more than anyone else. Not because they actually have better insights, but because they like to hear themselves talk. In our group, that person is Hazel.

This is potentially an even bigger problem because Hazel may be a greater threat to the Erica Go fellowship than I initially feared, sucking up to Paul and Jen and Daniel, constantly replying-all to emails sent to our listserv. And being memorable in class isn't a terrible campaign strategy—so I can't even blame her. It's essentially the same tactic I used to get elected as my sorority's PR director senior year.

When my poem is up, Hazel decides she's going to walk us through it.

"'A Young Ingenue Throws Up in a Toilet.'" She pauses for dramatic effect, then reads the whole thing. She has a severe case of *poet voice*. Her voice lulls at each line break, drawing out every syllable of the word. We all do it for some reason, but Hazel embraces it, speaking my lines as if it's a spoken word poem.

This is the clip the Academy has chosen
to present the nominees: all leg and mini dress
so pink you could chew me up, spit me out, don't
bother holding back this dance-greased
hair—how it frames the lipstick smear, my sour
throat, the clumped mascara. I clutch porcelain
like an award, sink lower until my back goosebumps
against tile—something like an acceptance
speech. I watch the performance in the mirror:
the gape of glossed lips, bunched neon fabric
against sallow skin, the frat house bathroom
light bulb flickering like paparazzi, my mouth
spills saliva and I squint, arch my back as if
I'm silk-draped on a magazine cover. Applause
rings my ears and my irises shrink blind
from the knock of someone opening the door.

"Okay," Hazel begins after I read it out loud, and I swear she licks her lips. "So here we have a one-stanza poem with a speaker who is sort of dissociating in her drunkenness and seeing it as a performance, hence the 'young ingenue.'

"I think what's working well is the specificity of each detail, like 'bunched neon fabric against sallow skin.' I'm not sure if the conceit is working, though. I question the speaker's motives for the performance, firstly, and I think it's overall just a mood board of ideas without any real thesis."

A mood board. Ouch. I've heard that before. All style, no substance.

I'm not allowed to speak during any of this, so I simply sit and scribble comments.

"I loved the motion in this," Penelope, the second-year, says. "Especially near the end, we get that, 'and I squint, arch my back as if,' and the slant rhyme is really satisfying in how it builds."

Will raises a hand to speak and I feel the swoosh of his hand in my stomach. He doesn't make eye contact with me.

"I disagree with the sense that this is merely a mood board. I think the conceit here is that the speaker enjoys the performance. She's actively participating, consenting—at least she thinks she's consenting. Or she's consenting because she knows the performance will be thrust upon her anyway. Like a young ingenue."

"Where do you see that, William?" Paul prompts.

"The line break at 'something like an acceptance.' I thought that was clever."

My face flushes with his praise and I look up from my notes. He stares at me, but his eyes are as unreadable as they were ten years ago in Mrs. Lincoln's workshop. I wish I had a clue how to read him.

The class continues for another minute until Paul sums up his own thoughts. Good visceral details, there's space to play with line breaks to create more unexpectedness, rethink some of the *I*'s.

We move on. August goes next, then Kacey. Then it's Will's turn.

Because we're near the end of the class, everyone has volunteered to read except me and Jerry. I pick invisible lint off my pants and rummage through my tote for a spare pen.

"Leigh? You haven't introduced a poem today—want to take this one?" Paul asks.

I feel my skin crackle like broken glass. I can't turn Paul down.

There's no good reason why I can't present Will's poem. No real public reason, anyway. I scan the words on the page in front of me for the sixtieth time in the last twenty-four hours, each letter a taunt.

" 'In a Pittsburgh Parking Lot, I Break Down,' " I begin and a shiver rips through me.

> I say, *you look really good tonight*
> like it's currency, and in your neon
>
> pink heart, the tip's not
> included so I try my luck: You burn
>
> the whole way down like vodka-
> laced Sprite, like a high school crush,
>
> your strawberry hair, glowing
> in autumn leaves' crunch. You'd read me
>
> Mary Oliver as if you were silk-
> caressing my jaw over candlelight
>
> and pancakes in a rusty kitchen,
> our cheeks February-flushed
>
> magenta. You're jealous when I thread
> myself tight into slick-lipped
>
> girls, as if I didn't drunk-drag you
> into my apartment, as if you weren't

sipping the amber-eyed Cambridge
boys. Just once you say you want to

kiss me as if you actually want to. Another
will invite me to her bed, champagne-sticky,

and pressed against her thorny neck
I will never feel more ugly.

That same night, I dream of your wrist,
and I choke in lavender.

After Will reads it, his smooth voice sinking through the words like melting butter, I speak once more.

"This poem is composed of twelve unrhymed couplets where the speaker is lamenting the loss of some sort of love interest. I think this poem does a great job of colliding down the page. Couplets were a good structure here."

I look back across the table to Will, who looks at me so neutrally I feel exasperation twine around my windpipe. Twenty-one-year-old Leigh wouldn't have believed me if I told her this is where we'd be six years later.

"I don't think it's clear what the conclusion is, though. Is the speaker jealous? Angry? Is he actually in love with her? Was he ever? The poem asks more questions than it answers, and the final couplet feels underbaked. 'Choke in lavender'? Why is that appealing to the speaker?"

August lets out a deep exhale. "Bro, this is intense."

Kacey snorts.

"I'm confused as to what's happening once we get to 'You'd read me Mary Oliver,' since the tense shifts," Hazel chimes in. "Not saying you shouldn't do it, but I'm jarred by the abruptness with which we're now in some other timeline."

"I think the speaker is imagining what life could be like with the love interest, since him saying 'You'd read me / Mary Oliver' is like the ideal state for the speaker," I butt in.

"How do you possibly get that from the poem?" Hazel asks.

Will's eyes jump to mine, and I realize what I've done. He looks back to his own paper and starts circling words. I don't know how to answer Hazel, so I ignore her and swerve to something else I've been thinking about.

"I think the poem could spend more time in the turn, when we get to 'I will never feel more ugly.' What if another stanza or two was added before the final couplet, lingering in the regret? There's an interesting combativeness between the speaker and the first love interest, so it almost feels like the thorny neck girl might be a better choice. If that's not the case, can we get another beat to understand why?"

I put my pen down, shocked by how many sentences I just said in a row in poetry workshop. Paul raises his eyebrows in deep consideration, then nods.

"I agree with Leigh," Hazel says, and I sit back, surprised. *Who'd have thought.*

As the class continues to debate Will's poem, I take my own pen and circle the word *Cambridge* on his page.

Tufts is in Medford, I write above the line. *Not Cambridge.*

*　*　*

The entire cohort, poets and prosers, funnels into Pete's post-workshop, ordering tall glasses of beer and cheap white wine. I sit next to Kacey and across from Will, trying not to stare or look away, either. Trying to act natural. What more can I do in the face of hot-and-cold behavior?

"I felt like Hazel didn't get what you were trying to do in your poem," Kacey murmurs, her chest oriented toward me, while Hazel is at the bar ordering her beer.

I bite my bottom lip. "No, I guess not. "

"It made sense to me," Will interjects, making no attempt to pretend he isn't listening. "The title set the conceit, and if you don't get that, you're actively trying to misunderstand."

I meet his eyes for a second, then two. He's leaning in across the wooden table, his hand loose around a sweating glass of beer. Hazel joins us and sits next to Will.

"So, workshop!" she exclaims. "What did you all think?"

"We were talking about how it's obvious that some people just don't get each other's work," Kacey says, and it takes everything in me not to kick her under the table.

Hazel takes a sip of beer. "Yeah, to be perfectly honest, I didn't understand a single word of Jerry's poem." She lowers her voice even more so Jerry, at the end of the long table, can't hear. "It was just, like, word soup."

Hazel is annoying, but she's right on this one. Kacey nods emphatically. "Like, *what*?"

"Your poem, though," I say to Will, emboldened by wine and the fact that we have witnesses. He's a deer in the headlights, but he plays it off casually.

"What about it?"

"I was surprised by it."

His face reddens, almost imperceptibly. "Mhmm?" he murmurs. I can tell he has no idea where I'm about to take this. I'm not sure I do, either.

Twisting the stem of my wineglass around and around, I land on: "It felt very female-gaze."

"Meaning?"

"I totally agree, Leigh, it was refreshing to see a male poet talk like that. The bit about wrists, for instance," Kacey says.

"I thought it was hot," Hazel adds, and I cross my legs tightly.

"Hot?" Will laughs, eyes glittering. She turns cherry red.

"It's like the shit women notice all the time. Women are into rolled-up sleeves and forearms and veins and eyebrows, and I feel like men are just, like...boobs. Y'all are much simpler," says Kacey.

"*Your wrist / and I choke in lavender,*" I recite part of his final couplet. "Your speaker hasn't even touched the object of his desire, and yet he's completely overwhelmed by, like, her fucking wrist." I pin him with a look and he doesn't avert his gaze, his eyes now as dark as his stout.

"It's very Victorian," Kacey says.

"There's like ass men and boob men and William's a wrist man," Hazel cackles.

"Hey, *the speaker* is a wrist man." Will smiles. Like this is a game to him.

"Riiiight." Hazel stares pointedly with a grin, looking at him through her eyelashes. "Convenient that we poets always have that excuse."

"Gotta have plausible deniability, of course."

I continue twisting my wineglass as they volley conversation back and forth. Hazel has pretty wrists, adorned with stacks of bracelets in mixed metals. Her fingers look smooth, her nails painted silvery black.

"Anyone need another round?" Kacey asks.

I shake my head, my glass still half full. But Hazel nods, says, "Actually, I think I need fries. I'll come order, too."

She and Kacey scoot off their stools and go to the bar, leaving Will and me alone at the end of the table.

"I'm glad you liked the poem," Will says softly before I can change topics.

"I never said I liked it. I said I was surprised by it."

Will grins. "I already read your comments. Lots of underlines. I think even a checkmark, if I remember correctly."

"I give everyone checkmarks. It's important to find the positive even in work that doesn't speak to me."

"Well, thank you so much for your positivity."

"You're very welcome. I'm thrilled you're always seeking improvement."

Will glances behind me to the bar where Kacey and Hazel are waiting to pay. Then his eyes flicker back, golden and speckled.

"So did you think it was me?"

I choke on a gulp of wine. "I'm sorry?"

"My poem. Was the *I* me? Or was it in persona?"

"Only you can say. I wouldn't dream of projecting," I bite out.

A small smile. His eyes move down to my fingers. He pauses before speaking again.

"Are you uncomfortable?"

I look around the table to see if anyone else heard. "No. What?"

Will leans in so close over the narrow table that his mouth is inches away from mine. "You can't stop twisting your glass. It's been nonstop for the last ten minutes."

I don't know what color my face turns, but something in my chest tightens and I move my hands under the table. "Weird habit."

"Mhmm." Something flickers across his eyes, and I can't interpret it, but I feel suddenly like I am naked in this bar.

The girls return, setting down beer and fries.

"I'm going to the bathroom." I stand, swallowing my last mouthful of wine. "And then I think I'll go home."

"So soon? It's Thirsty Thursday." Kacey pokes my arm.

I shrug, poking her back. "I really want to finish the reading for nonfiction."

In the dingy bathroom, I stare at myself in the mirror. Brown eyes, jut of collarbone peeking out from my striped boatneck. Full curve of hip in black corduroy pants. Eyelashes thick with mascara. I run my hand through my hair, my bangs slightly limp after a long day. I scan my body, looking for clues, something to romanticize.

When I open the door, he's there, waiting, as if I manifested him. He looms over me, leaning against the wall, hands at his sides. And for a moment, neither of us says anything. I peer over his shoulder to see if anyone else is in the small vestibule. He breaks the silence first.

"Leigh."

I fold my arms, carefully distributing my weight on my feet equally.

"I thought about it," I say.

"What?"

"It's not persona. And the speaker isn't *William*, either. It's Will."

His Adam's apple bobs and his jaw tightens, blink-and-you'd-miss-it. He takes half a step toward me and reaches for my wrist, gentle, feather-light.

"Do you want it to be Will?" he murmurs.

I feel like I can't breathe, like all the heat in my body is concentrated at my wrist, where his thumb meets his pointer. I try not to blink. I am twenty-one years old again, that afternoon at Middlebury imprinted in the blueprints of every movement I make. And he seems to know the effect he's having on me, because when my breath hitches, his hold on my wrist tightens just a hair. I've had only one glass of wine, but I am drunk.

"Are you in line?"

Jerry, coat buttoned, Fjällräven on his back and clearly needing to pee, is staring at us, oblivious. Will takes a big step back, and I release my hands from their tight cross.

"No, sorry, all yours! See you guys tomorrow." My voice is high-pitched as I walk from the vestibule, through the bar, and out into the night.

At home, I go through the entire conversation and workshop again and again. Entirely unsure of what just happened.

*   *   *

"Did you see it coming?"

Bridget peers through my phone at me, unblinking. Unknowingly, I've maneuvered the conversation to my parents—either by accident or by Bridget's witchcraft. They're not usually a topic I'm in the mood to discuss.

"No. I mean, I don't know. Yes? I had a happy childhood. I could tell they argued a lot, but it always seemed to end up fine."

"How did you react to the separation when they told you about it?"

"Honestly, it was a bad time for me in general. I was already struggling at work. That, plus my parents' big news…that's when I had that panic attack in the bathroom. I was obviously very upset."

"Why obviously?"

I sigh. "It's ridiculous to say out loud, and I know intellectually it's not true, but I think I thought it was my fault. That I could have prevented it."

"What makes you say that?"

"I don't know. I just feel like I should try to fix it."

Said out loud, it sounds ridiculous, but it's true. When you're an only child, you're part of a three-person clique. And when the equilibrium of the clique is off-kilter because two members are fighting, it's on the third to comfort and appease and fix in a desperate attempt to make everyone like one another again.

"That's a pretty big burden for you to carry."

"My mom complains about my dad to me, tries to get me on her side. *Can you believe he did this?* Et cetera, et cetera."

"It's not appropriate for her to talk about her relationship issues with her daughter. You weren't responsible for their marriage."

I shrug. "No, I guess not."

"Do you see yourself getting married?"

"Yes," I say right away. "But I know my parents' marriage isn't working out because they're too different. They're from totally separate worlds. I need to find someone who is like me. Who sees the world the same way, who understands me. Someone who doesn't want to change me. The problem is, I tend to be attracted to the *other* types of guys more."

"What type is that?"

"I've always wanted the scholar, the intellectual who knows everything about the world. I've always wanted someone I could chase. People I maybe couldn't get. Someone super smart and successful and worldly."

Bridget laughs. "Couldn't those words also describe you?"

"No, I mean, no. I don't think I'm dumb, of course. But there's still, like, this difference. You know what I spent the most time doing in college? It wasn't reading literature on the weekends like the people here." I laugh, thinking of my fellow English majors who flocked to the library's reading room with its dim light and austere bookshelves. That crowd—too pretentious for its own good—was never where I'd felt welcomed. Greek life maybe wasn't the perfect fit, either—I've stayed in touch with very few of my old "sisters"—but they never made me feel like I wasn't smart enough to be there.

"No, I was deciding if we should do blue Delta Gamma letters on a pink T-shirt or pink letters on a blue T-shirt. I was debating the merits of an 'Under the Sea' formal theme. Like, most weekends, I was hanging out with my big and my little discussing shit I'm almost too embarrassed to tell *you*, much less my cohort. You know, I love pink and pop music and shopping. That's the stuff I'm into. But I'm not into guys who are into the same things."

"So if you found a guy who also loved pink and shopping, you wouldn't be into him?"

I scan over my mental spreadsheet of every guy I've hooked up with or wanted to. "I mean, not as a rule. I don't know."

Bridget scribbles something in her notes and I narrow my eyes. "Do you have any other rules?" she asks.

"For what?"

"For life."

I frown. "What do you mean?"

"We all have internal rules we live by, that we've created for ourselves. You know, like, 'If you're not five minutes early, you're late.' That's a cognitive distortion. It's black-and-white thinking our brains develop as a shortcut to help us process a ton of information. They can create deeply ingrained patterns within ourselves." Bridget pauses. "I think you've created some 'rules' to follow to avoid pain."

"Like what?"

Bridget shrugs. "It sounds to me like you've created a rule for yourself that certain types of men are never going to genuinely love you, and so you should avoid them to avoid getting hurt."

I'm not sure why my eyes are watering, but I brush the tears away, embarrassed.

"But how is it a distortion if it's true? I *have* been rejected by guys like that, multiple times. In college, Andrew broke up with me because I didn't 'fit in' with his life. He essentially confirmed what I'd already been suspecting."

"He sounds like a jerk."

"Well, fine, let's talk about my parents again. They're basically proof that opposites shouldn't attract. They have completely different communication styles and interests. And here's what gets me: When my mom tries to get me to take her side, I do. She makes excellent points. Sometimes I even find myself telling her, out loud, that I agree with her. But then I feel unbelievably guilty that I just took sides, and I put myself in my dad's shoes, and then I'm on *his* side. The saddest thing about their marriage is that no one is wrong, no one is right. They're just incompatible."

"Is one example enough to be proof? To think that two people with disparate interests or personalities can make it work together?"

I shake my head. "No, but it happened after Andrew, too. There was this guy from high school I had a massive crush on. He was maybe a bit of a douche in school, but I can't explain it: There was always something there. The summer before my senior year of college, I went to a summer program at *his* college, and I ran into him. And I thought maybe he was going to be the exception to my rule. The rare hot, smart guy who liked me. But then he proved me right, too."

It's almost a relief to say the words out loud. In the years that followed that moment, I've revisited it with Gen, with my sorority big sister (in less detail), and once, drunkenly, with some colleagues at Coleman + Derry. The reaction has always been a defiant *His loss!* And sure, maybe. But somehow, it's always felt more like mine.

"How did he prove you right?"

"It's almost too embarrassing to discuss," I sigh. "I barely knew him at the time and I think over the years I've made this into way too big of a thing."

Bridget gives her usual noncommittal shrug and a smile. "We have time."

She's right. We have thirty minutes left.

"Basically, he made me feel safe. He apologized for being a dick in high school. There was a vibe. And for once in my entire life, I put my heart on the line. I *never* do that shit. I don't know what came over me, but it felt like a sure thing. It didn't feel like other guys or my parents' relationship. It felt like something else. And then he rejected me, plain and simple. So if that's where my 'rule' comes from, I think I have pretty good reason to believe it's true."

The words come out in a rush, and I take a deep breath.

Bridget nods. "When you say he rejected you—what exactly did that look like?"

As if she snapped her fingers, my brain is *there*—the sharp grip of that Sunday afternoon still bruising my skin six years later.

But I want her to know. So I tell her.

Chapter Twelve

THIS PUB IS BUSIER THAN you'd think on a Sunday afternoon in June. I'm not sure what I expected, but I just want a beer and some peace and quiet. The space is small and cramped and the bartender is a burly, bearded man who grunts when I ask for whatever's best on tap.

I'm worried. On Monday, the Bread Loaf School of English College Intensive begins, and I've already psyched myself out. My mind is on Andrew and his breakup speech, the words of which have swirled relentlessly in my head for the four days since it happened. *I just don't see us matching well long-term. Unsustainable. Too different. Too. Too. Too.* It had the echo of things my mom has said to my dad over the years: *Could you be more sensitive, Jeff? Why are you making yourself sick over nothing?* As if the mature thing is to strangle human emotions into submission, lock them in a cage, throw away the key.

But like adults, Mom and Dad have always worked it out. Andrew didn't want to work it out.

I'm stewing over the memory of his final touch—what felt like a condescending brush of my cheek—when I see *him*. The very last person I want to see the weekend before I start a creative writing course.

I thought about it, obviously. I knew he went to Middlebury. But I've tried to not give Will Langford much thought in the four years since I saw him on stage at Rowan's graduation. Though I did explicitly check when Middlebury's graduation was. Just out of curiosity. Just in case.

He looks exactly the way I remember him, but also nothing like the gawky, boyish high school senior with shoulders too wide for his chest. He's just as tall, his eyes just as intense, but he's filled out a bit. He's softer. Less untouchable.

"Leigh?" Will says in disbelief when he sees me. He's at the table closest to the bar, the almost-empty cups of probably a couple of friends scattered before him. "What are you doing here?"

He stands with his glass and walks to where I sit at the bar. I wish I'd worn something nicer. I'm in a shapeless tank dress with flip-flops—more of a running-to-Target look than a meet-your-old-crush-at-a-bar look.

"I thought graduation was two weeks ago." I tuck my hair behind my ears. "I figured you would've moved out."

It's something in the way he looks at me, maybe the slight flush around his neck, but I can tell he's had a few beers.

"Yeah, well…" He's upgraded his glasses to circular frames, far more in fashion than what he wore in high school. "It took me longer than I expected to pack up my place. I move out tomorrow. My parents are driving in tonight to help."

I study him, taking my time, before opening my mouth again.

"So, uh, how have you been since Rowan?"

His face twists into something blank. "Well, I graduated."

I laugh, but it's not with a lot of humor. "Yeah, I know."

He wasn't gregarious in high school, either—he talked more in class than out of it. But he never seemed unhappy. Just all-consumed with his studies—that signature soft, intense focus he had when he walked through the halls with a book under his arm. But the Will next to me now seems like he's been wrung dry.

"So what are you doing here?"

"I'm in the Bread Loaf summer intensive." I cross my legs and pick at my nails. "It starts tomorrow."

"Oh yeah. Good for you."

"Yeah."

He runs his finger down the sweat of the cold beer in his glass. I press my lips to my own glass and tilt it back until the liquid meets my mouth, but I don't drink it.

"Can I sit?" he asks.

Maybe it's because I know he's tipsy. Maybe it's because I just want to. But what comes out of my mouth is all bite.

"Oh no, no, I wouldn't want to bother you with any surface-level chat."

His eyes widen, and I know for sure he remembers.

"Damn." And then he sits down next to me at the bar.

I raise my eyebrows. "Good thing you went to a fancy college like this. Only really deep writers here, I bet. We were probably bringing you down in Mrs. Lincoln's class. I'm sure this place let you spread your wings and fly."

I let out a giant exhale. It feels *great*, honestly. Because of Will, I've spent the last three years of college afraid of my fellow English majors. For some reason, maybe because I'll probably never see him again, I don't care that I'm taking it out on him.

I'm so sick of making myself palatable and cool to people like Andrew. Like Will.

Will laughs. "Fancy college, eh? Don't you go to Tufts?"

My mouth gapes. "How do you know that?"

He shrugs and sips his beer. "Don't worry, my wings have not spread here. Been clipped, maybe. Torn off, perhaps. Cut, slowly, with dull scissors. Yeah, that one feels right."

Something in my stomach drops. "Oh."

Will keeps going, his voice more animated now. He looks past my shoulder and I get the impression this is all maybe for someone else. Maybe just himself.

"Everyone always tells you *Don't major in English if you want to make money.* But my dad's called that misguided advice for years. He says if you major in English, the world is your oyster. I think he expected me to come out with a book deal or, at the very least, a one-way ticket to the Iowa Writers' Workshop, but here I am, blabbering drunk in a Vermont bar. No job prospects whatsoever. Instead, I get the privilege of moving back in with my parents tomorrow. Gonna be a great summer."

He finally makes eye contact again and almost looks spooked. As if he shouldn't have said any of that.

I shake my head and roll my eyes. "Come on. You're very smart. Surely you *can* get anything you want."

His pupils are dilated, almost not a stretch of hazel left. "Historically, that hasn't been the case."

The way he maintains eye contact is too direct, so I swallow and look down at my hands. The silence presses thickly between us, and I'm immediately aware of how few inches there are between our knees under the bar.

"Why was it so bad?" I ask. "Why the dull scissors?"

He swallows the last sip of his beer, waves over the bartender, and orders an old-fashioned and whatever else I want. But he ignores my question. "How has it been for you?"

"I asked first."

"Sure, but I'm not going to waste this further with my boring melodrama. I'd rather hear about you."

Waste *this*. What the fuck is *this*? My cheeks heat, and I fight the urge to run my fingers through my hair.

"Well, I'm also an English major. College has been pretty good, yeah. I think after graduation I'm going to look into copywriting. For an ad agency or something."

"Copywriting. Cool. What made you interested in that?"

The truth is, that career path hadn't been on my radar until recently. But my big sis Marnie just graduated and is going to work in marketing; she said it's exciting and potentially lucrative and far more stable than, say, journalism or, god forbid, poetry, which isn't really a viable career path at all.

"I just feel like I'd fit in well at a place like that."

Will leans forward, just a hair, and I peel my hands from each other, palms flat on the counter.

"But do you think it would fit you?"

A vision of high heels tramples across my brain. I'm in glass-walled conference rooms, surrounded by colleagues who stare at me like I'm the brightest thing they've ever seen. We laugh and say acronyms like *KPIs* and *ROI*. It feels like a team sport, and I've always wanted to play on a team.

"Sure," I say.

He's quiet. The burly bartender comes back, delivers Will's old-fashioned and my cranberry vodka. Will tips his glass against mine and nods a *Cheers*. I feel the blood rush in my veins with the glass's impact.

"You know," he says. "Ever since that workshop in Mrs. Lincoln's class, I've felt really bad."

I shrug it off. "It's...whatever."

He shakes his head and leans closer to me, our knees knocking against each other. "No, I was an ass. I just..." He pauses, staring down at his drink. "I'd been having a bad day. I'd gotten into an argument with my dad, I remember..." He drifts off, his jaw tight.

"You were right about my poem, though." I sigh into my drink. "It was this sort of incomplete piece. I came into that class so desperate to impress everyone. I put things together that looked smart but didn't have so much behind them. I think I could fool everyone but you."

He looks down at our knees, hardly a millimeter apart.

"No. I knew you were the best writer in that class, and I think I thought being really critical, making myself sound smart...that I would feel better about my own shit. I was eighteen and insecure. I'm hardly better now unfortunately."

Despite the seriousness of his tone, I snort in his face. "You did not think I was the best writer in the class."

"Not only did you get into that class as a junior, which I couldn't do, but you were the only one trying things out. Not writing about the fucking moon or creeks or ash or smoke or whatever everyone else was doing. You had the freshest voice in the room. All of your work—the feminist poem, the story about your crazy aunt, the other poems...they were really fucking good."

Something restless in my belly takes over, and I feel like he sees me. I want him to see even more.

"My boyfriend broke up with me four days ago," I blurt out and the sentence falls between us like a dropped fork, landing with a loud clink.

"Oh. What happened?"

"Not smart enough to keep up with him, I guess."

"Is that what he said?" Will turns his entire body toward mine, his eyes wide and focused.

I shake my head. "He was stupid smart. Just, like, could rattle off famous writers and would constantly ask who I was reading and, you know, he's from New York and his dad's an editor at *The Atlantic* and I think it became obvious to him that I couldn't keep up. I just wanted to watch *Love Island* and he kept wanting me to come to readings with him, but it made me feel like a fraud. In many ways…" The words slosh through me, but I pause, feeling the alcohol in my veins fizzle. It's always so strange to know you're saying things you wouldn't say sober and yet literally be unable to stop yourself.

"What?" Will urges. "In many ways, what?"

I let out a small laugh and look at him. "I think I wanted to prove to myself I could get someone like you. The hot, deep literary guy who made me feel hot and deep and worthwhile by association."

I'll never forget what Will's face does in the aftermath of that sentence. His lips twist into a small, almost internal grin. Like it was more to the voice in his head than anyone else.

"Do you want to help me pack up the last boxes in my apartment?"

*   *   *

Will's apartment is the exact opposite of my brain at the moment: sparse and quiet. It's a small, slightly claustrophobic studio, and all that's left is a tidily made bed, piles of boxes neatly stacked in the corners, and a pair of jeans and a T-shirt on his bedside table, probably for tomorrow. The blinds are open but still down, so only splinters of late afternoon bleed into the room, the light fixtures otherwise packed.

"Do you want a drink or something?" he asks, and I nod. "Just need to find the glasses... maybe check in one of those boxes over there."

He points to a stack of three near the oven, and I start rummaging. While he goes through another set of boxes, I open the top box and find it filled with tattered notebooks and binders—remnants of four years where he didn't feel like he was enough.

There's a pile of what look like poems underneath some notebooks and I'm flipping through them, curious, when the word *Cleveland* snags my eye.

" 'In a Cleveland Parking Lot, I Break Down,' " I read out loud from the loose paper. It's the title of a poem. The page says *Intro to Fiction & Poetry II* underneath his name and the date, three years ago, from his freshman year.

I say, *you look really good tonight*
like it's currency, and in your neon

pink heart, the tip's not
included so I try my luck: You burn

the whole way down like vodka-
laced Sprite, like a high school crush,

your ashy blonde hair, glowing
in autumn leaves' crunch. You'd read me

But before I can finish the poem, the paper is snatched from my hands, my heartbeat racing so fast I swear he can see it. He holds the poem behind his back out of my grasp and I wrap an arm around him, trying to reach it. Still beer-buzzed, my movements are clunky, chaotic. With the hand he's not using to hold the poem behind his back, Will grasps my wrists together and holds them tight in front of my hips. He gives me a stern look, but his eyes are brighter than they've been all afternoon.

"Hey, I wanted to read that," I complain, but the words come out like breath, gauzy and soft.

He shakes his head. "It's not *for* you," he says, firm but not unkindly, and the way he emphasizes the word is strange. I wriggle my wrists slightly and he drops his hand, releasing me. Then he takes the poem and folds it, slipping it into the back pocket of his jeans.

I want another excuse to touch him, so I loop my hand again around to his back pocket, sticking my hand down so I'm touching his ass, grasping for the paper. His lips curl and he grabs my hand from his pocket and intertwines it with his own and then walks one step toward me and I walk one step back and we continue two more steps in silence until my shoulder blades hit the wall. The hand that isn't holding mine is on the wall near my waist, caging me in.

If I wasn't drunk, I probably would be more shocked at what is happening. But in my haze, I feel like somehow this is where we were both meant to be, what we were both meant to do. Some inevitable conclusion. I want to memorize five senses' worth of data to inject into every poem I write for the rest of my life. Touch, the warm slide of his thumb against my rib. Sight, the clutch of his pupils to mine. Hearing, his breathing low and shallow. Smell, whiskey and woodsmoke, maybe cedar. And taste—that one, I'm almost afraid to know. Maybe it's better not to know what I'm missing.

"Who's the poem *for?*" My voice is low and grainy as I stare up at him. The hand that was on the wall is now soft at the dip of my waist. He drops my other hand and tucks a loose strand of hair behind my ear before running his hand down the hollow of my cheekbone, a thumb over the corner of my lip. My breath hitches and I know he can hear it.

"Who's the poem *about,* then?" But Will either doesn't hear my quiet words or chooses to ignore them because he looks spellbound. He leans his entire body in until his hips are against mine and my skin is on fire. I swear he almost looks hungry. I place my hands at his sides, pulling him closer. He edges a thigh in between mine, and I feel him hard between my legs. If he's in a trance, then so I am, and I don't want to break it.

"Will," I whisper. "Who's the poem about?"

His hand traces my collarbone, a finger slipping under the neckline of my dress.

"Who do you think, Leigh?"

My arms erupt into goosebumps, and I rise onto my toes to meet his eyes.

"I…"

And that's when his parents walk in. I guess in our stupor he never locked the door.

"Mom's ready—" says a large man with the same bone structure as Will, and we tear apart like shrapnel, Will turning suddenly to the kitchenette to fuss with his pants.

"Who are you?" the man asks me, and it's a great question, honestly. My face turns crimson as I contemplate all the moves that have gotten me to this point.

A woman with shoulder-length caramel hair, wearing leggings and a long tunic, follows the man inside. They both stare at me as I struggle to come up with words. Will answers first.

"This is Leigh. Leigh Simon. Um, we went to Rowan together."

Will's dad looks me up and down and doesn't say anything. "We want to start loading boxes in the car. It's just outside with the trunk open."

Will's mom goes up to Will. "Have you been drinking?" She frowns with pursed, tight lips.

His dad lets out a long, loud sigh. "Isn't a rejection from Iowa enough? Do you have to become an alcoholic, too?"

Will flinches.

"I'm so sorry, it's my fault," I interject. "I wanted to grab a quick drink with Will before he moved out, but we just had a beer! I'm happy to help with the boxes—"

"We just ran into Katherine," Will's mom interrupts me. "I invited her to dinner with us. You never said you were still seeing her. I thought you'd broken up."

The color seeps from Will's face, and my stomach tenses as if I've been punched. "We did break up," he says to me. But something about this feels all wrong now.

"You didn't tell us she was going to Vanderbilt's MFA, either. Now, that's a good program," his dad says.

His mom turns to me, ignoring her son and husband. "Sorry,

we only made a reservation for four. Maybe I can call to see if we can add another."

"No, no, I have to be going actually," I manage, grabbing the tote I left next to the door. "Nice to, um, meet you." I force a small smile and walk out without looking back at Will.

But by the time I'm outside in the golden glow of mid-June in Vermont, Will has caught up with me.

"Leigh, wait." He's out of breath.

"Katherine?" I turn to face him, and I can feel my lips twist into some false smile, some defense mechanism.

"She's just a girl I used to date. I'm *not* with her anymore."

"Does Katherine know that?"

He wrings his hand through his hair. "She should, yes."

I laugh, and it sounds mean and I don't care. "She *should*. Okay. Well, great."

"Why does it matter?" Will stands up straight and rolls his shoulders back. "I haven't spoken to you since high school. So what if someone named Katherine exists and I have some complicated relationship with her?"

"Because you're writing these, like, love poems about Katherine, but if your parents hadn't walked in just now, I'm pretty sure we would have—"

He rolls his eyes. "The poem is not about Katherine, Leigh, and you know it."

And you know it.

There it is. The poem is about me, just like I thought. And *he* knows that I know. He knows I goaded him into saying it. He knows I needed to hear him confirm it regardless.

All he knows of me is what we've both watched from afar over the course of high school, what he read between the lines of my writing from class. The intimacy he's gleaned from that. And somehow, that's so, so much.

I've subconsciously taken a step toward Will. The alcohol's buzz still lingers, but it's wearing off and I can see the whole afternoon with more clarity with every second. I place my hand on his bicep, goosebumps forming on his bare skin.

"Okay, fine, I know it. And I want you to know that I'm interested in...this. Whatever it could be. Will, I like you. I've *liked* you. For basically all of high school. I mean honestly, I've thought about you for years even when I've dated other people. I still have all your comments from workshop, even the harsh ones. That's weird, isn't it? I don't know, it's just your writing and how you talk and your *face*. How you smell and stand. I like all of it. A lot. And I always have." The words fall out before I can edit them. Before I can morph myself into someone with more tact, more chill, more foresight.

He says nothing and—maybe I dreamed it? Did I not just offer the most embarrassing monologue of my life? Before my blood curdles, my low, shaky voice tries one more time.

"But you—you like me, too." An unsettlingly long moment passes. "Right?"

He shifts on his feet, looks back in the direction of his apartment, and my stomach lurches. My hand falls against my side.

I asked if Will Langford liked me. He said nothing. Of *course* he said nothing.

"Okay," I whisper.

Will's jaw looks so hard. His lips tense, his eyes vividly, devastatingly hazel as they adjust to the sun.

"I'm leaving tomorrow morning with no plan, no idea where

I'm even going to live. You have all summer, plus another year of college. You just got out of a relationship, and so did I."

"Right."

"I'm not…" He trails off, looking over my shoulder into the distance, no longer willing to make eye contact. "You're not…"

Something heavy drops to the bottom of my stomach. *You're not, you're not, you're not.*

I don't need him to finish the sentence. My imagination is good enough.

"Nice seeing you, Will." My throat constricts with the words, and I'm two seconds away from crying. "Have a good life."

I feel red and blotchy; he looks detached. Stoic. It wasn't worth it—being vulnerable. Letting him see me unedited. I cringe at how I laid myself out so naked for him, thinking maybe he saw what I'd seen. A tiny seed of commonality, something we could touch and hold on to. It was a mistake.

"Bye, Leigh." He turns, he walks back to his apartment, he doesn't look back.

And then I think, *I won't make that mistake ever again.*

Chapter Thirteen

"WHAT THE FUCK IS WRONG with him?" Gen's voice is so loud and shrill that I turn down the volume on my phone.

"I mean, I've revised old poems for college workshop before. It's not like anyone would know."

Gen sighs and ignores me. "That's a bold move, man. How the fuck are you expected to interpret that?"

I lie on the floor on my fluffy rug, staring at the ceiling, holding my phone over my face so she can see me. "The problem is, when I first read that poem six years ago, I only read the first few stanzas. So I have no idea what else he's changed since then. He changed the title. He changed the line to be a different hair color. *Your strawberry hair.* He could be talking about someone else."

She guffaws. "He's trying to not be so obvious, bless his heart. It's still about you. I know it, you know it, *William* knows it, my god, even that Hazel girl probably knows it."

I shake my head and give her a look that means *Stop*.

"Leigh, babe, come on. He's making a statement. This is your sign from the universe that he wants you back."

"He never had me. He specifically didn't *want* to have me."

"He's older and wiser now."

"This is the whole thing with poetry, Gen. You can never assume the speaker of the poem is the same as the poet. For all I know, this is a drastic revision he's made to an old poem because he got caught up and couldn't figure out what else to submit to workshop."

"Thank you, bitch, I've never studied poetry before," Gen says in a mock-grateful voice.

"Even if he does have genuine feelings for me, I'm done with his type. They think they like you and then six months later they're bored because no, you haven't read the latest poem du jour by the other establishment literary man he loves. I've been there, done that. It doesn't end well."

"What did Bridget say when you told her this?"

I get up from the floor and look at myself in the floor-length mirror on my closet door. "She said I should make a list of all the 'life rules' I've concocted for myself. We're going to unpack them one by one."

Gen whistles low. "So what I'm hearing is that Bridget doesn't trust your read on the situation, either. I love Bridget."

"I'm not an idiot, okay?" I go through my closet looking for something to wear to my Writing Center shift. "I acknowledge that there was a vibe, and there is a vibe, but I know better than to think it could be anything real. Look at the facts, Gen." I raise my fingers one by one. "One, you were there at Rowan when he disparaged my work in front of everyone. At worst, he's a prick. At best, he's a shitty communicator. Two, I literally told him I was into him in college—a very vulnerable moment, I might add—and he said very concretely that he wasn't interested *and* that we wouldn't work. He set a boundary—shouldn't I respect that?"

"Okay, yeah, but—"

"He's just toying with me now. I'm good for his ego. But this isn't real. This is Will Langford."

Gen sighs. "You undersell yourself so hard, dude. You undersell yourself and you oversell others."

"Let's talk about you instead." I'm unwilling to take this further. She's easily persuaded and launches into a detailed account of her team's daily stand-up, where she was once again outmatched by a colleague who stole her Instagram post idea and took the credit.

"These people suck." I completely commiserate.

Gen shakes her head back and forth as if she's a human blender. "Gah, I swear to god, Leigh, stay there and don't come back to marketing, because Jesus Christ…" She trails off with a string of expletives.

"I'm gonna try, at least," I sigh.

*　*　*

The 6:00 to 9:00 p.m. shift at the Writing Center is sometimes packed, sometimes dead. It depends on the weather—rain almost always means everyone will stay home; sun means business as usual.

On this Wednesday, it's pouring. So much so that when I enter the room, my sneakers are soaked and my white shirt is nearly see-through. Umbrellas only work when there's no wind.

Four of us work the Wednesday-evening shift: me, Will, Houston, and Susan, a British Lit PhD who never stops talking. But tonight, Susan is home with a sick kindergartner and couldn't manage to get anyone to cover her shift in time.

Will is significantly less wet than I am, probably because he has on sturdy black wellies and a knee-length forest-green raincoat, the rubber kind where water streams off in rivulets down your body. The only unprotected part of him is his chino-clad kneecaps—and those are deep brown from moisture.

"Wow," he says when he sees me, my hair frizzed, my bangs plastered to my face.

I hold out my mangled umbrella. "Sucks to suck." I throw it in the corner of the room to dry. "But maybe it's worth it if it means people won't come in tonight."

His eyes linger over my chest. I'm sure he can see the lace bra underneath my shirt.

"Do you want my sweater?"

"What?"

He gestures to my body. "I have a T-shirt on under this. Maybe if you don't want to sit in a wet shirt all night?" He's wearing a baggy cable-knit sweater; a white tee peeks out around the collar.

"Oh. I'm fine, but thank you."

He nods and I squeeze water from the strands of my hair onto the floor. Will laughs, and it's light and breezy.

Houston arrives and takes the first appointment of the evening. We wait, and then, out of the corner of my eye, I see a familiar figure on the other side of the glass entrance, wearing a bright-red backpack and a baseball cap. It's Lucas, and my entire body tenses.

"Fuck."

"What?" Will looks up again from his laptop.

"Lucas is here for his weekly peep show." Will frowns and starts taking off his sweater.

"Take it." He hands the sweater to me.

"Maybe it'll be fine."

Will presses it into my hands from across the table.

"Take it," he says, firm.

The sweater is still warm. I nod and mumble, "Thank you," then walk quickly to the bathroom to change, passing Lucas, who enters the UWC at the same time.

In the bathroom, I unbutton my drenched shirt in a stall and flip it over the door while I put on Will's sweater. It hits below my hips and maybe isn't what I'd pair with my light-blue jeans, but it's warm and soft and smells like Will—cedar cologne, pencil shavings, some musky scent all his own. I spend way too long looking at myself in the mirror, but it's just because I'm hoping to stall out Lucas.

No luck. When I come back, Lucas is waiting. Will stares for a few seconds at his loose sweater around me. His neutral expression looks like there's a lot of effort behind it, every line of his lips and jaw tense. I throw my wadded-up shirt in my backpack.

"Leigh, I brought you the revision of my essay." Lucas stands way too close as I lead him to one of the desks in the corner of the room. "I want you to read through the whole thing and fix the structure and then edit it."

I already feel slimy with his presence so close, so I concentrate very hard on the paper he hands me, just for something to do instead of thinking about how uncomfortable I am.

Will is clearly eavesdropping because he interjects from the main table, "Leigh, you only have thirty minutes—your appointment's coming in at six forty-five."

I know what he's doing and something blooms in my stomach, the sweetness of his lie.

"This is going to require an hour," Lucas says roughly.

Will shrugs. "Sorry, man, she has an appointment. If you need another thirty minutes, I'll be happy to take over."

I feel some rush of warmth across my skin, a strange urge to cry. Lucas is waiting, though, and he sits next to me, pulling his chair over. For the next thirty minutes, I am just thoughts in a body, some swirl of cells meant to cater to a man.

* * *

Houston leaves early, something to do with a date. Will and I are left to close up the UWC, turning off the computers and lights and tidying the consultation desks.

We're silent as he takes the left side of the room and I take the right. I hear the click and power-down sounds of each computer, the rearranging of pencils and pens. Once we're done, the entire room is darkened, save for the bright overhead light. Gilman Hall is empty at 9:05 p.m.

I finger the hem of his sweater. "Thanks for this, again. Just give me a second and I'll go change so you can take it."

He shakes his head. "You can give it to me later. I don't need it this second." A small smile.

I nod. "Okay, thanks. Well. Shall we?" I walk toward the door, grabbing my backpack, Will close behind me.

"Mhmm."

But when I get to the door, my hand hesitates on the light switch. I turn to face him.

"The thing with Lucas. You didn't have to. But I—I appreciate it."

He shakes his head. "It's nothing. I wanted to."

I nod, and we stand there for a moment in quiet, tense

stillness, two chess players before a match begins. I can't get my body to move, to turn off the lights, to walk out of this room with him. And he doesn't move, either—instead, his eyes jump to my mouth. A low exhale—maybe his, maybe mine. And then the energy in the air shifts. Under his focused, locking gaze, I go from Leigh the rejected to Leigh with the neon-pink heart and ashy-blond hair. The high school crush.

I feel his heat close to me and I smell him in the sweater and suddenly everything around me is Will. I can't see or think about anything else.

"Leigh." His voice is thick. He's maybe a foot away from me.

"Yeah?"

He lets out a deep, measured breath. "Just...just..."

And then he closes the distance between us, now two inches apart, and I'm confident he can hear my heartbeat. His fingertips, soft and tentative, settle onto my hip bones, and my brain goes dark. All my heat, all my thoughts, exist only where his hands are.

My hand goes to the center of his chest, almost a reflex, keeping just a modicum of distance between us.

His breaths are shallow and his jaw tightens and I feel hot, too hot, just—

"I'm going to kiss you, is that okay?" he says, so quiet it's almost a whisper.

My body thrums under his gaze, almost shaking in restraint. "Yes."

He waits a beat, either to give me time to back out or to muster up courage himself—but he moves another inch closer, his thumb gently tilting up my chin.

Whatever control I have left is shattered the second our lips meet.

He tastes clean and sweet, maybe a bit herbal from his Earl Grey tea. I fist my hands in his T-shirt and pull him roughly toward me, forcing him to back me into the door behind us.

He laughs into my mouth and his hands move to my waist, pressing almost too hard into my rib cage. I don't mind. I want even more pressure. Don't want even a centimeter of space between us. I grab his hips and pull them flush against mine and his teeth skate across my bottom lip in response.

Some sort of sound leaves my mouth—is it a moan? A sigh? I am nothing but where our bodies connect—the smooth skin of his bicep under my palm, the silken brush of his fingers against my throat, the jut of his thigh pressing between my legs.

That one in particular is very noticeable.

He twists his fingers in the hem of my sweater—*his* sweater. "I like this on you," he says as he pulls away and begins moving his mouth over my neck, slow and purposeful. My fingernails press deep into his shoulder blades, and the hairs stand up on his arms.

He bends his knees and suddenly he's picked me up, his arms holding my thighs. He walks me over to a desk in the corner where he sets me down. I spread my legs for him to step in between them and his hand creeps up under the sweater, over the cup of my bra. I trail a finger just an inch below the waistband of his pants until he shivers. He responds by pushing aside my bra and cupping my breast, a finger scraping over my nipple and shooting a deep feeling of want into my abdomen. It's a push and a pull, a call and a response. It's a rhymed couplet, this poem we're writing.

He's exactly how I imagined he'd be—in daydreams, early mornings alone in bed reading some filthy thing, and seeing his face instead of the male main character's.

In high school, I wanted Will to look at me so hard that everything behind me blurred into the horizon, into nothingness. In college, I wanted him between my legs, on his knees, begging, worshipping. After college, I wanted him to flatten me into a wall, all ten fingers splayed over my rib cage, watching him lose control, forget his name.

All three versions of Will stand before me now, each intoxicating in its own way. Each a terrible taste of something I know I can't have long-term.

"I've changed my mind," he breathes into my ear, biting the lobe softly. "I do want you to take off my sweater."

I can't suppress a grin, but his words, his escalation of this moment into something that would surely be even better, snaps me back to reality. That choking feeling in my throat, that this will be over before it's begun, jolts the recognition that we're in public, in a dark room with a wall made of glass. Something fragile.

Some inconvenient metaphor.

I hesitantly peel myself away from him and take a deep breath. He looks like I've doused him in cold water before I've even spoken.

"This is a bad idea," I begin, and watch his chest rise and fall, the dark pupils of his eyes.

"Yeah." He nods slowly. "Probably."

"It's just," and I jump down from the desk, smoothing out my, *his*, sweater. "You think you want this now, but it's a temporary feeling. It's just attraction, some sort of nostalgia for both of us."

He stares at me blankly but I keep going, emboldened by his lack of reaction.

"You know, like sure, maybe we keep it casual, classmates-with-benefits. But there's no way it ends well, and then what? We sit in the same poetry workshop for the next two years? I watch you end up with some girl like Hazel, have to workshop your poems about *her*? We both know this isn't a viable option."

He cringes but doesn't refute it, biting his lip as something flashes across his face that I can't read. "And the other option? Keeping it... *not* casual?"

"I already know you'd break my heart." It's almost too vulnerable a statement, but he always pulls them from me, doesn't he? It's hard to give him anything else.

The sentence lingers in the space between us, like the all-consuming waft of cedar I inhaled pressed against his chest minutes earlier.

"I... I just..." He pauses, and I watch his confused expression coil into something entirely detached, colder. "I just got carried away. Won't happen again."

"Okay, yeah." I nod, recommitting to my own statement, unsure why I feel a downward pull throughout my entire body. "I won't, either. Not again."

I grab my broken umbrella near the door. Will follows me out of the building in silence. I don't know where we're supposed to go from here.

Chapter Fourteen

THE NEXT FEW WEEKS ARE unbearable, each in their own lovely way.

It doesn't help, first, that I now know what Will tastes like. How he could angle my hips where he wanted them. How responsive his body could be to the brush of my fingers against his shoulders, his chest, his thighs.

I find this new information utterly distracting right before I go to sleep, at the Writing Center during our shared shifts, and especially in poetry workshop.

In fact, workshop has become a weekly two-and-a-half-hour torture session. It's a bad habit, I know it, but I scour every poem Will submits, looking for hints that they're about me. It's so pathetic I can barely tell Gen, even though of course I do.

The first workshop after the kiss, Will's poem is about a Christmas party gone awry, the speaker having trouble with his wife, shards of broken glass ornaments piercing his knees. The wife is moody and blond and angry and has nothing to do with me, unfortunately.

The second workshop after the kiss, Will submits a poem called "On a Wednesday, My Mother Wears All Black." I go through all the physical descriptions of the mother—*water-logged hazel eyes, mauve lipstick, mole-speckled*—to see if any of them could be me. None of them are.

"You're sick," Gen says, her whole body cackling over our video chat. "They're about his *mom*, Leigh. You're out here trying to see if he's sexualizing you in a poem about his *mother*."

"I'm going to hell," I agree.

The third workshop after the kiss, Will's poem takes place in some field in Pennsylvania where the speaker is drunk or high, contemplating his relationship with his father. It's the exact kind of poetry you'd expect from a straight white male poet in an MFA workshop, and I hate how my classmates coo over it, how I can barely understand it.

My brain does snag, however, on the word *lavender*, which reminds me of *I dream of your wrist, / and I choke in lavender.* Here, Will uses it to describe the speaker's drunkenness. My shampoo is lavender-scented. But so are a million other things.

I listen to "You're So Vain" by Carly Simon as a punishment that week, over and over, the chorus a reprimand.

The saving grace is that Writing Center sessions with Lucas, when Will is there, feel significantly better. Every time Lucas leans over my arm, or pushes my hand off his paper, or holds me longer than his appointment time allows for, I feel Will watching, his eyes protective even if he's across the room. It's hard to imagine him winning in a physical altercation against the bigger, more chaotic Lucas, but something makes me feel like he'd still do whatever he needed to kick Lucas's ass if Lucas crossed a line.

Today, Lucas is particularly *a lot*. His latest history essay needs serious work. Even though he's on the lacrosse team, he's clearly not here on a scholarship. He's smart enough but long-winded in his sentences, and massive parts of one section need to be cut. The problem is, since I'm not an expert in eighteenth-century Britain, I have to do a lot of question asking to coax out what should stay and what should go.

The other problem is that he interprets my questions as interest. In him.

"Great question, Leigh. The empire collapsed because—" My consciousness drifts off as the words get more specific.

"Leigh?"

I jolt back into reality. "Sorry, it's just a bit hard for me to follow. Never been much of a history buff." I send back a small smile.

"No, I was wondering what you were doing this weekend, actually."

As he says this, Will walks over in our direction near the bookshelf, taking a pamphlet about commas for his own session. I can tell he wants to linger near me and Lucas by how he pretends to look through the pamphlet first, before taking it over to his student.

"Oh, I'm not sure." My throat tightens. "We have an MFA party, I think."

"Let me know if you end up being free," Lucas says, his shoulders wide and imposing. "I'd like to get to know you outside of…this." He gestures to the paper we're working on.

I smile in a way that I hope reads as noncommittal. I don't know why I can't just say no to him in the moment.

Will walks briskly past us. I'm sure he heard this exchange.

"So sorry." Thalia taps me on the shoulder. "Your two p.m. appointment is here."

Lucas packs up his notes and his eyes linger on my face as we say goodbye. Across the room, Will's deep at work with his own student, his body positioned away from me so I can't see his face or profile.

Does he think about the fact that three weeks ago his tongue was in my mouth? Does it keep him up at night what *my* thighs felt like in his hands, on the same desk he's sitting at now?

Ultimately, I know it doesn't matter. This is what's best for both of us.

*   *   *

Luckily, I didn't have to lie to Lucas at all. Saturday turns out to be a beloved MFA tradition—the annual Halloween party. Which grad students love just as much as preschoolers do, apparently.

Penelope is hosting, which means the night will be high on both booze and production value. She believes all parties should have themes and sub-themes and occasionally sub-sub-themes, and this year is no exception.

The theme? Halloween. The sub-theme? Edgar Allan Poe. The sub-sub-theme? "EMERGENCY!"

"What does that even mean?" I'd asked her after workshop two days ago.

She replied with a glint in her eye, "It means the party is an emergency. I don't care what other plans you have, I don't care that I only decided to host three days before and forgot to tell everyone, I don't care if you don't have a costume. We're having this party because we *must*."

Can't argue with that logic.

When Kacey and I knock on the door of Penelope's apartment, she opens within three seconds and ushers us in. We're confronted immediately with dim mood lighting, courtesy of hanging floating (battery-operated) candles, a raven garland around the kitchen table, and a NEVERMORE flag arranged over the couch. At a bar cart in the middle of the room, she's prepared plastic martini glasses rolled in black and red sugar. The speaker is blasting retro spooky music, and a crowd of MFAers is already congregating in the kitchen.

Penelope herself is wearing some long black maxi dress that looks like it came from Anthropologie and a (presumably) raven-inspired mask that covers half of her face. "Etsy," she says when I compliment it.

Kacey and I were relatively bewildered at how to dress for this, so we went with the tried-and-true "just look hot" school of thought for Halloween. She's in a black faux-leather mini dress and a black veil that looks like it has spiders on it, and I'm wearing a black velvet dress with fishnet tights and a really good smoky eye. We're also carrying tons of cheap wine to make up for the lack of theme.

"Look who's here." August glides over. He's in a full black suit with a white scarf tied around his neck, clearly Poe-inspired, and he's mussed up his blond hair to look wild.

"The man of the hour." Kacey runs her hand down his arm. "Nice look."

I leave them to their flirting and pour a giant margarita into one of the glasses with black sugar around the rim. I want to be tipsy enough to relax but not *so* drunk that I start making bad decisions, especially when Will comes. I need to avoid being alone with him because I no longer trust myself to listen to my mind over my body.

It's all the more convenient, then, when he enters the apartment with a woman I don't recognize.

Wait. What?

She's pretty. Long brown hair, red lipstick, black nail polish. She's lanky, almost as tall as Will, and she looks expensive; I don't know how else to put it. Wide-leg jeans that fit her perfectly, an oversize black silk button-down. She's carrying a bottle of gin, because, of course.

She shakes hands with Penelope, and when Will leans in to say something to her, he puts his hand on her back before walking past me to the kitchen. When he does it, I feel the absence of his hand on mine. Because now I know how that feels—warm and firm and safe.

Kacey appears in front of me, holding a cup of wine. "Did William bring a *date*?"

I respond with a gulp of my poorly composed margarita, feeling the grainy black sugar against my lips.

Will and his date (?) walk up to us just as I swallow. He's wearing black pants and a white billowy shirt and he looks like a nineteenth-century poet, which is to say, he looks extremely attractive.

"This is Aria," he says, and the brunette smiles and holds out her hand to shake mine, then Kacey's. "She's a third-year PhD in art history."

Sounds about right. I guess it's not surprising he's pursuing a hot thirty-year-old with a humanities PhD. I stopped the kiss, so this is what I get. This is how it should be, anyway.

"Oh, cool!" I flash a bright smile to ignore the sinking feeling in my stomach. "Nice to meet you. So how'd you guys meet?"

Will's eyes trail to my mouth and then to my eyes. For once, I don't break eye contact.

"The Writing Center, actually," Aria chimes in, her voice velvety. "William's helping me with my dissertation."

"What's your dissertation on?" Kacey asks.

"I'm looking at twentieth-century women's domestic arts and how they've influenced New England identity today. I guess it must sound really boring, but yeah … it's been a fun few years so far," she says with a self-deprecating chuckle.

"Wow, impressive." I nod more than is probably necessary and take another slow sip of my drink. "Fun of you to come!"

I would very much like for this interaction to end but Kacey, oblivious, starts peppering Aria with questions about her PhD timeline (three years to go), where she lives (a ten-minute walk away), and where she went to undergrad (Brown, of course). Meanwhile, Will stares at her and nods at all the right moments, mirroring her smiles. I look down at our feet and see that he's oriented his to point slightly in her direction, which I once read on wikiHow is a sign that someone likes you.

Aria answers more of Kacey's questions and smiles and takes the cup of wine Will's poured for her. But then Kacey gets a look at my face and reaches to rub her thumb over my lips.

"You've got black stains all over you from that sugar," she laughs, and I flush red. Not the sexy image I want to portray right now.

"Excuse me, I'm just going to go to the bathroom." I leave the group to fix my mouth.

When I emerge, my lips re-glossed and ready, Will is leaning next to the door.

"Creepy, do you always just follow me when I go to the bathroom?" I frown.

"You look good." I watch his eyes sweep over my body, lingering on my fishnet legs.

"Your date looks good."

The smile dissolves from his face. He moves toward me a few inches and I take a step back to accommodate him out of reflex, the wall hard against me. He's so close and yet so careful not to touch me whatsoever. I have to tilt my chin up to meet his eyes.

"She's just a friend."

"It's important in graduate school to establish a support system, so kudos to you."

He takes a half step back, and I force myself to breathe.

"A month ago, you rejected me." His voice is measured, in control, quiet. He's just stating facts, and I know it.

The heat of the tequila burns in my belly. "And at Middlebury, you rejected *me.*"

He looks down at me, and something passes over his face. Like he's solved a difficult math equation, like he's had an epiphany.

"Ah, I see," he says, voice low and rough. "So we're even."

"Stop." The din of the living room music bleeds into the hallway so my words come out like smoke in wind. "You may think you know what my next move is, and you probably do. But I know your next move, too. Because for whatever reason, and I'm not sure what it is, you're going to stop this thing in its tracks if I don't. Excuse me for wanting to protect myself from whatever your current whims are."

His expression hardens, the long line of his lips a stone.

"I need another drink." I push past him before he can respond, colliding with his shoulder. Maybe on purpose.

Chapter Fifteen

JERRY IS DANCING TO TAYLOR Swift, and that's how you know it's a good party. It's not even one of her classics, the ones that get constant radio play. Instead, Jerry has his hands in the air, twirling his hips to some pulsing Taylor deep cut, beer in hand. He's in his *Reputation* era. Maybe he never left.

We've all gotten sloppy. August is six drinks deep; he's making out with Kacey on the balcony, pressing her so far into the railing it almost feels like she could fall off. Penelope and her gang of second-years keep taking videos using her custom-ordered Snapchat frame: a spooky black-and-white filter with the cursive letters QUOTH THE RAVEN: NEVERMORE. I dance next to Jerry and Christine, who begs DJ Morris to cater his playlist to her own personal tastes.

Funny thing about this cohort. If you ask them sober what music they listen to, it's all indie bands with long complicated names. When drunk, they want anthemic Top 40 romps about getting drunk in big cars and partying until sunrise—the frat house staples I lived and breathed.

Morris puts on some ska tune no one recognizes and the

groans are so palpable, host Penelope forces him to meet in the middle, and we get ABBA.

Aria and Will are very much not dancing. She's in some spirited debate with Wiebke by the bar cart, hands flailing, and Will looks miserable drinking his beer and talking to Hazel. I meander over to Aria and Wiebke because I deserve to make every bad decision at least once.

"Having fun?" I wrap my arm around Wiebke, who looks just as surprised as I do.

"We were just talking about how different it is in New York from North Carolina," Wiebke says, and Aria nods.

"Oh, you're also from New York City?" I ask Aria, who's slowly nursing her gin soda.

"Yes, and I must say, I do miss it. Only reason I got a driver's license was because I moved here for school."

"A bit harder to go to all those gallery openings and natural wine bars when there's no subway system," I say.

Aria nods earnestly. "Seriously, it's a whole different world over here." Gag me.

They go on and on about Wiebke growing up in West Berlin and Aria in the West Village and I have nothing to contribute. It makes perfect sense why Will would be attracted to a girl like Aria. Worldly and sophisticated, artistic and deep. Style and substance in equal measure.

"I've never even been to New York," I say. "Everything I know about the city comes from *Gossip Girl*, but I'm sure that's not a show for you."

Aria sputters. "Oh my god, no, I *love* that show!"

"Really?"

She nods, eyes wide, then launches into a passionate diatribe about the final season that eventually bores Wiebke so much that she floats away to another conversation. Aria and I continue talking, and I come to the conclusion that I both like her and hate her. She's beautiful and interesting and seems to maintain both lowbrow and highbrow interests—something I wasn't expecting. I wish her and Will nothing but the best and can't wait to watch their precocious Brown-legacy children grow up and go to New England's top boarding schools.

I continue to make the rounds, taking advantage of everyone's tipsiness by indulging in a bit of selfie taking and looser-than-usual dancing. In the hope of not having a horrific hangover tomorrow morning, I've been dutifully alternating liquor and water and am hovering the line between tipsy and drunk. It's a pleasant, respectable place to be. And if you squint, tonight's got all the makings of a classic Greek life party, albeit with a higher standard of alcohol. Just like back then, I sway and throw my arms in the air, swiveling my hips to a beat. And without writing to compare myself to or poems I'm barely qualified to analyze, it's starting to feel like home.

Until Will's tall form crowds into my peripheral vision, a seaside siren that threatens to take all of this away. But my mind, unfiltered with the aid of tequila and wine, ignores the warning. Instead all I feel is *want, want, want.*

And then "Mr. Brightside" comes on.

"This is my song," Houston yells, "this is my *song*!" and he begins dragging people into the middle of the room to dance. Even Morris stands up from the laptop to participate.

Will is pulled into the mob by Houston, and while he hardly resists, he just sways to the music. He never struck me as the dancing type. I only have vague memories of him at high school dances. How respectful he was—never the kind of guy to leech onto a girl and start grinding, a signature high-school-boy move. How handsome he looked in his button-downs, how awkward his hands were, dangling without purpose.

Aria's dancing near him but not *with* him, and the difference satisfies me. Somewhere during the pre-chorus he catches my eye, and the way he looks at me is unrelenting. I feel completely exposed. My heart races, and something pools deep in my belly. This time, I break eye contact first.

"More tequila," I say to Christine, who's been grinding on me.

"You better come back," she threatens, and I pat her shoulder. My eyes flit to Will, who is downing his beer, no longer looking at me.

I don't go to the kitchen, though, for a refill. I don't go into the bathroom to freshen up my bangs or my lipstick. Instead, I slip into Penelope's bedroom, the only respite of almost-quiet. I want to think without the too-much stimulation of the drunk MFAers around me. I walk in front of the mirror on her desk to look at my face, sweat-glazed and rosy, as I take in a four-count breath, a six-count exhale.

But then the door opens, sending in a beat of loud music and chatter. And Will.

"Hi." He stands with his back against the now-closed door.

"Hi."

He stays by the door, leaning. So casual. We look at each other for about ten seconds before he says, "Do you remember homecoming, my senior year?"

"I know I went." My body goes taut under his gaze. I'm near Penelope's desk, about six feet away from him, and I feel every foot of distance.

"Do you remember that 'Mr. Brightside' was playing when I bumped into you and spilled your drink on you?"

I shake my head.

"Yes you do," he says, storm-eyed, every atom of his attention focused on me.

The rapid pulse of my heart tattoos across my chest. "Yes I do."

"I was thinking of that moment just now, out there." He puts his hands in his pockets. "You were wearing this pink dress and the soda left this giant mark." He closes his eyes as if he's trying to visualize it. "I remember thinking how good you looked wet."

The way he says the final word is just filthy and its impact shoots directly between my legs.

I cross my arms. "Well, joke's on you. Gen pushed me into you as an excuse to make you talk to me. I'm surprised it wasn't obvious."

His lips settle into a small smile. "Nothing about you is obvious." He walks a few feet to my left and sits down on Penelope's bed, a queen with messy blue linen bedding. "Though I like to think I can read you better than most."

"You can." My voice is so low I almost can't hear myself. "I hate it."

He laughs, loose and breathy, and I know it's the beer that's helping. He leans back so his palms are propped up behind his shoulders, totally relaxed. Pressure threatens to build up inside me if I don't do something. His entire posture is an invitation, and I'm too tipsy to care that this is about to go beyond my original intentions for the night.

So I walk up right in front of him and put my knees on either side of his thighs, straddling him. I put my hands on his shoulders, blocking his view of the room, caging him in so all he can see is me. His jaw hardens, his lips part, and his hands go to my hips, holding them still. We just stare at each other for seconds? Minutes? I couldn't say.

"You're just like how I'd thought you'd be," he says finally, his fingers moving up and down my thighs.

"When have you thought about this?" My stomach does acrobatics, gymnasts somersaulting into some empty space.

He pushes my hips down so I'm sitting on him instead of hovering, making contact with his hard lap. "In high school." He presses his mouth to my collarbone.

"In college. And after," he says to my throat, planting an open-mouthed kiss.

"And ever since the barbecue." He pauses and then goes to my mouth. I let his tongue in immediately. My body arches into his chest on reflex.

If the kiss in the Writing Center was soft and hesitant, this is all urgency. Probably because we're tipsy. Because the door is unlocked. Because we know that for every time we give in, eventually one time will be the last.

"Can I?" He pulls his mouth away from me and slips his hand about an inch under my dress.

"Please."

He wraps one hand around my waist, pressing me into his chest as I continue to kiss him; the other, under my velvet dress, skims my thigh upward. My fishnet tights are flimsy, just held together by crisscross strings and a band at my waist. He grabs a handful of my ass over my tights and underwear and I roll my hips. He releases a loud breath.

"This okay?" he says, and I love how he checks in, again and again.

"Yeah, do whatever you want."

Somehow, that makes him even harder. I'm sure I'm blushing but we're in a dim room and I care less and less about the unlocked door. His hand goes back to the front of my body and slides a slow finger down the center of me, and I can tell I'm wet by the sudden cool feeling of being exposed to air.

"Fuck, Leigh," he hisses and I bite his lower lip, causing him to jerk his hips upward.

As if he's lost any remaining control he'd been attempting to hold on to, he spreads his own knees, causing mine to split wide open to adjust to him. I gasp and he groans and I can barely kiss him at the same time. I pull apart from his mouth and press my chest against his, pushing aside his loose cotton shirt until I can expose a shoulder blade to muffle my mouth on. He somehow snags aside my underwear from under the fishnets, and then it's just building, building, building. It's too much and not enough at the same time.

When my hips begin to buckle, he starts murmuring ridiculous things in my ear. How pretty I am like this, how he knows I need it, how crazy I drive him in workshop, how he can't write a single poem where I don't exist. In his stanzas, his lines, his words.

When the pressure becomes too much, he tells me to *just let go* and I do. My eyes roll back and my brain bursts into strings of words like *love* and *yes* and *Will*.

That last word reverberates like the repeating line of a villanelle, over and over in different forms, until the final quatrain blooms across my body. Some wild, quieting thing.

Chapter Sixteen

WILL AND I DON'T TALK on Sunday, but that's fine, of course. He's probably hungover, and I've got a bit of a headache, too. It would be weird to expect communication.

But then Sunday rolls into Monday and we still haven't spoken. I'm not sure what kind of text to send. *Hello, thank you for the orgasm, let's do it again sometime, but only as classmates, because nothing has changed and I still know deep down in my heart that you're exactly the wrong kind of guy and we inevitably won't last and who needs that stress in this economy?*

Gen vetoes this option when I text it to her.

When we left Penelope's room, the party was dying down anyway. That's kind of how these nights progress. Once Jerry attempts to breakdance, it's at its peak, and you really need to end. Also we ran out of wine.

But it *does* feel like something has changed. Will is more than my classmate, more than a friend. And definitely more than a guy I went to high school with. I'm so tempted to ignore what my intuition is telling me is right. That maybe William Langford *could* be a guy I could do forever with.

That's what makes this moment, in hour two of a long nonfiction workshop, feel so precarious.

Will's not talking. He stares at the essay we're reading—something long and winding I can barely follow myself—and all he does is drag his pen from word to word like he's trying to memorize the entire piece. He's never been the Hazel type, but he always participates. He's the kind of student that waits for the Hazels to take up space in the beginning, then chimes in near the end with something so introspective, so smart that the teacher probably goes home to her husband saying *that's* why she went into teaching in the first place.

"What do you think, William?" Jen Stewart-Weiss asks now, and Will is jolted out of whatever reverie he was in. I see a flash of embarrassment in his eyes. He puts his pen down.

"I'm sorry, could you repeat that? I was, uh, lost in thought."

Jen raises an eyebrow.

"What do you think of Sheffield inserting himself into the action?"

His face goes back to its usual coolness.

"It's always interesting in journalism when the writer has an opinion. But for me, in this piece, page four is where he starts to lose credibility. I have to wonder if Sheffield's participation is self-indulgent or genuine."

"Well said." Jen nods, and the conversation continues, Morris picking up on Will's point. Like he's dismissed, Will goes back to staring at the paper in front of him, careful to not meet my eyes.

I start running through all the potential reasons why he could be mad at me. The ways I've messed this up before it's even begun. I know I told him in the Writing Center I didn't think it would work, that whatever attraction he felt was just nostalgia—something purely physical. Some leftover chemical reaction from a bad experiment we started at Middlebury, a thing he would eventually regret. But two days ago, in the quiet of Penelope's room, he murmured, *I can't write a single poem where you don't exist.* Hot breath against my ear, his thumb dragging up and down in a constellation so perfect, it's as if he already knew my body's cartography. It didn't feel *just* physical. It felt years in the making.

Not a tipsy accident. Something fated. Something poetic.

I need to talk to him.

We walk out of the class, and I catch up to him as he zig-zags past lingering classmates and slow walkers, his gait stiff and determined. But I'm faster.

"Do you want to grab coffee with me?" I touch him lightly on his arm.

"Um." He pauses, looks around and over my head. "Sure."

It's the kind of enthusiasm girls dream about.

"So, what did you think of class?" I say, as we walk to the atrium café.

"Sheffield's a hack."

"Mhmm. Yeah. Agreed."

We take our cappuccinos to go. He seems lost in thought, anxiety stitched into his lips and chin.

"Want to just walk?" I ask.

He nods and we start meandering around campus, now leaf-strewn and rosy-cheek crisp in North Carolina's November, a light drizzle beginning overhead. Once we're out of earshot of other people, on a less busy sidewalk behind Gilman Hall, I take a deep breath, ready to launch into the soliloquy I spent the rest of class rehearsing in my head.

"Will, I—"

"I'm sorry. I should've texted you yesterday."

Okay. Not what I was expecting. I regroup.

"No, I mean, it's fine. We were both probably hungover."

He shakes his head. "I was fine yesterday. I wasn't that drunk on Saturday."

"Me neither."

We look at each other for a moment, parsing through the implication that what happened in Penelope's bedroom wasn't solely because we were under the influence of alcohol, but something far scarier.

He clears his throat. "I wanted to apologize." While I don't know where he is going with this, my chest tightens.

"Apologize for what exactly?"

"I know this is my fault. You very clearly said in the Writing Center you didn't want to entertain"—he motions to the space between us—"this, whatever this is, and at the time, I respected that. But once again I let myself get carried away, and then Saturday happened, and now I feel even more confused and…"

"And what?" My body is so still, I have to actively remind myself to breathe.

"You were right, what you said before. This *isn't* sustainable. And besides, we're here to write. Look at class today. I'm clearly getting distracted, and I can't afford to."

My throat dries, and there's a pang in my chest. But even in the face of information I don't like, my first instinct is to placate and nod, so I do.

"Yes, right. Of course. I understand that and I agree."

"And besides, you'd soon see I'm not…" He stops and gives me a long look, like he's holding something back.

I've never been good with silence. Have always wanted to fill in the blanks. Even as a little kid, with no sibling to play house with, I'd puncture the white noise of my bedroom with long, whispered conversations between Barbie and Ken—some tangled drama about who got to drive the pink convertible. They never listened to each other, but as long as I could keep them talking, I felt like we were getting somewhere.

"It's just physical attraction," I say, rolling back my shoulders. And of course it is. I've worked myself up, after spending weeks methodically working myself down, for nothing.

The wind brushes across my face harshly. Beside me, Will laughs. But it's not joyful; it's more of a low chuckle. Its edges skate across my neck.

"Right." His gaze is so intense I feel my face heat. I avert my eyes.

It's so strange, this thing. At Rowan, I would've died for the chance to hook up with Will Langford, the gawky, glasses-eyed kid who scribbled all over people's poems in red ink. For a moment in Middlebury, I thought something could come to fruition between us. Until it didn't.

But now that we're old enough and hypothetically available enough to really explore that physical attraction, that something *more* I felt hiding in his words on Saturday—it feels too fragile. Like it could crack open, seethe.

As much as my body wants it, my mind knows it's not a good idea. Bad enough that we're in the same cohort and competing for the same fellowship; those are small issues compared with what I know most deeply is true: Guys like him don't stay with girls like me. More important, they're not good for people like me. The ones who want to please. The ones who contort and twist to fit into whatever shape the other desires. I'm trying to move on from those old habits.

And so, on this rain-damp quad behind Gilman, the only words I have in my vocabulary are nods and *yes* and *right*.

"Let's just be normal then," I say to the silence.

Will nods with a weak smile. "Sure."

I reassemble my brain to live and breathe this new *normal*. Not because it's easy, but because I know, in the end, it's best.

*   *   *

After Tuesday-afternoon shifts in the Writing Center, Will and I usually leave together, sometimes getting coffee on our way home before we split off in opposite directions. But today, five minutes before the shift ends, he jumps up with his phone.

"My mom's calling. So I need to leave."

I look down at his phone, which is neither vibrating nor ringing. "Cool."

He does it again the week after—this time, to go pick up a prescription. He's a good liar, of course. His face neutral, his eye contact natural.

I know the truth, though. He doesn't want to be alone with me. I'm not sure what I was expecting when I asked him to be *normal* with me, but it certainly wasn't this.

September's impromptu pumpkin-buying trip feels like a completely different timeline. And it's all the more confusing because this is maybe what's best for me. Being Will's enemy was hard. Being his *friend*, if you could call it that, was harder. But being his nothing is maybe worst of all.

At first I convince myself it's great. This is essentially what

I asked for when I shut down our kiss in the Writing Center, and now I have the mental energy to completely dedicate myself to my fellowship application and my self care regimen against burnout, which consists of watching Netflix, listening to Gen's exploits with the local TV meteorologist, and going to therapy.

But as the weeks drag on, I find myself missing our poetry correspondence, his accidental grazes of my arm or back. Though in retrospect, I wonder if they were ever accidental.

In fact, his comments on my work have become irritatingly professional. Checkmarks, some underlines, and a paragraph to the side—about stanza length and similes, not unhurried musings about our classmates, high school gossip, whatever he read that week. And every time we're in the Writing Center together, I avoid sitting at the spot where he gracefully set me down over a month ago, his hand roaming under my sweater and my staccato breaths in his ear.

Some memories are easier to block out.

But occasionally, we have no choice. After workshop one Thursday, he ends up across from me at the bar, nursing his beer and avoiding eye contact. His shoulders are turned completely to the side, where Morris sits next to him.

"So who's going to AWP?" Morris asks the group.

All of us, even Jerry, raise our hands or nod. AWP, the Association of Writers and Writing Programs, holds a yearly conference of seminars, keynotes, and panels for writers from across the country. This year it's in Washington, DC, and Perrin is paying our entry fees; we just need to pay for transport and hotels once there. It'll be two nights of poetry readings and networking with writers, and while a lot of it sounds pretentious, I *am* excited to see Erica Go in person, as she's doing both a reading and a keynote address. I've only ever seen her read on YouTube and Instagram, and I would love to be able to introduce myself, just in case it gives me any sort of edge for the fellowship.

"Travel plans?" Kacey asks. "We should definitely split into cars or something so we can do this the most cost-effective way."

"And all be in the same hotel," Christine adds.

I cast a glance at Will, who definitely does not look back at me.

While drinking beer, we start searching for hotels and transportation. The conference isn't until after we get back from winter break, but it's something exciting to think about, so we start planning nonetheless.

"How are those fellowship applications coming?" Kacey asks the group.

"Jeremiah Brandon won't know what's hit him," Houston drawls.

"Damn, you really think it's gonna be you, don't you?" Athena punches his bicep.

"Fuck no." He scrunches up his face. "I think Jeremiah himself is going to politely request that I leave this program."

Athena snorts, and the rest of us laugh.

"All of you applying?" I ask the fiction writers. No one has outright *said* it, but it's obvious all the poets are interested in working with Erica Go except Kacey.

"Yes," Athena says. "And to be honest, it's ruining the vibe. Like sometimes on Wiebke's work I wanna make a constructive comment and then I think, *Nah, better the bitch doesn't know.* It's actual sabotage."

Wiebke laughs heartily. "That's her twisted way of saying she can't actually find anything to comment on in my work."

"Ohhhh shit!" Houston squeaks. "MFA trash talk!"

"And all you poets but Kacey are applying?" Wiebke asks, grinning.

I don't want to speak for everyone, so I don't confirm or deny. But Hazel pipes up immediately. "I'm applying at least. I hadn't actually read Go's work before, but she seems like a fascinating writer, and I'd love to work with her."

I bite the inside of my cheek. Jerry nods, and eventually Will does, too, unable to meet my eyes.

"Didn't think that was your type of poetry," Athena says to him.

He shrugs. "I bought all of her books in September and I've been making my way through them. I like her work more than I thought I would. I think doing the fellowship with someone who isn't one hundred percent like you is probably more beneficial than someone who writes in the same vein. Go's different from my usual, sure, but I think that's probably why she'd be good for me." He pauses. "Great, even."

I officially cannot stand this conversation any longer, the mixed messages and subtext far too much for me to handle. So I take my usual tactic before anything gets messier.

"I'm leaving," I announce, chugging the last of my beer and offering a halfhearted wave to the group at the long table.

"So soon?" Wiebke asks.

"Yeah, just tired."

People chime in with goodbyes and only when I turn back for another quick wave do I finally meet Will's eyes.

They're dark and velvety and dangerous. Not a small part of me wants to drown in them. I just don't know how to make this work. And I don't think he does, either.

Chapter Seventeen

♥

I REFUSE TO GO HOME for Thanksgiving. It would be my first with separated parents and I can't handle that right now, though I sell it to Mom and Dad on the basis of logistical hell. North Carolina to Atlanta for an eight-hour layover and then up to Cleveland, just for a long weekend when I'll come home for Christmas two weeks later anyway? Absolutely not.

Both my parents offer (separately) to pay for my ticket. But who would I take up on that? To accept one but not the other feels like no matter what, I'm rejecting someone. I beg them to drop it, and they do, reluctantly, as long as I promise to come home for Christmas.

Gen, bless her, decides to fly down using that sweet, sweet mid-level marketing manager money. She exits her airport Uber in a vivid cobalt-blue faux-fur jacket and denim miniskirt.

"Where did you even come from? LA?" I ask in disbelief, greeting her in leggings and a baggy sweatshirt.

"New England, bitch." She wraps me in a hug. "I thought I told you to tell North Carolina to expect me."

Only about half of the cohort went home for Thanksgiving. Particularly for the people from the West Coast, like Hazel, it wasn't worth the cost, either. For those of us who stayed in Perrin, Kacey invited us all over for a Friendsgiving and graciously said Gen should come, too.

I take her on an apartment tour that lasts twenty seconds given how small it is. She opens the refrigerator, surveying and nodding appreciatively at my condiment selection before walking into my bedroom, dropping her stuff in the middle of the floor like she's moving in.

"You're not wearing that to the party, are you?" Gen asks as she begins unzipping her suitcase.

"No, I'm going to wear my night guard, too." I shake the dental case perched on my bedside table.

"Okay, good, as long as you're accessorizing." She sighs in relief.

I end up in a forest-green sweaterdress and boots. We make the twenty-minute walk to Kacey's place, who greets us with a big smile, the smell of turkey and cinnamon wafting from the kitchen.

Tonight it's just me, Gen, Hazel, Kacey, and Jerry. Wiebke, not even an American citizen, had more pressing Thanksgiving plans than the rest of us.

The group introduces themselves to Gen, but she opts for hugs over handshakes. "Oh, I already know all of you. I literally stalked everyone on Instagram in August."

I pinch her shoulder and she shrugs. "Kacey's my main best-friend competition, Hazel's the mysterious artiste, and Jerry, I don't know, I feel like you're probably the smartest one here."

Jerry looks like he's just met a celebrity.

We gather around Kacey's table and set our sides next to her turkey and stuffing. I brought the pumpkin pie, which I texted a photo of to my parents earlier in separate threads. We pile plates full of food and sit around the table, passing red wine and serving utensils. Unasked, Gen gives an abbreviated history of our friendship (met in eighth grade, bonded over creative writing, she was the architect of my first kiss, et cetera).

"So you work in marketing now?" Kacey asks. "Do you do any writing yourself still?"

Gen nods. "Yes, but mostly erotic fan fiction." Jerry spits out his wine.

"That sounds amazing," Hazel says, and I turn to her in shock.

"You read fan fiction?" I blurt out. Hard to imagine Hazel stooping to something so pedestrian.

"I contain multitudes," she shrugs.

Thirty minutes into eating, the doorbell rings and Kacey gets up. "Oh yeah, I forgot that William was going to come, too." I could kill her.

Gen surely gets whiplash from turning her head so fast to face me. I shake my head subtly, as if to say, *I swear to god, act natural*.

In seconds, Will arrives with a bottle of wine and an apple pie, fresh and hot, which he blames for his lateness.

"William Langford, as I live and breathe," Gen exclaims, standing up. He casts me a quick look—the most intimately we've communicated in weeks—then allows her to hug him.

"Oh, right, same high school," Hazel says.

"That's fucking right," Gen says. "This kid here was the literary wunderkind of Rowan School. Also an asshole in workshop. Hope he's grown out of that."

Will flushes and Gen gives me a sly wink, which makes *me* blush, too.

"Nice to see you, too, Genevieve," he says. Kacey arranges another chair next to Gen for Will.

"Didn't want to go home?" Hazel asks Will.

"My mom went to Dayton to see my grandparents. But I didn't feel like making the seven-hour drive." I feel the familiar pang of acknowledgment that his family, in a different and undeniably worse way, is broken, too.

The rest of the dinner is relaxed. Gen catches Will up on the last ten years of her dating history (and luckily does not request the same from him), Jerry procures some links to Gen's fan fiction (he didn't ask—she *offered*), and I manage to avoid eye contact with Will for the entire dinner.

After eating our pies (Will's, unfortunately, is better), the group retires to the living room for Christmas music and Cards Against Humanity. Needing a break from socializing, I go to the kitchen to wash dishes. I feel someone behind me before I can turn around.

"Just wanted to get a glass," a low, quiet voice says.

It's Will. I look at him and offer all I can—a clipped smile—then turn back to wash a plate sticky with gravy. The cupboard with glasses is right above me, but I don't move.

He's behind me now and he steps close enough that I can feel heat radiate off his body. He reaches over my head to open the cupboard. If I leaned back a centimeter, we would be touching. How accidental I could make it look. I smell him and I feel him, but we don't touch. That would be too much.

I focus on washing. He grabs the glass but doesn't step away.

"Can I get some cold water?"

I nod and shuffle aside to make room. He fills his glass and stays close to me, silent for a moment.

"Nice that Gen came down to see you."

"Yeah, it was." I feel him nod and start to leave when I open my mouth. "Wait."

He freezes.

"Do you have something to say to me?" I ask.

"Such as?"

I frown, then turn completely away from the sink to orient myself toward his broad, lanky frame. "Such as an explanation for why you've become so distant."

He takes a deep breath, and I watch it move through his body. "I told you weeks ago. I think it's best if I focus on writing. The fellowship..." He cuts out.

"And yet, you're here." I look around the cramped kitchen, hearing the sounds of Kacey's high-pitched laughter from the living room. "You're being social. Normal. You're hanging out with friends. Why aren't you writing right now? You can be serious about school and still be nice to me, you know."

"Are we *friends*?" He lets out a hollow laugh.

"Yes!" I take a step closer to him, and this time, he's the one who takes a step back. "Look, I know it's been sort of a roller coaster of weirdness since we started here, but—"

"I knew you weren't doing the dishes!" Gen exclaims, moving into the kitchen with her glass of wine. I realize that, out of reflex, I've taken a massive step back from Will. "Y'all, your classmates are lovely and I'm of course extremely charming, but it's getting a bit weird that the only two people I really know at this party are hanging out without me."

I love Gen, but there's no doubt in my mind that she knew what must have happened and selfishly wanted to see it for herself. Because now she stands before us, sizing us up, cataloging our body language, the angles of our feet.

"I was just refilling my water," Will says coolly, then casts me a quick glance before leaving me with Gen.

"It's not what you think," I hiss once we're alone.

"An awkward fraught interaction between two idiots who can't seem to keep away from each other?" I glare and she grins. "Babe, what exactly do you want from him? I need you to explain this to me, because I don't understand what the problem is."

She's keeping her voice very low, because she knows I don't do intimate discussions in public at audible decibels. Still, I throw my hands up in frustration, almost knocking over a precariously perched wineglass I'd left to dry.

"Literally just a normal, friendly classmate relationship. Yes, I had feelings for him in high school, and yes, they resurfaced in college, but, Gen"—I drop my voice even lower—"when we kissed and then when we kissed a second time drunk, I did what Bridget always tells me to do. To see what the decision feels like *in my body* and react accordingly. And both times I felt like it was good and great but I knew it wouldn't last and that he'd inevitably reject me. I'm not interested in emotional pain for two years. I just want to *write*." I say the last word with a whine.

"Listen to yourself." She raises a perfectly manicured eyebrow. "*Both times I felt like it was good and great.* Your body was fine with the decision. It's your head that's getting in the way."

"You don't understand. I feel in my *bones* that this won't last."

She shakes her head with a sigh. "I think that's your mind, babe. Not your bones."

I shove her lightly in the shoulder. "We need to stop talking about this. They're probably out there thinking I'm having a breakdown or something."

"No, you're right. Better to mislead them," she quips, and I shove her again as she loops her arm in mine, walking us back out to the living room.

*   *   *

We get home stuffed and exhausted. Gen's here two more days, and because we have important plans to go on walking tours of campus and Uber ourselves to my favorite cake shop tomorrow, we don't talk much before we fall asleep. She dozes off almost immediately on the air mattress I've set up next to my bed, and I start absently scrolling on my phone.

But then I get a text from Will.

I'm sorry I've been distant.

I want to turn on the light and sit up, in order to put my full focus on those five words, but I force myself to stay in the dark so Gen can sleep. I see he's typing and my entire body feels like it's been put on ice in anticipation. I wait another minute, trying to formulate a response in case he doesn't say anything else.

But he sends another text before I get the chance:

I'm not really good at sharing emotions out loud so I'd rather write this to you. I know I've perhaps sent some mixed messages in the last few months but you're right that we're at this program for a reason. You want to reaffirm what you love about writing, and I need to get serious. College was rough for me, as you know, and I did some things I'm not proud of. I'm trying to prove I belong in this program. And even though my dad's not here, I feel a need to make him proud too.

I read the words over and over, utterly confused. Things he's not proud of? What is he talking about? Is this some strange, roundabout apology for how things ended at Middlebury?

He's still typing, so I don't say anything yet. I hate that he's done this right before I'm about to fall asleep, because however this conversation ends, I know it will keep me up all night.

A minute later, his reply comes in, a firm shut door to a relationship I'd only ever half hoped was maybe possible.

My concentration's slipping, I'm losing my grip in class. My writing's a mess. I can't do confusing or distracting right now. So if I'm distant, I sincerely apologize. But I think it's best for the both of us right now.

My mouth gapes and I let out a scoff that causes Gen to stir in her sleep. As I read over his texts once more, my mind compiles a supercut of the past four months, each moment more annoying than the last. Me on his shoulders in the corn maze. His groan into my ear as he slicked his finger over me at Halloween, my hips bucking against his chest. The flirty comments we've sent each other back and forth on our workshopped poems.

Gen was wrong. I feel it in my mind, my bones, my body. And I hate, so much, being right.

At this point, Will's rejected me three times. First in high school, when he rejected my writing. Then at Middlebury, when he made it crystal clear he wasn't interested. Now, again, when I stupidly tried to get closer, ignoring every signal he's sent. How come I never learn?

I need to stop this.

I send him back a single word: Fine. I wait for the dots to indicate typing. I almost will them to come, for him to fight me for more of a reaction.

But they don't. So I shove my phone aside and lie flat on my back, trying to lull myself to sleep with Gen's soft breathing.

I stare at the dim ceiling for the rest of the night.

Chapter Eighteen

♡

My parents' couples therapy isn't going well. How do I know this? Good question! My mom must've hired a transcriber, because the second I get home for winter break, she offers me play-by-play scripts that sound more like soap operas than the anxious meanderings of two people on the cusp of sixty.

"And then he said, *Well, if you wanted it that badly, you could have moved to Minnesota, who was stopping you?* Can you imagine? *Who* was stopping me? Your father cares so much about what his boss and his colleagues think, but when it comes to his own wife, I'm an afterthought. I'm just supposed to let go of any forward progress because ultimately, Jeff's comfort is worth more? I've let his anxiety dictate the trajectory of our lives, and he's totally taken that for granted."

My mom turns into the grocery store parking lot, her eyes wild even in profile.

"I don't know, Mom," I offer.

She turns off the ignition, eyes still fixed on the windshield. "He expected me, at the drop of a hat, to turn down one of the biggest opportunities I've ever been given. All because he was scared he'd never find a job or a boss he liked again. And you know what? I did it. Do you think Mayo is going to try again? Knowing I said no once? I never should have let him make this decision for us. I should've just taken the job."

Except he didn't *expect* her to turn it down. He didn't *make* her. She's a grown adult who made a choice to put family first, then regretted it.

But there are some arguments I know I'll never win.

"Maybe you shouldn't be telling me this."

She quickly puts on her sunglasses. "I don't have anyone else."

"Don't you still go on walks with Sheila? What about the people from your running group?"

We both get out of the car, and she stares at me over the hood. With her glasses I can't see her eyes, just shields of impenetrable black.

"We don't talk about our marriages."

Down the aisles, cart in hand, she continues. In the dairy section, she tells me how my dad, or rather *my father*, has neglected his health over the last ten months, blaming it on his anxiety. While inspecting berry cartons, she wonders if all of this could've been avoided if he'd just gone to therapy like she'd asked. In the frozen food aisle, she buys three pints of ice cream—Buckeye for her, mint chip for me, butter pecan for my dad. I raise an eyebrow.

"It's his new favorite."

"But you don't live together right now," I say quietly, as if saying it out loud makes it more real than it already is.

She shrugs. "We're trying to see each other a few times a week. Date night is on Wednesdays. That's what the therapist suggested."

In tiny moments like this one, I feel like it could all turn around. That the drama my parents are putting each other through is just a storm cloud on the precipice of a downpour. Something that will eventually pass.

Over the break, I relocate constantly to accommodate them. I spend the first three days with my mom, the next with my dad. My dad and his family get me for Christmas, my mom and hers for New Year's.

On the afternoon of Christmas Eve, I join my dad in preparing dinner before his relatives arrive. When I enter the kitchen, I'm assaulted by the smell of basil.

"Altering the stuffing recipe this year?" I ask Dad, who weaves in and out behind me with a giant pot. I skipped breakfast in preparation for our usual spread—turkey, stuffing, gravy.

"Seafood pasta. No stuffing. I know it's a change, but the turkey was really on your mom's side. I grew up with this. Here, taste. It's Grandma's recipe."

He hands me a spoon dripping with red sauce. If I close my eyes, I can still taste the salty richness of gravy on my tongue.

"Nice."

He places a gentle hand on my shoulder. "I know this is weird. We should talk about it."

I stiffen, leaning away slowly because I don't want to aggressively shrug him off when he's looking like that—all too-kind eyes and understanding. "I'd rather not."

"Honey, this is our first Christmas not celebrating with the three of us. I want to talk about it and hear how you're dealing with everything. Maybe you can even come to one of our counseling sessions. Pat mentioned that was a possibility—"

"Dad, Jesus, I appreciate the concern but it's too much. It's . . . suffocating. I don't want to talk about this. I don't think it's healthy. All this drama."

He raises an eyebrow and shakes his head with a small, sad smile. "You really are your mother's daughter, aren't you? I guess you'll have to just learn for yourself, but trust me, all that bottling up...eventually it has no place to go, and you'll explode."

Your mother's daughter. There's no doubt in my mind that he resents her, resents how her inflexibility and lack of empathy blew up what had been a good thing for decades.

"The sauce is good, Dad." I pick up the spoon, turn my back, and stare at the simmering pan, wishing it were something else entirely.

When Grandma comes a few hours later, I tell her it's the best-tasting thing I've ever had.

*   *   *

On New Year's Day, I wake up early, after a very non-eventful midnight, in my mom's new rental condo in Cleveland Heights, which looks like an interior designer came in and gave up. Everything is half done and all of it is new and smells too clean.

And what I noticed first when I saw it a few months ago was that I'm nowhere. At my childhood house, you can find boxes of Christmas cards from 2002, old marketing textbooks from my dad's college years, and half-empty ten-year-old condiments stuffed in the back of the fridge. Here, there's just pictures, moments in time without any of the tchotchkes that came with our shared lives together. I pause at faded Polaroids of us on vacation, sun-sleepy and burnt on colorful beach towels. I don't recognize the people in the photos at all. When was the last time my mom looked at my dad like he was everything in the world to her? Maybe an overpriced tourist gift from Florida could convince me it had happened, that I was actually there.

"Did you want to go on a hike in the Metroparks?" I ask my mom, still in her bathrobe, nursing a coffee on the couch.

"Isn't it cold? I was thinking we'd grab lunch with Grandma and Grandpa downtown."

I curl into a tighter pretzel on the couch next to her. "I thought you loved our New Year's morning hike." It's something we've done as a family as long as I can remember, bringing coffee and fresh donuts in a backpack as we slowly jaunt around the Rocky River Reservation, watching our breath make shapes in the cold.

"That was something your father liked to do." Her eyes stay on the TV.

"But aren't you guys doing date nights? Can't it be a date morning? With me?"

"It wouldn't be the same as before." She turns up the volume on the TV.

*   *   *

Three days later, I'm taking a virtual session with Bridget over FaceTime, in the parking lot of a home improvement store near my mom's condo.

"Was there any part of spending the holidays with them separately that you liked?"

"I liked that they both seemed miserable." I say it out loud and immediately feel like an evil daughter. But I also get a sense of relief from saying the words.

"What did you like about that?"

"There's a small piece of me that wonders if they could still get back together. Maybe this was a separation they needed for a while to test it out. Since neither of them seems that happy, maybe they'll reconsider."

Bridget nods, as if everything I'm saying makes complete sense. "And what would it mean, to you, if they were to get back together?"

I shrug. "I don't know. That they were wrong. That my childhood wasn't all a lie."

Something about those words doesn't feel truthful, but I can't pinpoint what it is. It's not like I think my childhood was a *lie*. I was there during the good times. The family vacations. The cozy nights in watching Nickelodeon, just the three of us. I know my mom and dad weren't acting. It wasn't a façade.

But when Bridget asks, I don't know how to describe what I'm feeling, and I pivot before it gets too uncomfortable.

"I'd like to talk about Will now, instead."

Bridget nods. "Let's do that, then. When we spoke before Christmas, you told me about how he texted you at Thanksgiving. He said he saw your relationship as too distracting. Have you guys spoken since?"

"Hardly." The word provokes an empty, aching feeling in my legs. "He doesn't go out of his way to avoid me anymore, but it's all just sort of tense and polite."

"And you don't like that?"

"No, it's fine," I blurt out. "I think it's probably a good thing. Every time we let our guards down, we just end up hooking up, and I get more and more confused."

Bridget's lips quirk up into a smile, but she quickly neutralizes her face. "What if, for the sake of a thought experiment, you were to just keep hooking up? Keep letting your guards down. How would that feel?"

I laugh. "It doesn't even matter. Will isn't interested. I told you, he very clearly said he doesn't have time for confusing or distracting. He wants to be there to write. Which is his prerogative."

"Didn't you also tell him you didn't want distractions? Right after you first kissed?"

"No, I told him this wasn't sustainable." Bridget waits for me to continue, and her silence feels like a push. "And it's not, long-term. Maybe, sometimes, it could be nice just to hook up. But I know myself. I can't really do that, and I honestly don't think it's his thing, either."

"What about after the MFA? Or after the fellowship application is due? Do you think he'd still consider your relationship a distraction?"

"Maybe not, but then we're back to how I don't see this working long-term."

"Isn't that coming from you, not from him?"

Something snaps taut inside me, and my voice comes out high and pinched. "He makes zero effort to convince me otherwise."

Bridget must sense that she's hit a nerve, because she backs off. I feel bad that I might have come off as harsh, but our session is up before I can convince myself to say something like an apology.

* * *

Back at my Perrin apartment in January, I'm in my usual spot at the window, racking my brain for something to write about.

I have a poem due for Thursday's workshop and a fellowship

application due a few days after that. One last shot to strategize the work that'll jump-start my new-and-improved writing career, far from the creativity-crushing briefs and subpar coffee at Coleman + Derry.

I take stock of what I have for the fellowship first. Parsing through the poems I've written for workshop, I read them in the eyes of Daniel or Paul or Erica, sifting through the ones that feel fit for their consumption.

"The Only Good Straight Men Are in One Direction" is a meditation on the sanitized appeal of the Boy Band Man, how the speaker would kill to be in the middle of their onstage huddle, high on musk and salt-dripped skin, pressed safe into eight-pack abs and long eyelashes.

"Taylor Swift Sleeps with Someone New for the First Time" is told in the voice of Taylor herself; drenched in red, white, and blond imagery, it's about her grappling with making art about someone she has feelings for.

Then there's a poem that takes the form of a *Love Island* audition tape, take three. Another two poems in my *Young Ingenue* series, told in the perspective of a made-up persona I've created, drunk on the performance of everyday life.

All of them feel well crafted. But do they carry the vulnerability other writers seem to be teasing out of themselves, like Kacey writing about her former eating disorder, Jerry about his alcoholic mother, Will about his dad's death?

Page by page, line by line, I scour the stanzas, looking for signs of life. In a way, I'm everywhere. A whiff between line breaks. A ghost in the nuance of a verb. It's like I've tried to be vulnerable but haven't figured out how.

I heat my kettle and light a cedar candle. Then I take the One

Direction poem packet, a thick, paper-clipped stack of all my classmates' comments. I've gotten to know everyone so well at this point that I know the writer purely by their handwriting. Which is good, because August never leaves his name.

Consider pushing this stanza to reach an even higher peak, Jerry scribbles in red, loopy letters.

Think these lines can be cut, Hazel writes, minuscule enough that I have to squint to read.

Heighten this ending :) Kacey circles.

I look at the last sheet in the bunch, and I know whose writing it is by the exacting, sharp cursive. While most of the comments I receive want me to push what I've written—asking for more tension, more drama, just *more*—Will's comments sound like this:

Linger here.

Can you explore this moment?

Gorgeous.

While everyone else asks for a performance, some heightened version of what I'm offering, Will just asks me to be more myself. The comments are so soft, tentative even, but also firm and confident, a reminder of what he's like when he touches me.

Stop, I tell myself. I blow out the candle and shake my head, watching the smoke fade.

My fingers tap-tap-tap across my keyboard, but nothing comes out. So I get up. Walk to my mirror and sit on the floor in front of it, cross-legged, close enough to catch every pore in the dim evening light. I fluff up my bangs. I run the pad of my ring finger under my eye, smoothing out patchy concealer. I try to write a poem in my head but still, nothing.

I change tactics. I run a cotton pad soaked with makeup remover over my face. There's something satisfying in seeing all the colors of me—beige, raspberry, charcoal. I step into the shower and let the heat shock my skin; when I get out, I'm dripping in front of my mirror. Normally, I avoid looking at myself naked if I can help it. But now, I linger.

When I dry off, I get into bed, my computer on my lap, and start typing. I take every emotion of winter break—every knife-sharp glance between my parents in their handoffs of me, every gut-drop my body's tried to carry—and spill them on the page. The Word doc fills before my eyes. I don't edit a single word.

When I wake up, the laptop is sitting, closed, on my chest. I open it, last night's poem stark and unruly in the morning light. I scan it once more, its words cascading into a whine, garden-variety neuroticism. The idea of seeing it next to one of Will's poems about his dad makes me cringe. For Erica, I'll stick with One Direction, Taylor, *Love Island*.

I save the document, close it for later. That's when I realize I'm still naked beneath my sheets. Cold and strange and exposed.

Chapter Nineteen

THE DAYS PASS, SLUGGISH AND winter-damp, and eventually it's March. We've settled into a rhythm—the mad dash of weekend writing, the pre-workshop anxiety on Wednesday nights, the post-workshop debriefs at Pete's. But now with the writing conference, that rhythm is disrupted.

I was always going to end up in a car with Will to AWP, wasn't I? While I'd like to blame it on some sort of logistical failure or fated inevitability, it came down to something potentially even dumber: my own ego. That, and the fact that there was no way in hell I was going to stomach a fifteen-hour Greyhound journey, despite Hazel's repeated soliloquies about it being "the most sustainable option *by far*." Kacey, for her part, was going with August after a rare public acknowledgment of their togetherness landed her a coveted spot in a second-year car.

Besides, Will and I are grown-ups. We have over a year left together in the program. We *need* to be able to coexist without my nervous system going haywire. So I asked him, in a highly roundabout way, to prove that *I'm* the mature one in this equation.

"Anyone else driving to DC? I really don't want to take the bus and I don't have my own car, of course…" I began, as if I didn't absolutely already know everyone's transportation situation.

"Oh, Will, didn't you mention driving?" Morris said, tapping Will, who was in another conversation with Jerry, on the shoulder. *Easy.*

"To AWP? Yeah, why?"

"Leigh needs a ride," Morris continued.

Will's body went taut as he looked at me, the entire drive playing across his face.

"I don't want to put you out if you don't have enough room," I said, not looking Will in the eye, but rather Morris, our strange liaison.

Morris laughed. "What? Will's driving and he has space. Don't you?" He turned to Will, who appeared to be biting the inside of his cheek.

"Yes," he ground out. "I have space."

"Solved it." Morris squeezed my shoulder with a smile.

As we walked out of Pete's, I caught up to Will, blurted out, "Sorry, you don't have to drive me, really. I can figure something else out."

He turned to look at me, and for a moment, I genuinely thought he was going to take back his not-really-an-offer offer. But then he loosened his shoulders and shook his head.

"It's fine. I'll pick you up at seven on Wednesday."

I nodded a thank-you and then we didn't speak for the next week.

Until now, when he shows up outside my apartment at seven on the dot. After he texts me to announce his arrival, I wait a minute before going down to his car, staring at myself in the mirror. Trying to see what I will look like through his eyes. It's an awful habit—viewing yourself via the lens of another—but now, smoothing out the divot in my chin and ruffling my bangs, it's the only language I know.

When I knock on the door of his locked car, Will flinches slightly, a strange reaction since he's expecting me. I hear the car unlock and open the passenger-side door.

"Hi."

"Good morning." His eyes sweep over me. It feels like scalding water the way his strained face takes me in. I shove my duffel bag in the back seat next to his leather weekender and we say nothing else until he pulls out of the parking lot and onto the road.

"Did you sleep well?" I ask in an attempt to fill the thick silence.

"No."

"That's too bad."

"Yep."

It's enough to make me resent him, how coolly he can respond to me. How nice it must be to not have to orient yourself to the comfort of others. How freeing.

We don't talk at all for the next two hours. I play on my phone, my eyes occasionally flitting to his hand on the gearshift between us, his fingers curling over the top. Before I can stop it, my brain serves me an image of those same fingers, large and unyielding, gripping my hip bones. I push it down before the flush has a chance to paint my cheeks.

Eventually, I have to pee. I suppress the urge for thirty minutes before I tell him we need to stop. He pulls into a gas station off the highway. When I come back from the restroom with donuts from the station, Will's filling up the tank and is on the phone, his foot tapping in an irregular rhythm against the pavement.

"It's a seven-hour drive," I hear him say as I approach. I want to stand outside the car to stretch my legs, but when I get closer, he opens the passenger door for me. I frown, shake my head, and make a big display of doing a quad stretch.

But he takes a step forward, toward me, until he has one hand on the open door and one next to me on the car, caging me in so I have nowhere to go but inside. We're inches apart; I can barely see past the blockade of his shoulders, and it unlocks a longing I've managed to suppress for weeks.

I stare up at him defiantly and he continues to *mhmm* into the phone perched between his cheek and shoulder, a woman's voice on the other end. He won't meet my eyes, and I watch him look over my head to the other side of the gas station. I insist on eye contact from the man who's avoided me for the last two months but is now crowding me against his car. It would only take a lean, a half step forward, to put my face in his neck and taste the salt of his skin, to tug open his jacket and find the crook of his shoulder where I buried moans on Halloween—

Please, he mouths, and the memory pops. I nod and get in the car before he gently closes the door, putting the phone back in his hand. I see his back while he pays for the gas, then he turns toward me and we stare at each other as he finishes the call. His voice must be low, because I can only hear a muffled sound through the glass. He doesn't break eye contact, and the look in his eyes carries no smirk, no amusement. But there's none of his usual sternness, either. He looks weary and for a second, I almost wonder if he's seeking comfort from my gaze.

He finishes the call and gets back in the car. We're silent until we're on the highway.

"Who was that?"

"My mother."

"Why wasn't I allowed to hear?"

He sighs. "I don't want you to see me when I'm like...that."

"Like what?"

He pauses and it suddenly doesn't feel like there's any air left in the car. "Cold."

I can't help but snort. "No, you're right. I can't even imagine what that would look like."

More silence. Eventually, I pull out the donuts I bought and hold a glazed one out to him. He accepts it.

"So what did your mom want?"

He shakes his head, and even in profile I see him roll his eyes. "She wants me to meet up with one of my dad's old colleagues who will be on a panel at AWP."

"Just to say hi?"

"No, to make the connection so I can network my way into a job after the MFA. I don't think either of my parents liked too much that I graduated college without one. My mother's taken it upon herself to make sure it doesn't happen again."

I stare at his hand on the gearshift, his knuckles white. "Ignore her. You turned out fine without having a job right away. Mostly."

There's a flicker of amusement in the corner of his lip, but it fades before I can memorize it and tuck it away for later.

"Peter really wants to see me. He hasn't seen me since...the funeral."

Will almost chokes on the last word. I know I shouldn't, but I can't physically stop myself from putting my hand on top of his. We haven't touched in months, not since Halloween, and his hand flexes slightly under mine.

"Leigh," he murmurs. But it's not a reprimand. It's a plea to stop the torture. I put my hand back in my lap before he has to tell me himself.

"Is this Peter a nice guy?"

Will nods. "Apparently every time I shared my work with my dad, my dad sent it to Peter, too. They were closer than I realized. Offices next to each other at Oberlin. My dad taught Intro to Fiction One and Peter taught Intro to Fiction Two. I guess my dad would warn Peter about the incoming students."

"So Peter's read your poetry." I glance at his profile and his focused eyes as he switches lanes to speed past another car.

"Yep. You know, he even mentioned one poem by name at my dad's funeral. 'Invisible Summer,'" Will says with a scoff, more to himself than to me.

"A Will Langford Greatest Hit?"

His eyes leave the road to look at me, something dark in his gaze. "No. But that's the only poem of mine my dad ever praised. Never got a single sentence of positive feedback on the tens of pieces I showed him over the years. Just that one."

"Some people are stingy with praise. It's a reflection of him, not your work. But hey, he clearly loved 'Invisible Summer' or whatever. You'll always have that."

His voice is so, so tight when he replies: "Right."

I want to hold him close enough that his pain is absorbed by my body. I want to take his face in my hands and run my fingers over the hard line of his jaw, melting the tension he's too stubborn to let go of. But he won't let me. He refuses to let me.

I suppose I shouldn't, anyway. I can't bear to be rejected again, knowing how jarring it felt the first, second, third time. There can't be a fourth.

"I'm sorry, Will."

He takes a hand off the steering wheel and runs it through his hair, maybe a self-soothing mechanism. His gaze meets mine for just two seconds before he turns back to the road, and in those shards of copper, sage, and seafoam, there's something soft and wanting. But it's over in a blink.

"What if you just talk to Peter? It's networking. Whatever, right? Maybe he could help you get something you love after graduation."

"No."

"Your dad showing his friend your work means he was proud of you, Will. It means he loved you and loved your poems."

"Stop. You didn't know him. My father had twenty-eight years to convince me he was proud of me, and he didn't, because he wasn't. I'm not going to cozy up to his colleague so he can help me out of pity and obligation when there are plenty of more...deserving writers."

"What are you talking about? You're just as deserving as anybody else."

Will grits his teeth and moves to the left lane to speed past a line of cars.

All the frustration I've felt for the last few months boils beneath my skin. I let it simmer, let both of us calm down before I speak.

"You're allowed to be happy," I say coolly, without looking at him. "I'm sorry your dad wasn't as generous with his feedback as he should have been, but just because he was famous or whatever doesn't mean his opinion was the end-all be-all. You're supposed to do this, Will. Instead, you're looking for ways out. Of being a writer. Of other things, too, maybe."

I watch the hollow of his jaw pull inward, the profile of his

Adam's apple bob. I can't explain it, but it's as if I see something unscramble in his brain in real time. But he says nothing more until we reach Washington, DC.

When we get to the hotel, he lets me out so he can find a parking garage. I jump out of the car and close the door. Before I can walk into the lobby, though, he rolls down the window.

"You're right," he says. "But you're looking for ways out, too."

And then he rolls up the window before I can respond.

*   *   *

Kacey and I wake up at 8:00 a.m. sharp to the annoying trill of our phone alarms in sync. After we all arrived in DC yesterday, we went out for sushi as a cohort, glasses clinking in frivolity, Will and I on opposite sides of the table. After a nearing-on-sloppy toast by Houston promising that the Perrin MFA program will "run this town" this week, we found our way back to the hotel where about half of us are staying. I'm sharing a room with two double beds with Kacey, Hazel and Wiebke are next door, and Will and Morris are down the hallway, a fact I tried to ignore as I fell asleep.

Today the agenda is all panels and some evening readings. Tomorrow will be about going to speakers, and then in the late afternoon, we'll begin the journey home.

Kacey and I sit in front of the mirror behind the desk and put on our makeup together. For a long day full of networking and readings with poets who are definitely cooler than me, I've chosen wide-leg black trousers, an oversize button-down, and pearl earrings—my signature accessory when I led Delta Gamma's PR meetings.

"What panels were you planning on going to today?" Kacey asks, scrunching up her forehead to apply mascara.

" 'Feminism in Poetry in the Age of #MeToo.' Then one about 'Reclaiming the Use of Meter in Modern Poetry,' and the last one before the book fair is about using the features of pop music to write poetry."

"Very you." She nods. "I'm going to the meter one, too. Should be fun."

"I'm just biding my time until the Erica Go reading tonight." I take a vial of shimmery liquid eye shadow and throw it in my bag for tonight's reading and bar run. "I want to get a glimpse of my future fellowship professor. Kidding." I grimace to make sure she knows I'm joking.

Kacey shakes her head so violently she smears her left eye with eyeliner. "No, no kidding. I genuinely think you'll get it. Jerry could never, it's just not remotely his kind of work. William is good, but no offense, he's like your standard poet bro. I say it's between you and Hazel, strongly leaning toward you."

"I really hope you're right . . . you just never know."

"I have a good feeling about this. When Erica reads your work, she'll see you're the one."

We don't bother making the beds and leave the hotel to make the short trek over to the event center where the AWP festivities are taking place. I enter the room for the first panel and see Hazel. We sit together and listen to the three poets and one moderator discuss how the #MeToo movement has changed poetry programs for the better.

An hour later, I meet Kacey and Jerry for "Reclaiming the Use of Meter in Modern Poetry." The crowd here leans significantly more male and poet-bro-y, all dressed in corduroy pants and denim shirts. Nonetheless, the panelists make me want to try out iambic pentameter—a first for me.

After a quick lunch, I head to the last panel but don't see any of my classmates there. We talk about pop music and poetry, and oddly enough, it's the session I find the least interesting. Maybe it's just that it's already familiar. Something I've mastered. Maybe I'm looking for new tools to add to my toolbox.

Most of us meet up at the restaurant Busboys & Poets for dinner, waiting around until Erica Go arrives at 8:00 p.m. for her reading. Everyone's buzzing with excitement, but especially me and Hazel, whose newfound interest in Erica's work makes me feel weirdly possessive.

"I'm more excited than I thought I'd be." Athena sips her second glass of wine. "Turns out fiction readings are fucking boring. Poetry is where it's at when it comes to live performances."

Will and Morris arrive once we're done eating; they said in our MFA group chat that they wanted to hit another reading with a famous literary fiction author. Will looks particularly good tonight, in gray corduroys and an airy button-down with a sweater-vest over it, that unruly lock of caramel hair hanging in front of his forehead. He looks like he's about to hop on stage himself.

They join us at the table, Will a few seats down from me on the opposite side. He glances quickly at me, then does a double take, and my entire face heats. I added smoky eye shadow around my eyes and unbuttoned my shirt a bit to feel more Poet at Night, rather than my usual Lost Sorority Girl. But judging by his look, maybe it was too much.

"How was y'all's reading?" Kacey asks.

"Incredible," Morris gushes. "You know who we saw in the audience? Colson Whitehead. He was sitting right in front of us."

"Guess who had to go shake his hand and get his book signed?" Will adds, a glint in his eye. We make brief eye contact across the table, and there's a thrill in being the one he chooses to show his sarcasm to.

"I'd be stupid not to take the chance," Morris says.

"Who was actually reading, though?" Kacey asks.

"Peter Merriman," Morris says between sips. "William knew him, so we were able to skip the line."

My eyes flit to Will, who I can tell is trying not to look at me. But I don't care. The smile that erupts from my mouth is genuine. He *did* it.

Once it approaches 8:00 p.m., the lights dim, and an overhead voice tells us that Erica Go is up in ten minutes. We cram into a small seating area in the back of the bar. At the front of the room is a stool and a microphone, and that's where Erica is sitting, about to read from her poetry book. The seats are a hodgepodge of stools, wooden chairs with backs, and the long bench most of us are packed onto. I slide in next to Christine, and because Kacey went off to pee, Will is next to me, two inches between our thighs. He surveys the room like he potentially wants to see if he can sit elsewhere, but stays put.

Kacey comes back and makes everyone scoot over to let her in, and suddenly Will is flush against me, our legs completely touching on the bench, the heat of him overwhelming.

"Sorry," he murmurs, and I shift only a centimeter, knocking into Christine, who doesn't seem to notice.

"It's fine." But my whole body is filled with the awareness of his proximity, and I barely register when Erica starts talking. We haven't been this close to each other in months, and I wonder if his body is reacting anything like mine is.

Even though I moved over a centimeter, he spreads his legs slightly, enough to have them touch my thighs again, and I can't tell if it's intentional. The contact feels so satisfying, and almost as a test, I put my hand flat above my knee, not touching his leg, but only slivers apart. He seems to register this; out of the corner of my eye, I see his eyes flicker down to my hand. He continues staring straight ahead, and I'm so tempted to put my hand away but feel as if now I need to keep it there to look natural.

After minutes I start to relax and focus on Erica, her poet voice so soothing and soft, everyone is barely breathing, hanging on her every word. She reads some poems I recognize, the ones that receive thousands of likes on Instagram. I love her words, her voice—and I want her all to myself in one-on-ones next fall.

She keeps reading, pausing between poems to make jokes or tell anecdotes that lull me into almost-complete focus. Almost.

What jolts me out of her voice is Will's hand next to me, the side of his pinkie pressing into mine. I know then and there that everything has been intentional. He doesn't look over at me, or at our hands, just stares at Erica as if mesmerized. I, too, don't look up, but I exert the smallest bit of pressure to his hand and then, as if he's teetering on some edge and needs to hold me still lest I push him off it, his pinkie is on top of mine, covering half of my nail, pressing my finger down harder into my thigh. The room is dim and I don't think anyone is watching us, but it feels like a delicious secret, and I feel my body crave even more contact, more pressure, *more*.

He keeps my pinkie pinned under his until the reading ends, then abruptly moves his hand away and stands. I get up, too, and we don't look at each other and my stomach swoops in anticipation.

"Drinks time," Christine says before I can open my mouth to say something to Will.

He turns his back to me and we file off of the bench and into the bar section of the space, where Kacey orders a bottle of wine for the group. We crowd around a table lit with votives in the corner of the room. As if he's a magnet, I stand next to Will, slightly closer than maybe is standard among friends. He plants his shoe right next to mine, our feet touching, and another shot of awareness wedges between my ribs, dripping down to my center.

"So what did y'all think?" Kacey asks the group.

"I thought it was great," Will says. "Her poetry has such a...pulse. It's just so much movement and *tension*." The way he says it almost feels like the universe is mocking me, and I cough to get ahold of myself.

"I will literally die if I get to work with her every week," Hazel gushes, and I press my tongue to the roof of my mouth, frowning. "Anyone else going to get their books signed?"

"Me," I say quickly, and pull out Erica's latest collection, *One Day I'll Be Famous*, which I bought earlier at the book fair.

Hazel and I make our way up to the front, where Erica's leaning against a table. There's a line, naturally. She talks to each person, sometimes letting out a big, booming laugh, before scrawling her name dramatically over the title page of their book.

Hazel's first. "Erica, I just wanted to introduce myself. I'm a first-year poet at Perrin."

Erica's face lights up. "So fabulous! We'll be learning from each other next year." She takes Hazel's book and opens it to sign, asking Hazel for her name so she can individualize it.

I blank out, completely starstruck. One day, maybe I'll be giving a reading at a cool city bar at the AWP conference.

"Hi there!"

Oh fuck, it's me.

"I love your work," I blurt out. "I've been reading you since high school."

Erica scrunches up her face in delight and puts her hand on her heart. "That's really nice to hear. Truly."

I have literally no idea what to say next, I'm already at the end of my pre-rehearsed script.

"Shall I . . . ?" She motions to my book, which I give her, wordlessly. "What's your name, baby?"

"Leigh. L-E-I-G-H."

She tries to scrawl, but her pen's run out of ink. "You got a pen with you?"

I rummage through my tote. I knew I should've taken the free pens they were giving out hours ago. "No . . ."

"Hey, you going to the keynote tomorrow? I'll sign your book after that. No problem."

"Yes, okay!" Maybe this is better. I can get the celebrity awe out of my system and plan a more impressive conversation.

"See you tomorrow," she says, and I nod three times too many.

We stay at the bar for another hour, talking about Erica and what seminars and readings we're going to tomorrow. Kacey wants to go to another bar for a second round, and Jerry wants to go back to the hotel. I'm too frazzled to stay out, and I definitely don't want another drink. I just want to get in bed and think about how to impress Erica after the keynote.

"I'm going back to the hotel, too," I say. "I'll take a cab with you, Jerry."

Will's eyes meet mine across the table. "Same."

Suddenly, the air feels thick and hot, crackling like broiled sugar, between us.

Chapter Twenty

JERRY ORDERS THE CAR, AND within five minutes, we're crammed into the back seat, me in the middle, everything from my thigh to my shoulder pressed against Will. Jerry is quiet on his phone the whole time, and I can't pay attention to anything, so I concentrate on my own breathing, and Will's—his low, deep breaths, slower than mine.

At the hotel, Jerry's on floor three, so he leaves us at the elevator with a wave and a *Have a good night* with an eyebrow raise.

Will and I get off on floor four. His room with Morris is an entire hallway down from mine, but when I stop in front of my and Kacey's room, he pauses.

"Do you have a moment to talk?" he says, and I feel my pulse so strongly I'm worried he can see it at my throat.

"Um, yeah." I unlock the door and we both go inside and look at each other. He runs his hand across his mouth and I feel like my entire body is a bottle of cola seconds before someone drops a Mentos in it.

"I think I'm going insane," Will says and the words pinball through me.

He stands in front of the door of the hotel room, his arms

crossed. He looks at me like he's a disappointed camp counselor after his charges refused to go to bed at curfew, once again.

I put my purse down on the table. Kacey's makeup bag takes up almost the entire rest of the space—a reminder that she could be back at any time.

"I'm not sure why you're the one going crazy." I walk up to him, leaving about two feet of distance between us. "You're the one making it worse." The recent memory of his finger, flattening mine to my thigh—so small, such a *nothing* I could be convinced I dreamed it—sears across my brain.

He takes a step closer to me, so close his heat radiates, but not close enough to touch. It's a position we've found ourselves in far too often over the past six months. The boots he's wearing must add an extra inch of height because he feels so imposing. Like he takes up the entire room.

"You could have taken the bus." His voice is even lower than usual.

"You could've not left with me and Jerry," I retort.

"Yeah, well, you could have not climbed on top of me in Penelope's bed on Halloween."

"And you could've not submitted *that poem* to workshop."

We stare at each other. He's stern and I'm seething and I can't think like this. The heat, his scent, the musky, salty cedar with some undercurrent of high school nostalgia—it's a heady combination that is no longer allowing me to think straight.

"What are we doing?"

Wide-eyed, I shake my head. "After Thanksgiving, *you* made it clear that you thought this would get in the way of your precious art." I bite out the last two words.

He inches even closer, so I'm talking more to his chin than his face. Not one molecule of me touches one molecule of him and I feel every single atom in the narrow ravine between us.

"Let me remind you," he murmurs above my ear, "you also stopped this in the Writing Center because you said, and I quote, 'There's no way this ends well.' And yet, here we are. Again and again."

The desire to scream builds in my throat. I'm choked by my own stupid logic. I think of Middlebury, of high school, of my parents' separation. The ways Will and I don't fit together.

The ways we could tonight.

I take a step back to see his whole face again. "Okay, maybe we just get this out of our systems."

Will laughs, but it doesn't reach his eyes. "Famous last words."

"No, listen, you've built this up in your head now for a decade. God knows why but you have. It's just this stupid physical thing. But the longer we put it off, the more 'forbidden' it's going to feel and the more we're both going to get off on that and turn this into something we both know it will never become, so let's just do this, put it aside, and then move—"

I can't finish my soliloquy because Will's mouth is on mine. One hand behind my neck twined in my hair, the other snaked around my waist, pressing me to his chest. My body freezes at the shock, and even more when he pulls away.

That's when I take what feels like my first breath in months.

"You can call it whatever you want," he breathes into my mouth, his forehead pressed to mine. He smooths his hands on either side of my waist, gripping me so I'm pinned against him, forced to feel his staccato heartbeat. "Get it out of your system, whatever. But at least for right now, I'm done overthinking this."

He moves to push my coat off my shoulders, and it falls to the floor. His hand trails down my shoulder, along my arm, to my hip. His eyes are black, so transparently full of want.

I teeter onto my toes to reach his mouth again and he immediately coaxes mine open with his tongue, deepening the kiss. I shove his coat off his shoulders and his hand goes under my shirt, underneath the cup of my bra, his other to the back waistband of my pants, running his thumb along my lower back. I pull off his sweater-vest and start unbuttoning his shirt, my fingers working quickly to touch his skin faster, faster. He grabs my wrists and holds them behind my back, more tightly than he needs to.

"Slow down," he orders. "If it's just this once, I'm going to take my time."

"You started it," I murmur, and he smirks against my mouth.

Releasing my hands, he resumes kissing me and walks me into the dresser at the side of the room with the mirror where Kacey and I put on makeup this morning. Just as my back hits the edge, he spins me around and crowds me into it, his chest to my back, until I see both of us in the dim light of the room, the dresser's edge digging into my hips.

Our eyes lock in the mirror, both of our chests going up and down quickly, my lips bitten pink and his neck flushed. His hands wrap around to my front, and he begins unbuttoning my shirt and kissing my neck, the faintest scrape of teeth turning me liquid.

"What I don't think you understand," he begins, and he says each word slowly, each syllable pronounced, the way he reads poetry in workshop, "is that I haven't built this up in my head."

He moves my unbuttoned shirt down my shoulders and unhooks the back of my bra, slipping that off, too.

"Because that implies that the reality isn't as good as my imagination."

I reach my hands back around to his chest to tug on his own unbuttoned shirt. He gets the hint and shrugs it off, our clothes landing in a pile on the floor. I want to close my eyes so badly— to lose myself in the *feeling*—but I want to look at him, too. I like the way his shoulders fan out beyond mine, the contrast of his hard chest against my softness, his arms lightly ridged with muscle, the way he looks at me like I belong to him.

"And trust me, my imagination is really good." He spreads his hand possessively across my stomach. "In my head, I've already had you every way I can think of." He cups my breast and runs a thumb over my nipple until it's pebbled and hard. "Spread out beneath me on my bed. Bent over the table in Gilman. On your knees in the mountain house."

"Will, please." I move to turn around to kiss him, but he tightens his hold, shaking his head in the mirror.

His skin burns hot against my back, and I lean into him, pushing my ass against his hard length. His fingers move to the waistband of my pants, unclasping them, and I help him push them down until they land in a flood around my feet.

"But despite all of that, it hasn't been true." His fingers run along the hem of my underwear and he makes eye contact with me in the mirror, a question in his eyes. I loop my fingers through the sides and pull them down, too.

He lets out a large exhalation, as if he'd been holding his breath for the last minute. He slides his hand down my stomach to the crest between my legs, his finger moving in lazy circles. It's almost embarrassing how heavily I'm breathing, how flushed

I look, how every bit of this is better than every daydream I've concocted in months.

"See, the reality has been so much better than my imagination that I really don't see how I can get *this* out of my system. I've already tried for ten years."

My breath hitches as he slides a finger inside me, then two, releasing something guttural from my throat. The stretch is so good and my knees buckle so hard that I have to put my hands on the dresser. He wraps his free arm around my waist, keeping me upright.

"And look at you," he whispers into my ear, his head in the crook of my neck, staring at me in the mirror. "How can I get this out of my system? I want to do everything with you."

I let out a whimper and a wave rides over me, forcing me to close my eyes for a second. I turn around to face him and unzip his pants and push them down.

"Stop making me wait any longer," I hiss. He captures my mouth in a deep kiss, and I feel the contours of his grin.

He's only in his boxers when I walk him backward onto the bed. When he scoots himself up to the headboard, I straddle him, his hands landing on my outer thighs.

"I brought condoms," he murmurs, taking the opportunity to trail his mouth down my neck and collarbone. The sentence crackles in my stomach—that he expected this, knew it. Wanted it just as much as me.

"Where? I'll get them."

"Wallet in pants back pocket."

I scramble to find his wallet in the pile of clothes discarded on the floor. I bring a condom back to him and he puts it on.

"You go on top," I whisper, and he wraps an arm around my waist, rolling us over. His hips press hot against me, my legs trembling until he places a palm lightly on my thigh, his thumb making small, grounding rainbows on my skin. And then when he pushes into me, it's slow, slow, slow. He looks up—a caesura. A deliberate pause in a line of poetry. I whisper *Come here*, and his mouth is on mine once more. My hand winds itself down his low back, pressing all five fingertips hard against his hip in encouragement. And then he begins to move, controlled and measured.

His thrusts are shallow until I tell him *more*; as if he were waiting for permission all along, he pushes in all the way to the hilt until I gasp his name. He's so overwhelming and all I want to do is overwhelm him back, make him lose control, so I roll my hips against him, seeking friction. He asks how it feels, how he can make it better for me.

When I feel pressure building, I close my eyes, lost in his smell and the sound of his deep breathing, in the horrific, decadent ache of feeling seen. Of feeling complete.

"Look at me," he says, because he wants to be seen, too. I open my eyes and his gaze sears through me like a bolt of electricity. It sends me over the edge and I explode into a million pieces, each one a different shard of the Leighs I am, and the Leighs I could be.

Chapter Twenty-One

You can't *REALLY* get something out of your system, can you? Because the second it becomes forbidden again, you want it even more. That's why diets don't work. Your mind may have some distorted idea of what you're allowed to have—half a cupcake, a stupid serving size of fries, some small tease of something meant to be enjoyed freely. But the body doesn't care. The body finds a way.

Because you're *supposed* to enjoy it freely. It's a lesson my mind has never learned.

Alone, waking up with Kacey fast asleep in her own bed beside mine, my body wants one thing. And that's the staggering weight of Will on top of me, under me, behind me.

After he left last night, I spent an hour alone in bed replaying everything we did together until Kacey came home and I closed my eyes, pretending to be asleep like a kid on Christmas morning.

Even now, spurts of last night fizz to the front of my mind. The soft hold of his hand on my throat. How dark his eyes were as they grazed over me in the mirror. The low sounds he made in my ear as I tipped him over the edge.

Could we even make this work? I grab my phone off the night-stand to text Gen. Instead I see a text from Will, sent an hour ago while I was still asleep.

That's not going to be the only time.

Fuck. The words flip my stomach upside down. I don't respond, though; just initiate a conversation with Gen.

What would you say if I said Will and I
had sex last night

Within thirty seconds, Gen responds:

BITCH! I would tell you that my co-worker now
owes me 20 bucks because she lost a BET

I suppress a laugh. Of course Gen had a bet going.

"What are you smiling at?"

I jump at the recognition that Kacey is now awake and grin-ning at me.

"Oh, good morning." I roll over to face her. "Just texting Gen. When did you get home last night?" An Oscar-worthy perfor-mance if there ever was one.

Kacey appears to buy it. "Maybe one a.m.? We ended up at a bar in Georgetown and once Houston threw up on a street cor-ner, it just sort of fizzled out. Didn't want to be too hungover for the keynote today."

"Mhmm, same."

Kacey smiles. "So you had a good night?"

Based on her tone, she clearly knows something happened. My eyes do a quick scan of the room, looking for an errant sock that's giving me away.

"There's a condom wrapper in our trash." Her face is pure grin.

God. I feel my cheeks heat. "Please don't tell anyone yet. Will and I haven't really discussed... what we're going to say, *if* we're going to say..."

"Yeah, yeah, of course." She sits up in bed. "Though honestly I don't think it's going to come as a shock to anyone. There've been vibes since day one." She laughs.

I pull the covers over my face and groan. It's not like I'm embarrassed—if anything, it's the opposite. I want *everyone* to know. But I still don't see a sustainable future here and I don't want it to crash and burn in a public way.

"I don't want anything to be weird." I pick up my phone and there's an additional thirteen unread texts from Gen.

"Hazel's gonna be devastated," Kacey quips. I send her a glare. "Kidding."

I take my phone into the bathroom, along with a new set of clothes for after my shower. I stare at Will's text again. My shower is longer than usual.

* * *

We pile into the conference center auditorium for Erica's keynote. I narrowly avoided Will at the hotel breakfast, but not because I didn't want to see him. I just didn't want to see him with Kacey or Morris or any of the rest of the cohort who might be lingering. I wanted to see him myself. To see how we'd negotiate this strange new thing.

We make eye contact immediately, as if he was waiting for me. He's wearing brown wool trousers with a sharp crease down the front, some cream knit, black boots, and a neat jacket over it all. As usual, it's too damn much.

He waits for me to catch up to him before we sit in a row. Kacey is on my other side and I can tell she's making absolutely no effort to not watch our interactions.

"Sleep well?" he asks in a low voice that's just for me.

I nod. "You?"

He nods back and then runs his hand lightly over my knee. "You look nice," he says, like it's simple. Like we've been dating for years. Out of reflex, I look around quickly to see if anyone saw.

His lips curl up slightly and he leans his mouth into my ear. "Relax." His breath against my neck leaves a warm trail that envelops my entire body.

The director of AWP walks to the stage to introduce Erica, who's wearing all-black with bright-pink heels. The room hushes before she speaks.

She begins her set of poems—a handful of ones she read last night in the bar, as well as longer ones I've only ever read in her collections. Her soft voice razes electric across the auditorium as she catalogs her childhood, her parents' upbringing in Taiwan, how she wanted so desperately to be famous growing up. Each piece is personal and sharp. Sometimes, when she talks about the racism she's faced, the poems are caustic. Other times, they're meandering and romantic, or heavy with pop-culture references I barely understand but want to. She sounds like no one else.

She could help me be the poet I know I could be.

There's a real gut-punch hearing her now that makes me feel

restless. She sounds so open and free. She doesn't write for toilet paper companies or Big Pharma. She writes for herself and for us.

I know here and now that I can never go back to Coleman + Derry. I want to do what Erica does, and she's the blueprint I can use to get there.

*   *   *

At the meet-and-greet after the keynote, we flock to a long table for crudités and wine. Will's next to me constantly, and it's a comfort. It feels so normal, like we've been together forever, except more so than ever, I just want to touch him. I feel the subtle heat of his body when he leans in to make a comment and I accidentally make eye contact with Hazel, who quickly averts her gaze.

Erica moves through the crowd, mingling, shaking hands. Unlike last night, when she was in a more casual setting, today she's got her professional cap on, making a performance of polite nods and soft smiles. There's something recognizable about the way she moves through the world, and I wonder if she ever feels like I do, the relentless pull of orienting yourself toward the opinions of other people.

"Go get your book signed," Will says into my ear, releasing a shiver across my body that I don't think he intended. I wasn't aware he'd watched my interaction with Erica last night. But of course he did.

"I don't want to annoy her." Even though Erica explicitly told me to come find her today, now that she's in this environment, it feels like I'm doing something I shouldn't.

Will pins me with a look, then runs his thumb across the front of my wrist. The touch is almost imperceptible, but from it, I feel just a little bit safer.

"Okay, fine."

I meander over to where Erica is talking to Daniel and Paul. I don't want to interrupt, so after pulling her poetry collection out of my bag, I pretend to get a plate of fruit, turning my back to them to look less conspicuous. I'll wait for a more organic opening.

Will watches out of the corner of his eye from across the room. He's now chatting with Kacey and Wiebke. I shoot him the smallest of smiles, his glance a *Good luck*.

Even with the din of voices in the hall, it's easy to hear Daniel's standard boom.

"We're just so excited to have you this fall, Erica," he gushes. "Really great class of poets, and I think you'll have a great relationship with the student who wins the fellowship."

Anticipation lodges in my throat, and I orient my back even more away from them, so they don't think I'm eavesdropping.

"Fabulous, so you've announced it?" Erica says.

"No, not yet." Daniel shakes his head. "We think we've narrowed it down to two students. This one student, William, is really special—a cerebral, intellectual writer, but with a real simmer of dark emotion underneath. But the other student we're thinking of for this is a poet named Hazel."

I feel the air sucked out of me. Even though he's not talking that quietly, I stop chewing the strawberry in my mouth to make sure I don't miss a word.

"Interesting voice. Plays with cultural and racial identity. Very fearless, a real firebrand in workshop. This may change, of course—there's still the First-Year Reading Series, but regardless of outcome, we're confident you'll enjoy the fellowship. And, of course, teaching the second-year workshop."

"I'm thrilled to hear it," Erica says. "Let me know when you can send over work samples, and I can contribute my own thoughts."

"We absolutely will do that," Paul says.

I'm too frozen to turn around, so I pull out my phone and perform a sense of busyness until I know for sure they've moved on. For all they know, I came to get fruit. No other reason.

Will's still chatting with our classmates, and I don't want him to look at me again because I'm afraid of whatever expression my face is making. I hunt for the nearest bathroom or spare hallway in the opposite direction of Erica, Paul, and Daniel.

You're not even in consideration, I tell myself and try to breathe through it. Reconcile myself to it. My favorite poet, my role model for over a decade, won't be working with me. Instead, Paul and Daniel are considering the people profs always consider. The poets who write MFA poetry—the standard fare, the kind of writing that blends into one voice by the end of a two-year program. The ones who write about salt and ash and smoke and the fucking moon.

I should've known. Always, always, the professors go with Hazel—the one who takes up too much space in workshop, the one who read all the right books in high school and makes me feel like my girliness is incompatible with serious writing. Or they go with Will—the absolute embodiment of a white upper-middle-class straight male writer in his loafers and expensive glasses and *New Yorker* subscription, writing about how Daddy didn't love him enough.

It's that last intrusive thought that causes my mind to jump to *What the fuck is wrong with you?* And what *is* wrong with me? How can I be so insecure? I *know* they're good writers. They'd deserve this. How can I even think such a thing about a man who, against all my better intentions, I'm stupidly in love with?

In love with. The phrase hurtles across my mind like a metal ball in an arcade game, hitting everything it shouldn't hit by accident.

In the bathroom of this hotel, I stare at myself in the mirror and hate what I see. A vision of jealousy, of inferiority. I want Will to get everything he wants because he is perfect and the smartest person I know and because I *know* he'd want the best for me, too. I want him to get the fellowship.

But I also don't.

And it's that tiny, seething undercurrent that I worry could ruin everything.

*   *   *

I don't tell him.

I don't want his pity, first of all. To be any sort of reminder that I can't compete with him. That I'm not on his intellectual level. I play the conversation out in my head—*Of course you're my intellectual equal, what an absurd thing to say*—and I can't explain why the logic doesn't work. I just feel it in my bones. The powers that be looked at me and decided *No, not good enough.* And for my weathered brain, that's more than enough to work with.

I also don't tell him because why would I? We're in this bubble now, some sort of honeymoon feeling, rose-colored glasses, et cetera, et cetera. When I left the bathroom after hearing Daniel and Paul's talk with Erica, I went back to Will and the warmth of his hand across my lower back, our "secret" relationship be damned.

"Just couldn't do it," I'd said about getting the autograph, voice low and gravelly, the threat of crying lodged in my throat. "Didn't feel like the right moment."

He didn't chastise me or say something useless like *It's never the right moment, you just have to do it*. Something my mom would say, or maybe Gen. Something that doesn't make you feel better, just inadequate. Instead he said, "Well, that's just fine. Another time, maybe." As if he trusted my diagnosis and handling of the situation.

It's like when we were in the mountains around Christine's parents' house, and I didn't want to cross the bridge. He didn't push me to do it. He found an easy workaround without making it a huge deal or embarrassing me. Another friend or lover might have—under the guise of pushing me to face my fears and ascend to some higher plane of personhood. But Will understands that having a fear of heights isn't a commentary on how whole I am, how useful, how fun, how wise.

At the same time, I shuddered slightly at his response to me not getting the autograph. His empathy, his *no-big-deal* of it all made me feel worse about my own mean thoughts. Because he has no idea how bitter and jealous some small part of me is. He's smarter than me, *and* he's a better person. Great.

The rest of the day plays out in slow-motion dissociation, like I'm watching myself and him and all of us from above. Will finds small ways to touch me—the gentle guide of a hand on my back, the brush of my forearm, a tap of the knee—and I know people see. I know Hazel sees, too, but it doesn't feel like a trophy, just a consolation prize.

Kacey grins at dinner, sitting across from us. She texts later, You guys look right together.

I try to see it, and I only come up with the conclusion that I've somehow scammed my way into this, too.

We drive back to North Carolina together. Will puts on the new Taylor album without me asking. At a gas station in Virginia, I watch him fill up on gas and he presses my hips into the side of his car just a little bit rough because he knows I like that. He whispers *Come home with me tonight,* and a mountain range of goosebumps erupts across my arms.

So that's why I don't tell him. Because as much as I want the fellowship and the validation that comes with it, I want Will, too.

I'm just not sure how long those two competing thoughts can coexist in my brain.

Chapter Twenty-Two

WHEN WE DRIVE PAST THE WELCOME TO PERRIN sign, I feel the weight of what-next, thick and opaque, looming over us.

"Do you want me to take you home?" Will turns his head to me. His flicker of a glance is quick—he looks straight back at the road again, but even in that single second I feel his want.

Despite everything with the fellowship, I'm no longer in any position to deny this. My body craves it too much.

"Nope."

He keeps driving, one left turn, one long stoplight where I feel every second beat across my body. One right turn, another left. And then we're in front of his apartment.

His small one-bedroom is clean and minimalist with stacks of books and literary journals on the desk next to his bed. The two-person dining set has white candlesticks with long drips of wax—something I might have rolled my eyes at last semester, because it's so on-the-nose for a moody writer. But now I just see Will, trying so hard to create comfort in the art that has only given him anxiety for years.

"Well, this is it," he says, and I drop my duffel on the floor. I already like how my stuff looks next to his.

"I like it." I do a lap around the perimeter. His kitchen is immaculate—cleaner than mine. I open the fridge to find oat milk, sriracha mayo, and a jar of pickled red onions he's presumably made himself.

I feel the heat of his body behind me as I close the fridge door. He snakes his arms around my waist, his palms flat against the planes of my stomach.

"Are you hungry? I can cook us dinner."

I nod. And then he makes us pasta. He salts the water heavily and adds sprinkles of MSG to the tomatoes, which he explains adds more umami flavor, and he brings over little spoons of sauce for me to check the progress. I have no idea what to tell him each time other than that it's good, then better, then maybe best.

"I didn't know you were so good at cooking," I say when he places plates of spaghetti on the table. I take a bite. It's excellent, of course. Smooth and acidic and rich.

He shakes his head. "I don't know how good I am at it, but I like the idea of perfecting something where you can know, pretty obviously, if you've hit the mark or not. It's not like poetry where I feel like I'm writing into a void and I can't ascertain whether my work is good or not."

"Your work is good, I assure you."

"I like that you think so."

I want him to tell me that my work is also good. I want the reassurance that I'm special, that I can make something out of a blank page. That I'm substance over style.

Maybe he doesn't think I need the reassurance, or maybe he doesn't actually believe it. But he doesn't say anything else.

"I think you're going to get the fellowship," I say.

"You don't know that."

Yes, I do. But I don't want to have that conversation. I want to fool him, even just for now, that I could get it, too.

After we clean up the kitchen, it's obvious that we're at the point of the evening where we have to decide what happens next. Should we "put on a movie" and get closer and closer until we fall asleep in each other's arms on the couch? Should we get right to his bed to continue what we started last night? Should I go home altogether?

But that last option doesn't really feel like an option at all.

Will sits down on his bed, removes his glasses, and puts them on his bedside table. I pace and he watches me. I go through his wardrobe, examining his sweaters and carefully folded pants, a small hamper with his Rowan School sweatshirt wadded on top. I have an urge to put it on, to feel him all over me.

"Come here."

I look around as if he could be talking to someone else. A small smile washes over his face when our eyes meet and he leans back on the bed. I'm stalling and he knows it. I'm not sure why. Maybe it's because I don't trust his attraction to me, even though I want it so badly, so I want him to force the issue. To prove that he does want me just as much as I want him.

I walk to the bed and stand in front of him, my thighs leaning into his knees.

"So did you get it out of your system?" His hands skim the sides of my thighs. It feels like he's pulling me down to the floor like quicksand.

"Yep. I'm all good now, thank you."

His hands grip my legs more roughly and he spreads his knees so I can stand in between them. Every emotion he's bottled up flashes across his eyes.

"Really." He winds one hand up the back of my leg, stopping at my ass, pushing me closer so that his face meets my chest. He breathes in deeply and lets out a muffled sigh against me. "The lavender has always driven me crazy." His other hand slinks under my shirt, tracing up my stomach.

"You've had it in poems before." My hands weave through his slightly overgrown hair. "I wasn't sure if they were about me or not."

He coaxes my thighs onto the bed so I'm straddling him and pushes up my shirt so he can press his mouth to my bare stomach.

"All of them are about you," he breathes, trance-like.

"Shut up, half of them are about your dad." I laugh.

He shakes his head and wraps his arms around my waist, flipping us over so I'm on my back, moving my shirt slowly up my chest until I lean up and he takes it off. "Sure, but they're still somehow about you, too."

Will's on his side, head tucked into my neck, his hand meandering across my body. He tiptoes across my collarbone, down the plane of skin between my breasts, across my waist. His hand stops where my legs meet and he slides it under my jeans, but over my underwear, and just cups me.

A deep sigh leaves my body. He dips past my underwear, his middle finger circling all the spots he knows I like until I'm squirming, restless under his hand.

"Take these off," he murmurs, his own breathing shallow as I unbutton the top of his jeans, my hand skating over him, hard already.

I lift my hips to shimmy off my jeans, leaving my underwear on, mesmerized by his deep concentration, how his brows furrow, his jaw tight.

"These too." He tugs the waistband of my underwear. I'm so self-conscious under his focused, magnifying-glass gaze.

"Do it for me."

He smirks, shaking his head. "I like when you do it yourself." He kisses me deeply, on top of me now, one hand propping himself up on the bed, the other trailing down my hip.

"But I like when you're in control." I press my hips up needily to meet his as he hovers over me.

"I know." He kisses my neck, his teeth snagging gently on my earlobe. "So do what I say and take them off."

A violent shiver runs through me. His eye contact is relentless as I hook my fingers into the cotton, pushing them down, down, until they're mid-thigh and he takes it from there. I think he wants me to be equally complicit in this. Unable to take a back seat, unable to be someone that has stuff *done* to them. He wants me to *do*, and he's creating the space for it.

His mouth trails down my chest, tasting my skin. Again, I run my hands through his thick hair, my nails on his scalp, pulling hums deep from his chest. How satisfying it is to turn him animal.

But then he starts sliding down the bed, his head suddenly between my knees.

"What are you gonna do?" I grasp for him, but he's far away, out of my clutches.

He raises an eyebrow as his hands go to my thighs, nudging them apart. "I want to go down on you."

I prop myself up on my elbows. "You don't have to."

He gets a strange look on his face, but his lips curl up. "Because you don't like it?"

I shrug. "Yes. No. I mean, I usually skip it when I've been with guys. I'm too self-conscious." I feel my face redden. I so badly want to be the kind of girl who is sexually confident, who just demands what she wants. But I never have been. I've always put others first. It's a trait that embarrasses me. Intellectually I know better, but something deep within my body keeps me so wound up.

He releases his grip on my thighs and presses his mouth to my kneecap. "You have no reason to be self-conscious. But if you don't like it, we won't do it."

I grimace. "It's just...I just feel like it's probably gross for you? I'm not a diligent shaver and I don't like waxing and I'm not embarrassed but I also acknowledge it's not like the gold standard—"

"Leigh."

Will leans over me, one hand on the bed next to my waist, kissing my neck and collarbone, his other hand skimming across my breast, moving aside the flimsy fabric of my bra.

"You have no idea how little I care about that. It's for me, too. It's not like some sort of sacrifice where I don't get anything out of it."

My pulse races, his words curling around my center to the rhythm of my heartbeat. "What do you get out of it?" It comes out a whisper so low I hardly recognize it as my own.

He breathes in deeply at my neck, as if trying to inhale every molecule of scent on my body. "It's like..." He looks up, dead in my eyes. "...watching you lose control and knowing it's all because of me."

I swallow. "Okay, then."

Placing my hands on his shoulders, I push him down and down until I can no longer reach him. He seems to like this.

I lean back onto the pillow and close my eyes. I feel his hands splay me wide, gentle and soft, and then his mouth is on me. My breath hitches and I try to concentrate on inflating and deflating my belly, willing the muscles to relax, to surrender to the subtle pressure of his mouth.

My back arches on reflex and then an arm across my hips pins me down into the bed, keeping me there while he works. Twisting, circling. I grip the duvet in my tight fists, and his other arm wanders up my stomach to capture a wrist, intertwining our fingers. Heat builds and sweat beads along my hairline. The pressure bubbling up in me is almost too much; I grip his hand with my nails.

"Oh my god."

"Relax. Give in," he murmurs, coming up for a second to bite, then kiss, my hip bone. I close my eyes again, willing myself to feel nothing but the sensation, nothing but Will. To forget expectations.

I exhale a long breath and a wave starts to rise. Every pulse of muscle an incantation. *Will, Will, Will.*

"Good girl." His voice is so low, so rough, that it's almost enough to take me over the edge. It half feels shameful—how desperately I've chased his praise throughout the years—but in this context, I can indulge without the baggage or the guilt. And I know that he knows it.

While his mouth zeroes in with every rise and fall of my chest, he starts to run his hand down my inner thigh, a body part I forgot I even had until he draws attention to it.

I can't think. I am just words on a page and he's the poet, arranging me how he wants, using alliteration, rhyme, white space. Every moan a couplet, every breath a sonnet. He creates tension and I barrel down the blank page until the turn, the final stanza, where he breaks the words open into something more beautiful.

"You're doing so well."

That's what does it. My brain slices into stars and a hymn of vibrations sweeps over my body.

He keeps his mouth on me until it's over, pulling from me every tense-and-release of muscle I have to give until my heartbeat relaxes to its regular cadence. I drag him by the hair back up for a kiss and taste some combination of us in my mouth. We stay like that for a bit—drugging kisses that leave me aching.

"You can give me one more," he whispers. And I do. I flip over onto my belly as he pulls a condom from his nightstand. He strips off his jeans before coming back on the bed, hitching up my hips, pressing into me teasingly slow so I feel every inch. We find a new rhythm as my fingertips dig into the crumpled sheets.

It shouldn't be this good, really. It hasn't been with anyone else.

His release, short and explosive, comes as he groans against my neck. And even when he's done, he winds me up one more time. I give it to him. Just like he said I could.

Chapter Twenty-Three

We lie in bed after, naked, limbs entangled, neither of us wanting to fall asleep. I finally force myself out of Will's arms to shower and when I return, he's reading in bed, his eyes drowsy.

"Hi." I move back toward him. I'm in underwear and one of his giant old T-shirts. He's in boxers now, too, and he does a long, feline stretch that causes his ankles to dangle off the bed.

I nuzzle into him, his arm looped around my shoulders, my head perched on his chest, listening to his steady breathing.

"Leigh."

"Mhmm?"

"We should've done this way earlier."

I laugh into his chest, but there's a pang of something inside me, too. The same feeling I felt at Middlebury, standing outside with him after confessing my feelings, waiting for the other shoe to drop.

It's easier to ignore it.

We drift off, and I reluctantly disentangle myself from his overwhelming body heat. Early the next morning, he rectifies it by pulling me into his chest, his hand skimming the swell of my hip, twisting my shirt in his hand.

"Sleep well?" he murmurs against the back of my neck.

"Mhmm."

He rises to heat the kettle to make us tea, his standard Earl Grey, and brings the steaming mugs into bed. We prop the pillows against the headboard and take slow sips. It scares me how normal this already feels, how comfortable and domestic we could be.

My phone buzzes, and my dad's face lights up on the screen. I sigh into Will's shoulder.

"Do you have to take it?"

"Yes, because if I don't, the Perrin Fire Department will be here in an hour to confirm I'm alive. He's done it before, and he'll do it again."

Will laughs as I roll out of bed and walk to the bathroom for privacy. I answer the phone on its last ring.

"Hi, Dad."

"Hey, honey. Did I wake you?"

"No, no, I was just reading in bed." In the mirror, I notice a faint hickey along my collarbone.

"I wanted to ask when your reading was. I'm just planning my calendar for the next month, and I want to make sure we can go."

"Who's *we*?"

He laughs as if I've made a joke. "Me and your mother, of course."

"Like *together*?"

"Yes! We want to come down together. Counseling's been good for us. Don't get me wrong, it's not like everything's solved, but we're on a good trajectory now. I'll spare you the details— Mom said you didn't want to hear them—but yes, we'll be traveling together and we both want nothing more than to see our favorite daughter blow everyone away with her genius."

Even before AWP, I'd been dreading the First-Year Reading Series, which is happening two weeks from now. Now that I know I'm not a front-runner for the fellowship, it feels like too much is riding on that one single night. But for my parents to be there together, on their way to working things out? It's the friendly audience I desperately need.

I give him the date and Dad says he'll—they'll—be there. By the time he hangs up, I'm art-directing the family photo we'll take at the end of the reading. Them flanking me on either side, color-coordinated and grinning. A Leigh sandwich.

I downright skip back into Will's bedroom.

"Do you want to go to the farmers market with me?" he asks from bed. My face must freeze up because he continues. "I go most Saturday mornings. They have a really nice cheese booth and—"

As he carries on naming the local farms he usually buys from, the promise of the day twists around my windpipe. It sounds delightful and *sweet* and couple-y and that's, somehow, what makes it feel like a danger zone. Yes, clearly we've begun the casual sleeping-together phase of our . . . friendship . . . but I'm still trying to reconcile the competing parts of my body and brain. Going to farmers markets together is what bona fide defined-the-relationship couples do. Which we are not. And cannot be. I still haven't gotten over how quickly he pulled back after Halloween, how firmly he broke it off (again) at Thanksgiving. My body's been taught that this isn't a sure thing, that every step forward comes with two steps back, no matter how much either of us wants the other.

I'm not sure if he senses my hesitation or realizes for himself what a dangerous game we're playing, but he backtracks. "Of course, we just got back from a trip and I totally understand if you need to unpack and relax—"

And because, unfortunately, I am me, I interject, "No, let's go. I, uh, am out of…cucumbers." Naming, like an idiot, the first vegetable I can think of. "And I needed to go to the grocery store anyway. So sure, I can come with you to the market instead. It's really good for the environment if we combine our errand trips together. Less, uh, driving."

"But," Will pauses, sounding worried, "cucumbers aren't in season. So the farmers market won't have them. If you need them, I can drive you to the store after…?"

"Oh, wait, sorry, I didn't mean cucumber. I meant, uh, *squash*?"

Will nods. "Yes, great, they will have a lot of squash."

"Excellent!" I clap my hands together. "Let's tackle those errands!"

* * *

Our very casual, just-classmates Saturday goes like this:

Will drives me back to my apartment to set down my duffel bag and change clothes. He waits in the car while I put on an outfit that I calculate to be equal parts charming and casual.

At the farmers market, I watch Will buy goat cheese, Swiss chard, and honey, while he attempts to help me sort through all the squash by asking what I plan on making with it. I lie about a salad and so we go with butternut.

He takes me to the grocery store for cucumber anyway because he refuses to believe I don't actually need it.

We end up back at his place, unwilling to separate after twenty-four hours together, and decide we can sit together writing.

Out of the corner of my eye, curled up on his couch with my computer on my lap, I watch him at the table. His brows are furrowed, making sharp creases that stay even when he releases them. He types a sentence, then closes his eyes as if in pain. I hear the tap-tap-tap-tap of the backspace key.

He carries on like that for a while. A flurry of keys, the angry backspace. A symphony only a stressed-out writer could understand.

My eyes catch on his Rowan sweatshirt again, visible through the open doors of his closet. I close my eyes and let my mind fill with images. Just something to work with on a page. I begin typing phrases in a Word doc.

> Chapped lips
> Blazer boys
> Plaid skirt girls
> The sounds of a pep rally

It's not much. My mind flits to the possibility of writing in the voice of Rory Gilmore. A poem taking place in high school. Coming of age.

> ~~The sounds of a pep rally~~
> ~~Cheerleaders~~
> ~~Loud cheering~~
> Cracked-voice cheers

Yes, that one. Nice. Specific. I like the prickliness of *crah* and *ch* in my mouth, how it conveys being on the edge of adulthood. I start moving phrases around, compiling couplets that sound like this:

She inhales root beer Chapstick
to cracked-voice cheers

"I think it's illegal to look that happy when you're writing a poem."

I'm broken out of my reverie by Will's voice, light and loose.

"This is hardly a poem. I'm just jotting down random things. Maybe it'll become a poem."

He stands up from his chair and walks behind the couch, close, his heat against my shoulder blades.

I lower my screen. "It's too embarrassing. You can see the finished thing in workshop at some point."

His mouth is on my neck when he says, "Show me."

"There's nothing to see. It's just the inside of my brain. I'm blabbering on the page."

"The inside of your brain is not *nothing*." His hand touches the screen and I comply, releasing my grip and letting him see.

It's not much. Just couplets that don't fit together yet.

His hands are on either side of me, caging me in from behind, and he takes the cursor and highlights a few in the middle.

She inhales root beer Chapstick
to cracked-voice cheers

off the lacrosse captain, smirking
like the rest of the needy

blazer boys. She just wants
to be friends

"This is interesting." He rests his chin on top of my head. I feel the vibration of his voice with every word. "I like the darkness here, even though none of the words, at face value, are dark. It's all between the lines, which is compelling. Feels like something hiding underneath. Maybe something darker. But also maybe something brighter, depending on where you want to go with it."

I tilt my head up to face him. "You're good at that. At figuring out what I'm doing before I even know. You're always the best commenter in workshop."

He releases my computer and walks back to the table. "I don't know about that."

"You are. Everyone else is so prescriptive. They want to, like, impose what *they* would do to a poem. You provide options. You're like the perfect reader."

The candle's light dances in the reflection off his glasses. His face droops when he turns to look at his own work.

"What are you writing about?" I ask.

"An elegy. But it's shit. Every word I come up with looks wrong on the page. Why do we do this to ourselves? Poetry?" He takes his glasses off and puts his hands over his temples.

Now it's my turn to stand up. I close the screen of his laptop and sit on his lap.

"We do it because we love it," I whisper.

He captures my lips in a kiss, then pulls back, his finger tracing my cheek until I open my eyes.

"Write your poem in your own voice. Don't do a fictional character this time."

My arms tense around his shoulders. "I'll leave that to the pros."

He chuckles and stands up, carefully depositing me on the floor. He goes to take a book off his bookshelf and hands it to me.

"'*Death Is a Peach We Refuse to Eat.*'" I read aloud the title of the slim poetry collection. "Sounds like a feel-good book for the bedside table."

"I think you'd like it. Every poem is like a meditation on the poet's phobias. Death, spiders, social events, whatever. He's into wordplay like you and he does a lot of modern pop-culture references, but it still has this vulnerable side that's really moving."

I flip to the back. The author photo is of a scraggly-haired man with gaunt cheeks and thick eyebrows, his lips thin and straight, not a smile in sight. I read his bio, and it's filled with the kind of keywords that would make Hazel's mouth water. *Ruth Lilly Poetry Prize, a Stegner fellow at Stanford University, previously seen in* Kenyon Review, American Poetry Review, and on and on. I know from his face that this man would've rather gagged himself with a spoon than gone to a Phi Psi party in neon polyester— unironically *or* ironically.

"Sounds interesting." I'm sure to Will it's a good book. But to me, it looks like the kind of poetry that makes me feel dumb. Totally inaccessible, just men complaining about man things—

"Go ahead—you take it."

"What?"

"I really think you'll like it," he says again, and it's with such earnestness that I already know my response. "And then hey, we can discuss." He smiles, running his hand across my back.

"Yeah, okay." I offer a smile and set the book next to my purse. "Thanks."

He scoops me back into his arms and we curl up on the couch together.

"Have you picked poems for the reading series?" he asks.

"I have a few options. Guess I still have some time. Have you? Decided?"

"Yeah." He looks off into the distance instead of at me. "They're two of the ones I submitted. For the fellowship."

"Ah."

"Yeah."

"It's funny you think you're going to get that." I grin, and for a second, I almost forget Daniel's words in my head. Will makes it so easy to forget.

He chuckles, then pulls me into his chest. "I usually get what I want." His voice, low and gravelly, in my ear, causes my throat to dry.

"Oh, yeah? I seem to remember you once saying that historically that hasn't been the case."

"I've turned over a new leaf."

"We'll see." I shrug him off, a transparent ploy to make him do what he does next.

He laughs and sharply draws me back into him. "Yeah, we will."

And in the dimming light of late afternoon, he shows me—how it feels, looks, tastes—when he gets what he wants.

* * *

We get into a routine. Sometimes, we go to my place, but more often his. I like all his books, how the entire place smells like him, how he cooks for me, and I feel like I've been plucked from my old, boring existence into a new role as his muse.

"Want to go to the store? I was thinking salmon for dinner," he says one night, as if I've been his wife for ten years. It's a thought that's both scary and delicious, the way it's taken root in my stomach like a weed.

I'm horizontal on his couch, my legs leaning off the arm, my laptop on my chest. None of the poems I've tentatively decided on for the reading series feel like they're working anymore. I stare at a Word doc of "Taylor Swift Sleeps with Someone New for the First Time," and the stream of couplets mocks me in its refusal to sound exactly how I want it to in my head. I've been tinkering with the same three stanzas for the last ten minutes. This followed, of course, twenty silent minutes spent reading old Hazel poems on my phone, trying to decipher what Paul and Daniel see in her over me—and how I can replicate it in my own work.

Here is where I start to build: lips trail
    kisses like a crescendo saved for later, like tracing

zig-zags on a steamed-up car's misty window
    and *no, not yet* as he tugs the hem of my dress

as I search for a chorus in his freckles

"Yes . . . let's," I murmur. I delete the last line of the poem with a huff and an eyeroll that's solely for myself. Hazel would never work with this subject matter, to start.

Will's in front of me now, kneeling next to the couch so we're at eye level. "Keep writing." He presses a light kiss to my temple. "I'll go, you stay."

"You sure?" I turn my head to face him. "I can be done soon."

He shakes his head and returns to his full height. "You're in the zone. Keep going and I'll be back in like forty-five."

"Thank you." I run my hand up his thigh as he stands over me.

When he's gone, I put my laptop to the side and stand up to stretch my legs. No good comes from staring at one poem for too long.

I pace the room, walk to his desk in the far right corner, see papers from workshop scattered over every inch. I think back to my Taylor Swift poem as I run my fingers over his words.

Forget Hazel. What would Will do?

Because whatever he's doing is working. Paul loves him, Daniel loves him, Erica's about to love him. Is it just our difference in subject matter? Is it because his poems deal with death, the ultimate obsession of all the great male poets before him? Or is there something happening on the line level—some facility with language he and Hazel have that's out of my grasp?

I pick up one of the poems on top, from workshop a month ago: "The Weekend Wake." It's a thin block stanza now covered in Will's obsessive notes, taken during class as we all talked about it. He managed to create a subtle internal rhyme that appears as a call-and-response in every other line, a faint heartbeat that fades as the poem ends.

It's the kind of finesse I can't even dream of.

I re-read two, three more of his pieces. They're better now than when I first saw them in workshop. They've had a chance to fester under my skin.

I walk back to the couch, flop down, and re-open my laptop, scanning my Taylor poem with fresh eyes. The detail, the aural satisfaction of words that ring into each other like wind chimes in rain—I have that, too. Just because two old guys love Will's poems doesn't mean Erica will. And doesn't Erica ultimately pick who she works with? Daniel and Paul's input surely matters, but I can't imagine they can override her in this decision.

It feels like a revelation. Like I could still be in the running. Who's to say next week's reading can't change things? Who knows what could happen when Erica hears *my* words out loud?

More optimistic now, I go back to Will's desk to arrange his poems as I found them. My eyes snag on a folder partially hidden under the mess. *OLD POEMS*, a Post-it note reads in his precise cursive, stuck to the front.

It's hardly snooping. I'm confident he'd show me, though bashfully, if I asked. Plus, a part of me wants to find the original version of "In a Cleveland Parking Lot, I Break Down," the one he tore out of my grasp at Middlebury. I want to read it in peace without his red-cheeked color commentary over my shoulder.

I flip through the poems, some dated from when he was in college, others not, a few dotted with stains, as if they've been man-handled into different backpacks over the years. The parking lot poem is nowhere to be found. But the last piece in the folder piques my interest. It's "Invisible Summer," the one Will mentioned in the car to AWP. The only one his dad ever praised. It's dated his senior year of Middlebury. Scrawls of messy blue ink drift between the lines, barely readable. It's reminiscent of my dad's illegible hand-writing. Definitely not Will's. The only thing I can make out is *Very effective*, underlined twice at the bottom.

I turn around the room, as if expecting Will to burst through the door. It feels too intimate to read this poem, to try to glean insight into his relationship with his dad back when Will's father was alive. So I scan just the first line. But as with every Will poem, you *can't* just read one line. He grips you by the throat and refuses to let go.

> What's between us—crushed
> juice like a dew-slick plum
> in high summer, my chin streaked
>
> with words unsaid, sickly
> sweet and sticky. How you let it
> dry there, how every word you said

There's more. A lot more. But there's something weirdly familiar about it, too, like I've seen this image before, of the plum. It feels like some brilliant classic literature reference, some callout I'm not well read enough to pick up on.

It's for sure the kind of thing MFA fellowship winners would know.

I take the poem back to my computer and Google "crushed juice like a dew-slick plum in high summer," expecting a Spark-Notes analysis of some Mark Twain image to be the first hit.

But it's not. The first hit is from the archive of a now-defunct online literary magazine, *Anathema*, dated several months before Will dated his poem.

I remember *Anathema*. It was one of the few poetry journals I read in college. It felt like they published more interesting, experimental work than the usual university journals, which went with whatever got the establishment's stamp of approval.

I stare at the door again. Have twenty minutes passed since Will left, or is it thirty?

There's no need to click the link. My stomach seizes up, my hands sweaty. Somewhere, in a distant shadow of my brain, I feel like I already know.

Don't click it. Don't click it. Don't click it.

But I do, and a long poem cut into three-line stanzas fills the page. It's called "The Summer We Stopped Talking" by Sophie Wright. There's a black-and-white picture of her and her messy bun next to her name; she's smiling into the camera in front of a backdrop of ivy. I start reading:

> The last time we spoke was crushed
> juice, like a dew-slick plum in the heat
> of summer, my chin streaked
>
> with words unsaid, sickly sweet
> and sticky, and you let it
> dry there, every word, every syllable

The poem continues in the same vein. A bit messy and unwieldy, snagging with *S*'s, its alliteration slinking menacingly down the page, like a snake. Like a repeated conversation between parent and child that never quite stuck. It's good.

It's the same poem as Will's.

I read both poems several times. I come up with a litany of reasons for why this could've happened. A hilarious coincidence. Maybe Will and Sophie watched the same shows, read the same books. It'd make sense then, why they were drawn to the same images.

Or maybe Sophie's parent sucked in the exact same way as Will's dad did, and there was no other way to describe the feeling.

I grow delirious with options and ideas, alternatives to explain why the smartest poet in the cohort—the best writer I know—would blatantly plagiarize another person's work.

But there's no good explanation.

The rest of the night is a blur: How I close the link, delete my computer's history from today. How I tuck "Invisible Summer" back into the folder, slip it under the explosion of paper on Will's desk. How, when we eat ice cream later, his thumb swipes over the corner of my lip to catch a sickly sweet drip; how, when we curl up on the couch to watch TV, his chin tightens, deep in thought.

But mostly, what I think about are all the words left unsaid. Unnerving and sour and sticky.

Chapter Twenty-Four

"HAVE YOU DECIDED WHAT YOU'RE going to do, Leigh?"

"What?" I jolt and look up at Hazel staring at me, apparently so interested in what I'm going to say that she's leaning far over the high table at Pete's, where the whole cohort has gathered after Thursday workshop.

"For tomorrow. Which poems are you reading?"

Oh. I watch Will; he's ordering a drink at the bar, his hip slumped against a stool, shoulders loose and tired. He looks more fragile somehow, breakable in a way that's always, maybe, been there. I just never picked up on it, even at Middlebury, when he was feeling so low.

Over the last week, I've had this reoccurring dream. I walk into Daniel's office. I bring out an exquisitely prepared PowerPoint—the case against William Langford getting the fellowship. I show him "Invisible Summer" and "The Summer We Stopped Talking," the copied lines highlighted yellow. Three-quarters of the page is yellow. Daniel's jaw drops and Erica appears out of nowhere, as dream characters are wont to do, and bestows upon me a golden plastic crown. The second I pick it up, it splinters, shattering with even the smallest pressure of my fingers. And then I projectile-vomit in front of all of them, a Leigh Simon dream signature.

I always wake up in a cold sweat, unable to fully look at Will sleeping next to me.

I don't even care that he plagiarized—I'm confident he had a good reason. I know he had a rough time in college. Maybe he was stressed, and an innocent homage went too far. Maybe he'd read the poem just before writing, Sophie's words sticking in his mind. It was just a class assignment, never published, a one-off lapse in judgment that hurt no one but himself. He was clearly disturbed when his dad showed it to a colleague.

And I certainly don't think he made a habit of plagiarizing, either—I googled a bunch of phrases from poems he's submitted to workshop, and nothing else came up.

So I already forgive him. But I haven't brought it up. It'd be shitty of me, to confront him with something he's surely ashamed of, right before the reading series, in which his performance could clinch the fellowship he wants so badly. I still think he's an excellent writer—a *natural*—probably the best in the cohort, regardless of what he did when he was twenty-two years old.

What I resent, though, is the *knowing*, the power it gives me. It's like I don't fully trust myself with this information.

"I'm reading one of my Taylor Swift poems and then I think the One Direction poem we workshopped a few months ago," I say as Will returns to his seat across from me with a beer.

Hazel nods with feigned interest. "Oh, those are fun. What about you, William?"

He shrugs, swirling the foam around in his beer. "One of the funeral series and then the Oberlin poem."

"Great picks. Those are some of my favorites of yours," Hazel says, and I internally roll my eyes. At least I think it's internal—until Will captures my foot between his under the table and squeezes.

"I am nervous as fuck about this reading." Houston slides into the seat next to Will. "Jeremiah Brandon is going to laugh me off the stage. If anyone has a Xanax prescription, now would be the time to speak up."

"You're going to do great, don't worry," I say. "You have an amazing voice."

"But is it the voice of a *winner*? Too much is riding on this. My IBS has never been worse." Houston loops his arm around Will's shoulder and pulls him into his side. "This guy here, though. Talk about the voice of a winner. Sultry, deep. I don't know how you ladies handle workshop with him."

I choke on my beer and look at Hazel, then at Will, who shakes his head, smirking. We haven't explicitly "announced" this . . . new stage of our relationship, because we're not celebrities and we don't presume that other people care. But clearly people know. Will has made no effort to not stand close to me in public. Kacey can't stop looking at us every time we're all together.

"This guy's not nervous at all." Houston slaps Will on the bicep.

Will takes a long sip of beer. "It's just a reading."

"A reading that the fellowship could ride on."

And my future career and happiness.

But Will just shrugs again, and it's a tiny bit annoying that he's not freaking out like I am. I suppose it's the classic confidence of the white, straight literary man. Must be nice.

I could take all that away, the dark part of my brain taunts.

But I won't. And I don't need to. I'm going to win this fellow-ship fair and square.

*   *   *

I haven't been with my parents in the same room together since the separation. When it happened, I was in Boston, they were in Cleveland, and it's not like you go home for a separation. It's not Christmas.

I wouldn't have wanted to be there, anyway. It's easier to pretend nothing is happening when you're working long hours in Boston rather than flying home to create a new normal you never asked for.

But I'm genuinely excited when my phone lights up with a text from my dad: Here in your parking lot! Getting to hang out with Mom and Dad as a full family couldn't have come at a better time. I run out of the building and see their car with the Ohio plate. My mom emerges from the driver's side and pulls me into a tight hug.

"How's my favorite daughter doing?" she asks, holding me close.

My dad steps out of the car, too, and waits for Mom to release me before hugging me himself. Back in the day, they'd dive into a shared hug, squeezing me in the middle. I guess it makes sense that even though they're mending things, they need to baby-step back to normalcy. These days, I'll take what I can get.

"How was the drive?"

They exchange a look, as if negotiating who should speak first.

"Good," my mom says. "But baby, I need to take some calls— I promised these patients I'd get back to them. Okay if I do that before dinner? I was going to check in to the hotel, anyway, so you guys should catch up without me and I'll join later."

It's her day off, but classic Mom behavior that she's working through it.

"Yes, of course."

And then she leaves me alone with Dad. I take him on a brief walking tour of campus, about which he has a million questions. I show him the main quad, overflowing with students tanning on a grassy knoll dubbed The Beach. I show him the place with the good coffee, the stately marble steps of Gilman Hall.

An hour in, I get a text from Will: How are the parents?

I text back: Mom went to hotel to work but I'm showing my dad all Perrin's hot spots. Writing Center is next.

He's quick with the reply: Will you show him the first desk to the right?

That's between you, me, and Perrin's night security.

"Who are you texting?" I look up at my dad, who has a knowing grin on his face. "It's a boy, right?"

"Maybe."

"Boyfriend?"

My brain jolts at the word. I shake my head. "No. I don't know."

"Is he coming to dinner with us? Or is he with his own family tonight?"

"Oh, um." I stare at my phone. "I didn't invite him...thought it might be too weird. But no, his family didn't come down."

Not that he invited his mom. He was dead set against it. "I'm not going to ask her to travel all that way to listen to five minutes of my poetry" was all he said.

I didn't argue. In the last week, Will has been strangely detached about the fellowship, and I can't tell if it's because he's so calm and confident it'll go great for him or because he's hiding the same kind of nervousness I am.

Dad shakes his head. "Invite him! That could be good, actually." He says the last sentence more to himself.

It's not that I don't want my parents to meet Will. I'm pretty sure they'll like him. But I worry that I'm turning this into something it's not. Will and I have clearly gotten over the hump of being too scared to touch each other. But that doesn't mean he's in this for the long haul.

I text him, though. I want him with me, despite my self-preservation instincts.

Would you like to come to dinner with us tonight?

He responds in seconds: Would love to.

*   *   *

My dad sits next to my mom, and I sit next to Will, and it's like a bizarre double date that no one asked for. I can read Will's body language easily—he's not good at playing a role like I am, and it's obvious from his back-and-forth gaze that he's uncomfortable. The only other boy I've ever introduced my parents to was Andrew from college, and he was so used to firm handshakes at networking parties with his famous editor dad that meeting two Ohioans who went in-state for college was small potatoes. By contrast, Will sits up pin-straight and keeps adjusting where he puts his hands: knotted in his lap, palms on the table, playing with his chopsticks.

The night started out fine—Dad and I drove to the hotel downtown to pick up Mom, who met us outside on the curb. Then we picked up Will to go to the restaurant, a small vegetarian Vietnamese bistro near campus. When he shook their hands, my stomach pinched. It didn't feel like this when they met Andrew. This felt heavier. More significant.

Now, though, my parents are being themselves—except dialed up 200 percent, with my mom stiff and aloof and my dad rambling and neurotic. I'm like a cruise director, shuffling us between palatable conversational topics, constantly checking in and making sure everyone's happy. I'd like to relax before I try to convince Paul, Daniel, and Erica that *I'm* the better choice for the fellowship than the man next to me, but it feels like if I let my guard down, everything will become awkward, fast.

"So the Langfords," my dad goes. "Doesn't ring a bell, but it's been ages, of course. Though, god, Leigh, it feels like you were at Rowan just yesterday. Weren't *those* the days! I remember—"

"Will was the grade above me, so we didn't have much interaction back then. But remember how I got published in Rowan's lit journal junior year? Will was the editor." I turn to look at Will. "God, that was so long ago, I doubt you remember that."

Will smiles. "I remember."

Dad nods with way too much enthusiasm. "Oh, right! She was *so* excited. And then I remember she got into that creative writing class the semester after and couldn't stop talking about it. We always knew Leigh would be some sort of writer. She was such a reader. We took her to all the *Twilight* book launch parties at this little bookstore in Hudson, and the *outfits*—"

"Oh my god, Dad." I flush, but Will just laughs, his shoulders loosening.

"I'm sure it was the same in your household, huh? Overloaded bookshelves, dragging your parents to Power of the Pen competitions?"

The bookshelves and writing competition trophies? Yes. But I know for sure Will's dinner conversations with his parents were nothing like ours.

Will just offers a small nod.

"So are your parents still on Coventry Road?" my dad asks. We had gone over where Will grew up in the car—about a twenty-minute drive from where I did, in the same city as Rowan.

Parents. I feel my throat tighten at the plural. I didn't think to warn Mom and Dad beforehand, but then again, I'm not sure of the etiquette for people whose parent has died. Is it best to conveniently just never bring them up?

"My dad, uh, passed." I look down at my food. "My mom moved to Dayton, actually. A few months ago. We have family down there."

"Sorry to hear about your dad," my dad says. Will nods and then I can breathe again.

"What does your mom do?" my mom asks in her first actual question of the night.

"Consulting for high school and college admissions departments, so she can really work from anywhere, which is why she moved. Most of her work is done remotely these days, or sometimes she'll travel to different schools. And my dad was a professor at Oberlin. He taught English."

"So it runs in the family!" Dad fidgets with his chopsticks.

"I guess so." Will smiles.

We start discussing school and once again Dad takes the conversational reins. My mom supplies just *mhmms* and nods. She's never been amazingly socially acute, but I still figured she'd be curious about the guy I'm introducing them to, with or without the boyfriend label.

Eventually, Will leaves to go to the bathroom, though I plead with my eyes for him to stay and not leave me with them.

Once he's out of ear range, I say to Mom, "Do you... not like him?"

She frowns. "What? Why would you say that? He's adorable. Very nice."

"You just seem tense." I look behind me toward the bathroom.

My dad lifts his wrist to look at his watch. "What time do you think we should leave? I looked it up on Google Maps, but the parking situation seems really tricky, and I'm worried we won't get a spot and won't be able to sit together—"

"You good, Dad?" I really don't need his anxiety exacerbating mine before this reading, so I can't help but ask.

He's a deer in headlights. My mom tenses her shoulders.

"Honey, can you pass me the soy—" she starts.

"I'm sorry, but I can't just sit here like this and pretend," my dad says. "Leigh, sweetie, we have to tell you something."

My mom glares at him. "What the fuck, Jeff. You can't be uncomfortable for two seconds, can you?"

"We can't just act like nothing is happening for the sake of decorum. If it were up to you, we probably wouldn't tell her at all."

"What? Tell me what?"

My mom raises her eyebrows at my dad, who grimaces. "The divorce has finalized."

It's like a brick hitting my face. We're all silent, letting the chatter of the restaurant fill in the gaps among us. I press my tongue to the roof of my mouth, waiting for a punch line that never comes.

"But you told me counseling was going well," I hear myself say. "You drove down here together. You're staying in a hotel together. I thought the separation was . . . off."

"We're staying in separate rooms," Dad says, voice low, as my mom shakes her head, rolling her eyes.

"We wanted to tell you together," she says. "I suggested a call next weekend. Not this weekend, for obvious reasons. But some of us can't read the room, it seems."

Now my dad rolls *his* eyes. "Anna."

"It's fine," I cut in. It's not fine, not even a little, but seeing them fight over this is just going to make me more upset. "Now everyone knows and everything is great. Congratulations on the big news."

We sit there in silence. I take a sip of my water every ten seconds, just for something to do, an excuse not to talk or engage. Will comes back, and I feel even more pressure to perform a sense of normalcy.

He puts his hand on my thigh underneath the table, but I move it off. My legs feel heavy enough. I hunch my shoulders and cross my arms, shrinking myself in the hope of disappearing.

We carry on as if nothing's happened, but my mom's gaze is somehow even colder, my dad's needier, guiltier. He keeps the conversation afloat, flitting from topic to topic, until we've run out of reasons to keep sitting there. The reading starts soon enough. When I stand up from the table, my limbs feel stiff, my heartbeat quick.

When we go back to the car to drive to the bookstore, Will opens the door for me and I get in without looking at him. For the fifteen-minute ride, my dad blabbers on about global warming and potholes and the hotel's air-conditioning. I say *mhmm* and *right* every ten seconds like my life depends on it. My mom is silent, and poor Will sits there like he has no idea what to do with any of this, which, of course he doesn't.

"Was a pleasure to have dinner with you, Will," my dad says, as we jump out of the car at the bookstore.

"Thanks so much for inviting me along."

"See you inside," I say to Mom as she goes to park.

Will, Dad, and I funnel into the store, my spine tenser than it's ever been, like only a carefully placed hammer could crack it. Two days ago, my biggest concern was the fellowship. Two hours ago, how I'd introduce Will to my parents. But now, it's managing the unruly emotions of my body. The last time I felt the same swirl of anxiety, dissociation, and guilt was in a Boston bathroom stall, taking deep breaths against the door after I'd bombed a client meeting. Then, at least, I could go home to my apartment.

Now I'm not sure where home really is.

Chapter Twenty-Five

♡

ABOUT A MONTH AGO, BEFORE AWP, I had a pretty good idea how my First-Year Reading would go.

I'd picked out the perfect outfit—a chic wrap dress, with Hazel-inspired loafers and chunky earrings, that made me feel like a sexy English professor. I knew exactly which poems I'd be reading: the two best I'd submitted in my fellowship application, "The Only Good Straight Men Are in One Direction" and "Taylor Swift Sleeps with Someone New for the First Time," fun, punchy pieces with bits of humor straight out of the Erica Go playbook. People would laugh and be delighted; it would be a bright moment of playfulness and accessibility amid a lineup of otherwise bleak, remote poetry.

My gut tells me that none of this is about to happen.

When we enter the bookstore, at least forty folding chairs have been set up in front of a podium and microphone. I recognize most people here—all the second-years, the first-years, faculty (including Erica, in bright-red lipstick), and a scattering of parents. Christine's sister, putting her hand over her mouth and giggling into Christine's ear. A tall Black woman who is clearly

Athena's mom sits in front. A graying mom and dad, flanking Morris, laugh in the corner.

A pang nestles deep in my stomach.

Will's hand on my waist brings me back. "Good?" he murmurs against my neck.

My mom's scouting for seats. "Yeah." I force a smile. He's unconvinced, I know it, by the way he glances at me a second too long.

My dad sits on my left, my mom on my right. Will goes over to Morris's family, who've saved him a seat, and shakes their hands. Hearty laughter blooms from Morris's mom.

Once the chairs are filled, Daniel Kitchener approaches the podium. His deep voice reverberates in the microphone, filling the small space.

"What a thrill to introduce tonight's talents," he says after welcoming everyone. "We're running a tight ship this evening, with each of our ten writers getting five minutes to share just a snippet of what they've been working on this year. I know I speak for the entire faculty when I say I am constantly astonished by our MFA students. Their curiosity to push boundaries, to try something unexpected. To evolve a voice that is singularly their own."

Erica's in the front row, next to Jeremiah Brandon. I can see her profile from my seat. I don't believe in a higher power, but I find myself trying to telepathically signal to her or the universe that that singular voice Daniel speaks of is *mine*. All I need to do is go up there, read my work, and she'll see I bring the same deftness with language as Hazel or Will, but my work is more fun, brighter, more like hers.

My breath wavers as I picture Paul, Daniel, and Erica discussing it afterward. *I'd like to propose Leigh for the fellowship, actually,* Erica will say. *She deserves this, don't you think?*

The first writer up is Wiebke, and then we alternate: poetry, fiction, poetry, fiction, with me in the middle and Will second to last. Each slot is only five minutes, a speck of time.

With just two people before me, my whole body is shaking. I will myself to stop and my leg jiggles, almost imperceptibly, but I feel it nonetheless—the embarrassing lack of control I have over my own body and its secret impulses. I wish Will had sat next to me instead of my parents. I want him to still me, like he always does.

Hazel's up, in a white tee layered under a black slip dress, looking cool and confident as she grabs the microphone to adjust to her height, then keeps holding it, like she's a pop star at a music festival. She reads two poems, neither of which I recognize from class—"Who I Am in Chinatown" and "I Teach a White Boy to Hike Up a Mountain." She reads them like steady drumbeats; they build to a crescendo. I don't know if I take a breath during one of them at all. I wonder suddenly if I've misunderstood Hazel—been distracted by her intense workshop persona, intimidated by her already-long list of published poems, threatened by her crush on Will.

Because her poems? They're fucking great. And based off the rapturous applause when she finishes, everyone else thinks so, too.

"Wouldn't want to follow *that*," Penelope, who's in front of me, whispers to another second-year. My spine goes rigid and I glance over at Will in the corner, smiling and clapping like everyone else.

Hazel returns to her chair next to two people who are surely her parents. They sandwich her on either side, her mom whispering something that makes Hazel beam. Her parents look at each other with proud smiles. *We did that. We made that*, they're probably saying, in that no-words connection partners seem to have after decades together.

The three of them look like a unit. A small, meaningful community of love.

Christine's up next, then me. My skin feels too hot for my body. My lungs too small, my heart too heavy. I can't concentrate on a single word Christine is saying. All I hear is some jumbled pattern of sounds, as if from a distance. Somewhere very far away.

People start clapping—Christine must be done—and I raise my hands, but I can't put them together, as if they're opposing ends of a magnet.

Hazel's dad drapes his arm over his daughter's chair, stroking the side of his wife's shoulder with the tips of his fingers. My mom's hands are grasped rigidly, my dad's flat on his knees, his knuckles white. That's when I notice neither of them is wearing their wedding ring.

"And next we have Leigh Simon," Daniel announces, and the room quiets.

Those words I hear. But they do nothing to me—I feel no jittery urge to stand up and get the whole thing over with, no proud *It's showtime!* inner voice. My legs aren't prepared to hold the weight of this, the feeling of muscles seizing within my body, the drowning lull of my brain.

"Honey?" My dad presses his hand to my shoulder, and I know I've waited too long. This is officially weird. I catch a wide-eyed look between Hazel and Christine, Daniel's confused gaze.

"I can't" is what I come up with, the only two syllables I can make my mouth form as I get up from my seat and run out of the bookstore.

* * *

My parents find me first, unfortunately. I've commandeered a lone bench across the street, looking into the bookstore's windows. The group of teenage boys sitting here scampered the second they saw me, the runs of mascara and nervous sweat across my face.

"What happened?" My mom puts the back of her hand over my forehead before I can answer.

"I'm not sick." I brush her off and stare at the ground, willing away tears. "I just couldn't."

"You know, you didn't eat much at dinner. I get low blood sugar if I skip a meal," my dad says. He sits next to me and drapes an arm over my shoulders. "What if we go back in and ask if you can read at the end? I'm sure that wouldn't be a problem, everyone wants to hear your poems—"

"What happened after I ran out?" I interrupt. I can't see much through the bookstore windows from across the street, just some front bookshelves. Part of me wants to take the opportunity to concoct some sort of medical emergency, whatever will seem least embarrassing.

Leigh Simon, failing so miserably at something as insignificant as a poetry reading. If I wasn't already out of the running for the fellowship, I definitely am now.

"We don't really know. Your mother told everyone you had a migraine and that they shouldn't worry because you get them all the time. That was about a minute ago. And now, we're here."

It's jarring how I have no sense of time. It feels like I've been out here alone for an hour, not minutes.

"Thanks," I say to my mom, who just nods.

We sit quietly on the bench. I half expect Will to come barreling out of the store, wild-eyed and looking for me, but he doesn't. It feels like a cut, revealing some sliver of loneliness that I've tried to bandage over and over again.

"I knew it was a mistake to tell her at dinner," my mom says in a low voice.

My dad scoffs. "If it were up to you, she wouldn't know at all. You'd rather keep everyone in the dark about how you're feeling, including me, pushing everyone away, snipping at anyone who tries to intervene—"

"Why did you marry each other?" I snap. "Why did you have me? How did it take twenty-seven years for you to realize you were so horribly incompatible?"

My dad's mouth drops.

My mom purses her lips. "Honey," she says.

I stand to face them, my vision glassy.

"I thought you were going to try. I thought you were going to therapy to make this *work*, because both of you wanted to still be a family with me. Did you try? Wasn't I worth trying for?" The words come out like broken rocks, syllables snagging on one another, a pummel of unsaid words I'd wrapped up too tightly in my brain.

"Baby," my dad says. "Of *course* you're worth trying for. How could you ever imply—"

"*She* implied," I hiss, pointing to my mom. "She implied when she said I was just like you. *You* implied when you said I was just like her. It's amazing, you know? I didn't pay a lot of attention in AP Biology, but it's wild how I somehow got the worst of each of your genes!"

It comes out a bit like a cackle, but now that I've started, I don't know how to stop.

"Stop." My mom glares at me, her voice rising uncharacteristically. "This is between me and your father. I'm sorry you feel like you've been looped into it, but this is the situation: We tried couples therapy, and it wasn't enough. We are fundamentally incompatible with each other at this point in our lives. Twenty-seven years ago, even ten years ago, things were different. But when you're in a marriage, even when you think you're really in love, you end up compartmentalizing the little issues. And sometimes you get too tired of doing that. I am too tired. Your father is, too."

Each word feels like a stone dropped in my stomach. She's teary now. I can't remember ever seeing her cry.

But regardless of her intentions, the words lodge themselves in me, the realization clearer and clearer in my brain. I never want to be a detail, a little thing to be tucked away, watching as the people I love grow tired of me, unable to do anything until it's too late.

* * *

About an hour after my parents drive me home, before going back to their hotel, to their separate rooms, I get a knock on my door. Sure enough, it's Will, standing on the welcome mat in front of my apartment door.

"Are you okay?" he asks immediately when I open the door, putting a hand on each of my shoulders.

The second our eyes meet, I feel naked. I'm unsure how to spin my emotions for him. I tried my best to wipe off my wet face before I opened the door, but my cheeks are still flushed with emotion, my eyes tired.

"Oh, I had a migraine." He deserves more than vague, but I don't have it in me tonight.

"I've never heard you say you get migraines."

"I haven't had one in a while, but yeah, I do. Don't look at me like that, I feel much better." I force a smile and let him in.

"Did you take something for it?"

"What?"

He leads me to the couch, dragging me onto his lap. "For your migraine. Do you take painkillers for it?"

"Oh. Yeah. My mom had some heavy-duty ibuprofen in her purse. But how was your reading? I'm so sorry I missed it." I run my finger down the line of his cheekbone, feeling the weight of the lie begin to suffocate me in guilt.

"It was fine."

I pull him in for a kiss, but he shakes his head and cups my cheek, his vivid hazel eyes worried and uncertain in the dim light of my apartment.

"I don't believe that you're okay. You seem off."

"Please—" My hand goes to the back of his neck. "I just got into a fight with my parents, okay? But I don't want to talk about it right now. I just want to hear about your poems and be with you. You're what makes me feel good."

He stares at me, searchingly, and I watch his pupils slide back and forth to look into both of my eyes, as if one of them will fib on the other. I offer a smile, and it's not forced this time.

Satisfied, he leans in to kiss me. I deepen it with my tongue, and he hitches his hand up my dress. I arch my body into his, and he smells like trees and cedar and belonging.

But I can't get out of my own head. Why does it feel like this is the last time we could be doing this?

"I'm sure your poems were the best of the reading," I whisper. "Maybe you can read them for me later."

"Mhmm, I can do that if you want." He starts unbuttoning my cardigan.

"You're going to get the fellowship. I just know it."

I hope any tinge of bitterness in that sentence is counteracted by the way I lean into his mouth. I don't mean it. I just can't help it.

Will gives me a lingering kiss, then takes a deep breath and pulls away from me. "Leigh."

Even right now, the way he says my name makes it my favorite word. His eyes shine bright and his thumb makes circles on the back of my neck, and I feel like he's about to tell me three new words that could also become my favorites.

But he doesn't.

"I pulled my name out of the running" is what he says instead.

I freeze on the spot, my stomach doing that familiar somersault, which so often happens in his presence. But this feeling is more like plummeting. I remove my hands from his shoulders.

"What?"

"Two weeks ago. I went to Daniel and said I didn't want the fellowship. I told him to delete my application."

I pause to process, and I don't understand. I get off his lap and pull my cardigan back over my shoulder. "Why would you do that? I thought you desperately wanted this."

He shakes his head. "I didn't want to be something standing in your way. I wanted it, yes, but honestly, Leigh, I want you a million times more, and you deserve it more than me." He moves to stand up and grab my hand away from my crossed arms, but I take a step back.

"So you thought I couldn't just beat you fair and square?"

His brows furrow. "Of course I didn't think that. You deserve it and I want you to get it."

"And the only way for that to happen was if you pulled out?"

"No. I didn't have to pull out. I just didn't want it, and I knew I didn't deserve it like you do. I'm sorry. I understand now how it may look—"

"I'm not being seriously considered anyway."

The words ring loudly in the darkness of my apartment. He scrunches his face, shakes his head. "What are you talking about?"

Tears threaten to build behind my eyes. "At AWP. I heard Daniel and Paul talking to Erica after her keynote. They said the poets they were deciding between were Hazel and you."

Realization washes over his face. His expression softens, and all I can see is pity.

"Why didn't you tell me?"

I scoff. "Why do you think?"

He shakes his head, frowning. "I honestly don't know."

"Because it's fucking embarrassing," I laugh. "I talked a big game. I really thought it was something within reach for me. But year after year, they pick the same type of writer."

Now Will crosses his arms. "What's that supposed to mean?"

"They pick the guy! Or the girls that, I don't know, workshop like guys! They choose the *unoriginal* poems that sound like every other poem to ever come out of an MFA program!"

His entire body stiffens, from shoulders to legs. My stomach pools with regret, some sour feeling. *Don't bring up the plagiarism*, my brain screams. *It's too low a blow, you have no idea what the context was, just shut up—*

"I didn't mean that," I say quickly.

"It's okay. You're right. I am unoriginal."

I brush it off, not willing to open that box. "No, I'm sorry.

That was too harsh. But you know what I mean. You and Hazel both write in a way that, if I'm being honest, *occasionally* reads as pretentious. It's fine, really. Your writing is good. I'm just frustrated that they seem to only ever pick a certain kind of voice."

"Yeah, you're right. They pick the people who are willing to be vulnerable in their writing. You wouldn't know what that's like. You only write poems in the voice of someone else. And I think it's because you're too scared to be yourself."

I gape at him. "So the only way for me to write *vulnerably* is to whine about my parents in a poem?"

It's mean, but I don't care. I don't *want* to write about my parents like Will does. I feel like I'm being as vulnerable as I can be in my poems—and why isn't that enough?

Will turns his back to me for a second, as if he wants to shield his face. He paces around the apartment, then shakes his head.

"You say you don't like pretentious, Leigh, but it's not true. You went to Rowan and Tufts and now you're in a fucking MFA program, and you're only interested in guys that look like me, aren't you?" He spits out the words, frustrated. "Maybe that's why I started going by William after Middlebury. Maybe that's why I changed my glasses. Maybe that's why I signed up for this stupid program in the first place. You *want* pretentious. You wouldn't be attracted to me otherwise."

I'm not sure what to say. My whole body churns with regret, but it's too late. The inevitable has happened.

So I dig in my heels.

"No."

He laughs coldly. "No?"

"I never asked for any of that."

"No. But you like it, don't you?" He steps closer to me, almost predatorily, takes off his glasses and musses up his hair. "If I was a frat guy from a party school, you wouldn't like this anymore, would you?"

Yes, I would, my heart screams out, *because it's you*.

But my brain makes the end calculation. A little pain now means less pain later, when *he* realizes being with me is a mistake. That I was never good enough for him. Just like my dad was never good enough for my mom; my mom was never forgiving enough for my dad.

Because Will can see it, can't he? I'll beg him to like me, contorting myself into some false person who will eventually disappoint him. Or, when things get to be too much, I'll push him away. Just like I'm doing now.

I am my father's daughter. I am my mother's daughter. I don't trust myself to make this work, and I don't trust Will to wait around and try.

"I'm not interested in your psychoanalysis." I wipe the tears off my face.

Will puts his glasses back on and takes a deep breath. "Leigh, sometimes I feel like this is just a self-fulfilling prophecy with you. You're looking for reasons why this won't work, and I have to be honest, it's pushing me away."

"As if you haven't done the exact same thing."

He bites the inside of his cheek. "I know, and that's fair, but I've apologized multiple times. I've tried to show you in the last few weeks how much I regret it."

There's a beat of silence. *Cut the cord*, my brain pleads with me. *Do it. Now. Quick.*

"You shouldn't have backed out of the fellowship. You're just going to end up resenting me, and then you'll leave me. I know it. You guys always do."

"Who is *you guys*? Your college boyfriend? Sometimes I feel like you don't even see *me*—like I'm just another lit bro that's going to break your heart. Is it simpler for you to understand that way? It's like you're reading a page and you're only looking at the font without reading the words. What am I supposed to do to make you read the words? What am I supposed to do to make *anyone* read what *I've* written?"

Tears drip down my face. A vision flits across my mind: Will's father, ignoring his writing, only interacting with the words that showed him the version of his son he wanted to see.

But I block it out. I've come this far. I'm going to see this through.

Because it's not about the Leigh I am now, the Will he is *now*. It's about who we'll be later. In the blink of a second, I play out the next twenty-seven years of resentment, each of us compartmentalizing our incompatibilities. There's only one conclusion. I just watched it screech to a halt an hour ago on a bench outside a bookstore.

"I don't want to end up like my parents. I'm just trying to protect myself, and I don't trust you, Will." The words scatter on the floor like dropped bowling balls, loud and clunky, rolling until they hit someone. And Will looks like he's been hit.

"Okay." His voice is full of restraint. "Before either of us does anything rash, I think we should pause this discussion. I can tell emotions are high, and I'm empathetic that you've had a bad night and are recovering from a *migraine*."

He says the last word like it's code, and I hate how see-through I am to him.

"I'm not going to resent backing out of the fellowship. You don't need to worry about that. But please consider writing work that's really *you*. That's all anyone wants."

I wipe the tears still glistening on my face and nod. The apartment is unbearably quiet and all I want is for Will to step closer again and lock me in an impenetrable embrace, a weighted blanket against the doubts percolating in my chest.

"What now?" I step closer to him, an offering, but he steps back.

"I'm going to leave now. I—*we*—need a break."

"A break." The word seems to echo in the apartment. In only two words, I'm transported back into my twenty-one-year-old body, walking alone to my apartment in Middlebury, watching Will slip away for the first time.

You're not…

Stable. Smart. Worthy. Enough.

"Just for a little while. There's a lot going on with both of us right now and maybe we should sort that out first."

Within seconds, I am a robot. It's as if he's managed to find the secret code to power me down, wrap me up in plastic, store me in a box. And I have absolutely no energy after tonight to make any attempt to break free.

"Yeah, okay."

His forehead crinkles and he waits a beat, as if he thinks I'll fight back. When I don't, he walks to the door, opens it.

"Good night, Leigh."

And with one short glance, he's gone.

Chapter Twenty-Six

BEING IN WORKSHOP WITH SOMEONE you're avoiding is hell. When you're fighting with someone, all you want to do is hide from them. To expunge the world of your existence, so you don't have to confront whatever catalyzed the argument in the first place.

It's a problem, then, that our second-semester workshops are first-years only. Meaning that I'm now in a smaller table in a smaller room, inches away from Will. And Erica Go.

It was *supposed* to be a delightful surprise. When Paul emailed everyone saying that he would be out of town this week and Erica would lead the workshop in his place, I had already submitted my poem, the result of a tense weekend when I felt like I'd ruined my entire reputation in the MFA.

Clearly, I can't do what I set out to do. *So fine*, I thought. *I'll give everyone what they want.*

I hate my poem. That probably means everyone else will love it.

Will sits across the table from me, his eyes down, focused on the poems in front of him. We haven't spoken since the night of the reading, the last six days a blur of skipped Writing Center shifts and stiff body language in nonfiction workshop. It's not like we've broken up—we never made anything official, after all—but the promise of something more, the thing that's lingered in our movements since AWP, feels like it's damaged. Badly.

"I am so excited to do this workshop with such an intimate group." Erica clasps her red-nail-polished hands on the table. "We're going to have a lot of fun together next year, once I've been officially instated as a visiting professor. Let's let today be a little preview of my workshop style. I tend to be a pretty active leader, but my role is still mainly to facilitate discussion. I hope you all talk more than I do."

Hazel is beaming so hard I need sunglasses to look at her. "Can I go first?" she asks, and Erica nods in delight.

"I Break Up with a White Boy at a Café" feels like it's part of a series, a follow-up to what she read last week at the reading. It's pithy and clever. And it's vulnerable. The speaker presents the boyfriend as an antagonist, but by the end, she's thinking of her own complicity. I'd never noticed until last week how mature a poet Hazel is. Everything is moody with sharp images, but there's a lot of her personality on the page, too.

"I love the call-and-response of the speaker and the man," Kacey says. "You go into the poem thinking the white boy is going to be the villain, and he still is, but it's much more complicated than that, isn't it?"

"Fantastic point, Kacey. What do you think, Leigh?" Erica asks.

I stiffen. Kacey already said my one observation, and I have nothing left. I scan my brain quickly, searching for something intelligent to say.

"The images." I pause, trying to edit the sentences in my head. Erica nods, and I continue, "The specificity of them really works for me, especially the ones that describe the café and the boy in the same way, like he's this sort of background music, sucking energy away from the speaker."

Erica's eyes light up. "Yes! I caught that, too! I wonder if it could even be heightened in the third stanza—"

Everyone continues discussing the poem. Then they stop. And it's my turn. I wish I'd submitted something else, *anything* else. But I didn't. And I already used a health emergency to get out of a bad situation. I have no more cards to use. I have no choice but to read my poem.

I begin:

Aubade for a Stranger

A doe waits in a field
of fire and salt and ravens

with empty eyes.
I am a lexicon of ash.

When moon fills this
landscape with shadows,

what will I see? And what
will see me?

On a Wednesday in October
a stranger crosses

my path. We meet next
to the dirty river

under clouded sky,
my limbs limbless.

A corpse is just
a body until it dies.

With the last line, my body's a corpse, too. It's as if I've cos-
played August. My face is bright red, my armpits soaked.

"Thanks, Leigh. Who wants to walk us through 'Aubade for a
Stranger'?" Erica asks.

Hazel volunteers, as usual. "So we have an aubade—an
early-morning poem—in eight couplets. Um, it's in first person.
Quite short lines. I think there are two characters in this poem—
the speaker and a stranger, but it's possible that the speaker *is* the
stranger."

I guess as the poet I should probably know. But I don't. I have
no fucking idea. I just tried to write something dark and edgy,
like everyone else does. If there's going to be constant problems
with my persona poems, fine, I'll swing the other way. See if they
like *this*, whatever *this* is, better.

That was my strategy, at least. But now that I'm here, the
words hanging in the air, I know I've made the wrong move. My
classmates have their faces down, reading or pretending to read.
Erica's head tilts as she waits for someone to begin.

"My issue is that there doesn't seem to be an entry point for
the reader. This is quite, uh, a departure from your usual work,

Leigh, and um, it's interesting, but I'm just not totally sold yet," Kacey says.

"I actually like it," Jerry says. "It's minimalist, and in that way it's quite striking. The images feel like they're coming from a consistent palette, and they're quiet but well constructed."

Will is frowning. Because we're sitting at a much smaller table than our usual first-and-second-year workshop, I can see his copy of my poem clearly. It's blank. He hasn't commented anything at all.

There's some more back-and-forth from Hazel and Kacey, but eventually it dies out into silence.

"Leigh, interesting piece." Erica's voice is kind, but her face doesn't have any of the bright curiosity I saw when I commented on Hazel's poem—I killed that spark with my stupid aubade. "I think there's lots to work with here, and you might start with reevaluating the voice. I agree with Jerry that the piece is very minimalist, but I question if that's the right vein for this poem to operate in. I think the most interesting part is the middle where the speaker asks, 'What will see me?' Maybe you could linger there, explore the feeling of being watched and potentially evaluated, instead of ending on this death of the self, which sounds slightly generic."

If there are eighty words to lace together diplomatically to say "you suck," Erica's found them. My stomach fills with cement, and I drown under everyone's pitying eye contact.

Will starts scribbling something small in the margins of my poem. When everyone passes the pages back to me, I read it:

This isn't you, and you know it.

I look up and his skin is flushed, like writing that on my paper required more than he wanted to give. I'm silent for the rest of class, supplying the bare minimum of nods and eye contact so that Erica knows I'm still, at least, listening.

When workshop is over, Will leaves the room like he's on a deadline. I weave in and out of undergrads in the packed hallway and catch him by the shoulder.

"I read your comment. Very constructive as usual. Truly, some of your best."

He stiffens, pausing in the middle of the crowd. Then he ushers us into an unoccupied classroom, careful not to touch me, and closes the door behind him.

"It frustrates me to see you self-destruct like this," he says coolly, leaning against a desk.

I laugh. "Are you serious? Jerry or you or August could have turned in that poem. I'm not going to be shamed for doing exactly what the rest of you have done since we got here."

Will crosses his arms and swallows a scoff. "You're wasting your gift and not listening to feedback. No one wants you to stop the pop-culture poems. People constantly comment on how great your language and images are. But you refuse to give us anything real. And do you want to know my theory?"

He takes a step toward me, his eyes flashing with irritation. I say nothing and he continues.

"You're so scared of people rejecting you that you're going to waste the entire MFA submitting surface-level stuff. Stuff that you can brush off if you get criticism because you don't truly believe in it, either. That's why you're probably not going to be a poet after graduation. It's not for lack of talent. You're one of the most creative people in the program. But what you're submitting?

'Aubade for a Stranger'? Those are choices. You could do so much more, but you're standing in your own way."

Surface-level. Not going to be a poet after graduation. In this dumb classroom with its oak desks and marble floors, I've never felt more blond, more exposed. I stick out like a neon-pink thumb, like a ditzy *girl*.

I know, on a cellular level, that there's nothing wrong with who I am, the things I like, or the way I dress. I've never subscribed to the *not like other girls* persona. In fact, I've spent most of my life railing against it, enjoying being the contrarian in a room full of English majors. The dumb sorority girl who's as excited about *The Bachelor* as she is the structure of a sonnet.

But this program, which at the moment Will is unknowingly embodying, makes me feel small and stupid and judged. And the problem with me is that when I feel judgment, I attack. Like a scared cat at a vet's office, claws out and ready for blood.

"Well, at least I only submit words that are my own."

The sentence fireworks in the air. Will's jaw is so, so tight, and the worst intrusive thought I have is how I want to run my fingers over his cheekbone, melt him into forgiving me. But we both know it's too late.

"What are you talking about?" But of *course* he knows. He just wants to make me say it. To torture himself, to make me do the torturing.

"I know you plagiarized 'Invisible Summer.' I found the original poem online. So I'm sorry, I'm not going to take poetry advice from . . . you."

Will's face has drained of color, his expression eerily neutral, like he knows there's nothing he can say to make his case. He takes a step back, like he no longer recognizes me. I immediately want to take it all back, to not be the kind of person who is so petty, so bitter, so unempathetic.

"How long have you been sitting on this?" His voice is low. I can barely hear it.

I shift my weight on my legs. "Two weeks."

"So instead of asking me what was up with that poem—which by the way, sure, feel free to just go through everything on my desk, why not?—you keep it to yourself to wield when you receive some feedback you don't like?"

I don't know what to say. I've always identified more with my dad, but in this moment, I feel exactly like my mother. My eyes tighten, my mouth opens, but the overwhelming threat of tears spilling over renders me immobile. So I just stare at my shoes and shrug.

"Are you going to tell anyone?" His voice lifts, like he's finally geared up to fight.

My body goes rigid. "Are you kidding? You think I *want* you to get kicked out of the program? What, I'm going to knock on Paul's door and show him an old poem he's never seen before? Pull up the *Anathema* archive and take him through it? For what? You think I'd spend—I don't know, ten years?—embarrassing myself in front of you, so desperate for you to like me, for you to maybe *love* me, only to throw it all away when it finally feels like it's mutual?"

Will closes his eyes, runs his hand through his hair. "I'm actually not sure anymore."

The air in this classroom is too thick, and I can't breathe. I'm infuriated by his short, plain responses. I'd rather he yell at me. The more he pulls back, the more it feels like he doesn't see me—and it's an invitation, one my brain eagerly takes, to push, push, push.

"You already dropped out of the fellowship, so it's not like there'd be a consequence anyway," I say, my eyes now dry and focused, my arms crossed.

His eyes widen and his mouth opens, but before he can speak, I spit out, "Jesus Christ, no. Okay? I haven't told anyone, and I won't. I'd hope you'd know that, but I guess not."

He stares at my face like he has no idea what to do with me. His hazel eyes, once electrifying splinters of color and just-for-me warmth, go cold.

"This isn't going to work, is it?" he says, and it's quiet and final and I feel my heart split open. Even though I asked for this.

My head bobs in acceptance. "Yeah. Probably not."

The pairing that shouldn't have worked but did. Until it didn't.

"Have a good spring break, I guess," he says, and then he leaves the classroom, shutting the door behind him.

The urge to cry is still building behind my eyes, but I suppress it, strangle it, tuck it in deep somewhere in my chest, where no one, hopefully, can find it.

Chapter Twenty-Seven

WHEN MY DAD ROLLS UP to the airport, I'm a shell of my former self. It's the situation with Will, and it's the stubborn dehydration of someone who refuses to drink water on a plane lest she have to ask the person in the aisle seat to get up for her to pee.

"Yikes," Dad says, opening the trunk for me to throw in my suitcase. "What's with the face?"

"I'm just dehydrated. It's good to see you too, Dad."

He gives me a big hug and closes the passenger-side door for me once I've jumped in. Then he hands me his water bottle.

"Do you want to talk about it?"

I told him the gist on the phone—I ruined things with Will, blah, blah, blah—and he dutifully asked the key questions: why, when, who. I gave the bare minimum reply to each.

"There's nothing to say." I look at my reflection in the window, my greasy bangs stuck to my face. "Sometimes relationships just aren't meant for the long term."

Dad guffaws. "You're twenty-seven and have had, what, one boyfriend in your life? Honey, you're too young to sound so jaded."

"Well, Mom's not picking me up with you, so."

I watch his expression morph into something much flatter. We don't talk again until he merges onto I-480.

When we arrive home, I half expect to hear my mom's clunky steps to the door to greet me. But I don't. It's completely silent.

I throw my suitcase in my childhood bedroom, then Dad and I sit on the couch, having pizza for dinner. Mom never let us eat on the couch; we always had to use the dining table. But my dad's free now to live however he wants.

"Are you happy?" I ask him once the pizza cools to cold and a commercial interrupts our home improvement show.

"I'm actually feeling okay." Nothing in his tone contradicts him.

It's hard to understand, then, why that feels so much worse.

*   *   *

"Bitch, this is unhealthy."

Gen's not wrong. But if listening to weepy pop songs on repeat for two days is unhealthy, just let me die, then. I'm not interested in health.

Gen is here because my dad let her in. Ever since I told her what happened with Will, she's been texting nonstop; the second I set foot in Ohio again, she announced she was coming immediately, as in flying from Boston. I said don't bother, that's ridiculous, don't waste your money, I want to sleep it off. Gen said, *Nah*.

Now she's here in my neon-pink room, which is stuffed to the brim with the vestiges of my youth. Dog-eared coming-of-age novels and old SAT scores stuffed in my desk. Every textbook from college. Every spare sheet of paper I touched in elementary school, including complex social charts we made at sleepovers, naming our crushes, allies, frenemies.

Gen paces, cleaning. I'm in bed on my side, wearing a sorority-date-party tank top and flannel reindeer pajama pants, scrolling aimlessly on Instagram and watching videos of people tempering chocolate.

"I don't understand how it ended," she says.

"It was never going to work."

"I'm not sure why you say that like it's a fact. You had one fight. Big whoop. That's everyone's marriages ever." Gen plumps the other pillow and climbs into bed with me.

I shake my head and prop my elbows up on the mattress. "Some of those marriages end. So maybe it's better to call it before kids get involved."

"Babe, there's a difference between a pattern of marriage-ending communication breakdowns and one dramatic fight based on insecurities on both sides."

"But it wasn't just the fight. From the very beginning, he's been wishy-washy."

"Well, maybe because you've been wishy-washy, too."

I glare at her. "Out of self-preservation."

"Who's to say he wasn't doing the same thing? You think he's so fucking different from you and that it's just your mom and your dad all over again, but from where I'm standing, you two idiots are exactly the same in some key ways."

"And what ways are those?" I sink my head back, deeper into the bed.

"You're both terrified to give in to this because you both ulti-mately think you're not good enough for the other," Gen huffs. "You think he's going to reject you the way your parents rejected each other, and he thinks, *Well, my own father whom I looked up to barely thought I was good at anything; this perfect girl won't, either.* Freud *was* right, I don't care what anyone says, It all goes back to the parents."

"He does not think I'm too good for him. Look at him and look at me."

Gen rolls her eyes so hard I worry they'll get stuck that way. Then she scoots closer so she's right in front of me on the bed, her hands on my crossed legs.

"Leigh, stop it. It's not that he's a lit bro and you have nothing in common. It's that he rejected you once and you can't handle it. You'd rather be the rejecter. You'd rather quit your job before you get fired and you'd rather preemptively decide all your classmates are judgmental than risk them judging you."

"At least I'm doing what I love and not wasting away in corporate America. At least I didn't sell out."

I hate myself the second the words leave my mouth.

Gen shakes her head and snorts. "A more insecure person would turn this into a giant fight that would take at least seven business days to recover from, but because I am, like, so mature, I'm going to let you get away with that, because I know you're hurting and confused and just being mean out of a desire for catharsis."

"Gen, I'm so sorry. You're right. I'm being a bitch."

Gen nods as if to say *Indeed!* It's the benefit of being friends with someone for so long. They know your triggers and you know theirs, and you can give them the benefit of the doubt. Will and I haven't had the chance to build that sort of trust.

"But to set the record straight, I loved creative writing in school and hey, that's why I read now. That's why I write fan fiction. To do what you guys do in your MFA sounds exhausting to me. If that's selling out, whatever. If writing poetry is what makes you happy, fabulous; do it. But there are ways to live a meaningful creative life without being a full-time writer."

I think of Gen at work, complaining about her colleagues. Complaining about corporate life. But it's never been more than your standard anti-capitalist annoyance. She's not shackled to her company. She doesn't feel tamped down the way I did at Coleman + Derry.

I place my hands on top of hers. "No, of course. I know. I definitely don't think the only way to live a creative life is to get paid to write poetry. I just want to write for myself so badly, my body aches for it."

Gen nods, satisfied. "We can get back to our regularly scheduled wallow programming now. I just wanted to clarify that."

I sink down into my pillows. "How am I supposed to go back to fucking poetry workshop and act like everything is normal when it most certainly is *not*?"

"Well, this is why they tell you not to commit incest, must I remind you."

"Yeah, you're right, post-breakup awkwardness is the number one reason against incest."

She flicks me with her finger. "Do you want to make an action plan? If you want him back, I think it's on you to make this right."

I close my eyes, the arguments for and against tumbling alongside each other in my brain. I'm not ready to consider any of them. The shell I've created has cracked open, and I just want to let it seethe for a bit. There's, somehow, a freedom in that.

"I have no idea what I want right now."

She grabs my hand, holds it tightly. "That's okay, too."

*   *   *

"This is a really terrible bread knife," my mom mutters in the kitchen of her condo. "I think I accidentally let your father keep the good one."

As with all school breaks, I do them in two parts. Four days with Dad, three days with Mom. I got here two days ago, and we've tiptoed around each other like the Big Breakdown didn't happen at all. We're supposed to have one final meal together before she takes me to the airport early tomorrow morning, but I'm on edge. Too much unsatisfying small talk, and suddenly I have the urge to just speak plainly.

"I broke up with Will last week," I blurt out before I lose the nerve.

She takes a second to look up from cutting the baguette. "I'm sorry to hear that, honey."

She resumes cutting. I stare at her and all the wrinkles that make up her face, noticing how my early wrinkles are developing in a similar pattern.

"Do you...do you want to talk about it?"

It's an olive branch, but I'm not sure I'm ready to take it. "No. I just figured you should know."

She nods, then begins putting bread in a basket next to the cheese board she's also assembling.

"You're never getting back together with Dad, are you?"

She looks up at me with the saddest look. "No."

"But why?"

"Honey, I've told you why." She stares into her glass of water. "I don't want to come home every night to conflict. My job is emotionally exhausting. Your father and I want different things in life, and that fact managed to squeeze us into a lot of arguments."

"Are you emotionally exhausted by me?" I ask, and the words shock me, that I actually permitted them to come into existence.

She looks as if I've hit her.

"What do you have to do with any of this? I'm talking about Dad."

"I don't think it's some huge leap to think that if he was too much for you, then I am, too."

"Stop it." I watch her force her face into submission. Slowly, she says, "Honey, just because Dad has been a good father to you doesn't mean he's been a good husband to me. Both of those facts can exist simultaneously. I don't want to be in a relationship with him anymore. That doesn't mean I didn't love him or that your childhood was a fraud. But you need to let me be done with him. Neither of our experiences invalidates the other's."

"I understand that, Mom," I huff. "I'm an adult." Though there's a small seed in me that wonders if I'm not being very adult about their divorce at all.

"I never claimed to be perfect." Her voice is tight, like she's about to cry. It's a subtle cue to my brain, a whispered taunt: *Feel guilty. You did this to her.*

"I'm sorry," I grit out.

She bites her lip and doesn't respond. I follow her into the living room, where we eat and watch TV in silence. I wait to hear my dad's breathless laughter from the place beside me, the other piece of bread in a Leigh sandwich. But it never comes.

Chapter Twenty-Eight

ON SUNDAY AFTERNOON, WHEN I arrive back in Perrin after spring break, I'm supposed to have therapy with Bridget. We had an appointment scheduled over spring break, but I didn't feel like doing it in Ohio. I wanted to be in my own space.

The clock is five minutes past, then ten. Bridget doesn't respond to her texts. I email her, too. Nothing.

I'm annoyed. I put on concealer for this.

Soon I start ruminating. Why am I not an important client? Why doesn't she like me enough? Is she like this to all clients? It's rude. I get up to make a pot of coffee. Suddenly, I feel the urge to pee, but I can't because what if she calls in one minute and I'm in the bathroom?

Five minutes later, I resent not peeing. I should have taken the risk because now I continue to wait, and every minute I wait, the more likely she is to call.

Just like that, my phone flickers with a video call. It's her. Twenty minutes late.

"I wasn't sure if you forgot about me," I say when her face appears on the screen. She looks completely nonplussed, like she wasn't rushing at all.

"How did that feel?" she says softly.

"I'm sorry?"

Bridget leans back from the camera, her face going out of focus. "When you were waiting for me, how did you feel? The last twenty minutes?"

I narrow my eyes. Is this a joke? Why isn't she just apologizing to me?

"I felt annoyed."

Bridget nods and her eyes go down, probably to where she's scribbling in her notebook. "Annoyed?"

"I was frustrated that this session wasn't a priority. Obviously I know things come up, but maybe a text saying you'd be delayed? We've been talking for over a year now and I don't know…"

"Go on. What else were you thinking?"

"Well, I wondered if you didn't like me as a client." I feel ashamed the second the words leave my mouth.

"And how did that make you feel?"

"Bad?" I raise my eyebrows. "I would be sad."

"Sad," she states again, totally neutral, which exacerbates my frustration.

"Yeah. I…want you to like me."

I feel my face turn beet red. My eyes sting, but I try to push the emotion down. How embarrassing. What if she thinks I'm obsessed with her? Some strange stalker with a bad case of transference. Of course I don't assume she's like my *friend*, of course she's not—

"So when I didn't come on time, your first reaction was, 'There's something wrong with me. I'm not good.' Is that right?"

My mouth is dry and my throat tightens. Having it put like that feels so stark. Uncomfortable.

"Yeah, I guess."

"Leigh, I intentionally came twenty minutes late."

"What?"

Bridget nods. "I wanted to see what your reaction would be."

My mouth drops open. "Is that even legal?"

She swallows a laugh. "Your first reaction, when someone ignores you, is to assume that there's something wrong with you. You assign your self-worth based on your perception of what others think about you."

"What would a normal person do?"

"You *are* a normal person. But a person who doesn't base their self-worth on other people might say, 'Oh, she's late. That's frustrating.' And that's that. They move on. They don't assume it's a commentary on themselves."

I laugh a bit. "Wow, what's that like?"

"Last session, we talked about your mom. How would you feel talking about her again now?"

"Okay."

"When your parents separated, how did they explain it to you?"

I cringe at the memory. I'd sensed tension for months prior, of course, an increase in digs about my dad from my mom via text and weary calls from my dad, but when you don't live in the house anymore, it's too easy to ignore. To pretend that nothing has changed.

Until I got the phone call. A video call, actually, with both of them—the last one I would ever receive.

"It hasn't been working," my dad started.

"We've decided to separate," my mom said.

It felt like a death.

"My mom said they realized how different they were. How they wanted different things."

"How did it feel to hear that?" Bridget asks.

"Shitty. Sad. Obviously."

"Obviously?"

"The three of us were good together." I scrunch my eyebrows, trying to force myself to remember. "I was happy, my dad was happy, I thought my mom was happy. Them deciding it no longer worked was a—"

I pause. Bridget waits.

"A what?"

"A rejection," I spit out.

"Of what? Of who?"

Something snaps deep inside my chest. "Of me! A rejection of me, okay?" I feel shame at the way my voice rises, but I can't stop it; the words continue to flow out. "She *always* said, 'You're just like your father.' Constantly. Even when it was a compliment. 'The apple doesn't fall far from the tree.' Dad and I are heart-on-our-sleeves people. Emotional. Needy. Sensitive. And Mom decided that wasn't working for her anymore. And Dad! He's always, like, oh, you push things down; he tells me I'd rather hide away than fight for something. Just like my mom does. So sure, it was a rejection of each other, but…" I pause to breathe, to unwind my fisted hands. "…it felt like a rejection of me, too."

Bridget nods like she always does: kindly. "How does it feel to say those words out loud?"

"I feel like I'm a narcissist," I scoff. "You arrive late and I think it's about me. My parents divorce and I think it's about me. What does that say about me? Am I egomaniacal?"

"No. But I think you've tied a lot of your self-worth up with other people's opinions. It's not that you think everything is about you. It just sounds like you can practice more self-kindness. Plus, there's an opportunity for you to do some work identifying who you are *outside* of the opinions of others."

"And how am I supposed to start doing that?"

"You could start by taking some time to just feel your emotions. Not editing them because of what you think someone else will like or what you think is appropriate. It's not a cure, but something like body-scanning meditation could be a tool for you to regain the trust between your mind and body."

"Sure," I say, because everything sounds smarter when someone else says it.

"What about your writing? You've mentioned the feedback that your poetry might be stronger if you were willing to be more vulnerable. Maybe a poem is a safe place for you to explore who you are."

I curl my legs up into a tight pretzel on the bed and sigh. "I've tried. You know, I write these poems where I pretend to be Taylor Swift or someone else famous, and while I'm channeling another voice, it's still me, isn't it? I mean, what would I even write about otherwise? No one I love has died, I haven't faced some major trauma, and I don't have any profound insights on the moon that haven't been covered by every poet ever. And I just...I can't bear to write some whiny poem about my parents divorcing long after I've moved out of the house and then have ten of my classmates deconstruct it. I want my professors to give me an assignment, tell me exactly what they want from me. And trust me, I'll deliver. A haiku, an ode, something in fucking iambic pentameter? Great, I'll do it. I've been doing this on my own anyway. But they won't tell me what to write, so I've been coming up with assignments myself. *Write a breakup poem in the voice of Taylor,* or whatever. And yet, it's never enough for them."

I take a deep breath and swallow. That felt sort of nice.

Bridget lights up. "It's not enough for you, either."

"Excuse me?"

She shakes her head. "You couldn't stand how limited you felt at your ad agency. How interesting that there, the parameters and restraints you talked about were a huge burden to your creativity. But now, when you don't have any, you feel entirely unsafe with your own voice. You've been so, *so* good over the last twenty years, maybe longer, at self-imposing these restraints—molding yourself to exactly what other people want—that when someone asks for vulnerability in a poem, you're at a loss. You don't even know what they're asking for."

Well, shit. I bite my lip, but my shoulders straighten, a bolt of energy injecting into them.

"Okay, I hear you. But what am I supposed to write about, like actually? Divorce? Life at an ad agency? A bunch of limericks about bid day? Jesus, how dull."

Bridget laughs. "I'm no poet, but what about...*this*?" She waves her hand in the air. "Your tendency to people-please, the frustration of being vulnerable, et cetera. Couldn't that be interesting to explore?"

I'm not sure what my face is doing, but Bridget gives a light shrug.

"Just an idea."

*   *   *

Going back to school when you have no idea where you're supposed to go from here is tough.

I start with a Monday-morning Writing Center shift, one that luckily Will doesn't share. I exchange pleasantries with Houston and some of the English PhDs as we wait for students to come in. Since it's the week after spring break and we're not exactly the hottest spot in town, hardly anyone does.

I'm scrolling mindlessly through Instagram when Houston nudges me, holding his phone up. "Did you get the email? About the fellowship?"

My entire body goes cold and I flick to my inbox. Indeed, there's a new email, sent five minutes ago. Subject line: Announcing next year's fellows, from Daniel.

My vision goes glassy as I scan the email for the shape of my name. I know it won't be there, but still, a kernel, hidden in the back of my brain, thinks, *Maybe you misunderstood their conversation at AWP. Maybe you have a chance. Maybe something changed at the last minute.*

It didn't. Hazel got it.

"Damn, good for Wiebke." Houston sounds genuinely pleased for the fiction fellowship winner, even though he just lost something.

I nod. It's a placeholder, really, for an emotion I can't name. "Yeah."

Houston leans closer, lowering his voice. "I'm sorry, man. You really wanted it, didn't you?"

I shrug and it occurs to me suddenly: I haven't really wallowed. Over my parents' divorce, maybe. I let the façade slip in front of Bridget. Over Will, hardly, but Gen's listening was helpful anyway.

But for this? My big stupid dream about being a poet? About never going back to marketing and pencil skirts and bathroom panic attacks? About leaving the MFA with a fellowship, networking contacts, a jump-start to publishing in all the best journals?

No, I haven't allowed myself to mourn at all. I micromanaged my mind, too scared to feel.

"Yeah, I did." I don't dare turn to face him.

Houston puts his hand on my shoulder, just for a second, and squeezes. I force the muscles around my mouth to turn up in a grateful *Thanks*, but my mind is elsewhere.

"For what it's worth, I really liked your Taylor Swift and One Direction poems."

I stiffen. As a fiction writer, there's no way Houston could've heard them, unless a poet showed him the early drafts I submitted to workshop.

"What? When did you read them?"

Houston's eyebrows raise. "William read them. At the reading. We all thought you...knew."

My heartbeat stutters and all I can do is shake my head. I didn't know. He didn't tell me. But it makes the sharp feeling in my chest worse. He wanted to give me my moment that I'd worked hard for. He wanted my voice to be heard, didn't he? And then I absolutely ruined it.

I make an excuse about needing to pee because I'm thirty seconds away from giving in. From letting every atom of my existence ache, freely. Just this once.

* * *

"Are you okay?"

The voice is soft and tentative and weirdly familiar. I open my eyes and see pointy-toed pink leather boots.

I look up in horror. Erica Go, in a glorious navy jumpsuit, is watching me cry on the floor of a bathroom in Gilman Hall.

I pat my fingers across my eyes, trying not to make the mascara streaks worse than they surely are. "I'm totally fine! I have allergies. Never been better!"

Erica laughs and slinks down like I'm a child who got her knees scraped during recess. "Honey, I've been there. You don't need to lie to me." She sits on the bathroom floor next to me. "Now, really, what's wrong?"

I stutter. "Wait, why are you here?"

"I came back to campus to sign some contracts and take some meetings with Daniel about next semester."

"Oh." I sniffle, the sound of snot curdling through my nose.

"But what's got you crying on the bathroom floor?" Her voice is kind and soft, a dialed-back version of her poet voice. I feel like I'm made of glass, like she can see through me.

"In a year I'm going to have to go back to Boston to shill diapers."

Erica bites her lip. "That is quite possibly the last thing I'd thought you'd say."

"I don't want to be in marketing. I want to be a poet."

Images of last year in the Boston office bubble up, me going through the motions of being someone who cares about teasers and headlines and preambles. Just thinking about it, I feel tense, my body rejecting it.

"Cool. So be one!" Erica pulls out a pack of Kleenex from her chic purse and hands a tissue to me, like all of this is easy.

"Just because I want to be like you when I grow up doesn't mean I can. Poetry isn't really an industry that's hiring. That's why I wanted your fellowship so badly."

"Ah."

The bathroom door opens. A girl walks in and gives us a funny look before going into the stall. Erica opens her mouth, but I shake my head, and she nods. We wait for the girl to finish peeing. The second she leaves, Erica starts again.

"You know, after my MFA, I worked as a hairstylist for five years before I ever wrote another poem. I had zero connections. We didn't have fellowships like this at Emerson. So I stuck to hair for a while. It felt easier. But regardless of what your hands are doing during the day, some of us are still writers. I wrote poems in my head while I cut bangs. One time, I accidentally gave this very corporate woman baby bangs because I was trimming a sonnet in my head. I was getting to the last few lines while I was cutting her hair and realized they all had to go. So she ended up with these bangs that were a few inches above her eyebrows. Can you imagine? Baby bangs at Deloitte? My poem turned out great, though. I submitted it to *Best New Poets* and they accepted it."

I stare at her in wonder. "And her hair turned out great, too, didn't it?"

Erica clasps her hands together, matter of fact. "Oh no. She looked terrible. She refused to pay, rightly so, and the salon fired me on the spot."

My mouth cracks into its first smile of the week.

"What I'm saying is, you don't need anyone's permission to be a poet. I think the fellowship is a nice opportunity, but it's just an opportunity."

"But I know myself. I need all the help I can get. I'm not the type who's going to write on the weekends and submit to endless journals and awards just for a shot at *maybe* being in *Best New Poets*. This fellowship was supposed to be my fast track. I'm not good at persevering through rejection. It's so much work and I am clearly terrible at dealing with it. Look at me. I was told no and now I'm sitting on pee-soaked tile crying to my idol."

Erica guffaws. "Nice way to treat your idol! Why didn't you tell me the floor was pee-soaked before I sat next to you?"

My mouth drops open. "No, I'm just being dramatic, I don't think it's actually—"

Before I can continue, she grins and shoves my shoulder lightly. Like, *I'm just joshing you, bitch.* Is Erica Go my friend now?

I shake my head. "So I'm just supposed to do *this* forever?"

"Fall and get back up? Yeah, I think so. What other choice do we have, you know?"

A low, rumbling *ugh* escapes my mouth. "I was hoping I was special." It's facetious, of course, but sometimes my subconscious desperately wants to be the exception.

Erica laughs. "You're not. I'm not, either. And isn't that the most comforting thing in the world?"

I'm not sure it is. It's no warm blanket or cup of coffee or the feeling of Will's hand on my lower back, that's for sure. But maybe I can get there.

"I really messed up things with this guy, too. I'm so fucking afraid of rejection that I rejected him before he could reject me. But he's perfect, Erica, really. I just feel like I'm not smart enough or cool enough or a good enough writer, and he's going to kick me to the curb decades from now when he realizes that. How am I supposed to risk that devastation? He already rejected my writing once in high school and then he rejected dating me at Middlebury. How am I supposed to ignore those things? Why did he have to reject me at Middlebury?"

As I speak, Erica nods earnestly, like she's absorbing every single word. She opens her mouth, and I'm prepared for mind-blowing, life-changing advice that's going to make clear what my next eight moves should be.

"I don't know why he rejected you at Middlebury. I'm afraid I don't know...anything about Middlebury. Or you, really. Or this guy."

"Oh, true."

Erica stands up then and offers me her hand. "I can offer some generic advice, though, that I think is pretty tried and true. I recommend getting used to being more vulnerable. It'll feel uncomfortable at first, exposing yourself, but it gets easier over time and there's really no downside. Only good things come out of being yourself and asking for what you need."

We stand in front of the mirror, side by side. Erica fluffs up her hair and retouches her lipstick. She gives me another tissue to blot away the gray splotches under my eyes.

When I'm done, she turns to me with a grin. "You're a poet, Leigh, don't worry. Only a writer would describe this dank bathroom floor as prettily as *pee-soaked tile*."

I snort and she laughs and then we walk out of the bathroom together.

Maybe not as fellowship mentor and mentee, but something closer to that than faraway strangers.

* * *

When I get back home, I don't feel like doing anything but writing.

It's not a common feeling for me. I'm motivated by deadlines and praise and prestige. It's why I could never have developed a poetry habit without the structure of the MFA. Why I probably never would've applied to the program if *Goldfinch Review* hadn't accepted that lone poem I'd sent in months prior.

But right now, I do it just for me. As an outlet, as a refuge. I fill up a Word doc with verbs like *tug* and *break* and *tussle*. I command every scraped-cheek tear into a flinty noun that threatens all the nouns before it. I add adverbs where past writing teachers warned me not to, lest I inadvertently dull the impact of an action. The tension that knifes behind the muscles of my face cuts phrases into stanzas. Every breath I take blooms into a loose rhythm, the kind that hurtles words down a page even when they don't feel like being pushed.

I write until I have nothing left to give and the words become simple again—one-syllable bites like *love* and *yes* and *will*.

My eyes snag on that final word—no longer a name, but a promise of forward motion. I close my laptop and reach for the book he gave me, *Death Is a Peach We Refuse to Eat*, which I buried in my bookshelf weeks ago.

I devour every single page, and when I'm done, I start again.

Chapter Twenty-Nine

THERE ARE ONLY SO MANY Writing Center sessions you can swap with people before you eventually have to go to your assigned time and date. I know Will will be there. I've tried so hard to avoid him after class, but at some point, you have to rip off the Band-Aid.

I see the back of his head first. He's in a session with an undergrad; he's wearing the green cable knit I like. And when the shift manager says, "Leigh, your appointment is here," I watch his entire back stiffen. But he doesn't turn around.

To my dismay, my appointment is Lucas.

"My professor wasn't very happy with my last essay," he says as a hello.

I remember the session. It'd been a tricky English assignment. I felt confident in how I helped him, but as he's the writer and not me, there was only so much I could do.

"How did you feel about the essay?" I keep my voice even-toned to avoid provoking his defensiveness.

"I appreciate what you did for my first essays, but I think this isn't working anymore. I think I may need to switch to a different consultant."

"You're welcome to do so."

This was obviously the wrong response. Lucas's gaze grips me by the throat. "Or maybe we can start doing these sessions like how I want to do them. I know you're a grad student, but you're the consultant. You work for *me*."

I don't want to make a scene. "Let's just take a look at this new essay. Hopefully we can begin a dialogue to make sure you get the most out of these sessions."

He nods, his eyes intense. I see them pore over me, like they always do. I hate him, and still I feel my body enter its problem-solving mode when it comes to solving this particular equation: How do I keep someone who is making *me* uncomfortable comfortable? How do I mediate? The people-pleaser in me wants to curl into a ball of nothingness. Docile, calm.

We work on the essay. He tells me that he wants me to fix the structure, the first paragraph, the conclusion. He wants me to fix the bibliography, the entire paper's grammar. He asks for more and more. It's not in my job description as a consultant to do any of this. And yet.

I rewrite the entire first paragraph for him, transforming it from scattered to cohesive, like I did as a copywriter with client briefs. He must like it because he puts a hand on my thigh under the table.

"See, you're good at this."

His breath crawls across my skin, and it's unbearable. It's not like the praise that would come from Will, how I reveled in it, how it made me feel precious, how it felt stabilizing. From Lucas's mouth, it feels hollow at best, gross at worst.

I shove his hand off me. "I shouldn't have done that. You're supposed to write the paper, I'm just supposed to guide you. And I actually don't work for you. I work for the Writing Center."

Out of the corner of my eye, I see Will at the circular table in the middle of the room. I'm not sure if he's listening. But his hands roll into fists.

"You're supposed to provide a service. That's the entire point of you. Now let's look at the rest of the paragraphs," Lucas says, low and quiet.

And that's when I snap. Docile be damned.

"This session is over." I stand up. "I'm no longer taking appointments with you. You can find another consultant if you want. And please don't touch me ever again."

Lucas's eyes narrow. He glances around the room and puts his palms up, as if he's the victim here. Then he stands and looms over me, leaning.

I look past his shoulder at the shift manager, who has a puzzled look on her face. I shake my head. *I can deal with this.*

"I think it's a bit inappropriate, Leigh." His voice is coated in defensiveness. "You're the one who's been flirting with me this whole time. But if you're not into it anymore, *of course* I'll see someone else. Don't want this to be too hard for you. But you're the consultant. You're the grad student. I'm just a senior with no power here."

I spit out a laugh. "Please leave."

Lucas makes a big deal of packing up his backpack, and that's when I notice Will talking to the shift manager at the front. Lucas leaves the room, and Will's expression is like ice.

I try to leave the center to take a moment before my next appointment, but Will stands in front of me at the door. It's the

first time we've really looked at each other since before spring
break.

"You okay?"

"Yep." I try to weave past him. "I'm fine."

"Leigh." He catches my wrist, light and gentle.

"I can handle it, thanks." Part of me wants Will to run after
Lucas, to pin him against a wall, to threaten him if he ever speaks
to me again.

But I don't need any of that. And Will gets that, too.

He nods and lets me go.

*   *   *

I've been writing a lot. The words fly out of me these days, and I
wonder how much of that is due to Will or Bridget or Erica, the
people who've challenged me in the ways I needed.

I'm submitting to journals again. It strikes me that I have
nothing to lose, that these editors around the country don't know
me and never will, that I don't need a fellowship to have permission to be a writer.

My phone pings with an email, and I sit up. It's *Goldfinch
Review*, responding to the poem I submitted last week on a total
whim. I wrote it after talking to Erica in the bathroom and having
another session with Bridget. The poem's about watching the end
of a marriage as a kid, grappling with the perhaps unfair feelings
I'd had all along. That maybe my resentment toward my mom had
been an easy way to cope, not a reflection of reality. A reality where
she and I have more in common than I wanted to believe. Can you
really be a bad guy when you're hurting and misunderstood, too?

Hi Leigh!

We are thrilled to accept your poem "Portrait of My
Parents, Who Look Like Me" for our Issue 109.
    Please let us know if your poem is still available.
If so, we will be in touch soon with our contract
and other details. Thank you again for considering
our journal! We look forward to your continued
support.
    On another note, we see in our system that we
received an email about your poem "Usually,
Two Lefts Off Belvoir Blvd," published last year in
Issue 106. So sorry we are forwarding it to you
belatedly. I don't think any member of our staff
caught it until now, but when we searched for your
name in our inbox, it popped up. Hope to hear
from you soon.

Best,
Priya Gupta
Poetry Editor, *Goldfinch Review*

And below is a forwarded email, and it undoes every rotten
thought I've had in the last two weeks.

Dear *Goldfinch Review* editor,

I read "Usually, Two Lefts Off Belvoir Blvd" by Leigh
Simon in the current issue. Do you mind please

forwarding her this email? We've lost touch and I would greatly appreciate it. Sorry that this is weird.

Thanks.
 —William Langford

———————————

Leigh,

I know this is extremely random. I should have contacted you years ago, after that day in June. I don't think I was really ready until I read your poem here.

"Usually, Two Lefts Off Belvoir Blvd" broke me open. I felt the words slither down the page in such a sly way that I was left gobsmacked by the end of it. The structure, the diction. I imagine you with those fancy long tweezers fancy chefs use to plate fancy dishes, choosing each word so carefully for its spot on the page.

I know this is presumptuous. I know very little about your life beyond your writing and our conversations in high school, but I feel strongly that I know you. I'm going to go out on a limb and say that this poem is actually about your relationship with your mom. It resonated with me and made me reconsider my own relationship with my dad, who died a few months ago from a heart attack. It felt almost too intimate. Like I wanted to look away but couldn't. I saw myself in it. Your words a mirror.

I know we barely know each other, but I've always wanted to. In high school, I harbored a crush on you, especially after our conversation at homecoming. You were the first person to look at me not like a disappointment, but like something worthy, which is why I was hopeful, at the time, that you had a crush on me, too. But it's always been my impulse to push away the things I like, the things that like me back. I think that's why I pushed you away at Middlebury. I regretted it almost immediately, though it probably doesn't matter now and you have long since moved on. Even so, I wanted you to know. You deserve better than what I could ever give, even though I wanted to give you everything you wanted and everything I had.

If it's not already obvious, I don't tend to do these kinds of things. I don't expect a response, I just wanted to say that. Please ignore this if it's too weird. I'm pretty sure it is.

I hope that things are well. I look forward to reading more of your work.

Yours,
Will

My eyes flood with tears. Part of me knows that it might not have changed anything, had the letter been forwarded a year ago when Will wrote it. I wasn't in the right place—I would have convinced myself he didn't mean it, that I wasn't worthy.

But if he *had* said this, before my parents' separation, perhaps right after Middlebury, six years ago, I would've believed him. I would've contacted him.

It's six years we'll never get back.

Looking at his letter with fresh eyes, after all that has happened, makes me realize one thing: It was never just physical. Or nostalgia. Or an itch that had to be scratched. This strange, horrific, beautiful thing has always lingered between us—in the nooks of my rib cage, the early wrinkles of his rare smile, the angles we made grasping for each other. Despite our superficial differences in taste or personality, Will sees everything I am and could be, and I see the same for him.

It was never a sure thing, but we made it one. And in that way, we're not like my parents at all.

Chapter Thirty

How do you show someone you've evolved? That you're better—because of them?

A large part of me wants to walk to Will's apartment, bang on his door, and tell him everything I wish I'd said two weeks ago. That he was right, that my arguments against our relationship were a self-fulfilling prophecy. I thought we wouldn't work together because I didn't trust his affection, and maybe even more so, I didn't trust myself. Trust that a people-pleaser could be exactly what someone has always wanted. Naturally, and not by design or by force.

But then I think of his face when I told him I didn't trust him. That he would leave me. That his writing was pretentious, unoriginal, too *much*. For once he looked at me as if I didn't know him or see him at all.

I think back to how it must have felt when Will gave his poems to his father in college. How his father ignored all the words Will had spilled onto the page except for the ones that weren't his to spill. Will must've felt so misunderstood in that moment. And even then, he kept going. Applying to the MFA, stripping himself bare every week, on the page, for us. Even when he didn't feel a natural pull to poetry like I did. Even when it made him uncomfortable. Something inside him pushed him to keep doing it.

I've never been as comfortable taking myself apart on the page. There's something about writing it all down and reading it back that's worse than just talking about your feelings out loud. When you write them down, they become permanent. They become something to judge and tease apart, and I've never wanted to subject myself to that.

But that's why I'm going to do it. To lay it all out there for him to see—take it or leave it.

*   *   *

A week later, in workshop, Will doesn't choose to read my poem out loud, which stings a little. I guess it's unsurprising, but I wanted him to do it. To hear my vulnerability spoken in his low, deep voice—the one I trust the most with my words.

I wonder if he hates my poem. If he didn't know what I was trying to do.

Instead, Kacey reads it, which I told her beforehand to do in case Will didn't want to. She gives me a sly wink before she starts.

I try not to watch Will's face as she reads, but I glance up now and then. He looks mostly neutral, maybe a little sad. It's hard to interpret him when he's trying not to be interpreted.

I read it aloud next.

"'All the Leighs I've Been—and One I Could Be.'" I begin
with the title and then launch into the rest of the poem:

The one who kisses boys on the dank bus
on the sixth grade DC trip, giving in
to cracked-voice cheers and the first of many
clammy hands to trace her outline against

         the one who shaves because a boy smirked
         at the tufts growing from her tight-crossed
         legs, a pre-teen unknowing, staring at

the one squeezed into black polyester, pressed
into the hungry groin of a boy swaying
to Top 40, grateful to feel so small like

         the one who inhales root beer Chapstick
         off the lacrosse captain, takes off her shirt before
         he asks, lies about her music preferences to

the one who can't hold her liquor or feel
guilty after dribbling peach vodka in a basement,
letting needy blazer boys touch

         the one who says she just wants to be friends
         before they have the chance to say it first because

the one who's a gymnast, twisting in a ball pit,
nursing scraped knees and just watching
the decadence of being someone else is also

the one who decides she is pretty
with the lights on, with arms uncrossed
and breath slow enough to catch.

I stop reading and something deep in my chest uncoils. It's the most personal poem I've ever asked for feedback on. It's not written in some noticeable persona. My name is even in the title. It has details from my real life. Things that could be criticized. Judged.

Kacey begins. "So here we have a poem with eight stanzas, most of them three lines each, and they go back and forth on the page. What I think is working well here is the turn at the end, which I assume is the 'one' that the speaker could be. I like how the poem has this quiet optimism at the end, and it really feels like a release of breath with the images Leigh is conjuring here."

I take notes on my poem as she speaks, then look up to see Will, scribbling on his copy.

More people chime in. Jerry questions the format—should all the stanzas be of equal length? Kacey wants some of the details to be more specific, particularly at the end. Hazel thinks the last stanza has the right idea—but could be even punchier. I nod even though I'm not allowed to speak. Their points are all good.

Will doesn't say anything, but he does look at me when everyone is passing their poems over. His face is almost never readable, but right now, for a few seconds, I see everything—every wrinkle, every divot, every facet of his eyes. And he looks like he has lost something precious.

When everyone's comments are in front of me, I put his on top so I can secretly read it while Jerry's poem is up for discussion.

Will's done his signature underlining when he likes things, question marks where he's confused, *Hmmm* when he wants me to linger in the moment. But in the margins, he's written this:

> *A fresh concept, universal emotion in the specificity of the images. Lovely as usual. The perfect mix of style and substance.*

If the praise is playing out on my face, he doesn't show it. His own poem is up now, and it's another in a series he's been writing all semester. The title is "Ode to My Father in Late August." As with everything by Will, it's suffocating and sharp.

While everyone debates its focus and its length, I start writing in the margins, in tiny script so it all fits, on the copy I'll hand back to him.

Will,

> *Every night I replay our last conversation in my head with a simmering regret I feel deep in my bones.*
>
> *And then I replay all the ones that came before it—at AWP, in your bed, at Middlebury, in Mrs. Lincoln's class. And the only conclusion I have, after parsing through every word we've ever shared, is that I am irrevocably in love with you. I can't make it go away. It hasn't worked for ten years.*
>
> *I'm so sorry for what I said. I let my jealousy and insecurity take over. You're an incredible, brave, original poet, and you've taught me as much about writing as any teacher I've ever had. I shouldn't have made you feel like you weren't listened to or*

understood. I love everything you've been, everything you are,
everything you could be.

I'm not expecting any response, I just want you to know
how sorry I am. How I wish I could take it back.

You once wrote that my words were a mirror. I could say
the same for you. I have never felt more seen or understood by
anyone else. I just wanted you to know.

When the discussion is over for his poem, I slip my words
around the room, back into his hands. I watch him straighten the
sheets and tuck them into his tote bag.

*   *   *

I don't feel like going to Pete's afterward. I can't bear sitting there,
drinking a stale beer, having to wonder if Will's read my note or
not. So I go home despite Kacey's pleading and turn on a reality TV show—a balm for my overactive brain. I'm braless in my
sorority sweatshirt when I hear a knock outside.

And then there's Will—his beautiful face a fishbowl distortion
through the peephole. I open the door. He's as looming as ever,
his eyes intense. I suddenly don't know how to move my body.

"I read your comment." Given his expression, I have no idea
how this is going to go.

"Will, I—"

He cuts me off. "No, wait. Please, can I just talk first?"

I nod. "Come in?"

I close the door after him, and he stands in the middle of my
living room. He doesn't seem to know what to do with his hands;

first he crosses them, then he puts them by his sides. I stand in front of him and the air between us is thick, but the magnetic pull is as strong as it's always been. There's nothing I want to do more than haul him up against me, but I know he's not ready for that.

"I don't remember ever saying to you that your words were a mirror." He's fidgety, like he can't balance himself right on solid ground.

"Maybe you just don't remember."

"I remember every conversation we've ever had."

A ping of want zaps through me, creating a lace like broken glass in my stomach.

"Well, you didn't say it out loud. You wrote it."

Will stares at me, and I know his mind is revising his data set to include written correspondence. Realization washes over his face and he puts his fingers on the back of his neck.

"The email to *Goldfinch*," he says. I nod. "Why didn't you say something?"

"Because I only read it last week. They didn't forward it to me, not back then. But when they accepted a new poem of mine, they found it in their inbox and sent it along."

Will laughs. Not a low chuckle, but a loud, nervous laugh that I see move from his calves to his shoulders. "Fuck," he says once he works the laugh out of his system.

Even though I don't know what's happening, I'm smiling, too. Because he is. Because I can't help it.

"What's so funny?"

He shakes his head. "I spent the first semester feeling so awkward around you because I assumed you'd read it and were just so uncomfortable that you were never going to bring it up. And if you weren't going to bring it up, why would I bring up a strange, stalker-y email?"

"I swear I had no idea."

"That was one of the first things I mentioned, at the barbecue, that you'd been published in the journal, and I remember waiting for you to say something, and then you never did. I tried to bring it up again at the pumpkin patch, but then that kid hit you with a gourd or whatever, and it didn't seem like a good time." He laughs. "I thought, either she's very uncomfortable or, more likely, she's just entirely moved on and isn't giving *this* as much thought as I still was."

I take a step closer to him. "It was such a nice note, Will. I mean, it made me cry. I just don't understand why you sent it to them and didn't try to get it to me more directly."

"I didn't have your email address or phone number."

"Yeah okay, but you could have like, I don't know, DM'd me on LinkedIn or something."

"I think part of me didn't want you to get it."

"Oh." I can't look at him. Tears coat my eyes and threaten to spill. I know he sees because he takes a big step forward and puts his thumb on my chin, coaxing it up so I'm looking him in the eye.

"I want you to know why…" He stops and takes a deep breath. "Why I copied 'Invisible Summer.' I only did it that once. I was stressed, not thinking, *needing* to just feel sure of a poem for once, and the second I turned it in, I felt so unbelievably guilty, but it got a good reception and even though I didn't deserve it, I took it. My dad had asked to see my poetry that semester and I gave him a bunch; I shouldn't have included it, but I did. Maybe as a test. And sure enough, it was the only poem he liked. Didn't say a single word about any of the others. Not then. Not ever. I can't bear to look at it, but I can't bring myself to throw that copy away, either. His comments are all over it."

I exhale, stepping closer, so that our feet touch. "He was an idiot. He had no idea what he was missing. I mean that. I've read two semesters of your work now, plus your high school stuff, and I love your poems. I love your voice and how honest you are in them."

"Thank you." He whispers the words, even though we're alone. "But I shouldn't have done it, and I have to live with that. Leigh, reading your work, seeing the joy you bring to it...it's made me realize that this isn't what I'm meant to do. It brings me too much stress. What I enjoy much more is helping other people with *their* work. I love workshop, and I actually like working at the Writing Center, as long as it's with students that can keep their hands off you."

I laugh, grabbing his bicep, pulling him against me for a second before pushing back in horror. "Wait, you're not quitting the MFA, right?"

He shakes his head. "No, I'm committed to finishing the program. Besides, I love seeing you like this. How your eyes flash when you figure out the perfect way to separate your stanzas. How the corner of your mouth tips up when you know you're about to say something smart in workshop. You always look shocked and smug at the same time, and I'd be too jealous if everyone else got to witness that but me."

"Okay, good. You're not allowed."

He grins. "You know I'm not great at opening up with my feelings." He tucks a strand of hair behind my ear. His hand is so warm, and I just want to lean into him. "At Middlebury, when you said you wanted to try this out, I wanted to, so badly. I was—I am—so attracted to you, physically, emotionally, everything. But I knew I couldn't live up to your expectations. I never do, not with my parents, with girlfriends, whatever. I didn't want to start something because I knew it would end and I couldn't tolerate that.

"But after my dad died, I don't know, something snapped. I read your poem in *Goldfinch*, and I couldn't help myself. I knew I still wasn't worthy of you, but I think I just wanted to reach out. Then when I realized you were *here*, I wasn't sure where we stood, and I didn't want to open this up, to open myself up again. I still wasn't in the best mental state."

"Will," I whisper. I drag my hand across his heart, but he keeps going.

"I'm exhausted by this, by myself. I feel like I have no choice but to give in." He pauses and takes a deep breath. "Leigh, I can hardly remember a time I wasn't in love with you."

His voice is tulle—soft, airy, lovely. It's a comforting contrast to the fast beat of my heart.

He continues, running his thumb along my jaw. "In high school, I thought you were the kindest person. The best writer. The most beautiful, even though it was a fraction of how beautiful you are now. You have always been the brightest thing in the room and I have never not wanted to be in your spotlight."

"I'm in love with you, too," I burst out before he can get another word in. I've already written it, but I want to say it, too, to make it more real for him.

His entire face smooths, as if he'd been holding in so much tension. And then he kisses me. It's a bit rough, the way he crashes his body against mine, the splash of his stubble against my cheeks, his hand knotted in my hair. But I give it all back, my hands tight around his neck, grasping for every bit of breath from his mouth, as if I need it to breathe.

"I'm so sorry," I whisper. "For everything I said. You were never pretentious or judgmental. I think I was. I was just insecure. I swear, I love your writing so much—"

He shakes his head. "No, I'm sorry. I was a prick. I knew I was being condescending and I shouldn't have made it about me at all. You were hurting and I was insecure."

It's kind of scary when you can see someone this clearly—when you can see them beyond the parameters within which they've permitted themselves to live. It requires even more vulnerability. Will holds my entire heart, every vein, every nerve of it, in his hands. And I hold his in mine, too.

He keeps me pressed tightly against his chest. "I love you," he says again, like he can't get enough of the words on his tongue.

"Show me," I whisper against his neck. And then I walk backward until my thighs hit my bed.

* * *

He doesn't need to be told twice. When I'm lying on my back, he braces his hands over my shoulders as I unbutton his shirt, my mouth hungry and desperate on his. I break for air and shuck off my sweatshirt, my leggings. When I slip off my underwear, I don't blink.

"Good," he murmurs. A smile creeps across his face as his gaze sweeps over my body. "Beautiful."

I unbutton his pants, and he roughly pulls them off, unwilling to waste a second of time not skin-to-skin. His mouth is on my breast, his teeth grazing where I'm most sensitive, and a sigh rushes out of me.

"Tell me what you want." He runs a finger down the center of me, slowing the chatty part of my brain down with every inch.

"Take these off." I grasp at the fabric at his hip, and he pulls his boxers off.

"Now what?" he urges, nipping at my neck.

"I want…I want you to put my wrists above my head and keep them there."

There's a glint in his eye. He does what I ask, his large hand just-tight-enough over mine. "You're so pretty like this," he says, reverent, stretched over me, his lips against mine once more. "Now what?"

I wriggle slightly under his hold, pressing my thighs together, need softly building. "I want you."

He nods, then tightens his hand around my wrists for a moment before climbing off me. The condoms he'd put in my dresser are right where he left them.

"Don't move." He punctuates each word. As if I ever would.

When he's back, he presses my wrists into the mattress, his other hand reaching between us to position himself. And then he's *there*, sinking into me, but only a little before he slants himself out of reach. He's teasing. He wants to hear me beg. To ask nicely. To state exactly what I want from him and how.

So I tell him. I write him an entire poem and I read it into his ear, each word hot and damp like his hand gripping my thigh. He groans in free verse, my own climax sharp like an end-stopped line.

Sometime after, we lie in bed, even though it's only early evening and not at all time to sleep. But he's worn out. I roll half on top of him and whisper, "Will."

"What is it?" His voice is thick with sleepiness.

"You read my poems at the reading. After I ran out."

One hazel eye peeks open, hesitant. "Yes."

"Why? I thought you'd wanted me to move away from the pop-culture ones. You wanted me to use my own voice, to be more vulnerable. Those poems weren't."

He props up on his elbows. "It doesn't matter. You worked so hard on them. Maybe they weren't as vulnerable as your stuff now, but your wordplay has always been the best in the class. Erica needed to hear them. Everyone did. And I wanted to give you the best shot at getting the fellowship—" He stops talking when I curl my hand around his arm. "Are you...was it okay? That I did that?"

I nuzzle into the crook of his shoulder. "Yeah. I think it might have been the moment I knew for sure."

"Knew what?"

My head tilts, and a vision flits across my eyes—us in Perrin next year, us in Ohio, us here in this bed and many other beds to come. The warm, buzzing feeling that threads across my skin when he looks at me like he is now. "That this could be a forever kind of thing."

He closes his eyes in an exhale, tucking me closer into his chest.

"But now I want to know. When was the moment you knew you were in love with me?"

He laughs, shaking his head.

"Okay, never mind, I'm being insecure, I shouldn't ask for constant validation—"

He cuts me off with a kiss, slow and indulgent. "I want to say high school, because wouldn't that be romantic? A decade of uncontrolled pining." His eyes are open now, and his fingers trace the jut of my collarbone. "But that's not quite true. I wasn't *not* in love with you at Rowan, if that makes sense. But I barely knew you, even though my mind filled in all the blanks it wanted to."

He pauses. "No, the moment I think the feeling truly solidified in my subconscious was at the barbecue."

"When I spilled water on you? How come all the great moments in our relationship happen after I pour my drinks all over you?"

He shakes his head. His nail drags down my shoulder, as if he wants to leave his imprint on my skin. "No. It was when you refused to call me *William*."

"Is that right?" I feel such an injection of serotonin behind my eyes I have the impulse to cry.

"Yeah." His voice is the softest caress against my ear. "Somehow you knew who I was before I did."

*   *   *

We're over a month into a post-Hazel-winning-the-fellowship world, and I'm surviving. It's hard, I won't lie, but it helps knowing, truly knowing, that she deserved it.

What also helps, obviously, is getting together (for good) with Will.

"How did it feel when you found out about the fellowship?"

Bridget asks as I prop myself up on my bed, holding the screen in front of my face. We haven't had a session for a few weeks, so I had a lot to catch her up on.

"Shitty," I admit. "But I don't think it defines my worth as a writer. They could only pick one person, and Hazel really is the best choice. She's a fucking good writer. I feel guilty for being so judgmental of her from the outset."

Bridget nods. "That sounds like a really healthy response."

"Leigh Simon's all grown up."

"I'm impressed," she says with a laugh. "In a little more than a month, you told a bad guy that he could go fuck himself, came to terms with your worth as an artist, and got a new boyfriend? Sounds like our work is done here." She winks.

"No!" I say, even though I know it's a joke. "I'm still a mess."

"I'm kidding. The work is never really done, but I think it's good to pause and reflect on the progress you've made, too."

I nod, and it's not to please her or to make her feel like she's been useful. It's because I actually want to.

The semester winds down with a sprint of activity. We finish up our classes, edit our writing, await our assistantship placements for next year. I want to get out of the Writing Center, so I apply to the *Perrin Review* editorship instead, but we won't find out who got what for another week or two.

We say goodbye to the second-years with a final party at Penelope's—one that's been dubbed the MFA Prom. Kacey didn't want to come. We found out last week that August's been cheating on her; she saw an incriminating See you over spring break ;) text from his hometown ex on his lock screen and confronted him. No one in the cohort dared say *I told you so*. We all know how seductive the straight white literary man—most of them, anyway—can be.

In the end, Kacey bucks up, puts on a revenge dress, and decides to enjoy the company of the rest of our cohort. Morris snags his usual DJ spot, this time with a more democratic playlist. The night grows loud and sloppy, and after a few drinks, Jerry brings his much-requested moves to the center of Penelope's living room.

"So what are you gonna do this summer?" Hazel asks the group of us that's lazing on couches, taking a dance break to cool down.

I'll be in Ohio, spending time with both parents equally. It'll be weird and emotional, but knowing Will will also be in Cleveland helps. He told his mom it's to visit some other relatives and friends, but we both know it's for me.

"Summer in Cleveland," I say. "Maybe a part-time job. But I mostly just want to relax. What about you?"

"I'm doing a yoga retreat for a week in July, but otherwise I'll be in Portland."

"Oooh, yoga. Got all your Lululemons ready?"

Hazel laughs. "No, I prefer the ones made of upcycled plastic water bottles, actually. Much better than virgin polyester."

"You know, I'm trying to explore a better mind-body connection, too. Maybe we can do some yoga classes at the rec center in August when we get back."

Hazel lights up. "Yes, let's do that."

Then Will's hand is on my shoulder, and I look up at him in his white button-down and navy blazer, unbuttoned to show a sliver of skin at his chest. He leans forward to speak into my ear.

"Penelope's bedroom is unoccupied, I see," he murmurs, and his words unzip my entire spine.

"I think I left my phone in there, actually." I stand up from the couch and let him pull me into his chest, his hand resting on the part of my back exposed by the turquoise dress I have on.

"Think we better go make sure no one has taken it."

"So full of good ideas, you are."

"I have a couple of other ideas, too, actually, that I'd like to show you."

I flush and pinch his arm through his blazer. He laughs and kisses my temple. In an instant, I drown out the pulse of the music, the sparkling chatter of my classmates around me. Right now, here, it's just me and him.

Everything we've been and everything we can be.

Epilogue

♡

I YEAR LATER

"Shall we?"

We're perched on Paul's doorstep, a ranch-style home twenty-five minutes from campus. Will's in his standard uniform—cuffed chinos, a linen shirt, a navy blazer—and I'm in a bright-pink sundress. I even wore lipstick. We look like we're off to a sorority luncheon.

"You knock," I whisper. He puts a finger on each side of my waist and pushes me gently into the door.

"You're the one making the speech tonight. I'm just here to make sure Houston doesn't get drunk in front of all of the professors and insist we play Fuck, Marry, Kill again."

"God, that was a good party."

"Go on," he says into my ear, and in his bedroom voice, he can make me do anything. I rap my knuckles on the door.

Within seconds, Paul is there, flanked by his cat, Stuart.

"Oh, good. We were just preparing for the toast." He lets us in as Stuart weaves in and out of our legs.

"I'm already so sad," Kacey says, walking up and giving massive hugs, even though we saw her less than twenty-four hours ago at graduation. It's a low-key affair when you're in the MFA program. While the undergrads take it seriously, putting down serious money on a cap and gown, we showed up in business casual and dipped the second it was done.

"Don't be sad," I coo into Kacey's ear.

"You're leaving me!" she fake-cries, then puts her hands on Will's shoulders and grips him tightly. "If you two don't come down from Boston every once in a while and visit me, I swear to god."

"We'll come, don't worry."

We say hello to the rest of the cohort, everyone idling on chaises and a large couch, drinking beer and chatting. Paul's house is gorgeous and rustic, filled with vivid paintings by his late mother, giving the ambience of an underground art scene in rural France instead of a Wednesday in Perrin.

Our whole second-year cohort is here, as well as all our professors, including Erica Go, who joins me in wearing hot pink.

"Everyone's here now, so I think it's time for a toast," Paul says, and starts handing us glasses of champagne. "On behalf of the entire program, I want to congratulate all of you on a wonderful two years. We"—he gestures to the professors in the room—"are so proud of everyone's growth. It has been a pleasure to learn from you."

Paul continues his speech as we stand in a circle—me and the nine other writers I was intimidated by two years ago, now a family.

"To the graduates," Paul says finally, raising his glass. We cheers, taking long, easy sips as we continue to mill around the room. Amid the chatter, we pass final copies of the *Perrin Review*, the last one I'll get to edit. Everyone in the cohort is signing them, like some strange keepsake in lieu of the traditional yearbook.

Will presses his *Review* into my hands and puts his hand on the small of my back. "I want to be the last person to sign yours," he murmurs, and I feel my cheeks flush. During the last semester of the program, he's gotten into the habit of writing ridiculous, flirty things on my poems. I can hardly imagine what he's going to write on this last piece.

"Don't write anything you don't want Gen to read." He simply raises an eyebrow.

People pass me their *Review*s and I try to think of clever, pithy things to write. How to capture the essence of my relationship with each of them. But it's a lot of pressure, especially for the people I'm closest to. On Kacey's, I freeze up so much I end up just drawing a heart and writing *Friends forever*, like a thirteen-year-old.

Once everyone has signed mine, I give it to Will, who pulls out his inky blue pen and scribbles a few lines on one of the inner pages.

"Don't look at it until I say so." He gives it back to me.

"Oh Jesus," I cackle, putting the journal next to my purse in the hallway.

We eventually make our way to the dinner table, which is more like three tables put together with fifteen mismatched chairs, and I start shaking slightly because I know it's almost time.

"The traditional goodbye toast!" Paul says. "And we start in the usual way, with our fiction editor for the *Perrin Review*. It's all you, Houston."

Houston, in cobalt-blue slacks, a crisp white tee, and dirty sneakers, stands with his glass. "I would like to dedicate tonight's bender to the entire cohort," he begins, to raised eyebrows from Daniel and Jeremiah Brandon, the fiction fellowship professor, "but especially to the four fiction writers who shaped my shitty words into something slightly less shitty."

Athena makes no effort to hide a snort.

"To Wiebke," Houston continues, holding his glass in the air, "*Danke* for your incredible story comments. You are not my mother, but somehow, you also are my mother, and I couldn't have made it through this program without you." Wiebke puts her hand on her heart.

"To Christine, the most interesting surrealist writer I've ever met. You pushed me to write weirder and weirder, and my work is better for it. To Morris, who brightened our days with stories that I still don't believe are true and the encouragement only a guy deep into his thirties could bring to us." Houston stifles a laugh and Morris chuckles into his drink. "And to Athena, my partner in crime. You're the only one who can actually keep up with me, which is not saying much, to be honest, but I love you all the same."

Athena, next to Houston, wraps her arm around his hips as he stands. Houston continues for a minute or two more, talking about his early days in workshop and what the program meant to him. I forget I'm on next; I'm so wrapped up in the wistful ache of knowing the ten of us might never be in the same room again.

We clap and cheers and then I feel Will draw circles on my knee with his thumb, an antidote to any lingering anxiety.

"Beautiful, Houston," Paul says. "And now perhaps our poetry editor wants to say a few words?"

All eyes are on me as I nod and get up, a smile breaking through my face, my eyes almost watering in anticipation. I take a deep breath.

"Two years ago, I was a very different person. I walked into Daniel's foyer and put on a brave face, but secretly I was afraid of every one of you."

I feel Kacey crying next to me already.

"I thought I didn't belong here. That you all would judge me—for not being good enough, for not having tattoos like Morris, for not reading the right kinds of books. And for a while, I so desperately wanted to impress all of you that I was constantly afraid of being found out. Of you learning I wasn't cool enough or good enough to be here."

I pause.

"But then, something shifted. Each and every one of you challenged me. To be a better writer. To be a better person. And I realize now that maybe I was the one who came in with preconceived notions and judgments. Not you.

"I'm here today absolutely in love with the entire MFA fam, which is really a strange cult. And trust me, I was in a sorority, so I know a lot about cults."

The group giggles, and I feel emboldened by Will's gaze, his hazel eyes bright.

"Like Houston, I'd like to thank every single member of the cohort, but especially my poetry clique. The four of you have impacted me in ways both subtle and profound, and I don't really know what I'll do, not seeing your faces and reading your comments every Thursday, like we've done now for two years.

"So cheers to Jerry, who I think secretly shares the same music taste as I do, judging by the last three parties." Across the table, Jerry offers a shy grin, toothy and happy. "Your writing is beautiful and dark and deep, your comments even more so.

"To Kacey, my cake companion. I knew on day one that this

could be a friendship that could last a lifetime, and I'm so glad to say now that I *know* it will."

As I speak, I see Kacey swipe the tears off her face and smile.

"To Will," I say, my voice faltering as all the eyes in the room move back and forth between us, "who I'm delighted to say has much improved his workshop technique since our high school days." Everyone laughs and I feel his hand on the back of my thigh. "It's been a long, strange journey. I hope you already know the impact you have on me every day, and the continued impact you'll have on me in Boston, too."

The table cheers and my shaking subsides slightly, now that I'm over the biggest emotional hump.

"And finally, to Hazel." I direct my glass toward her at the corner, where she sits, braless in a loose black dress, in the *full poet* look I used to laugh at. "Your writing amazes me every day, but even more so, your friendship. I'm going to miss our impromptu grocery trips and your hilarious comments on my poems, and I know for sure Stanford is not even ready.

"So to all of you, to my MFA fam: Cheers." I raise my glass.

* * *

As we eat, we discuss next year's plans. Hazel's accepted a prestigious Stegner fellowship and is moving to California. Christine is moving down to Florida with her husband for his engineering job; she'll find work once she's down there. Kacey will stick around Perrin to teach English composition classes to freshmen. The salary's horrific, but she loves it, what can she say.

"And Boston?" Erica leans across the table with a smile. "What will you be doing there?"

"I got a job as an adjunct professor at Emerson in their creative writing program."

"That is lovely!" Erica gushes. "Once you're there, let me put you in touch with my former classmate. She also teaches at Emerson now, and she's an incredible poet. I think you two would really get along."

It was impossible to decide what to do this fall. I knew I didn't want to go back to advertising—at least not for now. It's been too delicious to write for myself, to not have to deal with briefs or decks or client presentations where I morph my words to fit someone else's desires. And working for the *Review* made me realize that I liked working with other people's words, too, so I thought teaching could be worthwhile. All I know is: I want to keep writing, to keep doing it for myself, and to be with Will.

That last one came particularly easy.

"And what will you be doing, William?" Erica asks.

Will coughs. "You can actually just call me Will now. I think it suits me better."

It's my turn to smirk.

Daniel nods graciously, listening in. "Will Langford of Cleveland, Ohio, it is."

Will turns back to Erica. "I'm going to be an assistant at a literary agency, actually, hopefully to become an agent someday." He shoots a glance at me, and I can't help but grin. "But our goal this summer is just to find an apartment."

We continue talking until I get up to go to the bathroom. When I get out, Will is there, standing outside, and I jump in surprise.

"You have got to stop doing that," I mutter.

"Come outside with me for a second," he says, his eyes intense.

We stand out on Paul's deck, the air still heavy with humidity but rapidly cooling in the dusk of evening.

"Good speech." He leans against the edge of the deck railing. "Kacey and Hazel were wrecks. I'm pretty sure you made half the cohort cry."

"Not you, though, right?"

"You know it takes quite a bit for me to do that."

I take a step closer to him and trail my hand across his shoulder. My heart beats faster and faster and I should really just say it, the words, the ones swishing through my chest every day for the last six months. So I do.

"Will you marry me?"

His eyes grow so wide and he starts shaking his head, his lips curling, but I keep going. I'm determined to make the man cry now.

"I know this is crazy and it's only been a year, but also I feel like I've known you my whole life, and to be fair, I sort of have and I've loved you a lot longer than a year, and you are my person. You make me better and you're just—"

Will reaches into his pocket of his navy blazer and takes out a small velvet box before I can finish.

"Holy shit."

He pops it open and there's, naturally, a ring. A sweet small diamond, emerald-cut on a gold band, just like what I once showed him once on a Pinterest board as a laugh.

"Are you proposing?" I ask before he says a word.

"Yes."

"Did we seriously both plan a proposal on the same night?"

"Check your *Perrin Review* when you get a chance." He laughs.

My head is spinning and I can't see very well because my eyes are tearing up so viciously.

"Okay, so can I assume from this that it's a yes?"

Will laughs again, the most beautiful sound in the world. "It's always been a yes."

He cups my face with his hand, his other at my waist, holding me so tight against him I forget to breathe. I kiss him, hard, my hand running across his cheek, where I find a single errant tear.

"You accomplished what you came here to do." He laughs, wiping his palm across his face, and he's right in so many ways.

We kiss again, this time lingering and deep, and all I can think about is ditching this party and going home together.

"But do we, like, tell everyone? Right now?"

Will shakes his head, peppers my cheek with another kiss. "We can video-call the group chat tomorrow. Tonight, I want this all to ourselves."

So we go back inside, a secret shared between us, and I'm weepy and he can't keep from smiling, can't keep his hands off me.

The rest of the evening plays out too fast, too slow. But with Will's arm around me, surrounded by my fellow artists, I am at peace. And at home.

Acknowledgments

As someone once said about romance novels, I think, it takes a village—and so many smart, talented people helped me shape this idea into something real and better.

First, a hearty thank-you to my enthusiastic and patient agent, Hannah Mann, for advocating for me and this book, for accepting my neurotic, rambling emails, for shepherding me through this process. I love doing this work with you!

To my editor, Sabrina Flemming, thank you for taking a chance, for your always kind words, for understanding the book this could be. Your great ideas truly made this better and I'm so grateful to work together.

Thank you to Genevieve Gagne-Hawes, who worked utter magic on this manuscript with Hannah. I still remember the delirious, teary kind of happiness I felt when you first emailed me, after I sent what I thought was truly a crapshoot query. I am beyond grateful for everything you've done for my books. Thank you to Sydnee Harlan, who did a ton of behind-the-scenes work on this and always hyped me up in every email. And thank you to all the other folks at Writers House and The Artists Partnership who played any role in championing this book, including, but not limited to, Penni Killick, Tom Ishizuka, Peggy Boulos Smith, and Maja Nikolic. I am so appreciative.

Thank you to the rest of the amazing team at Forever, including Leah Hultenschmidt, Anjuli Johnson, Taylor Navis, Estelle Hallick, Carolina Martin, Caitlin Sacks, Laura Jorstad, Xian Lee, Sara Schaller, Lori Paximadis, and Becky Maines.

Thank you to my first readers, a real Who's Who of my contacts list. To Kate Levine, for, well, you know, and your keen eye in the therapy scenes. To Emily Richards, for your praise and love and thoughtful edit letter. To Emma Draughn, for your hilarious notes and fiction expertise. To Michelle Reed, for everything, and the absurd lit bro poem inspiration. To Zach Wendeln, for your insanely fast read and comments, for sticking in my life, for laughing at all my jokes. To Erin Crabtree, for your utter enthusiasm and romance expertise. To Vanessa Pan, for being my first reader, my person, my sister in smut.

And an extra special thanks to Anna Blake Keeley and Katherine Mirani. AB, your edits were intimidating and scary and helpful. If not for you, this would've been a dual timeline mess for no reason, and your line edits truly prevented me from such amateur mistakes—I'm immensely grateful for the hours you put into this and your love and support along the way. Finally, to Katherine, without whom there wouldn't be a book at all. Katherine, I hope you know how much I value you as a friend and admire you as a writer. You were with me every horrific step of the way. I take none of it for granted and I'm literally brought to tears when I think about all the ways you've supported me during this process. (Also I am once again asking for your romance novel.)

And beyond all these early beta readers, thank you to all my cheerleaders who gave me guidance and hype, including, but not limited to, Perrin "Prynne" Carrell, Kate Dwyer, Maggie Cooper, Ellen O'Connor, Roderick Go, Soumaya Ezzemni, Jiwon Jang, my fellow 2025 debuts, and all the other amazing writers I've connected with in the last year.

Thank you to my parents for always supporting my ambitions, for taking me to the Learned Owl book release parties, for cultivating within me such a love for reading and writing.

To all my English and writing teachers at Old Trail, Laurel, Hopkins, and Greensboro for teaching me so much. To my MFA cohort, you *all* are the most lit of the fam.

Thank you to Robin, who had to live with me during this entire process and manage my volatile ego. I gave Will your glasses and intelligence but know that you are better because you are real and mine and a tax lawyer, which is much hotter and more useful than a poet. I love you an extreme amount.

And thank you, Reader! I can't believe you're reading this. Thank you for making my biggest dream come true.

About the Author

Katie Naymon lives and writes in Stockholm, Sweden. Originally from northeast Ohio, she got her BA in creative writing at Johns Hopkins University and her MFA in poetry from the University of North Carolina at Greensboro.